The Goddess of Warsaw

ALSO BY LISA BARR

Woman on Fire

The Unbreakables

Fugitive Colors

The Goddess of Warsaw

A Novel

Lisa Barr

HARPER LARGE PRINT

An Imprint of HarperCollinsPublishers

THE GODDESS OF WARSAW. Copyright © 2024 by Lisa Barr. All rights reserved. Printed in the United States of America. No part of this book may be used or reproduced in any manner whatsoever without written permission except in the case of brief quotations embodied in critical articles and reviews. For information, address HarperCollins Publishers, 195 Broadway, New York, NY 10007.

HarperCollins books may be purchased for educational, business, or sales promotional use. For information, please e-mail the Special Markets Department at SPsales@harpercollins.com.

FIRST HARPER LARGE PRINT EDITION

ISBN: 978-0-06-338652-5

Library of Congress Cataloging-in-Publication Data is available upon request.

24 25 26 27 28 LBC 5 4 3 2 1

FOR BRUCE BALONICK

*In loving memory of the man who relished telling
everyone that he was my "first reader"—our thing.
Find a cushy cloud Up There, Bruce, and read this with
your favorite tequila. Miss you.*

I am not a has-been. I am a will be.

—LAUREN BACALL

If you want to see the girl next door, go next door.

—JOAN CRAWFORD

The Goddess of Warsaw

Prologue

The young starlet stares at me with her multimillion-dollar pout, sapphire eyes wide and mesmerized, but she doesn't fool me. I have seen that canned look in her last three movies. Sienna Hayes at twenty-seven is Hollywood's "It Girl"—on the cover of every grocery-store rag and getting paid more than any other actress in town. She is the fresh new face of filmdom, and I'm the stale, old "Living Legend" with the obvious wig and the barely there penciled-in brows.

She sits cross-legged on the couch in my library (rumor has it that those extralong stems are insured for $10 million). I can see why she is a major box office draw. "Fuckable" is what the studio heads in my day would have said about her, what they used to say about me behind my back—as if I didn't hear. But this young woman is not in my home to gossip or to braid my hair. She wants something from me. I know what it is, and I'm going to make her work for it. Let's see what she's made of.

"So . . . my agent said you needed to see me, that it was urgent," I purr, jasmine tea in hand, pinkie finger extended in a perfected side split as though I were the Queen of England. I allow the delicate cup to graze my mouth but not touch it. I take my time and see the unnerving effect this has on the girl, who is now wagging a shiny, red-lacquer-bottomed stiletto in anticipation. *Good.* I remain silent for two additional elongated sips. "What brings you here?"

The wagging halts, and the girl's lineless face the color of clotted cream lights up, reminding me of the fake oversize moon in my 1953 picture *Moon Over Monaco.* "Ms. Browning," she gushes. "You're the reason I became an actor."

I put down the teacup with a harder thud than I'd intended. *Oh God, spare me.* Holding my breath, I wait for the next predictable line. *My mother and grandmother have seen every one of your films.* I could write this highly disappointing conversation starter with my eyes closed.

"And now"—she leans forward, her gushing expression waxes feral—"you're the reason I decided to become a director."

Now we're talking.

"A director?" I feign surprise. When my agent first mentioned this, admittedly, I flipped. Who the hell does she think she is? The girl has been in the biz just shy of seven years. Add seventy-eight to that number and you're looking at me. Do the math. Yes, eighty-five. I have been a working actress since I was in my teens. "A little ambitious, wouldn't you say?" I arch my brow and lower my chin—my signature "look" seen in all my films.

Sienna slowly runs her fingers through her long, highlighted blond hair as though she were searching for a hidden treasure among those thick, enviable golden strands. I've seen that gesture too—everyone has. "Perhaps," she says, treading carefully. "But I'm so over the 'It Girl' label. That's not why I became an actress. I set out to do something real, serious, make movies that matter." She pauses. "I'm here because I want to direct a biopic of *your* life. Act *and* direct—call my own shots."

Call her own shots. Movies that matter—hah! So young, so green, so infuriatingly bold. I stare her down. *You think this is your big idea, Sienna?*

The sole reason *I* chose Sienna Hayes from among the slew of blond, blue-eyed cookie-cutter actresses who have yearned to portray me over the years, who were determined to take on the "glamorous" life of Lena Browning, filled with the clichéd revolving door of leading men, furs, flash, and crimson Rolls Royces, is because *she* wants to direct the film. Not some overpaid Hollywood hack I couldn't control. This girl, malleable and inexperienced, is perfect for what I need—to steer the chain of events.

"Interesting," I respond vaguely, betraying nothing.

Pushing aside the tea, I lean back with a dramatic arm drape over the couch. I raise my brow for an encore performance, only higher. These brows (which I famously refused to tweeze) have made headlines throughout my career. The most memorable caption that still makes me chuckle was splashed across the front page of the *Los Angeles Times*: LENA BROWNING'S EYEBROWS STEAL THE SHOW. Of course, I framed it. And yet, these brows, once lush statement makers, are now wilted. That's the curse of having possessed luminous beauty. It fades too quickly before everyone's eyes—and all you have left is shadow, a silhouette of what was once exceptional.

Cocking my head slightly, I observe the young woman closely, this baby director wannabe. Undeniably beautiful, Sienna Hayes is not the typical glorified stripper I see prancing around town. She is feline, elegant, and sensual, like a slow dance. This girl could take on any role she wants for any amount of money with a snap-snap of her fingers. *So why this, why now, why me?*

"You don't know me at all." I challenge her with my long, bony, bejeweled finger, keeping up the charade.

"I've done my research," she says, shoulders squared and determined.

"Research—*please.*" I let out a cackle. "Let's see . . . the men, the booze, the pills, the ups and downs. Tabloid fodder." I reach for my Chesterfields. I'm not supposed to smoke. My doctors forbade me once the cancer made its debut in my esophagus three months ago. But I have smoked my entire life. *These aren't cigarettes*, I assured the handsome young doctor. *These are a prop, just like that stethoscope around your neck. I'm not about to stop now.* Pulling my silk robe tighter, I lean toward Sienna. "My story—the one you *think* you know—like your own name, Miss Hayes, is pure Hollywood fabrication."

She flinches slightly. I admit, that was a low blow. Her real name is Sally-June Johnson, from a nowhere town in Arkansas, a pretty little girl whose single mother pushed her into kiddie beauty pageants to support her drug habit and then overdosed in her trailer. Sally-June found her. I do my homework too.

Sienna meets my eyes with a formidable gaze. "Clearly, Ms. Browning, you don't know me either," she counters boldly. And I'm admittedly impressed. She hasn't been in town long enough to earn the right to stand up to me. Not a shrinking violet. I like that. "I am here because I *want* to know you." Her searing baby blues ignite. "I know what they've done to me. I can only imagine what they did to you."

I throw my head back and belly laugh. But it's not a laugh; it's a lifetime in one sound. "That's the thing, honey . . . You've been around the block for maybe five minutes. You can't possibly even begin to imagine," I drawl. And I don't have a southern accent, but it works for this scene.

I think back to all the Hollywood moguls I encountered, with their fat bellies and chunky cigars hanging from their salivating grins . . . This girl is too young, too overpaid, to understand any of it—my past or my path. Perhaps I was too quick to roll the dice with her. I cross my arms, wait for her next move.

Wordlessly, Sienna stands, takes a breather without asking permission, walks around the room, and observes the shelves filled with photos and stills from all my films, my myriad awards, charity affiliations, honorary college degrees—all the razzle-dazzle and glitz. This is not merely a library, rather it's a makeshift Hollywood historical museum. Those personal items that really matter to me remain under lock and key in my bedroom safe.

She spins around on her high heel purposefully. "I want to get behind the façade, behind 'the Face.' They call me 'the Face,' too, you know." She folds her arms defiantly, as though she were my equal.

"No, I haven't heard that," I lie. And yes, maybe I am being a little competitive, but I want Sienna to know from the get-go that she is nowhere near my match.

She exhales deeply. "I hope to create something authentic so that young actresses can learn what it really takes to succeed in this brutal business—the climb without the illusion. You are a legend, Ms. Browning, a woman who did it all. You called the shots when no actress in your day could. You were the highest paid actress of your time and the first to make serious demands in your contracts and get what you wanted. The 'no crying' clause was groundbreaking. This is not just about you—it's about control. It's about teaching aspiring actresses that they can be the leading lady of their own careers."

She moves toward me with the grace of a catwalk model. "I want to know who you really are, what makes you tick. Forty-one films . . . every leading man who mattered, roles in which you were not simply arm candy, rather the main draw. You never married or had kids. Yet you gave birth to the term 'femme fatale.' I mean"—she points at me—"you are *goals*."

"Goals?" I counter with a sneer. "Please don't reduce me to that."

I stare at the girl. She has no clue. *Never married, no kids.* She should only know what happened to my husband and the baby growing inside my belly. Who can blame her? No one knows. But she's trying. A grandiose speech, as far as elevator pitches go. Some might even call it *moving*. She wants to create an indie film for a mainstream audience to take seriously. But can anyone really grasp the depths of hell in a mere two hours? I shake my head. This girl will never be the same after I'm through with her.

Sienna's eyes expand to saucers, her hands clutch her hips like a folk dancer. She is clearly not backing down. "I'm not here to pitch you, Ms. Browning. We can leave the bullshit to our agents. I came only to prove to you that I am worthy of you. Don't judge me. I may look a certain way, but it's not who I am. My sense is that your Hollywood story is not who you are."

Not bad. Taking an unintended deep breath that I can feel quake at my chest, I stand, too, sluice around the library for dramatic impact, feeling Sienna's hot gaze at my back. I pivot, then plant myself in front of her, peer directly into her captivating eyes. She is tall, practically my height. My once celebrated mouth is just inches from hers.

"Let's be clear. I am not a star. I am a comet—a ball of gas, rock, and debris camouflaged in a spray of light." My gaze narrows as if she were a lowly grip on my set. "Here's what you don't know, Miss Hayes, what the *Enquirer* has not yet uncovered . . . Browning is not my real name. It's the make of the gun I used to kill the Nazi who pistol-whipped my father to death."

She stumbles backward slightly, but I lunge toward her in my fur kitten-heeled slippers. "How's that for the Face? Did you know, Sienna, that I've killed more people in real life than my characters have in my movies?" The eyes pop wider. *Yes, yes, darling. Shall I keep going?*

"My life is not a manual for young starlets," I spit out, feeling the errant droplets dot my lips. "It is a survival kit for animals—daunting and tumultuous. Contrary to popular opinion, my superpower was *not* my looks, but my brain and my will to survive. My strategic ability to one-up all those men who tried to put me in my place. And I'm not talking about skirting Hollywood's infamous couches and scoundrels." My smoky voice morphs into a calcified whisper. "Are you ready for this, Sienna? Are you prepared to go the distance, to push aside the Walk of Fame Disney version and do something that's dark, harrowing, but real?"

"More than ready." The girl's breath is equally heavy. I feel the warm stream of it loll against my face. Her voice is raspy, too—not my level of depth, but in time she will get there. Sally-June Johnson from the trailer park, child beauty queen at seven years old, with her Crayola-blue eye shadow, cheap drugstore lashes, and microscopic sequined showgirl dress—a pedophile's centerfold—is ready to play me, direct me, *be* me. I see it inside her fervent flashing pupils, in the same way I know the exact shot my cameraman captures of me from any vantage point.

Sienna Hayes is about to land this coveted role, but with one caveat. "There is a nonnegotiable before I approve any of this." I am prepared, as always. I know my lines, my worth. "Nothing is free, Sienna. In my day, you paid the piper. In your day, you have options—you can *be* the piper. Different times . . . better times."

My voice softens slightly. I may be tough and tested, but I'm not stone cold. I have loved hard, been loved even harder. "Give me your hand, young lady." She obeys. "Smooth and lovely, with so much potential." I then let it fall to her side and show her mine. "Like a dried-up branch that snapped off a rotted tree." I laugh, but not really, as I gaze down at the canvas of brown spots, the skin so thin it could split open at any moment. I feel a burning sensation judder between my breasts, which my doctors warned me about. "I'm asking you one last time: Are you strong enough to direct what may take down everyone's distorted image of the 'Great Lena Browning'?" I have always found it extremely effective to talk about myself in the third person.

"Yes," she says without hesitation, her fixated gaze never leaving mine.

Surprisingly unintimidated, the girl reclaims my hand. I can see down her blouse, at the lovely twin mounds that gave her instant fame when she bared them for the camera. A mistake she can't undo. But when I look up, her eyes are keener, more intelligent than she's been given credit for. And that's why she is here, why she needs me. She yearns to be more than live feed for teen boy fantasies. It's a win-win.

Admittedly, with her flawless skin and sharp cheekbones, she is the perfect physical match to play the younger me—a woman who could seduce with her lashes while picking your pocket. An actress renowned for her Waspy looks but who is really a Jew. A woman who slept with countless men but loved only one. An assassin who killed for good reason and didn't think twice about the blood on her hands, only about the blood that stained her dress, because at the time she didn't own another one.

"This is not a 'Liz Taylor and her seven husbands' story." My voice is taut, unrelenting. "There will be betrayal, deception, death, blood, and revenge—all the cinematic goodies that your audience will devour with their buttered popcorn and Raisinets. But if I agree to this"—I transmit my seasoned stare that has brought decades of men to their knees—"then you're going to do the ending *my* way. I will be performing, and *you* will direct it."

"D-Do you mean . . ." she stutters as I return to the couch.

"Yes . . . the last segment of your biopic is going to be in real time. I intend to correct my past while I still can." I pour each of us more tea, then pause, chin down, cerulean gaze smoldering. "Do we have a deal?"

Her cheeks turn flush, her eyes glow. She's seeing Oscar gold. "Hell yes."

BOOK I

WARSAW

1943

Chapter One

I stare at Aleksander's long, muscular back through his sweat-stained matted shirt as he leads us underground into the grainy darkness of the sewer passageway. I imagine the naked contours of his body beneath the sticky material and my heart hammers. It doesn't matter that I am covered in rot, slime, and stink. All that matters is that I am near him. Despite the stench drowning my nostrils, his musky scent is intoxicating. I cling to it, inhaling his essence as my husband, Jakub, trails a few paces behind. I am sandwiched between the two men I love. Scratch that. One I love, the other I want to devour. Take a guess which is which.

Yes, I'm going straight to hell, even though, let's be honest, I am already here. There is no escape out of the ghetto—our prison sentence for being born Jewish. Right now, in the bowels of the sewer, we are trying to stay alive, smuggling supplies for ourselves and others. And yet, this death trap is no match for the lust eclipsing my heart, the constant unrequited craving. If I die tomorrow, I want him. Once. I'm asking you, God. You've taken so much already. Give me Aleksander and the rest of my fate is yours to play with. Do we have a deal?

Aleksander turns, as though cued. His forehead drips with adrenaline. "You okay, Bina?"

Am I okay? Do I laugh now or later? Not okay. Nowhere near okay. I'm walking through waste and contaminated knee-high water for food and medicine. Could it be possible that just a few years ago I was sashaying across a magnificent stage in a custom-made costume to a standing ovation? I must have dreamt that, not lived it. But the way Aleksander's green eyes sparkle—a magnetic glint in the shadows—somehow makes everything, even the worst of it, okay. If we die right now, right here, and his face is the last I see, that would be enough. Except it is not enough. I want him inside me, penetrating me, releasing me—then I swear, I will go, surrender myself to this cruel, bottomless night. My husband's hand suddenly clasps my shoulder protectively from behind, puncturing my duplicitous thoughts. I turn slightly. A sharp reminder: *Snap out of it, cheater.*

"Are you okay?" Jakub asks, as if Aleksander hadn't asked the same question just seconds earlier. There are only three of us here—he heard.

"Yes, kochanie. And you?" I touch my husband's arm and camouflage my guilt with an endearment. A lie covering a lie—my specialty these days.

Before Jakub can respond, we all jump back, startled, as a loud barrage of gunfire pounds above our heads, followed by piercing screams. Not screams of war, but the hauntingly familiar cries of more terrorized Jews. Like dominoes, we fall. Like stepped-on rodents, we flatten. It doesn't stop. The gunshots, the cries for help, the deafening silence, the repetitious sounds of unnatural death. Acceptable Murder—a Nazi Olympic sport—day in, day out. While we sleep. If we sleep. Will we ever sleep again?

We stop in our tracks, trying desperately to ignore the pervasive thought banging in our heads: *When is it our turn?*

Aleksander stops walking, points upward. "Damn it, those bastards showed up. That's not the information we got earlier. There's a good chance the exit may be sealed shut or surrounded. But still, we need to get Bina outside somehow." He searches his older brother's face for answers.

Yes, his brother. I know . . . I'm a terrible person. But not always. This war—this brutal attack against us—has changed me, destroyed what was once good, sensible, faithful. The three of us have lost so much. Aleksander lost his wife and my best friend, Karina, and their baby daughter, after their home was set on fire by the Nazis before we were herded into the ghetto. He survived the blaze; they didn't. And as for us . . . I glance back at Jakub, then quickly push away those images . . . I can't think about that right now, or the guns firing above us. Better to focus on Aleksander's muscular shoulders. Better to think about touching him—about anything live, kinetic. Move forward. Stay in motion. Outsmart them. The only way to survive this endless nightmare is to pretend that our past, the lives we once thought belonged to us forever, never existed. This is who we are now: smugglers, fugitives, burglars—those dregs of society we once called criminals.

My face is our ticket to survival. I have been able to fool the Nazis because of my appearance. I am a tall, willowy, blond, blue-eyed Jew—not the stereotypical mousy, cowering Jewess falsely depicted in their anti-Semitic propaganda, rather the dreamy breed of Aryan goddess seducing an entire nation. This face enables me to slip out of the ghetto to the Aryan side, past the ten-foot-high walls covered in glass splinters and barbed wire with fourteen tightly guarded entrances, without getting shot. I have been successfully smuggling food and medical supplies through the sewers for nearly two years. I pretend that I am one of them, move among them freely. But sadly, the Nazis are no fools. They are ravenous monsters, lurking at every corner, waiting for me to trip, fall, betray myself and others. One slipup, and this guise is over.

I glance again at Jakub and see the look I do my best to avoid. Pain, despair, and resentment rolled into one tormented gaze. My husband is forced to turn the other cheek for what I'm about to do. Smuggling has a steep price. Let's call it what it is: whoring for food and medicine. Yes, fucking for potatoes and antibiotics if basic flirting doesn't work. That's who I am now.

Jakub and I never discuss it aloud, but it's there, the silent executioner between us, permanently destroying what little we have left in our young, thwarted marriage. Those heavy-hooded accusatory eyes speak volumes. I see it, feel it, but act like I don't. This war has turned me into that kind of human—someone who ignores her husband's pain, who desires her husband's brother, who seduces for scraps of food and medical supplies, who steals with a counterfeit smile, to feed him, myself, others. Survival is not heroic; it is ugly. All those things you would never do in a normal, moral, refined life is now your only way of life.

Don't get me started on how many we have lost in this war. Thousands. Countless men, women, and children. Family, friends, neighbors. The ten-block radius of the sealed ghetto was once crammed with nearly four hundred thousand Jews. Thirty percent of Warsaw's population was Jewish, the largest Jewish community in Europe. But they have murdered so many of us at this point—including at least 99 percent of our children.

The three of us are among the sixty thousand Jews who remain. We used to be among Warsaw's elite. Aleksander used to be a celebrated painter. I used to be an actress. Jakub used to be the top journalist for *Nasz Przegląd*. We used to be wealthy. We used to drink fine wine and talk about books and art and theater. We used to laugh. We used to be secular, cultural Jews, mingling with the upper echelon of Warsaw society. We used to speak only Polish—not Yiddish, like most of the ghetto inhabitants. A maid used to wash my hair, and another used to lay out my clothes. Our so-called friends used to be loyal, until they eagerly handed us over to the Nazis like Beluga caviar on a platter without blinking an eye or pausing between shots of Żubrówka. We aren't just Jews, I tell Jakub. We are inhabitants of a planet called Used to Be.

Despite appearances, I do know right from wrong. The other Bina—the one who used to laugh hard and live large—would be mortified by my transformation. If Jakub's mother knew . . . but she's dead. Or his father. Dead. Or my parents and sister—all dead. Two sets of grandparents—gassed on the first transport to Treblinka. The baby I was carrying . . . dead too. The only light in all this darkness is that no one I loved and cared about will ever know the extent of my desire for Aleksander, my burning for a man I can never have.

I have been professionally trained to pretend and camouflage. The other Bina was once a drama major at the Warsaw Imperial Academy of Dramatic Arts, a top student. So much promise. Gifted, my teachers used to say, destined for greatness. Little did they know that my acting skills, especially here in the ghetto, would be the gift that keeps on giving.

It feels like hours, but it's only minutes before the shooting above us stops. We wait until the ear-piercing screams wane, the surrounding voices grow dim, and the careening screech of vehicles diminishes. We wait until the wait itself is unbearable. And then quietly, coolly, Aleksander lifts Jakub onto his broad shoulders.

My husband feels the movement of the unsealed sewer lid above us and lightly pushes it up, revealing a narrow stream of icy night air and light. He takes a panoramic view of the area, peers down at us, and nods, then quickly returns the lid to its place. Regaining his footing on the sewer floor, Jakub gives me one last lingering, heavily hooded look: Showtime.

Chapter Two

Warsaw, 1939

"G o out there, Bina. Curtain call. They're begging for you." Stach nudges me forward, toward the stage. We are huddled together in the wing after our opening night performance of our play, *Romeo and Juliet.* "Listen to it." He points to the theater's overhead wooden beams vibrating with raucous applause. "Opening night magic. Hear the thunder? That's for you, my friend . . . 'a rose by any other name.'" His face splits into a sly smile. I laugh aloud, cover my mouth.

I play Juliet. But Stach is not Romeo. According to him, he'd never be Romeo. You couldn't pay him enough zlotys to play Romeo, whom he calls spineless, a prancing daisy picker. Stach is the fiery, sarcastic

Mercutio, a loyal-to-the-end hothead, and indisputably the most talented actor on that stage. When he performs, the rest of us fade into the background like fairy dust. His booming baritone resounds like the voice of God commanding from heaven, especially when he's angry. As Mercutio, Stach is deliciously sinister and more than believable—he becomes his character. I love watching the audience devour his performance.

"You know damn well that the thunder is for both of us," I say, grabbing my best friend by the poufy material of his bloodstained white poet's blouse and pulling him back toward the stage with me. "Everyone knows you're the star . . . 'Ask for me tomorrow, and you shall find me a grave man . . .' You have all the best lines."

"Not according to my father. Didn't see him in the audience tonight. Big surprise." Stach laughs again. His shiny black hair appears almost blue beneath the glare of the stage lights cast in our direction. But his laugh is not a laugh—it is forced, soaked in pain. His father has never showed up to a single performance of his. Stach's mother, of course, is in the audience tonight—front row, hands clasped together with pride.

Stach Nowak is his stage name. His real name is Stanisław Sobieski, a descendant of royalty on his father's side. His father still calls himself a baron despite noble titles having been abolished. He hates that his sole heir has chosen acting as his profession—a "worthless hobby"—and shunned the family's lucrative steel business. "You'll never be a leading man," his father chides him at every opportunity. "And Sobieskis are never second best."

Though I would never admit it, his father is right. Stach will never play the leading man, the romantic prince, the dashing rescuer on a white horse. Despite his incredible talent and winning smile, his handsome face is marred by a large purplish birthmark spanning the entire left side of his cheek, like a slapped face; an imprint so glaring that even heavy stage makeup cannot conceal it. Stach calls it the devil's handprint. It's his signature, distinguishing him from all other actors and giving his characters edge and anguish. But it also relegates him to playing only the complex antagonist or supporting actor—Shylock, Iago, Claudius, Caliban. And yet, he always manages to steal the show anyway.

Stach pushes me toward the stage once again, only this time more forcefully. And I shove him right back playfully. "Get out there," he says, "before that ass Mateusz robs you of all the applause."

I glance toward the other side of the stage at the target of Stach's ire: Mateusz—that ass—Romeo obviously, approaching center stage, his white canvas shirt with its bell sleeves billowing as though he were strolling along a windy seashore, his wavy blond hair blowing in sync with the stage fan, his chiseled face held high, owning it all. Pompous and greedy, as usual. I glance at Stach and note the gleam in his turquoise eyes as he watches Mateusz, and then the spark vanishes before I can fully process it. The two men have despised each other since the first day of drama school nearly two years ago. Mateusz is in my class, and Stach, one year ahead of us, is indisputably the superior performer. But Mateusz, physically beautiful with a lithe build, penetrating almond eyes, and lush, womanly lips, embodies dreamy, poetic Romeo. He, of course, lands all the coveted leading-male roles. That birthmark ensures there is no contest.

Their rivalry is most apparent during practices, when they snap at each other, cut down each other, and I find myself thrust in the middle, like a mother separating two combative sons. It was intolerable until that day a few months ago when I learned that the incessant animosity was all an act.

We had just rehearsed the balcony scene and finished play practice after a long, hot day. I knocked on Stach's dressing room door to debrief and gossip, as usual. No one answered. The door was left ajar, so I walked in and saw all his belongings still there, but he was nowhere to be found. I called out for him and searched the entire theater. We always leave practice together. Strange. I returned to my dressing room to pack up for the night when I heard low, stifled laughter coming from the costume closet as I passed by. The costume closet was not actually a closet, rather it was a large storage room filled with stage props and set designs from past productions. I opened the door, walked in, and looked around. Empty. I must have imagined the voices. And then, just as I was leaving, I heard loud whispers coming from behind a floor-to-ceiling painted garden scene on the far side of the room, near the back door. My heart pounded. I'd know that sound anywhere—deep and booming—even as a whisper. And the other voice, I knew, belonged to Mateusz. It was the same undertone he'd make when his lips grazed mine in the final scene, when Romeo believes Juliet to be dead. Stach and Mateusz? My breath halted. I knew I should leave. Instead, I hid behind a large mural depicting a snowcapped mountain range and listened for just a bit longer. I had to be sure.

It was silent at first, and then I heard the bated breath, the shushing each other warnings, the rustle, the unsnapping of pants, the rousing laughter, kissing, groping, sucking, groaning—an orchestra of intimacy. I imagined it all without seeing any of it. I quickly tiptoed out of the room, squeezed through the door I'd left partially open, and leaned up against the nearest wall, my hand plastered to my chest, my heart racing. All that sniping and jealousy was a ruse. Why didn't Stach tell me? Tears filled my eyes. We have shared everything since we were kids making up plays together. I even told him about my conflicted feelings about marrying Jakub a few months ago. I cried in Stach's arms the night before my wedding, and he reassured me it would all be okay. He was the only person in the world who knew my truth. Why couldn't he share his secret with me?

The applause grows louder and Stach takes my hand as we line up for our final bows. Everyone believes he is in love with me, and Stach wants them to think that. I clasp his hand tightly. *I will always have your back even if you are afraid to trust me,* my palm promises his.

We stand still behind the heavy red velvet curtain poised to reveal what I know to be on the other side: Warsaw's elite. Celebrities, politicians, socialites, and everyone who matters in the theater world came out to see what was being touted as the best Shakespearean production in years by the "next generation" of Warsaw's finest young actors. There has been much talk of an impending Nazi invasion, but that did not diminish tonight's attendance. Every seat in the house was filled. The show must go on, our director had told us during our final practice earlier this week. Next week may be war, he intimated, but this week we would celebrate our beautiful production. Don't let fear stand in the way, he said with a proud fist raise. Do this for Poland. For the arts and our way of life.

I inhale the intoxicating theater air as the crowd applauds vigorously, demanding we show ourselves once again. The familiar heady aroma of "my theater" clings to my nose and to the back of my throat—an even mix of cloying and stuffy—as I watch the rising curtain slowly unveil the tips of my dusty-rose ballet slippers, my burgundy Renaissance gown with its jeweled embellishments, my pushed-up cleavage, my neck adorned with a jeweled sapphire choker, my face rouged with excitement, my long hair braided tightly into a single golden rope down my back and topped with a tiny claret cap laced with gold that reminds me of a yarmulke.

I meet the adoring gaze of my audience, feel the deep, umbilical connection, and I lovingly receive the glory. An indescribable rush moves through me as I slowly take my first bow. Stach grabs my hand again and Mateusz clasps the other. United, we raise our hands high overhead, as we take our final bow together.

This, I think as my body arcs deeply. *This*.

And then just seconds before resuming an upright stance, the clapping halts as though someone cut the lights. An unwelcome hush blankets the playhouse as a phalanx of soldiers and police barge through the door, led by one man dressed in full royal regalia, a throwback to another era. And not just any man—Stach's father.

"Landau! Bina Landau," Baron Konrad Sobieski shouts my name, singling me out. I glance around. There is only one thing that separates me from all the other actors onstage. I am the lone Jew. A Jew who doesn't look like a Jew, I've been told my whole life.

My heart palpitates when I see my father in the distance, rising from his seat to protect me, and then my mother pulling him back down by his sleeve, silencing him with a fearful warning glare. I see Jakub seated next to her, immobile and not blinking. And Aleksander next to him, his cheeks burning, and my best friend, Karina, with both hands pressed to her mouth in shock.

"Bina . . . Bina!" the baron bellows to a dead silent theater, his voice ricocheting off the walls like wayward bullets. My focus is on the rows of unearned colorful medals spanning his uniform—a man who is not a soldier, never served a day of his life in the army. Those noble medallions are always locked inside the velvet-lined family vault with the rest of Stach's family heirlooms dating back to the 1700s. Stach made me swear to secrecy and showed them all to me once when his father was out of town.

If this weren't so terrifying, the moment might be comical. Konrad Sobieski appears as though he'd jumped straight out of our Renaissance production as a raging Capulet or a Montague. But his unexpected presence is more than real—it is premeditated. I overheard my father speaking to my uncle several months ago, discussing how Konrad Sobieski was funding the National Democratic Party's anti-Semitic platform to rid Poland of its Jews, and using all resources available to make that happen. The NDP's thugs have been destroying local Jewish businesses for the past few years and recently escalated their destructive activities with ample financial backing, mostly, I presume, from the baron's own deep pockets.

Stach steps forward, his eyes blazing. "Enough! Father, stop this now!" My best friend's face is clenched, and the devil's handprint seems to darken and expand as his cheeks become increasingly inflamed.

"Stand down," his father retorts, his arctic glare returning to me. "Bina Landau, leave the premises immediately."

I find my voice, and it, too, echoes in the theater, attempting to match his. "Why me?" But the sound is hollow, young, desperate. Everybody knows why.

The baron's striking face resembles Stach's, only without the birthmark and permanently scowling. Suddenly, I recall a memory from a year ago that I pushed away.

I was visiting Stach at his home, when the baron summoned his son into the drawing room, knowing I could hear every word through the thin walls. "If you ever fall in love with that Jew, I will disown you," the baron sneered. "I don't care how beautiful she is. I don't care who her goddamn father is. You have humiliated our family enough with this acting business . . . but a Jew too? I will not allow it. That girl is no longer welcome here."

I wanted to defend myself, to barge into that ornate room and scream: A Jew whose father built your palatial home! My father, considered Warsaw's most prominent architect, built many luxurious villas throughout Poland and refurbished several landmark castles. He has been celebrated for his architectural innovation throughout the country—especially in Konstancin, the exclusive woodsy enclave twenty kilometers south of the city, where both our families reside.

The baron glares at me from the auditorium floor

and makes a panoramic sweeping gesture to the audience. "Why, Bina, why?" he mimics cruelly. "You are a Jew. There is no place for your kind among us, especially now." He turns again to the audience for support. "We must protect Poland first."

I don't hear the rest of the vitriol he is spewing, but I feel every rotten word course through my veins like poison. I see the ugly truth reflected in the eyes of all who applauded my performance just minutes earlier. I see my parents and family being escorted out of the theater by the soldiers. No matter that my father also designed this theater for the nation's most prestigious drama school. No place for Jews . . .

"This is not about her. It's about me, isn't it, Father?" Stach steps forward to the edge of the stage, one hand on his hip, the other clasped around the sword at his belt. His voice fills the theater, as though he were Mercutio back at it. The audience, mouths agape, are now sucked into this performance within a performance. "Leave Bina alone, damn you."

Konrad Sobieski's eyes storm over the challenge presented by his rebel son before a throng of witnesses, his only son, who rejects his noble bloodline as though it were a plague, not a gift. The baron's mouth parts into a punishing smile, as if he has been waiting years for this very moment: a public duel that he intends to win.

"Get out, kike!" he roars at me and then begins to chant, "Jewliet! Jewliet!"

I can't breathe. I'm frozen. I'm burning. Every conflicting sensation takes hold of me at once. I look to the theatergoers for protection, to the audience who loves me, but there is only silence, eyes lowered at half-mast. Those zealously clapping hands, the thunderous applause that shook the theater's beams just a short while ago, have tucked themselves away. A Jew among them. I never hid my Judaism, but I never flaunted it either. It didn't seem to matter. I am an actress, that's all I cared about. Everyone knows who my family is. Everyone. Many people in this audience have been to our home, attended our parties, drank our wine, ate our food, were guests at my wedding.

But now?

Even my director, the man who has mentored me, who calls me his star pupil, who insisted that the show must go on—*Do this for Poland*—is a mouse among men. He stares down between his spindly legs at his scuffed shoes, unable to meet my demanding gaze. Say something, anything. Stand up for me. But when he looks up, I see Jewliet clouding his eyes now too.

I take one last look at the theater I revered with all my heart, at the stained-glassed ceiling and ornate woodwork—my home away from home. I see the writing on the wall. That ovation was for Juliet, not Bina Landau.

Stach reaches for my hand once again, and I cling to its warm, safe familiarity. But it can't protect me. He squeezes my fingers to the point of crushing them and whispers between closed lips, "Go out the costume closet back-door exit. Use it . . . hide. I will find you."

Controlling the tears filming my eyes, I know this, too, is yet another lie. He will never find me. This moment may be our last. Everything is changing . . . and Stach will too.

I meet his crestfallen gaze, his eyes the color of the gem adorning my neck, and I feel a pain like I have never known before. "Don't let him win, Stach. Don't let him take away everything you love . . . who you love," I add quickly under my breath, knowing I will never have another chance.

He responds with a revelatory twitch. I yank my hand from his, turn with my back to the audience, and move briskly off the stage, leaving Juliet and all my other characters—those I have portrayed and those I never will—behind in a wake of dust.

Chapter Three

Warsaw, 1943

I glance around my dilapidated kitchen with its rusty sink, chipped brick, crumbling molding, smelly pipes, damaged plates, and mismatched silverware, and it is hard to believe that I once ate from fine bone china and never washed a single dish. Even our staff would never have lived in such squalor.

I think back to my other life. I allot myself only a few minutes per day to reflect, otherwise it is too painful, too debilitating. Our home in Konstancin was a who's who of Warsaw: politicians, industrialists, poets, novelists, playwrights, entertainers, artists, doctors. We lived among them, believed that we were an integral part of them. There was no us and them where we grew up.

Of course, we knew of anti-Semitism, heard about "incidents," but it didn't affect our insulated world. Somehow, we believed we were immune. How blissfully naïve we were. I now know that the lines in the sand had been drawn all along, festering like cracks beneath our rare Calacatta gold marble surfaces. We fooled ourselves into thinking we were above the common Jews of Warsaw and their "lowly" Yiddish, with our clipped Polish enunciations, stylish clothes, salons, live-in staff, influential status. And then later . . . after the invasion, all the payoffs and bribes my father and uncle doled out to keep us protected. It bought us nine months, before we were taken and thrown into the ghetto with everyone else. We should have left Poland long before the invasion in September 1939. We knew better. We saw the signs; small Jewish businesses targeted and destroyed. We were educated, worldly—we knew. But my mother insisted we stay, believed that our friends in high places would shield us, and my father gave in to her, as always. That blind foolishness cost us our home, our everything.

My father . . . God, I miss him. He was brilliant, kind, loving, but . . . with deep respect for the dead, he was perhaps the dumbest man I have ever known. Gullible and blind. He didn't see what was going on in our home right under his nose. Way before the Nazis destroyed us. I saw it all, at age twelve. I did not look like anyone in my family. My parents and sister, Natalya, were dark-haired, brown-eyed, and olive-skinned. I remember the intense way my mother would eye the man in charge of overseeing my father's construction sites—Pawel, my father's trusted right hand. And how Pawel would return my mother's furtive glances when he thought my father wasn't looking—but I saw it all. My mother was the greatest actress I'd ever encounter, the way she turned it on for Pawel and off when my father entered the room. And Pawel—tall, blond, slanty-eyed, swarthy, with an ever-present cigarette dangling from his full lips—could not hide his lusty gaze or the obvious: I looked more like him than my own father.

I hated my mother for that, for that flirtation, for betraying my first love. My father, a man who told me that I could become anything, that there were no limits. A man whose only fault was that his life revolved around making my mother happy. I often wondered how he could not know the truth. Didn't he hear how her breath dropped when Pawel entered the room? And yet, my father died blind to my mother's deceitful antics. His last word when the Nazis burst into our home and beat him to death with their guns and shiny black boots was her name.

As I lean against the kitchen wall and see my reflection in the small hanging mirror across from me, I can't help but think: *You are just like her.* I quickly look away.

Pressing up against the door, I hear the din of voices coming from inside the bedroom, where the secret meeting is being held that includes both my husband and Aleksander. A meeting I wasn't invited to. But I am showing up anyway. They just don't know it yet.

Jakub thinks I am at the abandoned convent across the street from our apartment building, where I teach drama classes to the handful of children who are still alive. I told my assistant to watch the kids for an hour while I returned home, so I could eavesdrop on the "emergency meeting" led by my husband. The group sitting on the other side of the door, in a circle of mismatched chairs, comprises the elite wing of Oyneg Shabbos, a consortium of journalists, novelists, playwrights, scholars, and a few prominent artists, like Aleksander.

They are secretly producing an archive documenting ghetto life, an attempt to preserve the truth so that one day people will know what really happened to us—our version, not the Nazi version. Preserve, like the jam we once jarred from our sprawling garden. Giant blackberries, so wild and tart and luscious. Another life ago, the life that was erased. The archive in my opinion (though no one is asking for it) is merely a pathetic passive resistance, an intellectualized way of fighting back to protect the memories of the dead and the almost-dead (there is no in-between in the ghetto). But documented history doesn't lie, Jakub imparts to his colleagues. Through diaries, drawings, essays, oral histories, and interviews, he is determined to gather all the evidence of our demise. He calls it dignity versus indignities. It is all so antiseptic, so far from reality.

What dignity? Open your eyes, Jakub. I groan whenever I hear those stupid words. Jakub is so much like my father, brilliant but oblivious to what is right in front of his face. All words, no action. Not like me. All action. And that's just one of our many marital problems.

I hear my husband's voice rise above the others. Deep, reserved, and persuasive, like a rabbi giving a sermon from a pulpit. I shake my head. That voice seems to work its magic on everyone but me.

"Whores," he says quietly at first. "I called this emergency meeting because those animals intend to make prostitutes out of our young women. I just got this document . . . I can't reveal my source, but it was slipped to me from a friend in the Judenrat."

A friend. Hah! My stomach turns. The "Juden

Rats," we call them. Twenty-four traitors appointed by the Nazis who rule over the ghetto with the support of the Jewish Police. Police—please! They are turncoats with batons who beat into submission other Jews who get out of line. Trained Nazi dogs. Three thousand strong—the Jewish Police, like the hoodwinked Judenrat, believe that if they collaborate, do as they are told, the Nazis will keep up their end of worthless agreements, and they will somehow survive the ghetto. Delusional, all of them. Worse than Jakub.

Jakub pauses, takes a sip of water. I hear the sip, picture the jump of his large Adam's apple. "The Nazis are demanding that the Judenrat organize two brothels of girls to be established outside the ghetto—one for officers, one for privates. According to the document, their poor soldiers are 'suffering from a lack of sexual relations' and 'getting venereal disease from casual encounters on the streets of Warsaw' and—"

"Pigs. Rapists. Pedophiles. We must stop this!" Minna Lipchitz shouts out, and I envision the jutting of her pointy chin. She is a mother of two. Her husband was shot dead in front of her in broad daylight on Świętojerska Street a month ago. Her eldest son, thirteen, is one of our prized smugglers. She also used to be a prominent historian who once headed the National Library of Poland.

"You're not going to like what I have to say, Jakub," chimes in another man whose voice I don't recognize immediately. "We are wasting time with these oral histories. The world needs to know what's going on here now. Getting out information and training couriers must be our prime focus."

I snap my fingers lightly. Szymon Berkowicz—that's who it is. The renowned children's book author, whose famous story, *Go to Sleep, Żabko*, about a talking frog, who after a long, twisty adventure finally falls asleep on his own lily pad, is—was—a staple in every nursery, Jewish and non-Jewish alike.

"Does anyone really care, Szymon? We will be wasting time with that too." It's Aleksander. "With all the lives we've already risked trying to send telegrams through couriers to our friends in Europe and the U.S., where has that gotten us?" His voice rises in a way I've never heard before, a mix of disgust and strength. "Has a single goddamn country lifted a finger to help us? We need to fight back on our own. Start smuggling weapons. Our words are no longer working for us, Jakub. We must all accept this."

"Aleks, that's enough," my husband says, cutting off his brother. "This is exactly what they want us to do— divide among ourselves—kill one another, do their dirty work for them. Let's not argue. Let's think. We need a plan. That's why we are here."

But Aleksander's voice waxes bitter. "I'm done thinking, planning, drawing, pretending. We're out of time. They burned my Karina and our baby girl alive, laughing and drinking while torching our home. Just imagine what they will do to our daughters in their beds. Would you have me draw that, too, Jakub?" I hear a chair push back violently, a sudden crash to the floor. "Enough with the archives. The only plan left— the only discussion—is to figure out ways to defend ourselves while there are still some of us alive left to do it."

My Karina. His Karina, my best friend. I shrink back against the broken brick wall, which pokes sharply into my back. Aleksander's pain is unbearable. His love for Karina clearly hasn't diminished, while mine for him has only grown stronger. I feel the heat rising in my neck. But he's right. Jakub and his precious archives, his opus, his dignities versus indignities. For what? If the world is indifferent to us now, just imagine how it will be in the future. No one cares, Jakub. No one fucking cares! I told him that in the privacy of our bed. Perhaps that's why he has never asked me to join this group. Too afraid of my rage, too afraid I might incite his brainy supporters to put down their pens and their pondering and to act.

Well, he's right. Exhaling deeply, I fling open the door and enter the room. Jakub drops his papers and looks up, as does everyone else.

"Bina, what is it? I thought you were in class."

"I was in class, Jakub. But now I'm here." I stare back at all of them. The core group of twelve, Jakub's tribe. "I heard everything. You're not going to be able to stop them. If they want prostitutes, they are going to get prostitutes." Hands on hips, I stare them all down. "We need to think ahead, take matters into our own hands immediately, before the Judenrat does it for us. I want to spearhead this endeavor."

"You? Spearhead prostitutes? Enough. Bina, leave." Jakub's reserve has fallen away, giving space to his own anger. So much suppressed anger.

I plant my worn-in shoes on the floor. The soles are so thin I can feel the slivery hardness against my calloused feet. "I'm not going anywhere. Look at what's really happening around us. The *aktions*, the mass deportations. We know exactly what's going on in those death camps." The tension builds behind my brows. *Everybody in this room knows.*

"Dignity," Jakub says emphatically, with a paper slam against his knee. I can tell the thud is softer than he'd intended. "We have to find normalcy inside this hell, if we have any chance at all of surviving."

My eyes scorch at his naïveté. "Don't fool yourself. No one is going to survive this place. No. One. It's a numbers game, a waiting in line until it's your turn to be slaughtered. We need to assume we have no chance of survival and work from that standpoint." I should stop right here, but I'm on a roll. "You are just following orders." I point accusingly at my husband and his band of intellectuals. "Working within their demented system. Accepting the unacceptable. And I simply refuse. I respect that you are documenting these atrocities, but it's not going to save lives." My eyes meet Aleksander's briefly. "Look at me." I challenge them all, changing tactics. "What do you see?"

No one says a word. They don't have to. "I will say it for you: I look more like them than they do. The Aryan poster girl. Let's call this face what it is. Use me. I can act. I speak German fluently. You've already seen that I can smuggle. And I'm not dumb." I turn to Jakub. "Let me do what I can do to get us information and get out information—to resist. Resist, not write. Resist, not sit and wait. Let me handle this matter so that maybe some of us can escape and live to tell our stories. Not die with our stories buried in some secret underground time capsule. Think about that, Jakub."

I feel the fervor burning inside my eyes, daring anyone to defy me.

"You're my wife. It's unacceptable, degrading," he mutters under his breath. I'm undermining Jakub yet again, I know. We are having an intimate fight out in the open. I am landing wild, humiliating punches in his boxing ring in front of the most gifted minds of Poland, his people.

"Look at me," I command the room. Now I'm Portia in *The Merchant of Venice*. "Let me be the madame of this brothel for those officers—the decision-makers. Allow me to watch over our girls who are going to be forced into their beds anyway. I will set the rules of engagement for those men. I will demand better food, hygiene—"

"You will demand?" Jakub interrupts with a laugh. But it's not a laugh. Everyone knows it's not a laugh.

I stand my ground. "I get it. They could easily get a Polish woman or a German woman to do the job— but having a Jewish woman inside overseeing their sex slaves is exactly what Nazis want. Just the way they have used the Judenrat and the Jewish Police to rule over us. Same damn formula. They are monsters, but brilliant tacticians. They know how beneficial it is for them to pit our own against us. We do all the dirty work for them. I have no illusions. But let's use them right back, Jakub. I will do what I can to protect our girls and, most importantly, give them purpose to survive—that is the only way they have any chance at all."

Jakub's face is pale, but I can see the hot shame sweltering beneath it. My heart thumps wildly. No one says anything, not even Josef Stromski, world-renowned philosopher and a nonstop talker, the type who revels in hearing his own condescending voice. But right now, Stromski is uncharacteristically mute, radio silent, paying attention.

"What about you?" Jakub whispers coldly. "You are the greatest beauty of them all. The prize."

I don't argue with that. "No one gets the prize until they earn it, win it, beg for it. It will be a game that I intend to win. That's how it works with those beasts. You're going to have to trust me."

Our eyes meet. *I don't trust you,* his soft brown eyes transmit. *I once loved you, but we are broken. I know,* my eyes transmit back. Still . . .

I turn away from Jakub, look to the others. They don't love me. They aren't married to me. Perhaps they are envious of me. Perhaps they are numb to me, thinking I am beneath them. But all of them want to live, and I'm offering more than just paperwork. I am proposing a way in which I would be the eyes and ears among our captors when they have their pants down, and are at their most vulnerable.

"Enough words," I announce. "It is time for action."

I stand before them: self-appointed leader of the whores. I have stooped to my lowest denominator, risen to my highest calling. By the looks on their faces, I have defeated my husband. A man who knows he is impotent against my desires. My eyes meet Aleksander's once again, but only for a wistful second. He, too, sees the possibility, the fight. A way out, a sick, distorted path to survival. It has come to this. My darkest hour and perhaps my greatest performance.

Chapter Four

I love watching Aleksander wash. It is the only activity in the ghetto that gives me pleasure. He doesn't see me because I'm hiding behind the kitchen door, eyeing him through the broken hinge, which provides a three-finger-wide span to view him inside the bedroom, which also serves as our washing area. We are among the lucky ones with two rooms for the three of us. Most ghetto prisoners are relegated a room for at least seven people. Jakub is out tutoring students, and Aleksander thinks that I'm teaching too. This is his moment alone, mine to savor.

Aleksander's solo bathing performance is so tender and raw. His beautiful, starved body is a Rodin come to life. It begins with the dampening of the washcloth, the slight twisting of material, using only the tiniest swipe of soap—if you could call it that—practically an air-kiss. Soap is a nonexistent luxury in the ghetto. That bar melting in his hand with the monogrammed *E* is taken from what was once the ritzy Hotel Europejski, now a dumping ground housing the Nazi invaders. They renamed it the Europäisches Hotel—Germanizing everything they conquered, wiping our country's history clean.

Jakub held his tongue when he saw the two small exclusive bars stashed inside the sewn-in pocket of my dress a month ago. Didn't ask how I got it. There was the usual pause. The shifting of the brow. The sharp, pained flicker of his eye, as though a shard of glass had fallen into it. The accusatory look. He understands, as we all do, that every single item smuggled into the ghetto comes with a cost. That bar of lavender-scented soap was in exchange for my body. A young Nazi soldier who thought he was having his way with a Polish girl—not a Jew. Two vials of antibiotics, a wedge of cheese, a kilo of flour, and three potatoes also came with the deal.

Watching that guilty soap graze Aleksander's body, I pretend it's my lips against his skin, determined to shut out the expense the bar cost my soul. Right now, I allow myself the indulgence. I am just a woman watching the man I love wash, and that's the place where I want to be—not the other.

My cheeks are flush, and I am unable to peel my gaze from Aleksander's naked back; if only I could touch it. Long and lean with a silvery sheen as the late morning sunlight casts a path of canted light over his skin. He bends over the tiny wash area and concentrates on cleaning his private parts, lightly touching himself, and I can barely breathe. I reach under my dress and place my hand between my thighs, feeling at once both the heat and unquenchable desire.

I allow myself just a few seconds of pleasure, and then open my eyes and remember where I am, who I am. His brother's wife.

Every time I'm near Aleksander, enveloped by his presence, I am reminded that I picked the short straw, married the wrong brother.

The truth, childish as it may seem, is that I saw Aleksander first. Before Karina got him. Before Jakub asked me to dance. Before I accepted his hand in marriage and made the single greatest mistake of my youth—the one I can never take back.

Karina and I had just turned nineteen, ripe for marriage, and decided to attend the fundraiser dance at our former lyceum. It was a reunion of graduates past and present and touted as the biggest social event of the season.

"Even the Blonski brothers are here," Karina whispered from our corner of the gymnasium. "Don't look, but they are across the gym, at two o'clock."

I waited three long seconds and then turned in their direction. The Blonski brothers were holding court in the middle of a group of eligible bachelors. They graduated well before Karina and I got to the school, but their reputation preceded them. Jakub, six years older than me, was making his mark as a journalist, and Aleksander, who was two years younger than his brother, was a rising star in the art community and a well-known catch.

My heart fluttered. Aleksander . . . I mean, look at him. Tall, broad shouldered, electric green eyes, thick sandy-brown hair, winning smile. And his talent . . . When Aleksander stared back at me and grinned slightly, I felt my blood sizzle, so much so that I looked away, played hard to get, and feigned disinterest. I even made a point to smile at someone else and completely turned my back to him.

When I finally pivoted around, I caught Aleksander still smiling my way and then realized it was not meant for me. It was for Karina. I glanced over at my best friend, and she was positively glowing. What have I done?

Forget Bina—her flirtatious gaze beamed two dimples deep—*she could have anyone. Pick me, and I will make you happy.* Aleksander began walking our way. I had been so full of myself, and now I couldn't stop this train from rolling. But I was only acting, damnit! And Karina, my best friend, with her naturally rosy cheeks, twinkly brown eyes, auburn curls, and just enough curve, stood to win the prize.

Accompanied by his brother, Aleksander strode right past me and asked her to dance. Her, not me. This left me no choice but to accept a dance with his studious sidekick, Jakub, with his dark wavy hair and kind, intelligent eyes. I jealously watched Aleksander whisk Karina onto the dance floor, both laughing as they twirled the night away.

I blew it. My heart was crushed, and it was all my own doing.

Spying on Aleksander standing naked, I think back to that pivotal moment. Not only did Karina and I marry our respective dance partners several months later—it was a double wedding—what a *simcha* it was (for Karina). I went overboard to mask my true feelings. I feigned happiness for my best friend, pretended that Jakub was my *bashert*—soulmate. I should have earned an award for my acting performances. The only person with whom I couldn't pretend was me.

And then, just a few months after the wedding, the invasion happened, followed by the brutal murder of my father, the burning down of Aleksander's home with his family in it. And then on July 22, 1942—a day forever carved into my heart—the first train destined for Treblinka took away the rest of our families, including my mother and my sister, and everything changed.

Except for this.

Funny, how war both entraps and frees you. What's the point of niceties, manners, morals, and suppressed emotion when you could die at any given moment? Hitler's assault did more than murder my family; it unleashed my hidden desire, which rose to the surface, smothering my conscience and any semblance of right and wrong.

What's left is the damp washcloth in Aleksander's hand, the lavender soap swipe, the elegant way he places the items on the top shelf over the basin, and then flexes naked in the mirror. I like to believe that he is reminding himself of who he was before. Darling of the art world, Aleksander was a sought-after painter who once exhibited with other avant-garde artists at the National Museum in Warsaw, before his paintings were removed and he, too, was booted out by the very same curator who had begged to showcase his works and then stole all his paintings.

Aleksander's hands fall loosely to his sides as he eyes himself in the cracked mirror; a jagged fracture cutting through the glass like a streak of lightning. I place both hands against my rapidly beating heart, when suddenly he turns toward me as though sensing the magnetic pull of my forbidden gaze. I suck in my breath as he grabs a towel, wraps it around his waist. There is nowhere to hide. I brace myself against the wall behind me for the imminent confrontation, as Aleksander's bare feet stomp across the hardwood floor in my direction. What do I say when he discovers I'm spying on him?

"Bina?" he calls out. I'm caught. The washing sessions are officially over. I try to mask my red-faced guilt.

Focusing on his probing eyes, I feign surprise. "Aleks, I'm so sorry. I didn't want to disturb you. I had forgotten something here earlier for class. Didn't mean to interrupt your privacy . . ."

He folds his arms firmly across his bare chest, raises a brow. "Yes, you did."

Yes, I did. But I say nothing, too afraid of what new lie might escape my mouth.

He shakes his head, and his damp hair sprays slightly. "I know you've been fighting with Jakub since that meeting. I mean, the walls here are paper thin." He searches my face. "I didn't want to interfere the past few days. But I could feel you trying to draw me into the argument, to choose sides. I know what I said at the meeting. And I agree with you, but he's my brother, and—"

I put up my hand to cut him off, relieved that this is his concern and not the spying. "You're right," I say carefully. "But I wasn't being entirely truthful right now. I also came to apologize. I knew you'd be here alone."

A truth snaking a lie. *I came to see you wash, to view the droplets sliding down your body like rain on a windowpane. The only way I can get through this terminal nightmare is to witness your beauty and imagine myself touching, tasting, feeling every inch of you.*

"Apology accepted." He smiles with teeth that are still nearly white, as everyone else's have decayed and become stained from lack of nutrition, fresh water, anything healthy or sanitary.

"Aleks—" I pause. There is so much more to say, but I stop myself.

"Back at that meeting, what you did, what you expressed, wasn't easy," he says. Still the damn meeting? Is he really that obtuse? "But I agree," he continues. "Enough with words—we need action. We can't pretend we are going to survive. We can't pretend that those barbarians will honor any agreements.

The truth is, I can no longer ignore my own feelings." He glances at the door, as if Jakub could walk in at any second. "I need to tell you something."

Finally. I brace myself, my hand clasping a loose brick sticking out of the wall beside me. He wants to tell me he feels the same, that he, too, looks at the sheet dividing his bed and ours at night and envisions my naked body. "I have joined the fighters—the ZOB unit," he whispers instead. "I've been secretly attending their meetings and training with them. I am going to help with the resistance from inside the ghetto. If I die, then I sure as hell am going to take as many of those Nazi bastards as possible with me when I go."

Training? Guns? Ammo? Secret meetings? How did I not see or know that Aleks is part of this? I spend three-quarters of my day obsessing about him. "Jakub is against those young fighters," I remind him. "Calls them troublemakers and says that they are going to make things much worse for us."

"Jakub doesn't know."

Like my father, Jakub sees nothing.

"I still attend Jakub's meetings. I still give him drawings for the archives, but I've been meeting in an underground bunker and—"

"Take me with you," I beg, my eyes trained on his.

He is silent for a long moment. "No, Bina. Absolutely not."

His penetrating gaze, deep green with mottled flecks of gold, reminding me of the jade marbles that my sister and I used to play with when we were little girls, sears through me. My body is ignited by the lavender scent of him. He must know how I feel. But he quickly takes a step back as if my nearness is invasive. My heart drops. Loyal to the end, that's what Jakub always said about his younger brother. I saw it, too, when he ran back into that burning house and reemerged with his charred wife and baby daughter dangling in his arms. And me . . . loyal only to him.

"One meeting. Please let me come . . ."

He exhales deeply. I can feel his mounting anger. "No."

"I know where it is," I persist. "I've heard the rumors. It's in the basement of that house on the corner of . . ." I stop when I see the rage visibly shrouding his face. But it's true, I hear things, the whispers about the covert resistance group springing up. So many whispers. There is breath, and then there is the breath beneath the breath—the only sound in the ghetto that matters.

"Bina, if something—anything—happens to you and it's my fault . . ."

Something already happened to me, Aleksander.

And it is your fault. I glance at the gray, threadbare towel around his waist, wishing I could yank it from his hands and drop to my knees. Wishing I could take him fully in my mouth right now, then lie together entangled across that tattered mattress shoved up against the window. Wishing more than anything that I could feel my skin pressed against his.

I look away, because if I don't, I will ruin this. His loyalty to Jakub is a nonnegotiable, a blood pact between brothers. When I glance up, I see Aleksander's steadfast fraternal devotion locked inside his clenched squared jaw. But something is changing. I know it because I studied body language, gestures, facial expressions, all the ways in which an actor morphs into character.

Aleksander's words are saying one thing, but his body, loose and agile, tells another story. It's in the way he leans in, the curl of his shoulders, the want in his cold nipples—erect like twin arrowheads against a smattering of golden chest hair. I can barely gather my breath. He is clearly fighting this thing between us inside his head. But perhaps, just maybe, not inside his heart.

Chapter Five

The apartment on Dzielna Street appears empty, deserted like so many buildings in the ghetto, but I know otherwise. All the action is happening down below, in the basement. As I approach, I see three teen boys loitering in the courtyard, and I'm not surprised. Everything in the ghetto moves in threes—especially the young smugglers. It takes three to get out: one to hold the top of the barbed wire, one to pull down the bottom, and one to slip through. But this trio is not the usual variety. They are clearly assigned guards trying not to look conspicuous. They have a ball between them, and when they see me, they start kicking it around. Their acting is terrible, and besides, I recognize one of them as I get closer—the tall, gangly one. Eryk Behrman. He drops off his younger sister, Dina, at my drama class in the afternoons on his way to wherever he goes. The kids lost both of their parents in the last roundup. A seventeen-year-old taking care of a ten-year-old. Ghetto life.

"Eryk." I acknowledge him. So, this is where you go.

His eyes widen when he sees me. "Mrs. Blonski, what are you doing here?"

"What are you doing here?" I counter. The two other boys are elbowing him. Eryk begins to blush, just as he does whenever he brings Dina to class and steals side glances at me. Dina is so painfully shy that she clings to her brother's arm until the last possible second. I watch Eryk peel her fingers off his skin, one by one, lovingly, protectively, and it breaks my heart.

Their parents were once famous violinists in the Warsaw National Philharmonic Orchestra and would lead weekly Friday afternoon concerts with other prominent musicians in the ghetto, playing in the center of Muranowski Square among the beggars—the children selling trinkets for food; the vegetable vendor who hocks only two items: cabbage and beetroot; the makeshift newsstand guy selling *Gazeta Żydowska*, the *Jewish Gazette*, the ghetto bulletin; the factory slaves selling bedsheets; and the dead and almost dead lying face down along the pavement, whom I would purposely squint tightly to unsee as I walked by. But there, in the heart of hell, was the ghetto orchestra, led by the breathtakingly talented Behrman duo. And for just a moment or two, I would stop and drink in Mozart, Beethoven, Brahms, allowing the symphonic notes to flow through me, ignoring the panorama of harrowing images, and think to myself: Yet somehow the music survived. Then, two months ago, the Behrmans and all members of their orchestra were seized from the square while playing. And now the music is dead too.

"I want to speak to Zelda." I stare down all three boys, my gaze moving deliberately slowly, resting briefly on each face with a look that says *I'm not leaving until I do.*

Zelda. I gambled with the name. Aleksander had told me that afternoon in his towel that Zelda would never agree to my presence. When I asked him who Zelda was, he stopped talking.

"Does she kn-kn-know you?" asks the youngest guard, a boy who barely has any facial hair. I half want to tell him to join my acting class, that I have helped several students who developed stutters and nervous tics in the ghetto. But right now, I just want to get inside the building.

"Zelda does not know me, but she will," I say. "The message is important. Let her know that Bina Blonski is here to see her." I pause, then, having a change of heart, I tell him, "And come to my class. It's at the convent on Nowolipki Street. I will help you get rid of that stutter."

The boy's gaze turns hard, older than his years, and I see the words form before he can push them out: "At this p-p-point, does it really matter?"

Eryk leaves the other boys at the entrance and brings me down to the basement bunker, pausing at the base of the rickety stairs, and tells me to wait here in this empty room, that someone will come for me. He then steals a quick last look at me before returning to his guard post. I glance around the large, vacant cellar with its sweaty, porous concrete walls, a long, scratched-up wooden table at its center holding a few half-filled scattered glasses of water and a dozen mismatched chairs along its perimeter. There are muffled voices coming from the adjoining room, so I wait. I don't sit or make myself comfortable. I stand in place, arms folded, just in case they are watching me, assessing me, which I'm sure they are. I spotted the small bullet-size holes in the walls as soon as I walked in. I'm not to be trusted. So, I remain still, play their game.

A woman finally emerges from the other room. She's around my age, early twenties, small in stature with a smooshed pugilistic face. Her nose looks like it has been recently broken; it is swollen and bluish on one side. Her short, dark, unruly hair is pinned back carelessly, and she wears a man's button-down shirt partially tucked into a pleated gray wool skirt with a belt that has roughly made notches. She is unattractive but carries herself powerfully, like a sheriff or a school principal. Her presence dominates the room. I straighten my shoulders to my full height and puff out my chest, determined to show that I am not intimidated or easily threatened.

This tiny woman is visibly unimpressed. Ferret-eyed and tight-faced, she circles me, eyeing me up and down rudely, then calls out loudly in Yiddish, "Why is the beauty queen here? I don't have time for this shit." No hello. No introduction. No why are you here? Not a care that I've been insulted. Just that. And that's the other thing about ghetto life. Manners no longer exist. People steal, lie, spit, walk over bodies strewn in the street as far as the eye can see— as though circumventing roadkill—but not before stripping the dead's shoes and snatching the contents out of their pockets, taking whatever is takable, seizing whatever is edible—doing whatever it takes to survive. Clearly, this woman is testing me, and I intend to pass.

"I came to fight," I announce, cutting to the chase.

She strikes me as someone with little patience for small talk.

"You." She laughs haughtily, and the mocking sound echoes off the barren walls. I know that cruel laugh, that sound. I have used it myself when I portrayed the evil stepmother in *Snow White* in primary school. I step forward, recognizing that I have only one chance to sway this woman before I'm dismissed.

"Just to be clear, Zelda—I assume that's your name—Aleksander Blonski did not invite me here. He told me to stay away. I invited myself because I want to help. If I'm going to die, it sure as hell is not going to be in a concentration camp in a poof of oven smoke. Like you . . . it's going to be on my own terms." I cock my head. Do not show fear. "And what is your problem with my face anyway?" I challenge, imagining my theater audience applauding my audacity.

Her eyes smile, but not her mouth. It tightens into a thin line like a worm doing a morning stretch. "Your face is too memorable, prettier than it has a right to be, that's my problem. But I'm listening." Her arms cross over her boyish chest like armor. Unlike most women, she is not unsettled by me, does not feel inferior. She is a huntress—not the prey, not minimizable. I'm starting to like her.

I lean forward, point my index finger between her

dark, unforgiving eyes. "I'm not afraid to do what needs to be done. My plan is to use my skills as an actress to get you what you want, what you need."

"You have been here thirty seconds. How the hell do you know what we want or need?" she snaps.

"A fighter needs two things: guns and ammo," I say, not letting her rattle me. "You can't fight back unless you can get to the Aryan side without getting caught. Lots of checkpoints. And I have done it numerous times." I touch my face, leave my finger on my cheek for emphasis. "It's because of this face." I pause, move in closer to her. "Because I look like them, I knew I could do it. I could have easily joined the cabaret with other actors and entertainers here. Café Sztuka begged me to join their entertainment troupe countless times, but I chose to keep a low profile, teach classes to the kids during the day, so that I could put my skills to better use and do what I need to do at night."

"Don't fool yourself," Zelda scoffs, dismissing me with a sharp wrist flick. "Low profile? Everyone knows who you are—Sabina Blonski, Maksymilian Landau's daughter. You can't hide that face, that pedigree, even in this shithole—even at night."

Our bodies are inches apart. Her breath smells of cheap cigarettes. She is baiting me, wants to see what I can handle. Am I tough or all show? I get it. "We can work together, Zelda. I can be useful," I insist. I know my worth and I'm not finished presenting my case. "Don't judge me before you know me. Don't criticize me before I've earned my stay here."

"Earned your stay," she repeats. Without taking her eyes off me, she snaps her fingers. Who does she think she is? Over Zelda's shoulder, Aleksander enters the room on command like an Egyptian eunuch. My heart races when he brushes past me, his shirt grazing mine. Our eyes meet briefly. Lips curled at the corners. Is he amused, impressed, or still angry? He was one of the voices I heard coming from the other room. He could have jumped in at any time to attest to my abilities, but he let me defend myself. Better this way. I will show him too.

I turn to Zelda. "I'm betting you have only a handful of guns here."

"Two," she admits. "Two goddamn pistols. That's our arsenal. It's a beginning. Do you know how much everything costs? Money that we don't have." She nods at Aleksander and then turns back to me. "So tell me, Sabina Blonski, how do you intend to earn your keep? Are you going to sell a family heirloom and buy us what we need? Have you even shot before?"

"Have you?" I counter. Two pistols against Nazi tanks? That's their resistance?

"You answer to me."

"I answer to myself. And I go by Bina, by the way," I retort. She may be the playground bully, but I am a worthy adversary. "And yes, I have shot. Plenty. I hunted with my father when I was a young girl. I am also pretty good at archery. Summers at the youth group." I stop as Zelda's face hardens. Entitlement and privilege have no place in this bunker. "I know guns."

She eyes Aleksander briefly. "What about that husband of yours? Does he plan to write about this in his silly archives? Does he even know you are here?"

"No," I say truthfully, feeling a lump form in my throat. Leave Jakub out of this.

But she has no intention of backing down. I can see it in her persistent glare. "Let me get this straight. Jakub Blonski, keeper of the truth, has no idea that his brother and his wife are joining the resistance movement that he and his smart friends oppose? Oh, this is too good." She moves in closer. "You know exactly what your husband thinks of us. Just like those traitorous fools in the Judenrat who believe that any form of resistance will provoke our sacred Nazi overlords." Her voice rises. "You know, Bina"—she spits out my name—"your husband and his posse are our real enemies—intellectuals with their faces so deep inside their books that they can't read the goddamn writing on the wall!"

She is not wrong.

"Zelda, that's enough!" Aleksander shouts.

But she ignores him and searches my strained face. "What will your husband think when he finds out that you are here breaking bread with us?" She points an accusatory finger this time. I see nails that are bitten down to the quick. "Your presence here puts us at a grave risk. Did you think about that before pushing your way inside?"

I say nothing.

"Tell me, how is this going to work, Bina?" she presses on. I want to reply that it works for Aleksander, but I hold back.

I clear my throat, attempting to buy myself a moment to think. "You're right. It's not going to work if my husband knows what I do for you. It will only work if he doesn't," I say honestly. "I choose to live. I choose to fight back. My husband chooses to write about it. And he will continue doing his work, his way." I meet her beady gaze squarely. "I'm not leaving."

Zelda picks up a used glass from the table and raises it high. "To marriage. L'chaim." She laughs mockingly, takes a swig, then slams it down.

Immediately, three young men from the other room

surround her like she's Cleopatra. Then they all walk out together into the next room, leaving me alone with Aleksander. I'm not sure what just happened, but Aleksander's expression is icy. Once Jakub and his precious archives were mentioned with such ridicule, his face changed. The lights went out. He is clearly struggling with my presence here, fuming that I invaded this part of his life, or what's left of it.

"You're playing a dangerous game here." His voice is muted, incensed.

"This isn't a game," I reply. "Not for me and not for you. It's survival. Need I remind you that you're playing too. You know exactly how Jakub feels. You heard what she said. How am I any different from you?"

He shakes his head. "We are not the same."

Zelda reappears, her boots announcing her entrance. She stops in front of me. "What can you bring to the table right now?"

"Right now?" I glance at Aleksander. "Did he tell you about the latest edict from Jürgen Stroop?"

Zelda gives me a look, like there's nothing she doesn't know. "I heard all about it. They want our girls to serve as their sex slaves." She begins to pace. "Bad news travels faster here than anywhere else in the ghetto. And you volunteered to be Queen of the

Whores." She rolls her eyes. "And your husband? He approves?"

Jakub again. Can't she just leave him alone?

My hands move firmly to my hips. I'm done with the taunting. "Despite what you think, Jakub is a good man, much better than I am. He still believes in history, preserving it, and in the future. I believe in nothing, only right now, what's at stake. His goal is to tell the Jewish side of the story, to report it, so the world knows the truth, even if we all are"—I search for the lone word, the darkest one that looms in my nightmares when I think of rodents and spiders and rats—"exterminated. My husband's efforts are admirable but won't save us. I am not admirable, but I have guts."

Aleksander is not blinking. His face is frozen, mouth dropped open, reminding me of one of his paintings from a series that he'd painted in our other life. "There are two choices as I see it—fight or flight," I continue. "Jakub has chosen flight—running away from the reality. It gives him purpose. I, on the other hand, plan to fight back and perhaps help save some of us in the process and, at the very least, take some of those monsters down with me. And I have a plan for our girls."

Zelda holds up her hand to stop me from speaking. "Keep your plan to yourself for the moment. You really want to help? I have a job for you. Something much more pressing." She glances at the door leading to the other room. More members of the resistance file in, at least twelve, an even mix of women and men. All young—most under twenty-five. I recognize several of them, but I say nothing, show no sign of recognition, as they take their seats around the long table or stand back against the wall.

"Before the guns, before the ammo, the smuggling, and now the whores, we must first clean up our own streets if we stand any chance of surviving. We need our people with us. Without that, we have nothing." Zelda closes in on me. "It's time to show Jews here and everywhere in Poland that resistance—not compliance or collaboration—is the only option left. We must get rid of the traitors within and send a powerful message immediately." Zelda's hot breath warms my skin. Her hands are balled into tiny, tight fists at her sides. I don't move a muscle. Woman to woman. Soldier to almost-soldier. I want to be part of this so badly I can taste it.

"I learned long ago that no one is to be fully trusted, Bina. No one, no matter what. So, I am only going to ask you this once." Her fierce deep-set eyes become murky twin puddles. "Your face . . . how far will you go to use it?"

Chapter Six

Jakub leans against the carbide lamp on the kitchen table, watching me closely as I clear the dishes. He knows I am up to something. The air is too thick and he's too well trained a journalist not to sniff out a story. Normally, he helps with the dishes, but tonight he sits across from Aleksander in silent anger, making a steeple of his index fingers, digging under his chin. I feel his distrust burning a hole in my back.

"What is it, Kuba?" Aleksander is the only one who uses Jakub's boyhood nickname and gets away with it.

From the corner of my eye, I see Jakub shaking his head. "The list."

The fucking list.

I heave a heavy sigh as I stare at the rusty trickle of sink water. I can't help it. The list is all we've talked about—argued about—for the past two days. The Nazi list of Jewish girls who will be plucked out of the ghetto for forced prostitution. Our Judenrat warlords were too cowardly to announce it or fight it. Instead, they ordered the decree printed on the front page of the *Jewish Gazette*, thinking it would absolve their own guilt, their part in throwing us all under the train. The *Gazette*, known as the bulletin of only bad news, is the ghetto's sole means of mass communication. When it first started, the creators asked Jakub to be its editor, but he refused. Like everything else in my husband's life, it all comes down to dignity. The *Gazette* is beneath him, a rag, not up to Jakub Blonski standards, no matter that it's the only news source in town. But after the latest decree was issued, he couldn't sleep. None of us could. And my role in it has pushed him over the edge.

Once I saw the decree in black and white, I couldn't sit still, wait it out, and do nothing. The second I read it, I made an appointment and went before the top brass of the Judenrat and two junior members of the Nazi command, without discussing my plan with Jakub first. I presented my case and volunteered to be the one to watch over all the girls. Yes, Queen of the Whores. I appealed to the Nazis by playing on their greatest fear—disease. I saw both young Nazis flinch when I mentioned syphilis. So I purposely stated it repeatedly, inserting disease and hygiene and syphilis into every single sentence, secretly enjoying watching them twitch. I told them I intended to make sure that every girl would be clean for the soldiers. That we should have nurses on board and at least a dozen "maids" on hand to keep the rooms tidy, the sheets changed—a job, I explained, that would be optimal for the younger girls. My goal was to save as many girls' lives as I could. But I didn't stop there. I also demanded warm blankets, better hygiene—soap, specifically—and most of all, more food to keep our young women "Nazi-worthy." I stressed that a Jewish woman from the ghetto was necessary to watch over the girls and keep them in line because they would trust her. I would personally stay with the girls, I emphasized, sleep in the same area with them. I did not lower my gaze. I showed no sign of fear, even though internally I was trembling. I wore my best dress—a now-faded blue Chanel midcalf form-fitting dress that I'd worn to the dinner party the night before my wedding to Jakub. I knew that every man in the Judenrat's office who heard my passionate plea saw not a prisoner or a Jew, but rather an elegant woman of impeccable breeding, who looked like God's gift to the Nazi libido. *You are the prize, Bina,* Jakub's voice echoed in my head. I knew my audience. And I sold it.

I sold it and broke what was left of my marriage simultaneously.

I drop the rest of the dishes in the sink, leave them there; I will get to them later. I quickly glance at my watch. Swallowing hard, I am barely able to look my suspicious husband in the eye. Zelda made me swear to secrecy. Too many lives are at stake.

One hour.

"Jakub," I say, curating a conciliatory tone, "please, let's not discuss the list. Go rest."

"Rest, Bina?" He slams his glass against the table, nearly knocking over the lamp and spilling the water. Here it comes. "Rest, goddamn it!"

Aleksander gives me a hard look when Jakub stands and stomps over to the window. His back faces us as he stares out at the convent across the courtyard, where I hold my acting classes for the children, many of whom are now orphans.

I nod back at him. Yes, I know. One hour. The clock is ticking. *Do something*, my eyes transmit silently. *Occupy Jakub. Find him vodka. Get him drunk. Whatever it takes.*

"Let's take our mind off things," Aleksander suggests when Jakub returns to his chair at the head of the table. "Perhaps play some cards? Bina, you're going to the Behrmans' now, right?"

"Yes, remember? I'm bringing the kids some soup." I purposely announced that activity this morning, but I repeat my plan for Jakub's benefit.

Forty-eight minutes.

"I will walk you," Jakub grumbles. Despite his anger, he is mindful of the eight o'clock curfew. A rule follower until the end. He turns to Aleksander. "Fine. I will be back in fifteen minutes. Cards then."

"Great, thanks. Just give me a minute." I muster appreciation. I'd already anticipated that Jakub would walk me to the Behrmans' apartment. So did Aleksander, who gathers the two small servings of the vile beetroot soup for me. Our tormentors have limited ration cards to three hundred calories a day per person. If they can't kill us with the typhoid, the death trains, slave labor in their sweatshops, then starving us to death still works like a charm. Smuggling food is our only option to stay alive. "The little girl Dina Behrman I was telling you about, Jakub . . ." But he's barely listening. I ramble on anyway. "She's been having night terrors since they took her parents. I have been working closely with her in class. Her brother told me Dina has gotten much worse and asked if I could help."

Aleksander gives me a cut-it-off neck swipe signal. "So, I may stay over there a bit longer until she falls asleep. I know it's after curfew but . . ." Aleksander's hard glance again. I stop talking.

"I will pick up Bina," Aleksander volunteers, then points to the top shelf in the nearly empty cupboard and tells his brother, "There's a spot of vodka waiting for you when you get back."

Jakub's brows knit together as he eyes the flask. "Seriously, you went to Manny's Bar with those thugs again?"

Those thugs. The Jewish gangsters on Mila Street. The thieves who live among us—but without them, we couldn't smuggle or survive. In the ghetto, professional thieves are the new heroes, saviors, teachers, our lifeline.

Aleksander's mouth breaks into a mischievous smile, and his eyes sparkle, and I can't help but smile back. "Yes, I went to Manny's the other day," he admits. "Get this . . . I traded Manny a portrait of himself for a pint of vodka."

We all laugh at that. We can't help it, and the release feels surprisingly good. Manny Abramowicz— the bar owner and jack-of-all-trades thief—is the most popular guy in the ghetto, self-anointed Mayor of Survival. Anyone who needs to barter anything starts with Manny and his boys, who were also crooks back in the other life. But who needs a self-portrait when we are all starving, dying by the second? Just Manny. Nothing in ghetto life makes sense. But it's also Manny, I think as I slip on my coat, who is making tonight happen. And those twin pistols that Zelda possesses—all Manny.

As I turn toward the door with Jakub close behind me, I purposely do not look back at Aleksander. We made it through the first hurdle, I know we are both thinking. A lot is riding on this. On me.

Thirty-six minutes.

As Jakub and I enter the courtyard to the Behrmans' apartment a few blocks away, he pulls me back from the door by the sleeve of my coat.

"What is it?" I ask, my heart seizing. *Please don't stop me.*

"Let's not fight, Bina. I'm so tired of fighting with you." His eyes look like his father's—baggy, sunken lids—a twenty-nine-year-old man who has aged forty years in the twenty-six months we've been here. And I hate myself right now. For hurting him, betraying him, humiliating him, lying to him. Everything I do is destroying this dignified man, breaking him down piece by piece.

"Jakub, I'm so sorry." And I mean it. For this. For what is about to happen tonight and all the nights after that. You deserve a wife who loves you, who would die with you and your precious archives. A wife who sleeps with you and thinks of you—not your brother. A wife who does not volunteer to be the ghetto madame. You deserve so much more. But I can only give you less.

I lean over and kiss my husband fully on the mouth, tasting the beet soup on my lips. But for this one solitary moment, I'm not lying. He pulls back, looks at me, his tired eyes shining and his permanently disapproving mouth smiling for the first time in forever. An eye glint—like his brother's—emerges for a split second, but then just as quickly, the muscle memory kicks in. He looks at me and sees the list. The spark extinguishes to a flicker and then it's gone for good. He releases my sleeve, turns, and walks away, not knowing that his wife, a serial betrayer, will soon betray him once again.

Chapter Seven

Where is Eryk? Dina was not supposed to be home alone. I look around the tiny one-room apartment, at the two mattresses splayed on the floor—one for her, one for her brother. She is sitting on her mattress, curled up with a book. Books are prohibited in the ghetto, but we do what we can to smuggle books for the children. She smiles when she sees me, then buries her nose right back inside the pages.

There is nothing left in the apartment, which was once rich with music, instruments, and life—even in the ghetto. What remains are just the basics: a wooden table, two chairs, a dresser, kitchen utensils, and photos of the Behrman family: the parents playing in the Warsaw Philharmonic, a prepubescent Eryk at a piano recital, a baby Dina playing the xylophone. Everything else, all keepsakes from the past, have been bartered for food and supplies. Everyone has done the same.

"Where is Eryk?" I ask Dina. "And why are you here alone?"

"Peter is coming. Eryk said he will be home later."

The boy with the stutter. I use a spare minute that I don't have to heat up the soup for Dina. I know better than to push for more answers. Zelda told me not to ask questions, to trust that she has worked out all the details from start to finish, and that everyone is doing their assigned part. The less I know the better, she explained. If I'm caught by the police or the Nazis, they can't beat nothing out of nothing. Another lie. That is all they do.

There is a knock at the door. "Who's there?" I demand.

"P-p-peter."

The boy enters holding a small suitcase. He is fifteen but looks twelve. This is who is watching Dina? My stomach knots. Zelda couldn't do better than that? I glance at my watch and sigh deeply. It's time. I've got to get out of here.

"Dina," I call out. She looks up timidly. "I need to leave. Your brother will be back soon, okay?" She nods, returns to the book.

"Peter," I whisper, wagging a finger. "Do not let

Dina out of your sight. Do you hear me? No matter what."

He nods. A child taking care of a child. "Wait," he calls out, and points to the small valise. "That's from Zelda. She said to put those clothes on."

I open the suitcase and see a belted black dress with a leather hook attached to it like a makeshift holster, a matching wool coat, and a tube of lipstick. Lipstick? Bright red, practically orange. A clownish color I would never wear in real life, but I don't ask questions. I follow instructions. The dress and coat—a set—not my taste, but good enough. And Zelda got the size correct. I wonder to whom the clothes once belonged. I try not to think about that and focus on what I'm about to do. "Turn around," I tell Peter, as I quickly undress and put my own clothes back inside the suitcase and store it in the corner of the room against the wall for when I change and return home to Jakub.

I take a deep breath, eye both children briefly, tell them to be safe, keep the door locked, and then I head out.

A man named Henryk waits for me in a parked car two streets away from the Behrmans' apartment. Though I've never met him personally, I have seen him numerous times driving around the ghetto. No one drives a car here. It's either a bike, a horse-drawn vehicle, or a rickshaw, unless you are a high-up member of the Judenrat. A car is one of the perks of being a collaborator. Henryk is the driver for the Judenrat's vice chair and clearly one of Zelda's boys—a plant. No wonder she gets all the information so quickly.

When I open the car door on the passenger side and climb in, Eryk is sitting in the back seat. He acknowledges me with a nod, but surprisingly doesn't really look at me. His eyes are steeled ahead. The fledgling resistance movement is about to send its first message to the Jewish Police . . . and I'm the messenger. *But what is Eryk's role?* I wonder but don't ask.

There is no question or doubt about the purpose of my mission. My first kill: a Jew turned policeman turned Nazi collaborator. Everyone knows him, fears him. He is head of the Jewish Police and goes by one name: Kapitan. He flaunts his power along every dirty, stinking block of the 1.3 square miles of ghetto, parading around in his chauffeur-driven rickshaw like he's King David—with his bright blue cap and sand-colored belted uniform, wearing a permanent smirk while wielding two well-used batons, one at each hip.

Kapitan is notorious for his cruelty. He has raped at least a dozen young women, sent hundreds of families to their deaths in the roundups—with lists that he personally presented to our captors. If a man was chosen for the transport, Kapitan took it upon himself to search for the missing wife and kids who were still in hiding and sent them on the death trains as well. He liked keeping murder neat and tidy, a family affair—no stragglers left behind. Like the other policemen on active duty patrolling the ghetto, Kapitan volunteered for his position, believing it would save his life. I smack my orangey lips together.

Not tonight.

Zelda's team has monitored Kapitan's movements and patterns for the past few weeks. He is a creature of habit. At 8:15 p.m. exactly, he exits police headquarters and heads to Manny's Bar for a round of drinks and to collect his nightly kickbacks. The bar is around the corner from the now boarded-up Café Sztuka on Leszno Street, the once splashy cabaret that Jakub, Aleksander, and I used to frequent when the ghetto was first sealed off before the roundups, and the same café that begged me repeatedly to join its performers, most of whom are now dead. Manny's Bar is the last bar standing in what used to be the ghetto's lively entertainment district, the premier let's-pretend-life-goes-on section, once consisting of five professional theaters, both Yiddish and Polish, a symphony, opera, live revues, and musical comedy. All gone now. When Zelda reached out to Manny for help, he didn't hesitate. He, too, was fed up with Kapitan's incessant demands, and more than happy to do his part.

I tighten the belt of my coat, grit my teeth. It's bitter cold even though I'm sweating through the wool material from nerves. The only thing worse than being in the ghetto is being in the ghetto during winter. No heat, barely any running water. Anything that comes out of a faucet is filled with rust and debris. My heart races and I can practically hear it pounding. We wait silently in the car until we see Kapitan toddle out of the bar and onto the other side of the street. His uniform is undone, his police cap is lopsided. He is drunk on his power, but not too drunk. That was the deal. Zelda told Manny that Kapitan needs to know exactly what is happening to him and why. Drunk then dead is not a lesson, not a punishment, not justice. Semidrunk, begging for his life, is the objective.

"It's time," says Henryk, the only words he has uttered all night.

Eryk leans forward, clasps my shoulder. "Be careful, Mrs. Blonski." Mrs. Blonski. A young man with ingrained manners, no matter how many times I've told him to call me Bina.

When Kapitan walks away from the bar and ambles

down the street, Henryk hands me Zelda's loaded 9mm Weiss pistol. One of the twins, I think, as I open my coat and stick the pistol securely inside the fitted holster attached to my dress.

Taking a deep inhale, counting to three, I close my eyes briefly and envision what I'm about to do. I get into character, conjuring up the strongest women I know: Joan of Arc, Medea, Cleopatra, Athena. Fierce, fearless, unstoppable. Once I leave myself behind, I can do anything.

I carefully get out of the car, taking pains not to make a sound, and walk on the opposite side of the street toward Kapitan, exactly as Zelda had instructed. I hear her voice in my head guiding me as I move briskly, anxiously, like a woman who knows she should not be out past curfew and is praying that she doesn't get caught.

Kapitan, of course, sees me and stops in his tracks, salivating like a hungry lion eyeing a terrified baby deer. I heard that in the other life he was a math teacher. He is only one-quarter Jewish, which makes him Jewish enough to be thrown into the ghetto. *Well, you are about to calculate this one wrong*, I think as I pick up speed. Show him how nervous you are—that's exactly what he wants. He lives for Jewish fear, gets off on it. I count to three silently in my head once again, anticipating.

"Hey, you! Stop! Where do you think you're going?" he slurs predictably. "It's past curfew."

I pull up my coat collar and keep walking, pretending to ignore him, my shoes clacking loudly against the cobblestones.

"You!" he shouts again even louder, his voice reverberating down the dark, empty street. Manny keeps his street clean of beggars and bodies. So it's just us. "I know you."

I stop, but don't look at him. This is it. No going back.

"What do you want?" I pivot slightly, holding my head high.

"What do I want? That's how you address the head of police?" He crosses the street, drunk but not too drunk.

"That's how I address a traitor." I repeat Zelda's script word for word.

"Traitor?" he roars. "You little bitch. I can save your life or put you on the next goddamn transport. Who the fuck do you think you are?" He charges toward me. I have mere seconds now. I reveal the terror in my eyes that he craves.

"You're in big trouble, young lady." He smiles, baring all his rotting teeth. *Big trouble*—clearly his two favorite words. I picture him standing in front of his math class, chiding a student caught whispering during one of his boring lectures.

Kapitan extends a sweaty hand and runs it along my quivering face, then squeezes my chin tightly, and I let him, keeping my eyes wide and unblinking. "You want that husband of yours and that brother of his to stay off the next train." It wasn't a question.

I swallow hard, feeling the press of the pistol against the tight waistband of the belted dress. He drops his hand from my face, and I can barely breathe. I take a step backward but try to keep him engaged. "What do you want from me?"

"Isn't it obvious?" He points to the nearby alley. "Walk in front of me," he orders, patting both batons at his hips simultaneously. "Where I can watch you."

My head is hammering. I feel the heaviness press between my brows as we make our way toward the alley. From the corner of my eye, I see Henryk's profile in the distance, for backup, just as Kapitan pushes me roughly against the side of the building. A broken brick rips at my back, but I don't scream. Instead, the pain wakes me up, sharpens my senses. Kapitan starts clumsily unbuckling his belt. And in that brief second when he takes his eyes off me, I reach inside my coat, step back, and shoot him point-blank in the chest.

His eyes spring wide open as the blood splatters

everywhere. He stumbles forward and grasps on to me. I push him off to the side, emboldened. I am certain this is not how Kapitan imagined he'd die—by a woman's bullet. I see the disbelief in his half-shut gaze, as he clutches his chest.

"That's for all the Jews you betrayed, Kapitan." I spit out his name as he cries for help. To no avail. Manny made sure no one would be walking down his street. I shoot Kapitan once again to shut him up and give him more pain, the second bullet to his stomach. *Make him suffer.* I hear the echo of Zelda's words. The fear gone, my blood pumping wildly, I watch this man's slow, dramatic death as though it were straight out of Mozart's *Don Giovanni.* The chest clutch, the tears blinding his eyes, the rattling breath, the furrowed forehead lined with drippy sweat, the calling out some random woman's name—dying but not yet dead, alive long enough to see who killed him, to feel it, and to know why. I feel drunk on my power over him. I reach up to shoot him once again—the final shot—when I hear footsteps quickly approaching. I point my gun at the intruder.

"Eryk, what are you doing?" I drop the pistol to my side.

"My turn now," he says, not looking at me. He is holding the bow of his father's violin. He pushes me aside roughly—no manners this time—and straddles Kapitan, who is beneath him grasping his last seconds of life. Eryk raises the bow high over his head and stabs the man right through his chest into the bullet hole, pushes it in with all his weight, and twists. "This is for my mother, you piece of shit. And for my father. May you rot in hell."

I stand back and let Eryk do it all, feel it all: the rage, the pain, the immeasurable loss, over and over. He repeatedly stabs the already dead man until the bow in his hand snaps in half. I wait it out, knowing Zelda gave Eryk this gift, avenging his parents' murders, the finishing touch. That was her plan all along.

Finally, I lead Eryk away, out of the alley, just as Henryk pulls up in the car. I climb into the back seat with Eryk, who is now crying. A killer back to a boy who'd lost his parents. At least he still has tears. The last vestige of humanity. Most of us have already gone numb.

"They're never coming back, Bina." No more Mrs. Blonski.

"No," I whisper. "They're never coming back." I lightly wipe away his tears with my finger, grateful for the wetness, that I can still feel something.

"Nor are we."

"Nor are we," I repeat, knowing that none of us is

going to come out of this alive. And if we do, we will have already died a thousand deaths.

"If something happens to me, Bina . . . can you . . ." The tears halt and the resolute gaze returns. This boy-man of the house at just seventeen with one family member left worth living for is about to ask me to protect the only person who matters to him. Dina once told me that her brother was a great pianist. Gentle, kind, shy. But not when he played the piano. Then, he seemed big and bold, different, she said, adding with a whisper, and kind of scary.

"I will watch over Dina," I assure him. "I won't let anything happen to her." I give Eryk the soothing words he needs. Comfort lies, empty promises—the good kind. *If I don't die first*, which I don't say, but we both think it anyway.

Henryk purses his lips together tightly, nods his tacit approval. Justice was done. We all know that by morning, word of Kapitan's death will spread like wildfire throughout the ghetto, and Zelda's message will be heard loud and clear: There's a price to pay for collaboration. We are fighting back. You're either with us or against us.

For the first time in months, I feel something akin to peace as the cold air from the open window wafts over me. I think not of my dead parents, my sister, the baby I lost, but of fat Manny Abramowicz—the only human who actually gained weight in the ghetto. And I understand now to the depths of my soul the dark, exquisite beauty of survival, the saccharine glow illuminating revenge.

Chapter Eight

The Sabbath candles radiate in the corner of the room in the bunker, which is filled with at least two dozen fighters ranging in age from the boy with the stutter to Manny the bar owner, who is in his late forties, and by far the oldest member in the room. Most of the fighters are not religious, but now more than ever, showing pride in our Judaism matters. I stopped by for just a few minutes at Zelda's behest, lying once again to Jakub that I was dropping off soup for the Behrman kids. Aleksander told his own lie. He is here too. Both of us separately promising Jakub we would return before curfew.

Zelda sits at the head of the long table, her charcoal eyes sparkling like stars against a black velvet sky. Tonight, she is the proud leader of a fledgling organization claiming its first victory. And I gave it to them: Kapitan's murder. There is no standing ovation for my performance, just a circular glow radiating from all directions—respect, and it is everything.

Zelda raises a tarnished goblet of wine. "To Twarz." Everyone laughs at her code name for me: the Face. The soft, admiring tone camouflaging her usual gruff pitch tickles my skin. She then gently places the goblet down and hands me a gift wrapped in crumpled old newspaper—the *Jewish Gazette*, which bears a death toll headline from two deportations ago. "For you, from all of us."

No one says a word as I stare at the gift. The silence is thick, anticipatory. My breath catches in my throat when I look up briefly and hold Aleksander's hot gaze in mine. My heart twinges, and I quickly look away, afraid my eyes will expose what is embedded in my heart. He is not standing behind Zelda, like her posse of young teenage soldiers, but leaning against the door-way across the room in the faded blue button-down shirt that I washed yesterday along with Jakub's shirts.

I take my time, stretching the moment, holding the gift as though it were a sacrificial offering. The only gifts in the ghetto are food. Even for birthdays—food. Anniversaries—food. Nothing else matters when you're starving. Smiling to myself, I recall my last real present.

My father had gifted me a pearl necklace—rare pink pearls—for my nineteenth birthday. It had a clasp with a diamond embedded in the gold. It belonged to my grandmother, who had the good fortune to die peacefully in her sleep a year before the war began. I traded that necklace within a few weeks of arriving in the ghetto, to a Polish guard for a bottle of aspirin, a dozen potatoes, and two pounds of sliced meat—a necklace worth all the sliced meat in Warsaw. But this . . . I stare at the shabbily wrapped present, fondle the length of it, and then slowly open it. My gaze returns to Zelda. She nods. It is what I think it is. I let the paper fall off and drop to the table. A bloodstained club. Kapitan's club, his blood. A symbol of victory. I blink back the tears. It is the most meaningful gift I have ever received. Zelda nods like a proud mother. I am one of them now.

A lone tear escapes its shackles, and I feel its slim wetness loll down my cheek, and I allow it. I look up with tear-dappled lashes. Aleksander, like everyone else, is smiling. But nothing—not even him—compares to Zelda's face right now.

"Mazel tov." She beams a smile that transforms her face, making way for unexpected beauty to shine through. The French call it *jolie laide*—ugly beautiful.

"Mazel tov," echoes everyone in the room.

"Today, we celebrate." Zelda raises the Sabbath

goblet once again. "We fought back, sent a message, and we were heard. People are celebrating Kapitan's death in the streets, Bina. A beacon of light in the Land of Darkness and Defeat. And this first triumph belongs to all of us here." She meets the shining gazes of everyone in the room, then gently puts down the glass, leans forward with both hands pressed across the table. "Make no mistake, they're coming for us. But yesterday, we came for them. We fought back. Shabbat Shalom."

"Shabbat Shalom," everyone responds in unison.

Zelda glances over her shoulder, signals to Eryk. He reaches inside his jacket and hands her the gun. My gun. The murder weapon. I recognize it because it has a lightning-shaped scratch along its sleek long-nosed black exterior.

Zelda puts the gun on the table next to the goblet, then takes out a black-and-white photo from the inside of her jacket and shoves it across the table in my direction. The smile is gone. "This man, Bina . . . His name is Dabrowski. He works at the Halstrom factory. You know where it is."

"Of course," I say uneasily. The factory is in the heart of the ghetto. It is the largest sweatshop, owned by a German-based company that manufactures Nazi uniforms. And Jews provide the free slave labor. No one lasts at Halstrom's more than a few months. Women and children are worked to death. Everyone knows it's a last stop.

"Dabrowski oversees the workers. A Pole who married a Jew—that's why he's here. A Nazi plant, another collaborator. They think we don't know. But he reports everything he hears to his Nazi handlers and has been rewarded handsomely. This traitor is particularly brutal. He doesn't just turn people in. He goes the extra mile—giving up names of those in hiding, and especially the 'troublemakers' like us. Names the Nazis never even asked for, ingratiating himself to those animals. He's number two on my list."

How many are on your list? I wonder.

"Twelve to start," Zelda says, reading my mind. "Between us"—she makes a circular motion with her finger, indicating everyone in the room—"in the next few days we will kill a tribe of those within our community who have betrayed us. But you"—she points the short, stubby finger in my face—"will take out Dabrowski."

Zelda lets that sink in for a few seconds, and there is pin-drop silence around the room. "And then, you are leaving the ghetto. Because this killing will make a statement. Every slave laborer in that factory will witness it. And everyone at all the surrounding sweatshops will hear about it, which is a good thing, the important thing."

"Wait—leave?" I interrupt. "Leave the ghetto?" I repeat, glancing at Aleksander. His mouth drops. It is clear he wasn't privy to this information.

"Zelda," he interjects, walking toward the table.

She holds up her hand. "Not now. We will discuss this later in private."

She turns back to me, ignores Aleksander's glare, the tightening of his mouth, the fists curling at his sides. "We need you on the Aryan side immediately. There are rumors of the next roundup coming soon. I heard this from my source in the Judenrat. And it may be the worst murder train of all. We hear Nazi commanders are being ordered to clean out the ghetto, and we must be ready." She glances at her comrades. "Let me be clear: this roundup is not going to go like a Swiss train as usual. For the first time, there will be consequences. And not just dead collaborators. Dead Nazis too." She glances around, dares anyone to challenge her. Her eyes rest on Aleksander, whose cheeks are bright red, clearly upset with her. She clasps her hands tightly together. "Now, everyone, leave us. I need the room alone with Bina."

She nods at the young men lurking behind her and smiles slightly at the young woman standing with them. A pale-skinned, scrawny, freckle-faced redhead with riotous coils of curls. No more than eighteen or nineteen years old. I wonder what she does for the team. Everyone leaves. Only Aleksander remains. He is not going to let Zelda push him around.

"Zelda." His arms are crossed and the muscle pops in his jaw. "I'm fully aware of Bina's capabilities. But it's my brother we are talking about here."

She dismisses him with a wrist flick. "Your brother has his nose in books while everyone is dying around him."

"Damn it, Zelda, let me kill Dabrowski. Not her." He points at me without looking at me. I shrink slightly at the anger in his voice.

Zelda's hard gaze is slightly mollified. I sense that Aleksander is among the very few who could get away with challenging her. "We all make sacrifices. We will talk more later. I have a different assignment for you. Now please, go."

Zelda waits until Aleksander stomps out of the room, and I realize I haven't let out a breath. She leans forward. "It's best if this remains between us. There is an apartment already set up on the Aryan side—a safe house—close to the ghetto, just on the other side of the wall. You're going to kill Dabrowski, then you're going to get us ammunition, guns, grenades. There is no other option. The next roundup, like I said, will kill most of us. We must be ready to fight back. There's an organization on the outside sympathetic to our cause, an arm of the Polish resistance called Żegota. They are friends. Do you hear me? We don't have many of those. These are Poles who care about us and about what the Nazis have done to our country. I got word that they are willing to help us get what we need. That's why you must go immediately and arrange for the transport of weapons."

I struggle to keep my voice even. "Let me get this straight. You want me to shoot Dabrowski dead in broad daylight, then leave the ghetto. What am I supposed to tell my husband? And what about the girls? The list?" I shake my head. "I went directly to the Judenrat. I pleaded my case. They know who I am. My plan is to protect the girls. I can't just leave in the middle of all this—especially now."

"Guns and ammo are our only priority." Her voice is deceptively calm, like a still wind. "And you *can* leave, if you're dead."

"Dead?" My eyes widen.

Zelda laughs, but it's not a laugh. There is no smile, no warmth, no twinkle. "You think they are going to agree to you babysitting pretty young Jewish girls that they intend to fuck and discard? The Jewish Nanny? Wake up, Bina! It's all very admirable, but don't fall asleep like the rest of the ghetto idiots. The Nazis will agree to your terms and then turn around and break the agreement before you can blink. They will use the girls, kill them, and then rape and kill you too. There is no happy ending here. No escape. No hope. Do you understand me?" She bares her teeth. "I don't talk about this . . . But do you know what those animals did in Warsaw right after they invaded us? It was October first, 1939, exactly one month after the invasion. They rounded up forty young women between the ages of eighteen and twenty years old. I know this because my younger sister, Raisa, was one of them. She got all the looks in the family. They passed me over, seized her while we were having dinner, took her to an apartment on Piusa Street that belonged to a Jew. They shot him dead, of course, threw his body out the window, stripped the girls naked, made them dance, abused them, raped them, and killed them all. My beautiful sister was studying to become a nurse. Don't kid yourself, Bina. That will be your fate, too, and all those girls on their goddamn list. No one is going to be saved or spared—no matter what you promised, or what they promised you. Clean sheets? No diseases?" She laughs that non-laugh again. "Just like those trains to Treblinka—all those lies they told us to send us to the death camps. Work, good food, even beaches— hah! We jumped on those trains willingly, like we were going on holiday. Fools! Now we know the truth, we have the evidence. Fighting back, taking them down for the world to see—making them hurt, too—is all that's left for us now."

I press both palms on the table, lean forward. "I'm not stupid. I know the end game. But I want to give those girls protection and purpose. Get information out, teach them to act as couriers, listen, find out Nazi plans, get—"

"Do you hear me? No one cares!" she shouts. "The world has forgotten us. The Polish government-in-exile makes all kinds of false promises to us. We are out of time. We are going to die here! Let's take them with us. That's the only goddamn plan!" Her voice intensifies, and I can feel the walls shake.

"But the girls . . ." I persist.

"Not one of those girls on that list is going to become a whore under my watch. Do you understand me?" she yells, then coolly pulls two homemade cigarettes out of her pocket, lights them, sends one my way, sits back, and takes a long drag. "You are going undercover on the Aryan side to get us guns and ammo, period. We need you. Really need you now. You came here bragging about your Aryan face, your skills as an actress, as a hunter. What was it? In summer camp? Hunting with your dead father? Well, I believe you now. You proved yourself. You killed Kapitan, the worst among us. You're one of us now, so act like it." She grounds out the cigarette carefully to finish it up later, removes a pistol from inside her pants, and slides it across the table. "I'm giving you three bullets. That's all I can spare. My hope is that you will need only one to do the job, and you can return the other two." She stands. "Say goodbye to your husband tonight. Pack a small bag, just the important things. A good coat. Warm socks. Sturdy boots. Undergarments. One elegant dress and shoes. I will bring you a few other necessary items. You will meet me at the Behrmans' apartment at six tomorrow morning. From there, you will head to the Halstrom factory and follow my instructions." She pauses. "After you do what you need to do, you're going to die, like I said."

I stand too. "That's not happening."

Zelda's gaze remains cold, unblinking. "Bina Blonski is going to die. New papers and a new identity will be waiting for you. You're going to shoot Dabrowski in broad daylight, in front of all the laborers. There will be a dead blonde on hand with a bullet hole through her face to show the Judenrat and their Nazi handlers that you didn't get away with it. Believe me, there are plenty of dead blondes to choose from among the bodies lying on the streets. She will be wearing your clothes. Aleksander will know this, but not Jakub."

"No, I can't do that." My breath hitches. "Jakub must know."

"Jakub is against us. Jakub would turn us in. He can't know the truth. Do you understand me?"

"Aleksander will never agree."

She flicks her wrist. "Leave that to me."

"Either I tell Jakub, or I'm out." I can't do that to him. He needs to know the truth. I owe him that at the very least.

She lowers her voice threateningly. "If you tell Jakub, it will put Aleksander's life at risk. Is that what you want?" She waits for my reaction. "You think I don't know?"

Our eyes meet. *She knows.* Just like she knows everything.

"I thought so . . . Now go, home. Follow the plan."

Zelda wins. Bina Blonski is about to die.

Chapter Nine

From the corner of my eye, I see the small suitcase waiting for me near the door of our apartment. My heart pounds. This is it. I look at Jakub. Finally, we are quiet for the first time after twelve hours of fighting. The blame game as usual, and now it's goodbye.

I told him. A watered-down version of the truth.

Jakub sits on the tattered green couch across from me, a leftover from the Polish family who once lived here and relocated to the Aryan side. Jakub's endless paperwork is splayed across the coffee table, his makeshift office. I glance down at his life's work for what may be the very last time. His precious archives. The history of the Warsaw Ghetto. From October 1940, when the German officials first decreed the establishment of the Warsaw Ghetto, to . . . no ending yet. But we all know how it ends.

"You're leaving. Just like that," he says once again, throwing up his hands.

"It isn't 'just like that,' Jakub. How many times do I have to explain?" I sigh heavily, gearing up for the next round. "I couldn't sit back and wait to die. I had to do something."

"Was I even a factor in your decision, Bina?" He swallows hard. I watch his large Adam's apple go north, south, and north again. "Did you ever love me?" The one question that has been on his lips the whole night and probably the nearly four years we've been married.

I hold my gaze steady, prevent my eyes from fast blinking, my body from fidgeting, my lips from quivering, my words from escaping, keenly aware of all the telltale lying signs, praying my acting is good enough. "Of course I love you." *I just love your brother more.*

He points to the suitcase, the tone of his voice escalating. "You know, you're a terrible wife, but a great actress. No one pretends better than you." He wants to hurt me right now, so I let him. "No wonder they picked you to go to the Aryan side to serve as a courier."

That's what I told him. Courier. Delivering messages to the outside world, particularly to the Polish underground.

A plea for help. A risky job. Many of the girls who served bravely as couriers never made it back alive. A lie and a truth. I just don't tell Jakub that the messages are a plea to procure guns, ammo, dynamite, and raw materials to make grenades. This much I owe Zelda.

"I couldn't continue teaching drama classes and playing pretend," I tell him for the umpteenth time.

"All you do is play pretend." Jakub's forehead scrunches tightly. He is much too young to have those deep-set creases. How many of those did I give him?

My husband wants to hit me. He never would, but I see the rage roiling inside the tightening coils of his fists, as though clutching everything I have ever done wrong.

"And what of the girls, those on that despicable list that you were so keen to save just days ago? Yesterday's news?" The meanness, the sarcasm, begins to spew again. He used to be so gentle, so patient. I've done this to him. "Have you already forgotten about your big show at the Judenrat? I have heard of nothing else from my colleagues."

Queen of the Whores. His band of intellectuals probably remind him at every turn, and even when they are silent. Jakub sees the shame I brought down upon him in their clever eyes.

"That hasn't changed. There's a plan for the girls

too," I lie again. My God, it's become so easy. I pray that Zelda does have a plan for them as she promised me. I glance quickly at my watch. I must go. She is already there, waiting for me at the Behrmans' apartment. I rise slowly from the chair.

"So that's that."

"Jakub, please." I try to shut out his rapid-fire accusations to take one last, lingering look around the two-room apartment—our prison and refuge. I spent all night cleaning, doing laundry, to leave our home in the best shape possible. I turn away so my husband can't see my face. Can't see me eyeing the washbasin in the distance, the tiny sliver of lavender soap next to the faucet, and envisioning his brother slippery wet and naked as the sunbeams eclipse his lanky body. My eyes water slightly. I will only have those images in my head. I'm leaving Aleksander too.

I take in the little life we created and place my hand over my rapidly beating heart. There's a good chance I will never see this place again. There is an even better chance I won't make it back alive. But I'm willing to take the risk. Why? I wonder. Why can't I die with my husband, hold his hand, and wait for my number to be called to the death train like the other wives? Die clinging to those precious archives? I look away. It's not my fate, it is Jakub's.

Inhaling deeply, I grab my thick wool trench hanging neatly over the chair in the kitchen. Jakub follows me to the door.

"You killed Kapitan," he announces, his hand covering mine on the doorknob, not ready to release me just yet. "It was you, wasn't it? I suspected you were up to something that night you brought soup to Eryk and his sister. I saw the lying in your eyes. When Kapitan was found murdered the next day, I thought to myself: Was it Bina? She lies, but could she kill? Could she go that far?"

Yes, Jakub, my eyes confess, but I remain silent. And now I'm about to go even further.

Five minutes. I must meet Zelda in five minutes. And Jakub still wants to fight. Our last moments together will be spent bickering.

"And my brother? Is Aleks part of this? Is he with those radicals too?" he presses, now blocking the door with his body.

"It was all me, only me." I will never betray Aleksander. "And I'm not sorry for killing that man who sent so many of us to our deaths. My only regret is not having done it sooner." I straighten to my full height.

His face tightens. "Who the hell are you? You killed Kapitan, and yes, the world is a much better place without that bastard. But they will find you, Bina. And if they can't find you, they will come after me and Aleks. You put us at great risk. You know that, right?"

My heart is no longer pounding, it's crashing. I know that. So does Aleksander. It is the most troubling piece of all. Jakub now knows that I am willing to sacrifice him for the big picture. That if I am discovered, he will pay the price for my actions. That's how it works in the ghetto—the crime of one family member is a consequence for all. That's how they have us cowering like beaten dogs. Sweat trickles down my temples. Jakub can see it. I need to go, but I don't want us to end like this. I point to the table with his precious papers. "The archives . . . I will be on the outside. Please, let me help. Let me get your work into the right hands."

Jakub glances at the table. He realizes that his murderess wife is his one chance to bring the story of the ghetto beyond the walls. But he doesn't want to give me the satisfaction. His forehead furrows, a thousand lines making their presence known. He is wrestling with himself, and I don't have time for his painfully time-consuming analytics.

I move past him, walk to his worktable. "I need to leave immediately. But let me do this one thing for you."

He exhales hard, says nothing, just nods. I take that as a yes and pick up the first stack of papers. His own reporting. The book he's working on, rigorously documenting daily ghetto life. His insights, his creation. There is so much more, but this pile means the most to him.

"I will protect it," I vow, pressing the papers to my chest. "I will give this to someone who will make this matter. I promise you."

He nods again, but with some extras: a deep squint, a head tilt, and a tight pressing of his lips—a look I know intimately. It is the same intense expression when he slipped the ring on my finger, when he buried our dead fetus, when he orgasms.

"I know you think my work means nothing," he says with resentment. "That the archives are a waste of time. History will prove you wrong."

Guns matter. Food matters. Freedom matters. But to Jakub, the stories matter most.

I open my suitcase in front of him to stuff the papers inside. And when I look up, his eyes meet mine, only with less hate. I had stuck our wedding picture on top of all my clothes. Beneath it (which he doesn't see) is a photo of Aleksander and me by the sea, our backs to the camera—a silhouette of his body near mine, not touching, with just enough air between us. Karina and Jakub were also there that perfect summer day, but lounging on the beach blanket. Jakub took the picture. He thought it was artsy. If only he knew.

No more words are exchanged between us. We are done. I'm glad he saw the wedding picture. Tears fill his eyes as he pulls me in close, just like he did the night I murdered Kapitan. His embrace is hard, demanding. It's over, we are over. We embrace everything we lost and everything we will never have together. I am late for the mission, but it doesn't matter right now. I want to savor Jakub one last time, hold on to the quiet between us. Zelda will have to deal with it. Dabrowski will have five minutes extra to live. Feeling the jutting bones of my husband's thin, sunken-in chest against me, I whisper one lone truth into his ear. "Live, Jakub . . . Just live."

Chapter Ten

I stare out the small attic window from the fourth floor of the apartment building on the Aryan side. The ghetto is just one street over. That's how close I am. From my vantage point, I see the whitewashed apartment buildings directly across the street. But also, in the space of six inches of windowpane, I can make out the slope-roofed, redbrick tenements peeking out from behind the ten-foot-high ghetto wall, smothered with glass and barbed wire. I wrap my arms tightly around myself. I am here, free, and hell is within walking distance. Is this what it looks like, feels like, to everyone who is not a Jew?

I'm free yet trapped, a captive in this tiny attic, awaiting my next move. It's been three days since I took out Dabrowski, three days I have been anticipating instructions from Zelda. How much longer?

The kill itself was surprisingly easy. Almost too easy. I replay it inside my head at least once an hour. New details are added each time I relive it. How I strode into Halstrom's sweatshop wearing a simple black dress, sturdy shoes, that same dramatic orangey lipstick (for good luck, Zelda had said laughing; she knew I hated the color), and a navy beret. No disguise, just me, Bina Blonski for all to see. I carried a fresh loaf of bread, as though bearing a gift to Dabrowski.

Everyone turned to look when I entered the factory, strutting down the aisle toward their boss, who was sitting at his large desk at the helm of the warehouse cramped with at least one hundred rows of sewing machines and laborers. I noted Dabrowski's cushy, dark leather fanback chair that looked like wings behind him. Comfort and compensation for his betrayal.

As I moved toward him, the laborers stopped their sewing machines for only a split second, knowing that any pregnant pause in their fourteen-hour workday would yield a harsh beating meted out by Dabrowski himself in front of everyone. Making an example is the Dabrowski way, according to Zelda. He would ruthlessly beat the starving women and children into submission with a rod if their work wasn't completed to his satisfaction. I can tell by the man's smug, mustachioed face and his neatly combed, oily black hair that he relishes his power over the slave laborers. A coward. I see the gleam in his eyes as I approach, noting the bread in my hands. I am fully aware of what I look like: a "thank-you" being sent his way. I smile back seductively and know with every inch of my body that I am going to enjoy this.

"Bina Blonski," he announces with surprising familiarity. I stop in my tracks. Does he know me? We've never met before. "Why are you here? And is that for me?" He points to the bread. His voice is oddly melodious, like a tenor. It doesn't fit the man. And then I see the picture of a young boy on the console behind his desk, realizing that his son was once in my acting class a few years ago, in the beginning. A son who is now dead. Not from starvation or deportation, but from typhus. So many students have passed through my classes over the past few years in captivity. Countless have died from illness, starvation, shot while smuggling, or rounded up onto the death trains. I do recall that Dabrowski's wife always brought the boy to class, and I feel momentarily bad about the son—a sweet, affable child. I push away any empathetic thoughts and focus on the remaining tortured children in this hot warehouse slaving away for this sadistic bastard.

I smile broadly, and in my loudest speaking voice, which resonates throughout the chamber, I announce,

"Yes, it's for you. I came to deliver a message." I wore very strong perfume. Part of the seduction, Zelda said. Let Dabrowski smell the scent of death before he rots in hell.

"After your first kill, Bina, I promise it only gets easier," she explained when we debriefed in the Behrmans' apartment right after I took out Kapitan. "Once you decide you are no longer a lamb but a wolf, everything changes." Zelda leaned forward with her untamed eyes. "Everyone I have ever loved has been murdered. I'm numb to the point that I now circumvent the dead on the street, become irritated when I see bodies blocking my path. I'm no longer human, Bina. That's why these animals are going to pay. For stripping away my humanity. Revenge is redemption. You'll see."

I saw.

"You have betrayed the Jews of the ghetto," I told Dabrowski. "We will never forget and never forgive." The sewing machines stopped cold. Everyone's eyes were glued to me. Dabrowski's mouth dropped open, and as he reached for his desk drawer, I pulled the gun out of the bread loaf and shot him point-blank. One bullet, smack between his eyes. The man's head exploded, blood splattered onto my clothes, his desk, and the wall behind him. And then there was total silence, reminding me of that momentary lapse between a show's final line and the audience realizing the play is over.

At once, the entire room of slave laborers erupted with enthusiastic fists pounding against the tables and feet stomping the floor. The rich, pulsating sound was magnificent. I saw the triumph in their eyes when I turned and walked back toward the doors, felt the ground quaking beneath my feet. I murdered their tormentor in cold blood, and they were all still alive to see it. Not a Nazi. Not a man. But a woman who took out their enemy with a gun concealed inside a loaf of bread. Ahh, the stories that would be told. The victory I witnessed in everyone's almost-dead eyes meant everything to me. Justice for those who couldn't fight back.

You were right, Zelda. So right.

And then Zelda's well-oiled machine went to work. Her boys were waiting for me at the factory's entrance, wearing masks. The two Jewish policemen who had been assigned to guard the factory door were tied up and gagged. Two of her fighters whisked me out of the factory, and two others stayed back to clean up Dabrowski's murder. One of the masked men gently removed the gun with the remaining two bullets from my hands and whispered, "I'm bringing this back to Zelda, Mrs.—Bina." Eryk. I squeezed his arm but said nothing. It was all a blur.

Dazed, I was immediately brought to a deserted apartment nearby. My clothes were removed, even my shoes, and my attire from head to foot was quickly replaced. The same young, skinny redhead I had seen in the bunker dressed me, had my suitcase with her. Her name was Tosia. Fierce and smart, she moved swiftly. I learned that her family had been seized in one of the first roundups while she was on the Aryan side smuggling food. Alone in the ghetto, she joined Zelda's unit. Once I was changed, Tosia led me to one of the more discreet wall entrances, where two more policemen—resistance plants— were waiting for me.

Tosia handed them a fistful of zlotys to pay off the Polish guards on the other side, who would then quickly bribe a young Nazi guard to leave his post for ten minutes. Hands fed greedy hands. I could hear the smack-smack echo of the palm clasps. All Zelda's orchestration. I was then removed from the ghetto, shoved into the back seat of a waiting car on the Aryan side, and pushed onto the floor. A tarp was thrown over me. In less than fifteen minutes, I was stripped of my ghetto citizenship.

Gossip in the ghetto moves at the speed of light. By nightfall, everyone would hear that Bina Blonski, daughter of Maksymilian Landau, killed the collaborator Dabrowski. She would also be pronounced dead, her murderer still unknown.

All skillfully curated by Zelda. *Please, Jakub,* I beg inside my head, *don't ruin this.*

The young, elegantly dressed Polish couple who drove the getaway car barely spoke to me as they speedily set me up in the attic apartment. The room, the size of a large closet (much smaller than my own closet in my other life), contained the bare minimum: a cot, a sink with running water, a small toilet, an old wood stove, a tiny table with one chair, fresh linen, towels, feminine hygiene necessities, and floor-to-ceiling shelves packed with basic supplies, including three loaves of bread, cheese wedges, vegetables that were not yet rotted, sugar, tea, and a bottle of vodka. A feast by ghetto standards that I was told to "make last until you receive further instructions." No names, no introduction. The faceless couple moved in and out, as though they were never here. Who are they? Does Zelda know them? The answers may never arrive. With nothing here but a few random books that I found in the closet, I stare out the window and wait impatiently for my next instructions.

The knocks come on the fourth day, in the middle of the night. Three hard knocks, two taps, followed by three hard, just as I was told. I wait with my ear pressed to the door, then softly ask, "Who is it?"

"Me," a voice whispers. "Let me in."

Me. My breath catches, my heart drops. Him. Aleksander.

I fling open the door, pull him inside, shut the door quickly, and then lock it behind me. I hug Aleksander tightly—an appropriate embrace, not the real one I feel inside. "Tell me everything."

And then I see it before I hear it. Bad news. His expression is morose. He looks gaunt, exhausted, thirsty, dirty, covered with cuts and bruises, dried blood smeared across his face. A man on the run. He stinks of sewer.

I act quickly. "Drink, eat, Aleks. Sit, then speak." I give him water, tear off a large piece of bread (a day's worth). He devours them both. How long hasn't he eaten? What happened to him? I get a wet cloth.

"May I?" I ask, before tenderly cleaning the lacerations on his face.

His breath is choppy. "Two days ago, another roundup. They came after me and Jakub in the middle of the night, after Dabrowski's murder. They kicked down our door. They know it was you. Everybody does. Things were crazy, bedlam. We were pulled out of the apartment by the police, beaten up, and brought to the

Umschlagplatz the next morning. The trains were waiting for us. I was"—he shakes his head, unable to finish the sentence—"pulled out of line by . . ." He squeezes his eyes tightly, as though trying to ward off the memory.

"Jakub?" I whisper, too terrified of his answer.

He doesn't need to say another word. He can't. But I know anyway. Aleksander was saved by one of Zelda's plants in the police. Jakub is on his way to Treblinka.

I brace myself against the table, feeling like I'm going to pass out. "It's my fault. Jakub told me this would happen. I risked his life to murder Dabrowski. And yours. Aleks, I'm so sorry."

Tears roll down his cheeks and every inch of me feels his pain. A man who loves his older brother, who feels guilty for surviving when Jakub will not.

"Does anyone know you're here?" I muster.

He nods, wipes his face with the cloth. "Zelda sent me. There's more . . . always more. There was an incident right after the transport. Once I got away, I hid in the bunker. But I was filled with so much rage, Bina, that I went back out, defying Zelda's instructions. I found the young Nazi piece of garbage who pushed us onto the train, and I slit his throat. Eryk threw a grenade to cover me—" He starts to choke on his words.

I hold my hand to my heart. "Not Eryk, please don't tell me Eryk too."

He shakes his head. "Not Eryk. Peter . . ." He can barely push out the words. "I got away. Peter was with us too. He tripped and they shot him dead."

And that's when I cry. No tears for my husband, who was sent to the death camp, but an all-out bawl for the boy with the stutter.

Aleksander's voice fades with pain and exhaustion. "Zelda, the guns . . . there's so much to discuss and I've got instructions for you." He points to his shoe. Whatever it is, it's embedded inside the rubber sole.

"Sleep," I command, pointing to the cot. "You haven't slept in days. Just a few hours, and then we will talk. Please, Aleks, just rest."

"No sleep. Too much to be done."

"Two hours. No more. I will wake you. I promise."

Reluctantly, he collapses on the cot, closes his eyes, and he's out. I pull up the lone wooden chair in the room and watch over him, guard him with my whole body and soul. No soap this time, no nakedness, no sun beating down on his gleaming wet skin. This Aleksander is broken, racked with guilt. I stare at his sleeping frame. The matted hair, the cuts and bruises covering his face, his shirt—the same blue one he wore the day I left the ghetto—now blood-stained. He desperately needs a wash. I lean forward, tenderly push back a lock of fallen hair from his eyes. He is mine to protect.

He begins to snore, and I press my hand over my heart, thinking back to the Brothers Blonski—the orchestra of snores at night in our apartment. I begin to shake, my whole body tightening with remorse, knowing my husband paid the ultimate price for my actions.

Jakub, where are you? Dead? Gassed in an oven? Is this how it ends for you?

I grab the thin blanket from the bottom of the cot and wrap it around my trembling shoulders, allowing the soothing sound of Aleksander sleeping to wash over me. *I love you*, I tell him silently. *I have loved you since the first time I saw you. I wish I didn't, but I do. And I'm so sorry for what this impossible love has done to our family.*

The snoring stops, and Aleksander begins to violently toss and turn, and I yearn to hold him in my arms and stop the nightmares that are consuming him, but I don't dare. Instead, I wait it out, watching the shadows of night prowl across the wall.

After an hour or so he quiets. I stand, pace, then stare out the window and observe the burning ghetto through the window. Zelda needs us now more than ever. Whatever it is that I am supposed to do, it all begins before the sun rises.

Chapter Eleven

It is still dark and misty out when I wake Aleksander. I had let him sleep for nearly four hours. He lies in bed, rubs his eyes, and stares at the ceiling, confused, as though trying to recall how he ended up here. He slings his legs off the cot, sits bolt upright, and faces me. "Christ, Bina, what time is it?"

"Almost five a.m."

"What!" He jumps out of bed.

"It's okay. You needed it," I tell him.

He stretches, comes to the small bistro table where I made him breakfast, a thin slice of bread, a chunk of cheese, a cup of tea. He stares at the food and sits. "Thank you for this. I dreamt I was painting again . . . back in my studio, looking out the windows into the yard. Remember those windows, Bina? Floor to ceiling. So beautiful. You could see the lilacs blooming for miles, and the poppies—all that color." His eyes light up. "Even my favorite brushes were surrounding me. I felt them. I could even smell the turpentine, the linseed oil. It was all so goddamn real. And then . . . came the fire, destroying everything." He rakes his hand through his thick, dirty hair, looks away.

"I understand," I say gently, leaning up against the sink, not mentioning the thrashing that went on in the cot. "I've had countless dreams in which I'm onstage, the audience is clapping, and I'm so excited that it feels like I'm drunk. But it all ends the same way . . . Just before I take my final bow, the curtain comes down with a crash and smothers me as though it were alive."

We both remain silent for a few minutes, lost in thought, pondering all the double meanings. "After you eat, wash up. There's a clean shirt for you too. Then let's talk." I gesture to the large bowl next to the sink that I already filled with water for him. "That, by the way, is my bathing area." I laugh. "Not exactly the Hotel Bristol."

He sniffs himself. "I stink."

"Eau de ghetto." We both laugh.

I force myself to look away as Aleksander peels off his clothes. I make myself fake-busy organizing when there is nothing to do except to make the bed, which consists of one sheet and a wool blanket. From the corner of my eye, I see the bright bluish-purple bruises lining his back, where the police beat him with their batons. My eyes water, thinking of those traitorous brutes, wishing I could kill them all. He takes the cloth with water and washes his face and chest, then dries off, slowly buttoning up the clean shirt as he looks out the window with a faraway stare.

"You can see it from here," he says with his back still facing me. "The tops of the buildings, the barbed wire and broken glass embedded on the wall meant to tear us to shreds. They really are monsters."

"Yes," I reply simply, as he looks down at the shirt.

The shirt once belonged to Jakub. I use it as a night-shirt. I know Aleksander is picturing his brother wearing it, and it's unbearable for both of us. I had nothing else big enough to give him but that. He walks toward the cot, picks up the mug of lukewarm tea on the way, and drags the lone chair with him for me.

"Sit. Let's talk," he says, pointing to the chair.

"You mentioned a grenade that Eryk threw," I begin as I sit across from him. "How was that even possible? Where did we get it?"

"We didn't get it. We made it." He pauses. "Tosia."

"Tosia? The redhead?"

He nods. "She studied chemistry for a year at university before she was kicked out, which basically qualifies her as our bomb maker." He laughs, but the smile seems to slide off his face. "We smuggled in some raw materials. It's crazy, isn't it? I mean, I'm an artist and now a killer. That girl is a bookworm, and now she's our bomb maker. But brilliant and surprisingly confident for someone so young."

I feel a sharp twitch inside my chest. Am I jealous of freckle-faced, scrawny Tosia? Yes, I answer myself. I'm jealous of anyone Aleksander admires.

He reaches for his shoe at the side of the bed, rips out the sole carefully, and then removes the scrap of parchment paper stuck to it. On it is a scribbled address. He hands it to me. "Memorize this, then tear it up. You have a meeting there later today," he explains. "It's already been arranged through Zelda's contacts. I'm going to wait here for you and pray that you are successful so I can return to the ghetto with good news. We need it." His expression clouds over. "We must get the guns and ammo immediately. We simply can't wait. There's going to be another roundup soon, and from what I'm hearing, most likely the final one."

My throat constricts. We are both thinking of Jakub on the last train. I feel his presence here with us now, looming larger than life, in this microscopic room.

Aleksander leans forward, his elbows on his knees.

"This will be their victory lap—rounding up the last of us—those who have been hardest to kill, miraculously evading death. Zelda and the team are working on building alliances with other groups in the ghetto. We must put philosophical differences aside, unite, train people to fight, construct more bunkers and attic passageways between the deserted apartments, and build more tunnels into the Aryan side. But we are outnumbered, outmanned, untrained." He puts down the cup of tea, his cheeks fill with air. "This really could be the last of it, the end of us."

I let that sink in. Aleksander is not a pessimist nor a complainer. If he says that, I believe him. I shudder, and my mind goes to a place where it shouldn't. *What if we don't go back? What if we run away together now? We made it out. Free. Let's flee to the forest, Aleks. Let's start over.* I feel the forbidden words press at the tip of my tongue, but I swallow them. *Zelda.*

"We will never be free," he says, as though reading my thoughts. "Even if we survive somehow. You get that, right? We have seen too much. We will never unsee what they've done to us. And we owe it to Zelda and to the others." He points out the window, gesturing to the ghetto in the distance. "It wouldn't be hard to run and join the Polish resistance, the partisan units in the forest, or even find a way to steal across the Russian border, but I could never live with myself. I won't stop you, Bina."

"I would never leave . . ." *you*, I say only inside my head.

Our eyes meet in a way they have never met before. Straight on, with force. He breaks the intensity first by glancing down at his hands now resting in his lap; there's nowhere else to look. Beautiful, veiny, and calloused from countless brushstrokes, fingernails permanently lined with pigment.

"Revenge is redemption." He whispers Zelda's motto with a fight gesture. "That's all we've got left." His face turns ashen. "Everyone I loved is dead, and now Jakub is gone. Everyone except for . . ." He doesn't finish the sentence, but I feel the muted word with every fiber of my being. You. I shout it inside my head.

You. You. You.

I can't help it, can no longer stop myself. I reach out and touch his haunted face. My finger tenderly grazes the course bristles casing his chiseled jawline. I feel my skin flush, my heart beating wildly, until his green eyes morph from sparkling jade to a deadly grenade. Anger, disgust, hate, betrayal. I don't know which. I can't read his revolving expressions fast enough. I yank my hand away as though it landed on hot coal. What have I done?

Aleksander's glare is so aggressive that I feel pinned

down by it. "They are relying on us." His voice is rough, punishing, trying to pretend that touch didn't happen. If only it hadn't.

"And we won't let them down." My voice is strangled by the thick mucus filling my throat.

He stands abruptly, making the necessary space between us. He walks to the window, but there is no escape from me in this matchbox-size compartment. The weighty silence expands and suffocates. Jakub may still be alive. How could I have touched him that way?

Aleksander turns to face me, and I'm barely breathing. "Between us, Zelda believes the final *aktion* is going to happen on Hitler's birthday, on April twentieth. That's less than four weeks from now. It is Stroop's chance to show off, deliver a birthday gift to Hitler— meaning us. That's why we need to move fast. We are all out of time."

Aleksander's voice rises to a near shout, and I quickly shush him. He points to the scrap of paper with the address on it that was buried in his shoe and is now curled up on the small wooden nightstand. "The group egota is our last shot to get weapons. A lot is riding on you."

"Zelda briefed me before I got here," I tell him, still trying to pretend that touch didn't happen. "So, who am I meeting? And what exactly am I asking for?"

He scratches his head. "The contact is a bit of a

mystery. They call him 'Motyl'—Butterfly. A code name, obviously. Take any weapon that they can give us—I mean, anything. I'm going to make you a wish list. There's money."

"Money from whom?" I raise a brow. "Manny?"

"Who else? The King of Thieves, of course." Aleksander laughs, then stops cold. "They seized Manny's wife and kids while he was working and put them on the same train as Jakub. Manny is unhinged, ready to blow up the Reichstag."

Something mercurial darts through his eyes as he picks up the piece of paper with egota's address and waves it. "This is our defining moment. If we fight back, Bina, if we don't get on their last death train, and instead we blow out Hitler's birthday candles before Stroop does, then we win even if we lose."

Chapter Twelve

I brought two disguises with me from the ghetto, per Zelda's instructions. One is sophisticated, a custom-made midcalf, midnight-blue silk dress with a bow at the collar, shoulder pads, and a belted, cinched waistline (a Schiaparelli from my other life). The other is a peasant woman's guise—a faded yellow babushka, a pleated drab wool skirt, a frayed beige blouse, and work boots (gifted from Zelda's closet). What I wear depends on where I need to be to get the guns and ammo—city or countryside. For the 3:00 p.m. meeting at Marszalkowska 120, I dress up.

The busy street is one of the main thoroughfares of Warsaw's city center. It links Bank Square in the northern sector with the Union of Lublin Square to the south. It is filled with those going about their lives normally, as if an entire race of people is not being massacred on the other side of town. I feel disoriented and slightly faint, as though I have parachuted in from another planet. This is the most difficult role I have ever played—acting like one of them while knowing I'm a walking target. I pass couples, families, shopkeepers, peddlers, old people, young people, beggars, and bankers. Life as I once knew it, in what was once my Poland, carrying on without us. I think about the lovely palaces and the beautiful baroque buildings in the city center, all seized by the Nazis. My Poland. Not anymore. Probably never was.

Armed Gestapo are standing at each corner as far as the eye can see, scoping for troublemakers, liars, Jews—me. I purposely stroll by them extra slowly, guiltlessly, as if I don't have a care in the world, as though the fear surging through my body doesn't exist. I project confidence in my fancy dress, with my hair pinned back stylishly, lipstick (rose-tinged, not orange), and smoky eyes that were once all the rage before I was thrown into the ghetto. Bina Blonski is dead, and Irina Zieliński has come to life. A woman of means, a woman in control, a woman about to go shopping despite the Nazi presence, perhaps stopping along the boulevard for an ice cream cone.

Pretend you belong. Don't let up for a minute. Aleksander's warning words pound inside my head with each dainty step I take. I also recall his reaction earlier when I finished dressing, twirled around, and said, "So do I look Aryan enough?"

His eyes lit up, not with anger this time but admiration. "You look the part," he said. But then, just before I left the apartment, he grabbed my arm tightly, the angst shadowing his face. "They are smarter than you think, Bina. They are highly trained dogs combing the streets sniffing out Jews. You can't slip up even a single detail. Everything we discussed . . . don't forget. Be careful, and come back." His piercing green eyes held on to mine.

"I will, Aleks, I promise," I respond, lingering just a little longer, wishing he'd never let go of my arm.

As I cross the street and scan the buildings for the right address, I tell myself to stop thinking of him. Stay in character. I pat the fake identification papers inside my purse to reassure myself. The guy who prints the *Jewish Gazette* also has a side job forging identification. Irina has my same birth date, born in the same town; her job is teacher. Everything is identical except for the name. Zelda says that the best lies are those built around the truth. Let's hope she's right.

Smile, I tell myself. Irina would smile.

I find the building. It is an ornate three-story town-house, attached to various townhouses in pastel colors—peach, pale pink, butter yellow, and milky blue—the last one on the block, and my target. Two large beautifully carved Grecian vases line the arched doorway filled with bright yellow daffodils, reminding me of the lush gardens behind my childhood home. The gardens were once my mother's pride and joy. She would take her morning tea outside every morning, luxuriating in front of her favorite daffodils and corn poppies surrounded by tall, manicured pine trees. I feel a sharp ache inside. *Stop!* I chide myself. *Bina Blonski is dead. The gardens are dead. Your mother is dead. Stay in character.*

As I make my approach, I take note of everyone around me: a middle-aged couple near the building im-mersed in a conversation, perhaps even an argument. Two young women conversing animatedly with books in their hands. At the end of the street, two young men in business suits sharing a smoke. All so natural. But nothing is natural. Everyone is in twos. They all have their eyes trained on me, pretending that they don't. I'm an actress; I know bad acting when I see it. Those are guards. Most likely egota watchdogs.

I loiter for a few seconds, pretend that I'm looking

for something in my purse, to give my contact ample time to approach me. One of the women walks my way, clutching her books to her chest with a cigarette aimed in my direction.

"Excuse me, do you happen to have a match?" she asks sweetly in Polish.

"I'm sorry." I shake my head. "I don't."

"Irina," she mumbles under her breath. Her eyes are wide, boring deep inside mine, examining my reaction.

I pick up on it immediately. "Motyl," I respond, as Aleksander had instructed me to answer.

She nods, glances up at the large, draped window on the second floor, checks the street, then signals to someone. The door opens a minute later, and a clean-cut-looking young man wearing a pressed suit and tie smiles cordially from the doorway and gestures me inside with a slight nod.

"Go now," she whispers without moving her mouth as she walks by me. "He's waiting."

Motyl, or whoever he really is, sits facing the window when I enter. Why is he staring at drawn drapes? His thick blond hair peeks over the top of the large leather chair—a power chair belonging to a business executive or a high-level government official. And the desk itself is a work of art. I notice it immediately. English, ornately carved with mother-of-pearl inlays and ornaments. My father had a similar desk in his library. I stare at the back of the man's head, wishing it were my father in that chair. I clear my throat and stay put near the door. When he finally swivels around, my heart stops. I reach out to the nearest wall to catch myself from falling. It can't be.

Stach.

My best friend and partner in crime, wearing a suit and tie, rises in slow motion, mouth agape in equal disbelief. He grips the edge of his desk to brace himself and barely gets the words out: "Bina? You're 'Irina'?" His jaw drops. "Lock the door now," he manages.

Shocked, I turn, lock the door. Stach is Motyl? How is this possible?

His voice trembles as he comes around the desk and faces me. "You're alive."

I inch toward him, barely breathing. The shock waves between us morph into stillness, immobility. He snaps out of it first, grabs me, practically squeezes the breath out of me—the old Stach. "You're alive, goddamn it," he repeats, whispering in my ear. "So thin. I feel your bones, Bina."

"Bina is dead. It's Irina now," I whisper back. "Motyl . . . You're the Butterfly?" I am stunned. His hands drop from my arms, and he points to his face. To the large port-wine-stain covering the entire left side of his cheek—a deformity that has defined his whole life. It could be a butterfly, a handprint, a lobster, a puddle, a Rorschach test—whatever you want to make of its shadowy crimson form.

"I wanted to be called Spider," he cracks. "Something manly and elusive, but I ended up with Butterfly."

We both laugh. I cover my mouth, to control all the emotions spilling out at once. There is too much to say, too much we both don't know, when at one time we knew the minutiae of each other's life.

He assesses me from head to toe. "They starved you. You're barely there and yet, oddly, more beautiful."

My smile tightens. I no longer feel compliments when I once lived for them. "I've aged a hundred years."

He takes my hand and leads me to the plush leather couch and sitting area in the corner of the large office, near an open bar. "Tell me." He searches my pained face. "Your family? Your father? You know I always loved your father."

Everybody loved my father. I feel the tears building behind my eyes. Stach speaks as though I've been away on a long trip or got lost in the forest. He knows exactly what happened to me, to my family. Everyone knew about Maksymilian Landau's fate. He was one of the first prominent Jews in Warsaw murdered by the Nazis. Surely his death was widely reported after they carted us off. I wipe away the perspiration gathering at my temples. How could Stach in his tailored suit and tie in this plush office possibly begin to comprehend what really happened to us? How could anyone but a ghetto Jew understand the horrors?

I gaze deeply into his compassionate eyes. Stach did love my father, who welcomed him into our home like a son since he was a little boy. I swallow back the lump rising in my throat and the resentment blackening my heart. "They beat him to death, Stach. Just before they threw us into the ghetto. My mother, my sister, my uncle . . . sent to the death camps. And . . ." I reel off my family's murders clinically, as though I'm reading a prescription aloud. He knew them all. "Jakub was sent to Treblinka in the last roundup. Probably dead too."

Stach's face darkens, his fists clench. "I didn't know for sure," he manages, but I barely hear it.

I turn away from Stach's probing gaze. I can't go down this dark, bottomless hole. Instead, I try to regain my composure by taking in the rich office décor, a style I was once accustomed to. At its center is a large chandelier with dripping crystals, and on the far wall is a vibrant Matejko oil of a historic battle. We also had a Matejko in our home. It was of the astronomer Copernicus. It hung in the Great Room. My grandfather had purchased the masterwork directly from the artist himself and gifted it to my father. Whatever this egota organization does, it clearly does not lack financial resources.

"Bina," Stach interrupts my thoughts, bringing my attention back to him.

"Irina," I correct him softly.

His eyes well up. "What happened to your family and to the Jews of Poland and throughout Europe is unforgivable, unimaginable. I am doing all that I can to help, and I know it's not nearly enough. My father"—he clears his throat loudly—"is, no surprise, leading the Polish-Nazi Alliance. He is Hitler's point man in Warsaw. He rides around with their officers in fancy cars draped with Nazi flags. I'm so ashamed." He gestures to the door. "They don't know who my father is. I couldn't bear telling anyone the truth."

"You're not your father," I say flatly. *And you really believe that they don't know who you are, who your family is?* I reach over and grab my old friend's hand, a hand I once knew so well but that now feels only distantly familiar. Truth is, I don't recognize either one of us anymore.

Stach's gaze calcifies, and his thick blondish-brown

brows narrow harshly. "There's more. You don't know all the things he has done."

I know enough. I gently remove my hand and squeeze my eyes tightly to block out another faraway memory, one that I will never share with Stach. Ever.

He stands, returns to his desk for a pack of cigarettes, lights up two, hands me one. I examine it. The good kind—French, finely rolled, with what I presume to be top-notch tobacco. I can smell its superiority. I don't smoke regularly, but right now I need it.

Stach's assistant knocks and asks through the closed door if we would like tea and biscuits. Tea and biscuits? I roll my eyes. If only this were high tea at the Bristol. Everybody knows why I'm here: guns and grenades. This is not a tea-and-cake outing. But my stomach growls its response loud enough for both of us to hear.

Stach eyes me painfully as he calls out, "Thank you, Andrzej, yes. Please leave the tray at the door. As I was saying, several months after you left—"

Left! my eyes shout accusingly, stopping him mid-sentence.

He meets my burning gaze with an apology. "Were taken, seized," he corrects himself. "I was in *Hamlet* at the theater." He throws his arms up defensively when he sees my mouth drop. "Yes, goddamn it, Bina. Your father was murdered, you were kicked out of your home, sent to the ghetto, and I was still acting." He takes a long drag on his cigarette, and I feel the rage firing up in my belly. I'm about to burst, but I remind myself that life went on without us. Stach is here now.

He continues. "Two years ago, I played Hamlet. The leading man for once. Not the scene-stealing support- ing actor. For the first time, Mateusz and I changed places. That day, we were in dress rehearsal for the show. After we were done rehearsing, I heard loud clapping coming from the back of the auditorium." His hardened gaze is now far away, as though that sound in the theater were echoing in the air around us. "I didn't see them enter . . . my father with a group of Nazi soldiers. They walked together toward the stage, just like they did to you. A repeat performance. I knew exactly what was coming when I saw my father's face. You know that sadistic look of excitement in his eyes when he's about to inflict pain."

I nod, biting my bottom lip so hard I taste blood. Of course I know. It's the face of my nightmares.

"The Nazis walked past me and, instead, pulled Ma- teusz right off the stage and beat him to a pulp in front of me. I tried to stop them, but two Nazi thugs held me down and made me watch as they yelled, 'Pervert, criminal, faggot.' I begged, cried, screamed for them to stop hurting him and to take me instead. My father just stood there rejoicing. And then—"

Stach stops speaking. The brutal memory is clearly too much to handle. He finishes the last of his cigarette, gets up and pours himself a tall drink from the bar, finishes it in one swallow, and quickly refills his glass. He turns to me. "Those beasts kicked the life out of Mateusz's beautiful body and destroyed his face with their boots, laughing as he cried out for his mother. They pulled him out of the theater, broken and bloody, and shoved him into one of their long black cars. I later heard he'd been transported to Auschwitz. He was wearing his costume, Bina. He was sent to Auschwitz in his Horatio costume." Stach walks to the window, pulls back the thick drape slightly, peers out, then closes it. "I hear a homosexual's fate is worse than a Jew's."

"Unless you're a homosexual Jew," I counter, suddenly resenting Stach and his cushy office, his assistant, the tea and biscuits at his disposal. I begrudge his one pain, one loss, when mine are so numerous and unending. Yes, he has suffered, but not in the way we have suffered. And yet, I remind myself, he's here helping us.

"They did unspeakable things to Mateusz in Auschwitz." Stach's voice diminishes. "He is dead, I made sure of it. I paid someone inside the camp to shoot him quickly and stop the daily torture that my father ordered be done to him."

Stach's face contorts with so much agony that my bitterness stops and compassion kicks in. The old Bina. I allow myself to remember handsome Mateusz, Romeo to my Juliet. Stach's loss is immeasurable because it was exacted by his own father. A man who despised that his son was an actor, a homosexual, and my best friend. A disgrace at every turn. Most of all, Konrad Sobieski hated the birthmark that marred his son's handsome face and stained the family name. Every day of Stach's life, he made his son pay for those things that were inextricably part of him.

Stach chokes up. "The same night they took Mateusz, my father kicked down my bedroom door and said, 'You are alive only because of your mother. You repulse me. I am sick just looking at you.' So I left that night for good. When my father went to sleep, my mother gave me what I needed to escape. She heard about Mateusz. She knew who I was, what I am. Despite fearing the wrath of my father, she robbed our family vault—filled with her own inheritance—and loaded a bag with enough gold and zlotys to feed an army. She begged me to leave the country for my own safety. That night was my last at home."

"Why didn't you leave? Go anywhere else—London, America—and live your life?"

Stach exhales deeply, and I feel the heat of his cigarette-infused whiskey breath. "I could have gone anywhere, Bina. I have papers. Visas. Money. Contacts. Everything I'd need to escape this hellhole was at my disposal. But sometimes, there are things bigger than you. Sometimes there are moments greater than your own small life. Instead of running away I decided to run toward. I came to Warsaw and used my finances and contacts, joining those who are like-minded and helping to establish egota. I don't regret it for a second. It's given me purpose, my life meaning."

He gets up and pours himself yet another whiskey, downs it in one gulp. Stach is drinking much more heavily than I remember. He then opens the office door, nods at his assistant, and brings the tray of tea and biscuits and chocolate truffles inside and places it before me on the coffee table. My mouth waters as I reach for a biscuit and then another, forcing myself not to shove the food inside my mouth with both hands like a glutton. My one-time impeccable manners long gone, I make a clean sweep of everything on the tray as Stach watches and drains his latest drink as though it were water. Up close, his face is puffy. The birthmark fleshier. Stach, I think sadly, has become a man who drinks to get through what he must. We are both hardened shells of our former selves.

"Stach," I whisper, licking the crumbs off my lips, not wasting anything.

"Yes, time to get down to it." He cuts me off with a glass slam on the table. "Guns and ammo."

I square my shoulders. "We will take anything you can give us. Time has run out. We have strong information that the last roundup of Jews may be the final one and coming anytime soon. We need your help immediately to fight back. I can't leave here empty-handed."

"Bullets are no match for tanks." He folds his arms tightly.

"No, bullets are no match at all," I counter, crossing my own arms. "We have no illusions. Winning is impossible. We just want a victory. Some of us may even survive. But if we don't, we intend to die our way, not theirs—and take as many of them with us as we can when we go. We must set an example for Jews across Europe that while the world has turned a blind eye, we can still fight back, even if we don't win. Fighting back is the win."

"David versus Goliath." He purses his lips. "Now, I'm afraid the answer is no."

"No? Your response is no!" My voice drums with anger, and suddenly I don't care. "I was told you could help." I close in on my old friend with a tiger's snarl. "Why, damn you?"

He smiles crookedly, and I want to slap him. "Bina Blonski swearing? Now, that's a first. What I meant is that I refuse to help if this is your suicide mission." His piercing turquoise gaze turns icy, a look that reminds me of his father. "Look, Bina, I thought you were dead. And yet, here you are. We are here together, reunited. It means something. You mean something to me. You were the sister I never had. You accepted me with this hellish mark across my face. When others made fun when we were kids, you always defended me. Your parents welcomed me into their home with open arms despite my raving anti-Semitic father." He shakes his finger in the air. "I know you heard me with Mateusz that day in the costume closet, but you kept it to yourself. I mourned you when I heard they took your family away. I couldn't get out of bed for nearly a month. It was unbearable. The only way I could survive the loss was to act—to be someone, anyone but me. And now you're here—a gift—still alive." His face contorts in the same way it used to when I beat him at chess. "I'm not willing to lose you again. No matter what. You are going to live, Bina/Irina, if you're the one damn Jew I save." He leans forward, inches from my face. "If not, no deal."

My fists clench. "This is not some romantic knight-on-the-white-horse moment in one of our stupid plays.

My people are dying in there, nearly extinct. I need to fight with them." My voice rises again. I am not leaving without the guns. I will kill him first. "This is not about you or us."

"And you will fight for them, just not with them," he argues. "You will deliver all the weaponry that I will get you and pay for with my own goddamn money. But it ends there. You stay out of the ghetto fight. And that's my deal. Take it or leave it." He reaches out and touches my boiling cheek. I swat his hand away, and he can't help but smile. "I know every expression you make. I've studied you my entire life. This is not just about fighting in the ghetto, is it? I know you . . ." He points a finger again. "It's about the brother, isn't it? Is he still alive? Is he part of this? Funny, you haven't even mentioned him when he used to be all you talked about."

My hot face turns beet red. Stach is the only person who knew of my true feelings for Aleksander. I glare my response but admit nothing, hearing Zelda's voice inside my head. *No one is to be fully trusted, Bina. No one.*

His eyes widen. "So, he is alive. Do you still love him?"

"Yes, he is alive." I disclose only that.

Stach is not giving up. "Tell me, Bina, what chance do your fighters have if you are dead? Zero. You need to stay on the outside, to orchestrate and move weapons. Look at you. You were able to walk the streets loaded with Nazis. A Jew in their face and they didn't even see it. You are much more valuable to your people out here, and you know it."

"Fine, I won't fight," I lie, throwing up my hands in a dramatic surrender, knowing that there is no way in hell I'm leaving Aleksander behind. That there is no way I can or will honor this deal. Not when survival is at stake. I will say and do anything. I will lie and steal and make false promises even to my one-time best friend and brother.

Stach flashes his beautiful, wide, omnipotent smile, the one that lights up his face and captivated his audience every single performance. "I'm an actor, remember? An even better one than you. Everybody knows that. So don't lie to me, Bina. There's nothing romantic about dying for love. Does the brother love you back?"

"No," I say truthfully. Then I think back to when Aleksander held my arm, the terrified look in his eyes when I was about to walk out the door. "Maybe . . . I don't know. It's complicated."

"So, you're willing to die for unrequited love?"

"Yes," I say adamantly, daring him to challenge me. "Would you have died for Mateusz? Would you have gone to Auschwitz to be with him on his last days, even if it meant they would be yours too?"

He presses his lips tightly together. "Yes."

Our eyes lock. We have always been equally stubborn. He extends his hand again, this time, an olive branch. I take it. "Give me the goddamn list," he says. "You must have a list."

I open my purse and dig out the list embedded inside the lining: one light machine gun, ninety pistols, six hundred hand grenades, and raw materials for Molotov cocktails: nitroglycerine, sodium nitrate, wire, nails, thin glass bottles, and wood pulp.

"Wood pulp and glass bottles? You can't be serious," he says. "Stroop and his men will laugh in your face."

"Can you get me what I need, and fast?" I demand, ignoring the sarcasm.

"Of course . . . and more." Stach doesn't take his eyes off me as he gets up and walks to his desk. He removes a key and then unlocks the middle drawer. He hands me a thick wad of zlotys. "Take this. You will need to pay off all the schmaltzovniks along the way—those fucking Polish blackmailers are even worse than the Germans. Give me three days to get this together. I will start with this pathetic list and build from there. You will get a message where to be for the pickup." He glances at the plate of biscuits that I singlehandedly polished off. "And more food and supplies will be sent your way."

"Do you know where to find me?"

"I know."

Of course he knows. The young couple who brings me supplies must belong to Żegota. I take all the remaining chocolates that I can fit inside my small purse. I feel the pity in Stach's eyes without even looking at him. Yes, Bina Landau is now someone who stuffs her purse with leftovers. I close the purse and stand. It's late and I must get back to Aleksander with the good news.

"Thank you, Stach," I say with all my heart. "Don't be fooled by the pretty dress and the lipstick. I have become an animal. They turned me into that. You're either a hunter or hunted. There's no in-between. Manners no longer exist. And I'm truly sorry about Mateusz." I pull him into another tight embrace. For a moment, body to body, the connection feels like the old us. "It has meant everything to see you again."

He holds me back by my shoulders and his eyes pierce mine. "Don't be fooled by the fancy office, the priceless art, the suit and tie. And I lied to you earlier. I'm not just here to help save Jews. I'm here because I'm going to do all I can to destroy my father and his

Nazi empire in Poland." His gaze turns savage. "And then I'm going to kill him."

I stare at Stach, searching his tortured face, my heart pounding recklessly. "Here's the revised deal," I tell him. "Get me as many guns as you can, and in return, I promise to help you give your father exactly what he deserves."

Chapter Thirteen

Aleksander flings open the door before I even knock. He must have been watching for me from the attic window. Our building is across from a hospital, a strategic decision. There is constant action, so much so that a woman walking alone on the street is hardly noticed. I can only hope that a car or truck transporting ammo manages to get lost in the frenzy too.

"I'm back," I say sheepishly, dropping my purse at the door, standing before him. Aleksander looks like a mess. His hair is sticking up in strange places and his eyes are wide as though having seen a ghost.

"I was so goddamn worried. I was about to come looking for you." He moves in closer, just inches away. "Four hours? What the hell happened over there?"

I loosen the bow of my dress, which now feels like a

noose. "We are getting the guns, ammo . . . everything you asked for on the list. Everything." My face shines, triumphant but exhausted. I feel the heat warming my skin. Aleksander grabs me in a victory embrace and twirls me around. I laugh, and so does he. Good news for once. I'm careful to peel away from him first. I'm not making that same mistake again.

"You must be fatigued. Sit," he commands.

I sit on the chair, and he takes his place on the cot in front of me. I flash back to Stach's office. "Wait, first a little something to celebrate." I pop off the chair, reach for my purse, and pull out the flattened chocolates that I grabbed off the tray and the extra biscuit I took from Stach's assistant's desk on the way out of the office. I also brought back four Gauloises. His eyes light up. I hand him the chocolate and cigarettes. "It's not beetroot soup." I laugh, as he savors one of the chocolates, careful only to nibble a corner of it, making it last, ghetto style.

He beams with delight. "Now tell me everything slowly. Start from the beginning."

I wipe my hands, my voice waxes serious. "Motyl is Stach."

"Sobieski?" He raises a brow. "Your Stach?"

"Yes, my Stach. Do you believe it?"

Over the next hour, I unpack it all: the Nazis

stationed on every block, Stach, Żegota, Konrad Sobieski, Mateusz's murder, the weapons arriving within three days, the thick wad of zlotys stuffed inside my dress for bribes . . . and then, I hesitate, but share what Stach demanded of me.

"He's absolutely right," Aleksander says, nibbling another corner of chocolate. "You are much more valuable to us out here than inside. And Stach is the head of Żegota—a fucking miracle. You do understand how big this is for us, Bina." He stands, unable to sit, too excited, and begins pacing the tiny room. Five strides take him from one end to the other. "We have a real chance of survival. And . . ." He catches his reflection in the small oval wall mirror, starts patting down his wild hair. "We can bring more than just weapons inside. With Stach at the helm, I'm thinking food, medical supplies, perhaps even building materials for more bunkers and underground tunnels. We can move couriers safely across the border with their help. With you as our point person out here . . ." His eyes spark, and if I didn't know better, he seems almost inebriated. But he's right, there is now real hope for us.

"But I want to help inside the ghetto. I want to fight with Zelda, Eryk . . ." *And you.*

I quickly look down and pretend to fix something on my shoe before he can read the desire in my eyes.

But I feel his gaze burrowing through me, and I know he sees it all anyway. When I look up, the light in his eyes vacates, and the uninvited tension between us resurfaces. Suddenly, we are joined by the others: Jakub with his hooded, accusatory glare, Karina in her wedding dress, ghostlike, lounging on the cot. I remember that exquisite ecru lace dress, those dimples and curves, that bawdy infectious belly laugh I once loved—everyone loved. I exhale deeply. *Just go, please,* I beg them both inside my head.

Thankfully, our spouses vanish, and all that remains between us are the sounds of night—ambulances, traffic, sirens, and faint outside voices.

I can't pretend anymore. Slowly, my eyes meet his, and this time, I don't turn away. No more secrets. We know what's at stake, what this is. What do I have to lose? My pride? I lost that a long time ago. He knows how I feel. He's an artist, trained in detail, observation, and nuance. He has seen the dance in my eyes whenever he enters a room. He knows. And now he is returning to the ghetto to fight, perhaps to die. What if I lose him and never tell him how I feel? I swipe my hands and stand. I'm done hiding.

"I don't want to be away from you," I whisper, my voice shaking. "I can't bear it."

It's out. I put a name to the tension. He moves in

closer; his voice is deeply measured. "I . . . I kept picturing them catching you, Bina. Those animals raping or shooting you on the street. It was . . ." He stops speaking, presses his hand to his heart, and mine is beating uncontrollably, each word a revelation. "You are not alone here, okay. I feel it, too, and wish to God that I didn't." He squeezes his eyes shut briefly. "But I can't. Do you understand me? I can't do it to Karina, to my brother . . . my daughter. How could I live with myself?"

I say nothing at first. I roll his words over in my mind. *I loved you from the beginning. Not Jakub, you. You, you, you.* I yearn to spill everything, but I hold back. My face burns like I'm standing next to a bonfire.

"Once," I say, my voice barely a sound.

"Once," he repeats, twisting his mouth, his eyes unblinking, pained, tormented.

"You're leaving tonight, aren't you?" I quickly change subjects as my heart splits into a thousand tiny pieces. "They are waiting for you, for the good news. You must go back and tell them."

"Yes," he says softly.

His emerald eyes wax tender and then cloud with guilt, but suddenly, I see the other—the desire, the strain against his pants—a truth that can't be hidden, can't be controlled. My heart regenerates. He wants me too. Once. One sin. One time. His body is saying yes, even if his mind is fighting it, throwing red flags at him. I ignore his mind, choose his body.

I rise and begin to unbutton my dress, undo the wide belt at my waist and let it fall away. He watches, frozen, but doesn't stop me.

Once is all I get. *We* get. And I'm taking it.

I step out of the dress, and it puddles around me. I move toward him, skin and bones in my tattered silvery gray silk undergarments. I wish he could have seen me before, at the height of my beauty—when I was fuller, shapelier—not like this, at the end of it. *You're barely there and yet, oddly, more beautiful.* I hear the echo of Stach's words, and I cling to them, wishing they were true. Aleksander's hands are flexing at his sides. He wants to touch me. He's resisting. I give him more time.

I turn, walk toward the sink, fill a small basin with water, take a cloth and dip it inside. I turn around so he can see me, can decide. I dab the cloth and slowly trace it down the side of my face, along the length of my neck, and pull down the straps of the slip and let them fall, revealing my breasts. I hear the heavy intake of his breath as I make circular motions with the cloth around each nipple, then down my torso, slowly, gently, washing in front of him. He doesn't move a muscle, just watches me with unabashed intensity, the way I used to watch him. I feel the ardor in each unguarded exhalation. He's losing his resolve. I know because I know everything about him. I have studied him, the way I've studied lines in a play, memorizing every detail. I also know that he is painting me inside his head. I see the way his eyes dart back and forth, absorbing me, filling a blank canvas with color, detail, and form. Not his brother's wife, but a woman, a muse, standing before him, challenging him to use his imagination.

I'm burning for him, and I can't wait any longer. I reach up and my hand trails his set jaw with feather-like strokes at first and then becomes more demanding. He doesn't stop me, doesn't shame me. His eyes are equally kindled. I bring his face to my right breast, and he greedily takes my nipple into his mouth. Hard, wanting . . . not tentative, like . . . *Don't think about Jakub. Keep him out of the damn room.* I close my eyes and will my husband away, then remind myself to open them, to see it all, so I can remember every movement of Aleksander's face, his body. For later. And all the laters after that.

Untethered, he scoops me up, carries me to the cot, and lays me across it. He doesn't take his eyes off me as he quickly strips naked. There are no surprises. I know every inch of him. The chiseled face; the defined jaw; those broad shoulders belonging to an athlete, not an artist; the long, sculpted torso joining into a perfect V; and at its center his manhood is now throbbing, demanding. I sit up as he stands over me, and I take him fully into my mouth. I hear his heart pounding rapidly above me—or is that mine?

"Lie back and spread your legs," he orders huskily, pulling himself out of my mouth just before he finishes. He, too, wants this to last. Taking his time, he deliberately kisses and explores his way down the length of my body until landing between my thighs. It takes everything inside me not to cry out as I run my fingers through his thick, wavy hair and experience the exquisite tango of his tongue, mouth, and skilled fingers, as he readies to enter me.

Our eyes lock as he thrusts himself inside me, over and over. "Don't stop," I whisper. "Don't ever stop." I grasp his firm buttocks and squeeze him tightly to me. Skin to skin, breath to breath. Neither of us closes our eyes, not even for a second. I don't want to miss a thing. I want to devour him. I could die right here, right now, and it would be enough.

But it will never be enough. I will always want more of him, more of this, more of what I can never have again. Our fingers are twined as we climax together, a synchronous muffled cry, and I hold on to the fervent sound for as long as I can, until it slips from my throat, through my hands, and fades into the night. We say nothing when it's over. Words elude both of us.

A wave of sadness climbs over me as I lie in the afterward, ensconced in the crook of Aleksander's arm, inhaling his scent, listening to his steadying breath, the satiated snore, feeling the elusive tenderness of this precious moment. I touch the air next to the fringe of his long eyelashes. I want more. So much more.

I don't want to forget a single breath or sensation. Jakub's face flashes through my mind. *Yes*, I think guiltily. *I must write it down.*

The flame of the small candle on the table sways sultrily, casting a crown of radiance over the wall behind it. As night turns into morning, I cling to the only man I will ever love. Once. Just once.

Chapter Fourteen

It's been twelve days since Aleksander left my bed. Does he think of me? I have never felt so isolated, so alone. I now have books to read, courtesy of Stach. He made sure the apartment was stocked with the classics he knew I once loved, among them *The Doll* by Bolesław Prus, *On the Niemen* by Eliza Orzeszkowa, and our mutual favorite, *The Wedding* by Stanisław Wyspiański, also a play that we once performed together in school.

Like everything else in this distorted version of life, the books are not merely books. They serve as a cover. Hidden beneath those books are well-concealed bullets and materials to make grenades and other homemade devices. Żegota smugglers had snagged discarded boxes from the Tarabuk bookstore that had been tossed out into the alley behind the store, to transport and camouflage the small weaponry my way. The ammo is transferred from my apartment to an open manhole in the courtyard of Zlota 49 on the Aryan side that leads directly to a makeshift tunnel into the ghetto. With Żegota's help paying off the myriad Polish smugglers, we have created a working assembly line straight into Zelda's hands.

All the action happens in the middle of the night. I try to sleep during the day, so I am awake for the nighttime activity.

I look around the tiny, cramped apartment filled with enough food and supplies, even an old foxhole-type radio, to get by. I leave only when I must, which is rarely. I have not seen Stach since the day I went to his office. All communication is delivered through the young couple who brought me here. Residents in the apartment building believe that I am the woman's younger sister. It's not a stretch. We bear a strong resemblance to each other—tall, blue-eyed, lissome blondes. Our relationship is believable, which is half the battle. All it takes is one person in the building to rat me out and the entire operation would fall apart. Every move on everyone's part is fragile and calculated down to the most minute details.

I sit on the chair, reading by candlelight, when I hear the three hard knocks, two taps, followed by three sharp pounds sounding off in the middle of the night. Panic courses through my body at the familiar yet still startling code. I jump up, press my ear to the door. "Yes?" I whisper loudly.

"It's me," responds the young, familiar voice. "Bina, let me in."

Eryk. Here? My heart drops. Did something happen to Aleksander? Something bad. I know it. After easing back the bolts on the door, I pull Eryk inside by his sleeve and quickly lock the door behind him. He stinks of sewer and rot.

"Eryk, what happened? Is it Aleksander?" My heart lodges in my stomach. Please say no.

"No, it's Dina . . . they took my sister. Rounded her up with the other girls from the school last night. Stroop. The edict demanding sex slaves . . ." Eryk is trembling, trying but failing to control his tears. "You need to help me. You need to—"

"Sit, sit." I lead him to the table, give him water, a slice of bread and cheese, my mind whirring wildly as I sit across from him on the wooden stool that the young couple brought for me on their last visit. The edict. Girls to whores. It is happening. Zelda promised she would take care of it . . . and I believed her. My heart slams furiously. And now they've taken Dina. Barely ten years old! I'm filled with dread as I stare at

Eryk. Don't show him you're scared. He will break. Dina is all he has left. I reach across the table and take his hand. I notice his fingernails are bitten down to the quick. "Slowly, Eryk, breathe . . . Tell me."

Still shivering, he starts to speak but his voice is strangled. I jump up to grab a blanket and wrap it around his shoulders and move the stool closer to him. "I knew about the edict. Everyone did, but I thought Dina was safe. The edict said the Nazis were rounding up girls between the ages of fourteen and twenty-two for their officers. But now"—he looks as though he cannot bear the sound of his own words—"they changed their minds after a grenade was thrown and killed one of them. One! One in retaliation for the hundreds of thousands that they've murdered. Those sadistic fucking bastards." His face drops into his hands. "Dina will never survive. You know my sister—scared of her own shadow. She was sucking her thumb when they took her, and I couldn't stop them. Please, Bina, you've got to help me. I can't lose her. You promised me."

Don't cry, I warn myself, forcing my voice to remain steady. "I need all the facts so I can think this through properly. First, do you know where they've taken the girls?"

He nods. "Zelda heard that they are being held in the

basement of the Great Synagogue for four days before being transported somewhere else. It's now day two, and here . . ." He hands me a letter, but reluctantly. "This is from Zelda. Instructions for you."

I rip open the hastily sealed envelope and read its contents in shock. I look up at Eryk's face, the dilated eyes, slightly quivering lips. "You read this, didn't you?"

He is about to lie but changes his mind. "Yes."

"And you're not just here to deliver the letter, but to break your sister out of the synagogue," I say flatly. "And you will get yourself killed within minutes, maybe less. How will that help Dina if you're dead? She needs you alive. You're all she has left. Do you hear me, Eryk?" My voice is scolding, harsher than I intended.

His eyes fire up. "Did you read what Zelda wants you to do, damn it! Read it again, Bina!" he yells, jabbing his finger into the letter. "Dina is going to be dead by day four!"

"Keep your voice down," I warn him. I stand, walk to the window, turning away from him so I can think. Down the street, a group of people are gathering at the hospital's entrance at this late hour. Dina, my shiest student. She couldn't even perform in front of the others. She hid behind a desk when it was her turn to recite her lines. So instead, I had her work on making scenery, cutting cardboard and other skimpy odds and ends that we foraged from the factory dumpsters. She was happiest blending in, head bent, not being noticed.

"How many girls did they take?" I ask. Get all the details. Think, think.

"Around a hundred." His voice scrapes. "Most are from the Beit Ya'akov school. They raided the school during the girls' morning classes."

"The religious school." My heart sinks further. Virgins. Every one of them. Orphans, nearly all of them.

"Why was Dina there?"

He starts cracking his knuckles. "I sent her to that school because they have a good music teacher there, and a piano. Dina is an even better pianist than I am, a natural, so talented. If only my parents could hear her play." He can't hold back now. He starts to cry. I return to the table and embrace him, hold him close to me. "I tried so hard to do everything right for her, to protect my sister the way they would, but I've failed," he laments.

A child raising a child. My stomach twists in knots. Dina doesn't stand a chance.

He looks up. His eyes are wet, his face streaked. "Please, don't do what Zelda asked you to do. Promise me."

I squeeze my eyes shut. "I need to think this through

properly. But tell me"—the words fall out before I can stop them—"is Aleksander okay?" So selfish amid Eryk's pain, but I must know.

Eryk wipes his face with his dirty sleeve. If I were a better person, I would go get him a clean cloth. But I'm not. I must know that Aleksander is safe before I can think straight about anything: the girls, Dina, Zelda's demands.

"He is staying with Zelda now. They are both hiding in the basement of our new bunker on Mila Street. It belongs to Manny the bar owner. It's big, lots of rooms for everyone, and much better coverage. Aleksander couldn't go back to your apartment because people believed he was on the death train with your husband, and Zelda wants to keep it that way. So he's working underground, instructing others on how to use the weapons that you've been sending us. He's busy helping Tosia make grenades, Molotov cocktails, and whatever else is needed to stockpile." My stomach lurches at the thought of Aleksander with the "brilliant" Tosia.

"How many fighters do we have?" I ask. At least Aleksander is alive and safe for now.

"Between us and the other resistance group, we have close to fifteen hundred fighters, which includes children," he says. "Everybody who can help is contributing. Those who can't fight are building bunkers, cleaning out attics for passageways between buildings, gathering supplies, foraging food. The older kids are babysitting the younger kids and training them to smuggle. You should see those daredevils." Eryk's eyes light up with pride, and it warms me. "Small enough to fit through the wire, too young to understand, but still not ready to die. Everyone is prepping for, you know, Hitler's birthday."

I sit across from him again and sigh deeply. Yes, April twentieth—the day that may be our last, just shy of a few weeks away. Not nearly enough time to do everything we must do to survive.

"I've got something for you." Eryk stands, heads over to the door, picks up the large satchel that he was carrying on his back when he walked in, places it on the table, and opens it. He dumps out a change of clothes, a hard piece of bread, a flask of water, and one of the pistols I had sent last week, and then carefully removes something long wrapped in cloth.

He cradles the large package like a swathed baby. "This was my father's. His greatest treasure, given to him by his grandfather. We buried it underground near our apartment when we first arrived in the ghetto to save it. When my parents were taken, I was very worried it would be discovered. So I reburied it in the cemetery with its own marked grave, knowing no one would dig it up. Dina knows about it too. I explained to her that if anything should happen to me, this is hers to be used in an emergency in exchange for food, medicine, passage, whatever she needs. But now this happened." He thrusts the package toward me. He twists his lips together, trying to hold back his emotion. "It's worth a lot. Trade it for Dina's life, for her freedom."

I unwrap the cloth, stare at it, then at him. A violin.

"Is it?" I implore, steadying myself against the thin edge of the table.

"Yes. A Stradivarius." His deep brown eyes bore into mine. Eyes that have aged overnight. "Don't let them rape her. Don't let her die, Bina. Swear to me now, and I will return to the ghetto tonight and fight. If you can't help me, then I'm going to do whatever it takes to save my sister."

We stare at each other without blinking. I think back to when Eryk stabbed Kapitan with his father's violin bow, the violent thrusts into the man's bloody chest. He was once a gentle, well-mannered boy, a gifted pianist with so much promise, and now he is a fearless warrior willing to give up the last remaining family heirloom to save his sister, who may already have been raped, already killed.

"Zelda didn't want you to know her plan." I state the obvious.

"No, she didn't," he admits.

If it was my sister trapped in that basement of hell, I would do exactly what he is doing. Dina is all Eryk has left in the world. What else is there to fight for, live for, die for?

"Go back to the bunker," I instruct him. "Tell Zelda I got the letter, and that I will find a way to reach the girls." I grab his hands in mine and squeeze them. "I won't let anything happen to Dina. No matter what. I swear to you."

Eryk searches my lying face. But a lie camouflaged with hope is the only thing that will stop him from his own suicide mission.

"Sleep for a few hours first," I urge him tenderly, the younger brother I never had. "And then go back before the sun rises. I will wake you."

Like Aleksander, Eryk doesn't argue. Like Aleksander, he is about to fall on his face from exhaustion. The boy trusts me, and what have I done to deserve it? In the ghetto, it's every man, woman, and child for themselves. It's either you die, or I die. That's what they have done to us, stomped out compassion, the human touch, turned us into serial liars. And yet, Eryk foolishly believes that I'm his one ray of hope. A woman with no morals who slept with her husband's brother and her dead best friend's groom. And who would do it again and again, if only she could.

Once I hear Eryk sleeping, I fill his satchel with food and medical supplies from my reserve and return to the window, my only connection to the outside world. I think of the magnificent Great Synagogue in the center of Warsaw, where the ghetto's daughters have been stripped down, held in the basement, awaiting their fate. How can I possibly do what Zelda wants me to do? *Don't let those bastards win* was the last line of her letter. I wrap my arms tightly around my bone-thin body. There is no other option. Somehow, I must get inside.

Chapter Fifteen

I enter Stach's office wearing a simple black skirt and a faded but clean white blouse. The couple who brings me supplies also brought me more clothes. Stach smiles, then laughs. "You look like Maria."

Maria was one of my family's maids. Young, pretty, smart Maria, the daughter of our head chef. I glance down at my attire. He's right. This was our female staff's uniform. Black skirts and starched white blouses.

"What I would give to trade places with Maria right now," I quip.

His smile fades quickly. "More importantly, why are you here? It's too dangerous. I told you not to come, no matter what. Unless it's an emergency."

"It is an emergency."

He points to the door. On the other side of it sits

his assistant at his desk. Stach lowers his voice. "I'm having suspicions about him. We believe there may be a mole in the organization. A Nazi plant. I'm watching his every move these days." He motions me to the couch, but I remain standing.

"I need you to get me inside the Great Synagogue right away."

"Inside the synagogue? To pray?" He laughs, sees my face, and stops immediately. "What's going on?"

I inch closer. "Ninety-four girls were seized from the ghetto and are being held hostage in the synagogue's basement. The Nazis intend to use them as sex slaves, and most likely will kill them when they're done. They are children. All virgins, religious girls. Most are orphans and have already been through hell. We know that they are being held there for at least two more days, being prepped for their Nazi tormentors."

Stach sighs deeply. "Who ordered this? Stroop?"

I nod. "Who else? He sent an edict before I left the ghetto, demanding our girls be used to help alleviate his soldiers' stress. You know how it is, round-the-clock murder can be taxing." I feel the lump forming in my throat. "It's all so much worse than I thought, Stach."

He walks over to the coffee table, picks up the pack of cigarettes lying there. We both sit on the couch close together. He lights up a cigarette, offers me one, and I take it. "What can I do to help?" he asks.

I gather my thoughts, focusing on the fresh flowers in a crystal vase in front of me, realizing I haven't seen a vase filled with fresh-cut flowers in three years. "I need you to get me inside the synagogue as soon as possible. Also, I need"—I pause—"one hundred cyanide tablets."

He falls backward into the cushion of the couch. "Oh, is that all? Jesus, Bina. Cyanide? Let me get this straight. You want me to magically transport you inside a heavily guarded fortress so you can help murder those girls before the Nazis can? Are you out of your fucking mind?"

"Yes, maybe," I hiss back, pop off the couch, and begin to pace. "I don't know what else to do. These are children, who will be raped and then murdered. No happy ending here. No escape. I was given orders to help them die with dignity. So yes, it's fucking crazy, but this world we live in is fucking crazy." And then I remember Dina, my promise to Eryk. It doesn't end. "And there's another issue . . ."

Stach holds up his hand. "We are not done with this one yet. I won't do it. You're going to get yourself killed. There is no possible way to do what you want to do and come out of this alive."

"Believe me, I know," I say, straightening my shoulders. "But there has got to be a way inside. You can do something. You must know someone . . . must have something on someone. That's how these things work, am I right?" I want to remind him that he managed to get someone to shoot Mateusz dead inside of Auschwitz, but I hold back. I see the look in his eyes. He's already thinking that.

He turns away, but I won't let him. I grab Stach by the shoulders, make him face me. "Goddamn it, help me! You know someone."

"Keep your voice down, and I mean it." He pushes me off him, fighting like we used to fight, like a brother and sister.

I point my finger between his eyes. "You are going to help me, period. I'm not leaving here until you do. Damn it, Stach, think!"

His pupils dart back and forth, and I know the truth without Stach revealing it. There was a time when we used to finish each other's sentences. He does know someone . . . someone in a very high place. It's written all over him. A homosexual Nazi? I implore with my eyes.

He nods without moving his head. Even secrets have secrets.

I don't ask the details. "Go to him now," I command.

"I need you to get me inside the synagogue before it's too late and I have no options."

"You already have no options." Stach's smooth forehead breaks out into a sweat. He grabs another cigarette, heads to the bar, pours himself what is clearly not his first drink of the day and nowhere near his last. He pivots with the refreshed whiskey in hand. "You are playing a dangerous game here for both of us."

Playing it safe no longer exists. "And there's the other thing . . ."

He raises his glass in a mock toast. "To the woman who is never satisfied."

I run my fingers through my hair, limp and lacking in luster, when I once possessed a golden mane. "I need you to save one girl. Get her out, into the forest, somewhere, anywhere, safe." I point across the room. "Hide her behind that bookcase. I don't care. Whatever you need to do, just do it."

"Why, who is she?"

"She is my student, and I care about her and her family. She is barely ten, Stach. Most likely the youngest one there." I look away, then turn back to him with my eyes blazing. I let out a deep, elongated breath. "I was pregnant, you know."

"Was?" He searches my face. "When, what happened?"

If I say it aloud, then it makes it more real. But if I don't . . . I take the drink from his hand and swig hard until the glass is emptied. "The day they killed my father in our home, they beat me up badly and dragged me out of the house by my hair. I was three months pregnant. I lost the baby the day I arrived at the ghetto, only to be told later by the ghetto obstetrician that the damage was so great I will never be pregnant again." I bite my lips, deciding whether to tell him the whole truth. "Your father was there, in our home, watching," I whisper. *Your father orchestrated it. If you could have seen his face, Stach.* But I say none of this. I don't have to. Stach knows. I see him picturing his father's evil sideways grin. Konrad Sobieski made no secret of hating my family, especially my wealthy, successful father, who Stach secretly wished was his own.

Stach lowers his head and his upper body curves as if he's trying to make himself as small as possible.

"You didn't do it, Stach," I tell him. "He did. They did, not you."

He raises his watery eyes. "I will help you. All of it. I will get you inside the synagogue, find you the pills, save the girl. Damn that despicable bastard to hell."

"I have something to offer you that might help," I say. "It's not here. But if you need to trade it for the little girl's life . . . It's a violin. Extremely valuable. A Stradivarius."

He places his hand to his forehead. "Seriously, Bina. What are you doing with one of those?"

"The girl I told you about, she's from the Behrman family."

"Why is that name so familiar?" he asks.

I roll my eyes. "Because we saw them perform at least a dozen times at the symphony together." If only I could be sitting and gossiping with Stach at the symphony in my parents' box seats.

"Yes, of course, I know who they are. Keep the violin for now." He walks over to his desk, searches for the key, unlocks the middle drawer, grabs a thick wad of cash—he seems to have an endless supply—and a pistol. He shoves the cash inside his coat, the pistol into his waistband. "But you are not going anywhere. Stay here, in my office," he orders, and I'm instantly reminded of when he played King Lear. Same bullying tone. "I will be back in a few hours."

"And your assistant, the mole?" I gesture to the door.

"I'm going to send him out on a meaningless errand that will take him the rest of the day." He pauses, grabs his overcoat off the coatrack. "Please, don't do anything stupid."

Chapter Sixteen

S tach returns nearly three hours later. His clothes
are in disarray. "You will have fifteen minutes
inside the synagogue. That's it," he says breathlessly.
The top buttons of his shirt are misbuttoned. What did
he do to make this happen?

I pause, worried that I may have pushed him too far
with his Nazi contact. "He could have killed you."

"The less you know the better." We are at that
stage now, I think. Hiding things. No one is to be
trusted. Even me. "Bina, none of this—whatever you
do, whatever happens—comes back to me or to this
office. Under no circumstances. Even if there is a gun
to your head. Are we clear?" His eyes search mine.

"Perfectly. Thank you." And I mean it.

"Fifteen minutes. That's it. Not a minute more." He hands me a satchel. "The pills."

"Did you rob a chemist?" I laugh.

"No." He shakes his head. "But a girl who works for a pharmacist and is one of us, she did."

Enough formality. I fall into Stach's burly arms and hug him hard. He smells of fresh whiskey. He clearly had more than the one he downed here earlier. This war has ruined all of us. "I won't forget this, Stach."

He gently pulls away. "There's a car waiting for you behind this building. A black Fiat. You will get specific instructions from the driver. He's one of us. You need to put on these clothes first." He hands me a drab skirt, a beige headscarf—a schmatte, my grandmother would have called it—old, worn-in shoes, and a ragged blouse. "And put black circles under your eyes. Here's some makeup. You're still too pretty. You don't want to draw any attention to you."

I smile wanly. "Am I to play the part of the Dour Synagogue Maid?"

His eyes expand. "That's exactly what you're going to do."

It's 5:40 p.m. The car is waiting for me in the alley. The driver is clean-shaven, around thirty, wearing a dark suit and a black bowler slung low. It's hard to see him clearly. He is staring straight ahead like he popped out of a gangster film. He rolls down the window, cocks his head slightly. "Irina?" he asks in Polish. His deep-set eyes are mismatched and penetrating, an arresting silver-gray in one eye, the other a muted brown.

"Yes."

"Get in."

I climb into the back seat and focus on the tiny strawberry-blond curls sneaking out from under the back of the man's hat, too nervous to think about what comes next. When he looks up, I meet his intense gaze in the rearview mirror. *Those eyes.*

Once we turn down Tłomackie Street in the southeastern tip of the district, I see the magnificent Great Synagogue up ahead. My heart aches. The synagogue is one of the grandest structures in all of Warsaw, designed years ago by Leandro Marconi. As the story goes, Marconi was my grandfather's chief competitor, commissioned to build the magnificent Renaissance-style structure. My father would say that his father never got over losing that commission to Marconi.

But Marconi lived up to his reputation. The sumptuous golden-bronze synagogue is considered the most imposing in all of Europe, with its Corinthian columns and larger-than-life Ten Commandments tablets suspended at its roof. The only thing missing from its ornate façade are the two giant seventeenth-century candelabras perched at the grand entrance. Rumor has it that the synagogue's rabbi saw the writing on the wall and managed to have those treasures removed and smuggled to safety before he was captured and sent to the death camps. And yet, the gleaming building, with its iridescent tiles at its crown, still stands strong despite being devoid of its candelabras and its Jews. This structure was once the epicenter of Jewish life. My family were members.

We were not religious, but growing up, we lit the Sabbath candles on Friday nights and celebrated the High Holy Days. My father enjoyed going to the synagogue on those special holidays, relished the prayers and contemplation in the immense sanctuary. My mother tolerated it—calling it the Jewish Duomo—but appreciated that we were always seated in the front row alongside the rabbi's family. No one could dispute the splendor of the synagogue, with its two thousand seats filled with Poland's most prestigious Jews, especially on Rosh Hashanah and Yom Kippur. Sermons were delivered in Polish rather than Yiddish, like most of the other synagogues in Poland. The Great Synagogue was meant to cater to families like mine, Eryk's, Aleksander's, and all the members of Jakub's archive committee.

The car slows down, and I see the Star of David twinkling at the apex of the synagogue's domed roof. I close my eyes briefly and allow the nostalgia to move through me for the very last time.

The driver stops the vehicle a block away. He turns and hands me papers. "These will get you through the door. They are signed." He speaks in perfect Polish. But I also detect subtle notes of something else. German perhaps? Who is he? I wonder. What else does he do for Żegota? I don't ask. I have one mission, and whoever this man is, all that matters is that he is making this possible.

"There was another woman assigned to this particular job," he explains, then clears his throat. "She is not going to make it. You are taking her place. That's the cover story. Are we clear?"

That wasn't a question. I nod.

"You are required to do the final check of the girls," he continues, explaining the job. "That's your assignment. A different group of maids came earlier in the day. They hosed down the girls . . ." The driver's face is cold, his incongruous eyes are unblinking. *Hosed down the girls*. I think I'm going to be sick. I look away, not wanting him to see the revulsion. He checks his watch, gestures to the synagogue. "You tell the guards this . . . now listen closely: 'Ich bin für den letzten Schliff hier.'

It means, 'I am here for the final touches.' Can you say that, Irina?"

"Yes." I repeat the sentence in perfect German. *Final touches. Final solution.*

His blondish-red brows rise in unison. "Your German is surprisingly good."

So is your Polish, I think. *Who the hell are you?*

"Keep your head low," he commands, like a man used to being obeyed. "The girls are in the basement. You are allowed only fifteen minutes once you're inside. That is all that could be arranged. Use the time wisely."

Fifteen minutes. How can I do everything I need to do?

"I will be waiting for you here." He points again at the synagogue. "You will have three sets of guards to get through. The first hurdle is at the entrance. You tell them: Pokojówka—maid. Nothing else, just that. Then, you will be sent to the back entrance. That's when you will say what I told you to say. You will then repeat the same sentence to the guards on the inside." His mouth tightens. "Polish first and then German twice. You got that?"

I feel chilled. Nazis and their unbending rules. I stare at him. *You are clearly not Polish.*

"And the girl," he adds with a sharp squint. "Tell

her to pretend that she is dead. Someone will come for her. Warn her not to move. Jews will be brought in from the ghetto to clean up the bodies in the morning. She will be removed and brought to safety."

The way he explains this with zero emotion. I don't trust him. "Please, don't let anything happen to her," I beg.

"That will be up to her," he says impassively, and I wonder what Stach has on this man, or worse, what Stach sees in this man.

The driver turns around, faces the windshield. I glimpse both of us mirrored in the glass reflection. "Now go."

I walk along the gravel road toward the synagogue entrance like I'm walking the plank. The two guards at the entrance are watching me, amused. I climb the synagogue steps slowly, trudging, tired like a maid would move. I keep my gaze plastered to the ground, as the driver instructed. I stop in my tracks when I see boot tips pointing in front of me.

"You!" a Nazi guard calls out in German.

My breath quickens. I don't look up. "Pokojówka," I say timidly in my best Polish peasant accent, then hand him the papers that the driver had given me. My throat tightens as if there were two hands clasped around it.

A minute or two passes in silence. My heart is a ticking time bomb.

"Gehen!" He gestures finally to the back side of the synagogue, where another guard duo awaits, exactly as the driver had laid out.

Now comes the German. I repeat the "final touches" sentence, hold my breath, and I am admitted inside. Exhaling deeply, I walk toward yet another armed guard, repeat the same sentence. He points me to what looks like a storage closet, which I assume contains the cleaning supplies. The guard has a Polish interpreter standing next to him repeating instructions in Polish to ensure that nothing is missed in translation. "White nightgowns. Sterilized," the man orders. "The girls need to be dressed in white before the officers arrive for inspection. If any of them have rashes, we are to be informed immediately. If any are coughing with croup or you spot any sores on their bodies, we must be informed. Understand?"

I nod without looking up. I feel chilled. I don't know who is worse: the Nazi or the traitorous Polish translator.

May you both get syphilis, I scream silently with my eyes glued to the marble floor, knowing that "informed" means immediate death. *Oh, you will be informed all right.*

I drag two large bags stuffed with the white cotton nightgowns from the closet toward the basement, where another armed guard waits at that door. How many of them are there? He doesn't help me with the bags. Instead, he opens the door and presses his gun to my back. "Fifteen minutes." Then with a little shove and a chuckle as I stumble, he closes the door behind me.

Fifteen minutes to kill ninety-three girls and save one. I touch my stomach, where the pills are taped around me in a small bag. I had asked Stach for a few extra tablets, should I need one as well, only he didn't know that part.

With trepidation, I walk slowly down the creaky basement steps. Unlike the rest of the synagogue, this dungeon space is filled with floating cobwebs and furred with thick dust. The maids certainly didn't clean this area. I imagine they will not be bringing the officers down here. I picture them parading the girls in the main sanctuary, on the *bimah*, the platform in the synagogue from which the Torah is read. I envision young Dina down here and the others, their cries of sheer terror as the sadistic guards make examples of a few of them to shut them up and ensure that they follow orders. Zelda was right. Better to die with dignity than live through this hell, to be used, abused, broken, discarded, and then sent to the death camps or shot dead on the spot.

I blink my eyes rapidly, not knowing which way to look. The girls are all huddled together in various corners of the massive basement—naked, freezing, starving, an entanglement of flesh, bones, and limbs. The older girls seem to be consoling, protecting, the younger ones. As I walk toward them, the talking and tears stop immediately. The girls all cower in silence. Trained dogs. We have been taught to do exactly what those barbarians want. They've broken us. They won.

I square my shoulders. Not this time.

I see Dina in a corner. Skinny like a knife. White as if the color has been sifted right out of her. Her terrified eyes are wide like saucers and her mouth drops open when she sees me. I also recognize many other girls who have been in my classes over the past few years. "Mrs. Blon—" I hear a few call out.

I shush them immediately and make the cut gesture across my throat. No one utters another word. They understand hand signals. Except for one brave girl who comes forward. I recognize her too. Her father is the editor of the *Jewish Gazette*, the same man who made my fake identification. Lilah, I believe her name is. She is around sixteen. I have seen her passing out newspapers in Muranowski Square. A confident girl, a born leader, a wheeler-dealer. She will make the decision for the others, I can tell. She is the one I must convince and do it quickly.

The girl's hair is long, dark, and straggly. She is medium height and clearly was once a curvy girl who has been starved to the bone, but her curves remain. They will come after her first if they get their hands on her. "We know what those Nazis are going to do to us," Lilah says. "I saw the edict in the paper. So did everyone else here. How did you get inside? Did you come to save us, Mrs. Blonski?" Her voice is numb and clinical.

There is no tiptoeing around this. No time. "They are going to bring you to a hotel, turn it into a brothel, make you their whores, and then kill you," I say. "Rape then death."

She nods, understands, doesn't cry, nor do any of the others listening in. We have all seen so much death and destruction that it's become the norm, not the exception. "If you're not here to save us," she asks, "then why are you here?"

I blow the wind out of my cheeks. *I'm here to help you die.* "I am with the resistance in the ghetto. We are all going to die, but how we die is the issue at hand. I'm here to give you a choice."

"I see . . . death by their hand or ours," Lilah reflects quietly, exhaling deeply, tugging at the ends of her hair, a nervous habit; a giveaway that she is still a girl, not as strong as she seems. "Just like Masada."

"Yes." I nod sadly. "Exactly like Masada."

The story of Masada, a fortress and symbol of the ancient kingdom of Israel, is one of the most powerful historical tales depicting the Jews' heroic last stand against the Roman conquerors two thousand years ago, in which 967 Jewish men, women, and children fought until the very last moment and reportedly chose to take their own lives rather than endure enslavement or death at the hands of the encroaching Roman army. Every Jewish child learns this story, not to romanticize death, but so they will stand up and fight for their Judaism.

"That's why I'm here." I lift my shirt, pointing to the black satchel taped around my stomach. My breath hitches in my throat. "I have pills . . . there will be a seizure, perhaps loss of consciousness, and then it's over. Over, before they can get to you. And they are coming for you tomorrow."

Lilah looks behind her at all the other girls. "We've talked about it. We would rather die than be violated and destroyed. And here you are, our angel of death. I was in your class, you know."

"Yes, I know," I say, trying to prevent my eyes from welling up. They all need to see me strong, but especially her. "You were a good actress, and then you left because your father needed help after—"

"After my mother was murdered," she interjects. "And now it's my turn."

I reach for her arm, which stubbornly remains at her side. "I'm sorry it has come down to this, Lilah. You are so brave. Tell them all exactly why I'm here. I've been given fifteen minutes, and we are now down to eight." I glance at the watch Stach had given me. I remove the satchel of pills from around my stomach and hand it to Lilah, then I point to the bags. "Put those nightgowns on to cover your bodies. Take the pills. And you will be buried Jewishly . . . I was promised." I lie. Let her believe that. Let her and the others die modestly in a white nightgown, virginity intact, trusting they will be buried Jewishly. So many lies.

"And you?" Lilah asks accusingly, folding her arms over her ample breasts. "Tell me about your death with dignity."

I feel feverish. "I am staying here on the Aryan side, smuggling weapons into the ghetto so that those who are left can fight back, die with dignity, too, and kill as many Nazis as we can before we go."

"Make them suffer," she says coldly. "Make them bleed and pay for what they have done to us." She turns and looks at all the girls, who seem to trust her, their naked, courageous leader. The things Lilah could have done with her life. "This is a mitzvah," she tells them. "None of us will be violated. We will all die by our own hand—our choice, not theirs. I didn't envision my life ending like this. But here it is. Let's do this together before they come for us."

My heart pounds. How can I save Dina? How can I kill ninety-three girls and keep one alive? What kind of a monster am I?

"Lilah. There's one more thing," I call out. She turns.

"One of you must live to tell the story. A witness to what happens here after I go, someone to say Kaddish." The Jewish prayer for the dead. Most of these girls are religious. The Kaddish means something. I put on my best act for a teen girl who is about to choose death for herself and all the others. "I was given word that a Christian family is willing to hide one girl, the smallest, the youngest," I lie again, but it's all I've got. A bottomless reservoir of lies. I turn to see all the haunted, frightened faces. Every inch of me is howling inside. I will never recover from this.

"Her," I say, pointing at Dina. "She is so small. She can hide."

Lilah nods and then recites a verse from the Talmud. "'Anyone who saves a life is as if he saved an entire world.'"

Lilah says this just as I'm wondering if there is even a God anymore.

"Do you have paper, anything to write on?" she asks. "I want to send you with a letter, so we are not forgotten."

Three minutes.

The only thing I have on me is the permission papers to get inside the synagogue. There is a pile of charcoal in the corner. I point to it. Another girl runs to get a small piece of charcoal. I hand it to Lilah. Probably stupid on my part. I may need these papers again. But these girls are about to die, I won't refuse them anything.

Lilah writes quickly: *Remember us. We died pure. We died brave.* She signs it. I stuff it inside my shoe. "I need another piece of paper." She glances at Dina. "For her too."

The basement door opens, and a guard shouts down, "Pokojówka!"

"Almost done," I respond in Polish and wait for the translator to interpret.

One minute later, the door slams shut. I let out a sigh of relief. "You will never be forgotten," I tell the girls as I wipe the tears from my eyes. So many beautiful young lives lost . . . but mostly, I cry for Jakub. Now I understand what those archives detailing history, interviews, testimonials, meant to him. Proof, evidence of our existence, for generations to come. *Forgive me, my husband, for ridiculing you.*

"Come here," I call out to Dina. "Quickly."

Dina looks to the other girls, glances at Lilah, who nods. Dina is covering her private parts self-consciously as she walks toward me. I kneel before her and whisper, "Eryk came to me. I promised him I would save you. Dina, these girls are going to take pills and die before the Nazis can hurt them. You will keep one pill with you if you are captured. Hide it, okay? For now, you are going to live. Do you understand me? You must live." I beg the child with my eyes. "Your brother will come find you, I promise. But you are going to have to be very, very brave."

She puts her thumb in her mouth. I gently remove it and take her small, shaky hand inside my own, speaking loud enough for the others to hear. "You have been chosen by the girls, Dina. You are the smallest. Can you stay alive? For Eryk? For them?" I point to Lilah. "They need you to stay alive to one day tell their story. You will have to hide beneath their bodies and pretend you are dead. Can you do that, maleńka?" My tone is motherly, endearing, sugar-coated. I want to scream.

"Take me with you, please, Mrs. Blonski." Tears

fill Dina's eyes, and she clings to me like a necklace. If only I could. But I can't. We will both get killed.

"Now!" the guard shouts down.

I peel Dina off me, look at Lilah one last time. The fate and last fight of the ghetto's daughters is now in her young hands. She straightens her shoulders valiantly, places her hand to her heart. Gratitude. This courageous girl is thanking me for giving her poison— thanking me for sparing her a brutal, abusive death at the hands of our tormentors. This is how low we have come: death by choice is the best option in a world of no options.

My heart rips straight down the middle and tears are slick on my cheeks. Words elude me, falling away like ash descending from the sky. I am not religious, but I look up at the cobwebbed beams. *God, if you are there, make it quick, make it painless. Watch over them.*

I turn to go. My fifteen minutes are up.

Chapter Seventeen

I open my eyes and see a chandelier hovering over me, the crystal prisms dripping down like giant raindrops. To my left, bright yellow daffodils are arranged beautifully in a vase at the center of the coffee table. The morning sunlight seeps in through an opening in the drapery and sends a striped beam across the couch and onto my leg. As I slowly sit up, a wet cloth that must have been placed on my forehead falls to my lap. Stach, sitting at his desk, meets my puzzled gaze.

"You fainted," he explains. "The driver brought you back here last night, and you fell to the floor. It must have been—" He stops speaking.

I rub my eyes. "I was dreaming that I was performing in a play. The curtain came down, wrapped around my neck, and strangled me." I hold my breath and release deliberately. "I was in hell, Stach."

"Bina," he says gently, then walks over and sits next to me on the couch, pats my leg.

But I don't want to be patted or pitied. I remove his hand. "The girls, are they—"

He swallows hard. "Dead. There have been sirens blaring all night long. You did what you had to do," he says, lowering his lashes.

I think of Lilah, those squared courageous shoulders, and the others. It's all too much to bear. "Dina?" I plead with my eyes. "Please tell me . . . at least that."

"She is alive." His eyes brighten, but the pupils dart quickly in both directions. "I made sure of it."

"Are you lying to me?"

You can't pretend to another actor. We both know that. He sighs deeply. "Here's what I know. The cleaning team assigned to prepping the girls for the officers' visit found them. One of the maids is also one of us. Somehow, she managed to quickly hide the girl in a storage closet. Then Jews were brought in from the ghetto to remove all the dead bodies—"

"Wait!" I hold up my hand to stop him from speaking. "Is Dina still in a closet?"

He nods. "She needs to stay there, until we are sure

that all the Nazis have evacuated the building." He glances at his watch. "Which is anytime soon. That maid . . ." He looks as if he is about to reveal something important but stops himself. "What matters is that the girl is alive and hopefully still safe. That's all I can tell you right now."

Hopefully safe. No guarantees. That's the best anyone can do. Tears sting my eyes as I picture timid little Dina alone among the dead, hiding in a suffocating closet filled with spiderwebs, sucking her thumb. It's gut-wrenching. But Stach has risked so much to make this happen. She's alive.

"Thank you," I say. "The man who helped us, who brought me back here last night, with the crazy eyes, who is he?"

Stach purses his lips tightly, as though deciding whether he is revealing too much. "A man, like me. He is with them . . . and us."

A man, a Nazi, who loves men. Who lives in secret. So many secrets.

"Why is he helping us?"

"Why does anyone help? Because he's on the wrong side and knows right from wrong. He has done a lot of bad things. He is forced to be here, forced to serve with them. If he doesn't, he puts his own family at risk." Stach's jaw pulses. "He is also forced to hide his sexuality. I met him that way. He is risking a lot helping us, but he hates them too."

I stand. "I need to return to the ghetto, Stach. I have done all that I can do. My people have weapons, and the girls will never be Nazi sex slaves. Never be anything . . . period. I don't want to be here anymore. I must go home."

"The ghetto is now home?" Stach says coldly.

"The ghetto is the only home I have left." The ghetto is Aleksander, Zelda, Eryk. It's where I'm going to die. I feel my cheeks burning up, furnace bright.

Stach reaches over and places his large palm on my shoulder. His eyes are no longer warm, empathic; they are calculating. There is a hardened look that reminds me of Zelda, of his father. "You made me a promise. Before you go back . . . I now need something from you."

Chapter Eighteen

The knocks come in the middle of the day, two days later. Three hard, two soft, three hard. I grab a kitchen knife, just in case. I ask who it is. When I hear her voice, I'm relieved and open the door. It's the woman, one half of the couple who always come here together. Anna—not her real name. No one's name is real. Her blond hair, which is usually pinned back and tidy, is a tangled mess. Her blue blouse with a faded sunflower print looks wilted, slept in. Her eyelids are swollen red.

"What happened?" I demand.

"Sit," she commands. None of our usual pleasant small talk when she brings me supplies. I hold my breath.

"The day after the girls' suicide, the Nazis burned

down our headquarters and took Motyl." She barely scrapes out the words. "Someone inside our organization betrayed us. We thought the mole was his assistant, but it wasn't. He died in the fire."

I left Stach's office that same day around noon. It must have been shortly thereafter. "Stach?" I grab her hands and shake them. "Is he alive, damn it?"

Anna releases a long, heavy breath, the worst kind. She pulls her hands away, squeezes her eyes shut, and covers her mouth. "You don't want to know."

Interrogation. Torture. Death. The day-in, day-out Nazi specialty. I fall into the nearest chair. Stach is dead. There's no way anyone survives that, especially those considered traitors. My vision blurs and my heart wrenches as the horrific details of my best friend's final moments unfold. I hear Anna's voice, but only vaguely, like random breaths moving through the air with no discernible sound. All my fault. The girls, the synagogue, Dina, the pills—every single risk Stach took for me.

"Five people died in the fire, including Darek."

My heart feels like it stopped beating. Darek was Anna's fake husband, who joined her when she made deliveries. Darek gave his life to help me, help us. "I'm so sorry." Tears roll down my eyes. I can't hold back anymore.

"He was my cousin. His real name was Stefan." And then Anna cries too. This stoic woman who always keeps it together, who is all business and caution, breaks. I get up and comfort her. "Beasts! Animals!" she cries into my shirt, then looks up. "Motyl's father was there, you know. He sat in that shiny black Nazi car and watched our building burn down and his son being dragged out of the building. Motyl thought no one knew who his father was, his prominent family, but we all knew. It's his . . ."

Birthmark. No disguise could ever cover that.

"We had a plan," I say slowly, the fire burning inside me, enveloping me. "Stach and I were going to—"

"Yes, I know about the plan. I am part of it too." She points to her large purse and a wrapped package perched next to it, signaling the items meant for me. "That's why I'm here. The plan is still going into effect tonight, only without Stach. They are going to pay for what they did to us—especially his father."

"Anna," I begin.

"My real name isn't Anna."

"Mine isn't Irina." We lock eyes. Same age, similar in appearance, same stubborn fighting spirit. In another life, we might have been friends.

My thoughts spin as I search her face for answers. "I must know . . . the little girl at the synagogue. You were the maid, weren't you? The one who went there the next day, hid her in the closet, saved her." I beg her with my eyes. *Please tell me the truth. Tell me Dina is still alive. I need something, anything right now, to keep going.*

Anna hesitates, but her blinking eyes tell me yes. But that's all I receive. No one is to be trusted. I get it. "Jews were brought in from the ghetto the next morning to clean up the bodies," she whispers. "Before that, I quickly hid the child in a dark closet as fast as I could. She was terrified, but not crying. Not a word. Mute. She looked haunted, in shock from all she had seen. I can't imagine what it was like for her to wait inside that closet. Motyl snuck back into the synagogue right after the Nazis abandoned the building. I believe he got the girl out. The plan was to take her to the Bielanski Forest because it's the closest, and then move her from there. But I don't know what happened after that. They raided our office before Motyl could debrief me. I was on my way there to meet him when I saw the fire in the distance."

Stach saved Dina and lost his own life doing so.

"All I know for certain is that someone from inside our organization betrayed us." She pauses. "Like I said, we thought it was the assistant. Now we don't know. You are not safe here anymore, Irina. They are looking for you, for the woman who gave the girls the poison. There's a manhunt underway." She leans in. "I admire what you did. Brave, selfless. What those monsters have done to all of us . . ." Her wet, red-rimmed eyes light up. "Motyl loved you. I could see it in his eyes when he spoke about you."

Not the way you think. She presses her lips together, raises her brows. She knows that too. "Pack up your things," she commands, switching gears, taking a quick inventory of the room. "I will take one suitcase with me now. You can retrieve it later, after tonight's mission. You need to get out of here. Everything has been compromised."

"Where are you taking my bag?" I ask. I know it seems insignificant given everything else, but its contents are all I have left in this world: photos, Jakub's manuscript, Eryk's violin.

Anna doesn't answer. Instead, she gets up off the chair, walks to the window, pulls back the curtain slightly. I see her staring at the six inches of ghetto. "You can see it from here . . . that must be hard."

"Yes," I say. Hard doesn't begin to describe it. I finish packing, close the suitcase, and put it aside.

She pivots slowly, gracefully, hands on slim hips. "I was once a dancer. I studied ballet. My old studio is not too far from here. The ballet mistress who owned the studio was Jewish. A few weeks after the Nazis invaded, they stormed our class, barged through the door. I have never been more terrified. We were practicing. They shot Madame Sosia dead in front of us. She had mentored me since I was a child. She was strict, difficult, brilliant, talented, and kind. We all loved her. I'm here, doing what I do . . . for her. She was more of a mother to me than my own." Anna's head dips forward, almost afraid that one truth could lead to another.

Your truth is safe with me, my eyes tell her silently. She nods back, her dusty-blue eyes sinking deeper into their sockets as she proceeds to give me detailed instructions for the mission ahead.

As I listen to the blueprint of the implausible plan, I realize that there is a good chance tonight could be my last. I point to my small suitcase in the corner of the room, already feeling the emptiness of its departure. "If something happens to me, his name is Aleksander Blonski. Please give everything to him. Tell him . . . that I loved him."

"You're not going to die tonight. It's their turn now." Anna's forehead creases as she bites her bottom lip. "After you do what I've instructed, the driver— his name is Lukas, by the way; he's the same driver who brought you to and from the synagogue—he will be waiting for you, and then a little later, for me. If anything happens . . . memorize this." She hands me an address. "No one knows about this location, okay? I'm trusting you. It's the ballet studio. It's deserted and boarded up. There are blankets there, some modest supplies and food stored in the closet. Your suitcase will be there. There's a large window that opens on the right rear side of the studio building. You will need to climb in. It's where I still . . . never mind."

It's where she still lives, still dances.

This information is a gift, a dangerous disclosure, and we both know it. She points to the items she left for me on the table. "This is not going to be easy. Everything must be exact. Are you sure that you know what to do?"

"I'm sure." But I'm sure of nothing.

Anna takes my suitcase, turns to go. With her hand resting on the doorknob, she gracefully twists backward and observes me one last time. Her lovely, pained face hardens into a mask. *It's us or them.* I nod. I know. And then she quietly leaves. I stare at the closed door, thinking that two women who might easily have been friends, who share creative passions, have been turned into assassins, doyennes of death.

Chapter Nineteen

After Anna leaves, I shed my clothes and the drab material pools at my feet. I carefully put on the fancy dress and T-strapped pumps that she brought me. I close my eyes and guiltily inhale the deliciousness of refined black lace, remembering what it was like to wear something this sophisticated and experience the tingly anticipation of getting ready for a special occasion. I think back to the large oval standing mirror in my old bedroom, and to my personal maid, Justyna, who laid everything out for me on the bed, then helped me dress for the evening while we'd gossip together about the guests. I can even picture the admiring looks on everyone's faces when I'd enter the room. I used to live for that moment. I reluctantly let the memory go. Somebody else's life.

I wonder to whom the dress once belonged. A Pole? A Jew? Have I ever crossed paths with her? I turn the garment from front to back, eyeing the intricate stitching, the train of tiny pearl buttons lining the length of the spine, imagining Aleksander slowly undoing each delicate gem, his fingertips lolling against my flushed, exposed skin.

I pull back my hair into a tight chignon at the base of my neck and apply the bright orange-red lipstick that Zelda had sent with me—my good luck lipstick—and then tone it down with a lighter shade over it. I apply kohl liner around my eyes to create a smoky evening look. I glimpse my face in the small wall mirror. My insides vibrate. I can do this.

Before I leave the apartment, I check my purse for the third time: the thick wad of zlotys, the Irina identification papers, the good luck lipstick, and the two addresses Anna had given me. Memorize them, she said, then rip them up. I do both. I glance over at the coat lying flat across my bed—the "package." Not exactly a package, not even close. It's a beautiful handmade herringbone evening overcoat with its lining ripped out and resewn with flattened dynamite inside, collar to hem. I carefully slip into it, my fingers quivering slightly as I belt it closed.

This is for you, Stach.

Seven o'clock exactly. Walking briskly in the balmy night, I move as fast as I can in the weighty coat and dress shoes that are at least one size too small. The air is cool and breezy against my face, and I suck it in. I pass the hospital, where there is, thankfully at this hour, still a mad rush of pedestrians gathering at the entrance. I slow down when I spot a Nazi guard at the street corner yelling at an old man to show his papers, and I'm able to circumvent them by blending in with a group of others doing the same. No one wants to be caught in transit, harassed by a Nazi. My heart pounds as Zelda's voice fills my head. *Stay focused. Look like you belong.*

In the distance, near the park, I spot the car parked exactly where Anna told me the driver would be waiting. I see his silhouette—Stach's lover. The same man with two different-colored eyes who drove me to the synagogue and then dropped me off at Stach's office just before I passed out. Same man, different car. Anna said that Lukas has been her right hand since they captured Stach. He was the one who obtained the dynamite for us. Perhaps I misjudged him. He rolls down the window and I cinch my shoulder blades together, meet his impenetrable gaze, and nod. He motions for me to get in the back seat.

"Not the maid this time?" he comments after I close the car door.

"Off duty," I respond lightly from the back seat, directly behind him. "How are things going so far?"

"In motion." He squints at me through the rearview mirror, then turns on the ignition. "Look under the seat. Be careful. It's loaded."

I reach my hand beneath the leather seat and feel around until I find what I'm looking for jammed into a secret cut-out compartment, most likely not the first weapon hidden in there. I remove the pistol, keep it low to the floor. A Browning P35, the exact make I'd requested from Stach when he told me his plan. My eyelids suddenly feel hot and heavy. He and Lukas must have worked out the details together before the building was set on fire.

Sweat trickles down my back. Stach . . . don't go there now. I stroke the barrel of the gun with its sleek bluish-black finish, and exhale deeply. "Anna, is she all set?"

"Yes." A man of few words, the driver is not wearing a hat tonight, so I can see him clearly in the rearview mirror. His forehead is wide and shiny, his nose straight and upturned, his square jaw is clean-shaven, and his reddish-blond hair has been trimmed neatly, cropped close to his head. No more little curls peeking out of a hat. He is attractive albeit in a stern dour way, like an unsmiling banker. It's hard to tell if he's thirty or forty. A Nazi turncoat. Who was he before he came here? What exactly does he do when he's not moonlighting as a driver? How is he able to do this without getting caught? I raise a brow at him in the mirror. And when did he have time to get a haircut between the synagogue suicides and the Żegota bombing?

"What now?" I ask, putting the gun back inside the seat compartment as he wends his way through side streets. Up ahead, I see Café Ali Baba all lit up, and I recall the old days, that giddy feeling I'd get whenever I entered the theater district. I feel a tug in my chest, knowing I will never experience that again. Anna told me that the Nazis transformed the cabaret into a "gentleman's club" filled with handpicked Polish beauties to entertain Nazi officers and their partners in genocide: upper-class Polish sympathizers.

Lukas points straight ahead. "That's the target. Anna is already inside. Everything is in motion." He parks in a semishaded area with a clear frontal view of the café and speaks to me through the rearview mirror. "Once you get inside, give her the coat, and immediately find a way to slip out the back door, which is near the bathroom. Timing is crucial." His voice is frosty, no-nonsense, no level of camaraderie. His Polish is impeccable.

"Yes," I tell him. "I went over all this with her."

"This is my operation." His slitty eyes expand, shooting darts almost childishly. Mine, not hers, mine.

For now, we wait. There is no curfew for Nazis. The club starts getting packed over the next hour. Lukas lights up a series of cigarettes but doesn't offer me one. I dislike him—my first impression sticks—and focus on the three gleaming black vehicles now pulling up to the entrance with jarring oxblood-red Nazi pennants draped over the hoods. The Reich VIPs have arrived.

The security guards at the club's entrance leap forward in sync to open the car doors for their superiors, and it's almost comical. My breath halts when I see him exit the middle vehicle. Konrad Sobieski, the baron, dressed in white tie attire, throwing his head back with pompous laughter, joined by his collaborators, who have donned their Nazi finest for a late night of drink, business, and womanizing. Conquerors who steamrolled our country and make it a point to flaunt their robust victory everywhere they go.

"Fifteen minutes," the driver mumbles.

Fifteen minutes. Like everything else on the Aryan side. Fifteen-minute slots determining life or death. I think about the dead girls in the synagogue basement.

Their blanched faces and ghostly nightgowns, and Lilah, the brave sixteen-year-old leader who would rather die than submit to sexual torture. Suddenly, any hesitation about what I'm going to do and the potential danger looming dissolves like sugar in water, and everything inside me lengthens and strengthens.

"Go now," the driver orders. "I will be here waiting. Walk slowly. Speak Polish and throw in German words, as though you've worked hard at practicing them. Smile, bat your eyes, make those guards at the door wish that it was them in your bed, not their superiors. Look like you belong." He turns to face me, emitting one last two-toned stare, those unsettling pupils frozen in sync.

It's the way he pauses, the thick lull in his breath, telling me what we both know to be true: I may look the part, but I will never belong.

Chapter Twenty

F our Nazi guards exchange lewd smiles as they assess me from head to toe while checking the Irina papers. It is obvious to all who I am: one of the handpicked Polish women brought to the club as décor and dessert; dolled up to keep the officers happy and, in turn, off their low-level backs. Satisfied with my identification, the guards step aside and I sluice forward between them. I can practically feel the heat of their desire pummel my back, hear their carnal thoughts: *One day she will be in my bed.* I tilt my head, tighten the belt of my explosive coat, and keep my eyes fortified against their stares.

Sorry, boys, that day will never arrive.

When I enter, Anna is behind a podium—the hostess—greeting the guests and herding the escorts into a corner. I do a double take. Understated, practical Anna has morphed into a bombshell, an exquisite belle of the ball, in a long, sylphlike, pale-blue silk gown complemented by a sheer cream-colored scarf wrapped loosely around her neck. Her gold-spun hair pulled back into a perfect knot radiates beneath the gleaming tea lights above her. Her pearl drop earrings shimmer and her lips are shaded a deep, provocative crimson. She looks nothing like the distraught operative of several hours earlier who had just lost her cousin in a fire. This version of Anna belongs onstage or twirling atop a music box. She sees me and her face remains blank, showing no recognition. Several of the Nazis address her flirtatiously and with familiarity. This is clearly not her first day on the job. Smuggler, maid, lady of the night. This woman is a chameleon, a better actress than all of us.

"Follow me," she says coldly, gesturing me over to the other extravagantly dressed women huddled together in the corner. Several men loitering in the reception area stare at the lineup of beauties with unabashed hunger in their eyes. I observe the young women as I walk over to join them—seductresses of Warsaw doing what they must do to survive. We all have our roles. And for now, I'm one of them.

"Excuse me . . . may I stop quickly in the ladies'

room?" I inquire softly of Anna, but loud enough for the other women to overhear, knowing that she is waiting for me to ask this question.

"These are things that should have been taken care of before you arrived," Anna snaps, motioning with her head inside the club. "The gentlemen are waiting." She then ignores me and surveys each of the half dozen women in front of her one by one. "First, everyone, hand me your coats and wraps. They will be here in the reception area under my watch, waiting for you when you leave." She takes all the women's coats and mine last, eyeballing me as though still irritated by my bathroom question. She then points to the lovely young brunette in a red silk dress standing next to me. "You, go to table one. And you and you, table two in the corner by the stage. The others, go to the third table to the right of the stage. I will be there shortly to make formal introductions." She glances at me with a raised brow. "Let's make this quick."

I walk behind Anna. She even moves differently here, struts through the club as though she owns it. I am fully aware of all eyes turning to get a better glimpse of us as we zigzag toward the back, to the bathroom. I'm careful to keep my gaze down, not wanting to be recognized, especially by the baron. Anna is mindful not to walk anywhere near his table—table one, of course.

"Hurry," she whispers under her breath when we arrive at the bathroom. "Flush the toilet, wait one more minute, and then you will go out the back door." She motions to the dark wooden mahogany doors in the distance.

"What about those guards?" I ask nervously, seeing the stalwart backs of their uniforms. There are three of them.

"Leave it to me."

When I emerge from the bathroom, Anna leads me to the back exit. She speaks to the guards in perfect Polish-accented German. "This woman must be removed from the premises now. Unfortunately, she is"—she clears her throat to showcase her distaste and lowers her voice—"on her period. And you know that will simply not work this evening for our esteemed guests. Please escort her discreetly to the street without anyone's notice. Danke schön."

The guards' eyes widen with comprehension and revulsion, and I want to laugh aloud. Nazis and their irrational fear of anything impure. I'm out the door and ushered to a side street in less than thirty seconds. Brilliant, Anna, just brilliant.

The driver's face is expressionless when I approach the car. "Mission accomplished?" he asks when I get inside.

"Yes," I say, my voice breathless. "But will Anna get out safely? And how will we get the baron? And what about those other women?"

Lukas runs his hands through his close-cropped hair. "Anna knows what she's doing."

This explains nothing, as usual. Thirty minutes later, I see the baron exiting the club alone, Heil Hitlering the guards standing at the entrance. He adjusts his white bow tie, glancing up and down the street as though expecting someone. My hands ball into fists against the leather seat. From this far away he looks so much like Stach, minus the birthmark. Film-star dashing with his wavy blondish-graying hair, thick brooding brows, and athletic shoulders, prominent cheekbones, and piercing azure eyes—a man who had been unfairly gifted yet chose to bathe in a sea of cruelty and manipulation.

He glances back at the club, pulls out a cigarette, checks his watch. My mouth drops open when Anna walks out the entrance a few minutes later, hips swaying with a sexy, self-assured smile. She loops her arm through the baron's, too comfortably, as though this isn't their first rendezvous. What is happening here? Is this for show? A trap?

I reach my hand under the seat, carefully remove the gun from the compartment, and keep it low to the floor, prepared for anything.

As they walk in our direction, Anna's gown shimmers beneath the streetlights, her silky scarf billows behind her in the breeze. She throws her head back with laughter as though the baron has said something amusing, and my stomach turns. Then, suddenly, like a rebuke from heaven, the sky explodes. A ferocious boom shakes the car, and Anna and the baron fall to the ground. The baron stumbles as he tries to get up, helps Anna to her feet. She lifts her dress, peels off her high heels, and together, they break into a run. I sit bolt upright.

"What are you doing? Get down, damn it!" the driver barks at me. "Hide under the blanket, now!"

From my vantage point on the back seat floor, with the blanket lifted slightly, I see the flames fanning the car window, a twisted mural of orange, charcoal, and black smoke, and then I hear a secondary round of reverberating blasts coming from the direction of the Nazi club. I let out a loud gasp. The coat was loaded, but *that* loaded? Anna must have planted more explosives. Excitement rips through my body. I did this. Nazis being blown to smithereens, getting exactly what they deserve. Finally. Then my heart sinks, and I envision the other images. The ladies of the night trapped inside. The smiley brunette in the sparkly red dress covered in blood. The collateral damage of killing Nazis . . . Don't think about that now. Focus, breathe. Think of Zelda, Aleksander, Eryk. If the resistance can do this on the outside—the Aryan side—then we sure as hell can fight back from inside. We, too, can take those monsters by surprise, inflict real unexpected damage. Death—theirs—not ours, for once.

The driver rolls down his window and calls out in Polish: "Anna, Anna—over here! Do you need help? Come, get in quick!" He acts as though he is a concerned friend who happened to be driving in the area at the exact time of the explosion.

"Can you help my friend too?" she shouts back breathlessly, her voice fighting to be heard above the mayhem.

Her friend? *Please be acting.*

I clutch the pistol tightly to my chest. What if she's the mole? What if I am being set up? What if Lukas, the baron, and Anna are working together? *No,* I tell myself, recalling her tears earlier. *I must trust her. She is all I've got.*

"Get in quickly!" the driver responds. My skin prickles with anticipation and fear.

"Sit in front," I hear Anna tell the baron.

The baron quickly enters the vehicle, swearing in Polish, demanding the driver take him straight to the head of police. As Lukas drives away from the explosion, Anna makes eye contact with me on the back seat floor, her dirty feet placed lightly on top of my scrunched legs. She quickly removes her silk scarf, wraps the ends tightly around her hands, reaches over to the front seat, and strangles the unsuspecting baron from behind, using the top of the seat as leverage to pin him down. "Irina, now!" she orders as he begins to kick and scream and fight her.

I don't hesitate. I get up off the back seat floor and shoot the baron in the thigh. I could easily have killed him. But we want him to live. That's the plan. I heave a sigh of relief. Anna has not betrayed me. The goal is to get information, find out if Stach is still alive. The baron howls from the bullet wound, struggles to remove the scarf compressing his throat, his eyes bulging with understanding that this car ride and the explosion were premeditated.

I lean forward, ensuring he glimpses my face, as I press the muzzle of the gun to his temple. His skin goes pale, and his forehead breaks out in tiny beads of sweat. I can't help but smile. If only Stach could see this right now.

"We are going to kill my father, Bina," Stach told me that day in his office. "No one else understands the history like you do. All I want is to make him accountable for his crimes and see my face when we do."

Now it's just me, Stach. My face that he will see. This is for both of us.

"Remember me?" I ask the baron, relishing the haughty sound of my voice. I jab the dark barrel of the pistol even harder while Anna tightens the reins around his neck, maneuvering his head as though he were a horse. He begins to choke and cough simultaneously, a crackling wet symphonic sound.

"You're alive," he manages.

I smile broadly. "Yes, unfortunately for you, still here." I shoot him in his other leg to make my point, as the driver whizzes through side streets. Blood is everywhere. The baron is wounded but not dead yet. No one flinches. I look at Anna. She nods. This is where this must happen. Right here, right now.

She forcibly maneuvers the baron's head in my direction. His eyes are terrified; a vein protrudes like a lightning bolt from his forehead.

"Bina Blonski," he spits out with what little strength he has left. I ignore the name reveal, but I can tell the other two are taking note.

I stare into his hateful eyes. "You destroyed your son, murdered the man he loved, killed so many people I loved." Bitterness fills my mouth. "You were a Nazi even before they took Poland."

"I—" he manages.

I reach over and slap his face; his cloudy pupils roll back. "Shut up." I am Zelda now. My eyes glisten as my mentor's tough-as-nails spirit claims my voice, now commanding and frighteningly potent. This man has haunted my life, my dreams, and I need answers. "Where is Stach? Is he still alive?"

I nod at Anna, who loosens the reins so he can speak. He coughs uncontrollably, and then he laughs. Laughs! Amid his impending death. It is the same sick, sardonic sound of my nightmares, coming from the back of his throat and emitted like a gargle. But here, in the car, so close, that vile sound echoes from one car door to the next, from Anna to the driver, until it overtakes me. I can't help it. I lose my resolve as a suppressed memory surfaces like a genie let out of a bottle, and I can't seem to stop it.

I was twelve years old, in school that day, not feeling well. The school nurse decided to send me home. She tried contacting my mother to pick me up, but there was no response. And my father was away on business. So I walked home, which was relatively close, six blocks away, in the middle of the day, alone.

Standing in the foyer of our palatial home, I called out for my mother. No answer. Our maid looked away when I asked where she was. So did the butler. I ran upstairs, feeling hot and clammy, calling out her name repeatedly, but still no response. When I stood at my parents' bedroom door, I turned the knob, but it was locked. I heard a mix of voices coming from inside the room. My mother and a man's deep baritone. A voice that wasn't my father's. And then I heard the man's hearty laughter. I froze, certain it was Pawel, my father's assistant. How could she do this to my father? Barely able to breathe and flushed with fever, I ran into my room across the long hallway and stood behind the door, but opened it a crack, watched and waited.

Finally, the man tiptoed out of the bedroom, holding his shoes and carrying his jacket. My eyes were glued open. Only it wasn't Pawel. I cast a veiled glance just to confirm, but my brain couldn't absorb what it was seeing, and then I blacked out.

Years later, when the Nazis pummeled down our door and pistol-whipped my father to death, I saw Stach's father standing cross-armed in the arched doorway of our dining room, my mother crying out to him—calling him by his first name—begging him to make the Nazis stop hurting my father. But the baron ignored her. The very last words my father heard as he cried out my mother's name were my mother calling out that man's name.

I knew then, and I know now.

"It wasn't Pawel," I whisper hoarsely from the back seat, the gun still aimed at the baron's head. "It was you." The words barely form. His eyes up close are the same almond shape and shade as Stach's, changing from blue to green like a Siberian husky's. *Like my own.* I swallow back the bile forming in my throat. I wave the gun at him, feeling the burn rising in my face. "You despised Jews, destroyed us, and yet you were in love with my Jewish mother."

"She chose him," he spits out.

I don't look at Anna, but feel the intensity of her surprised gaze upon me, and I don't even want to know what the driver is thinking.

Him. A punishing affirmation. My father. My mother chose my father because it was expected of her—a Jew must marry a Jew—but secretly she loved this ruthless villain. How long did the affair go on? From the beginning? Before that? The rage inside me intensifies, hitting a boiling point until it has nowhere to go, filling my head with smoke, debris, and darkness, until there is no difference between what is going on inside the vehicle and outside. I feel the repressed memory snake along my throat, like the pale-blue scarf tightening once again around the baron's neck. It was him in her bed. His blond wavy hair splayed on my father's pillow. Him. Lucky my mother is dead or I would kill her too.

The baron's voice rattles with one last solitary breath. "You're my . . ."

I shoot him in the face before that word can make its way out. Before the ugly, inconceivable truth rears its head in front of witnesses. I won't allow it. Won't admit to it. Won't hear of it. Never! His arrogant royal blood splatters the same color red as a peasant's across the windshield, on the driver, and on me. Anna screams. This was not the plan. I'm frozen, dead silent.

The driver accelerates. Wherever he is headed, I don't know, don't care, can't feel anything except for the reverberating heat of the pistol burning against my hand.

I was specific with Stach that day in his office when he told me we were going to murder his father and he needed my help. I said I must have a Browning P35— that it was symbolic. "Symbolic of what?" he asked. The Browning was the same make used to bludgeon my beloved father, the man who raised me, cherished me, laughed with me, told me I could become anything I wanted to be.

The Browning falls limply into my lap. I could have been anything, but now I'm this.

The driver stops the car two streets away from my apartment, where the night began, by the park. In the distance, I see the swings, the slide, a sandbox. I look at Anna quizzically. Why are we back here? I thought that I couldn't return to the apartment because it was too dangerous. The baron's slumped-over blood-soaked body is now covered by the blanket I was using. Ambulances are swarming the nearby hospital. Anna tells Lukas, "Are you crazy? It's not safe there. Let's go. Irina is not getting out, especially now."

"Nowhere is safe," he responds, eyeing me with a sharp squint in the rearview mirror. "But she needs to get out immediately otherwise we're not safe either. I can't be here, Anna. You know I can't be in the middle of this." He glances out the blood-splattered window, turns to me with those crazy eyes. "You need to go. Anna and I must get rid of the body and this car and figure out next steps."

"Damn it, Lukas, her dress is covered in blood. She can't go anywhere looking like that."

He lets out a hard sigh. "You're right. We will get rid of the body and then come back for her. If we are pulled over like this, at least we can say we happened to be driving near the bombing, tried to save this man by bringing him to the hospital. Our papers are rock solid. Hers are not. And more importantly, there is a manhunt for her." His eyes wax empathic. "I'm sorry, Irina. You've done stellar work tonight. Hide behind the apartment building. Over there, behind those large garbage bins. We will come back for you in an hour or so, after we take care of this."

"And if you don't come back?" I ask, which is the more likely scenario.

"I'm coming back for you, I promise." Lukas reaches inside his coat pocket, hands me several large bills. "If something happens unexpectedly, there are smugglers roaming the park." He gestures out his window. "Use this to get help. Keep the gun, Irina, but get out. Now. You must."

I glance at Anna, who nods, squeezes my arm. Lukas is right. I am the weak link. I don't hesitate. I jump out of the car, then walk without looking back, hearing the screech of wheels as the car careens away with the only two people left on the Aryan side who can help me.

Chapter Twenty-One

Two hours have passed since I ran into the nearest alley and hid behind a cluster of garbage bins. I feel my chest caving in. I can't breathe here amid the stench and rot enveloping me. No one is coming back for me. It's obvious. I'm on my own now. I want to scream at the top of my lungs. I can't go back to the apartment. Someone could be there right now waiting for me.

I hug my trembling body, press the loaded gun to my chest. I could try to get to the forest somehow and join the Polish resistance. But look at me. It's the middle of the night and I am wearing a bloodstained evening gown.

There is only one option. The most unsafe place in the world is now the only safe place left for me to go. Home.

All fourteen of the ghetto's entrances will surely be

heavily guarded, especially after the nightclub explosion. The only way back inside is to go underground. Sewer or tunnel. And it will cost me plenty. I check my purse for the umpteenth time, stare at the thick wad of zlotys nestled between my false papers. I must go through the park, where I can hide, and from there I will have to choose between the closest sewer or a makeshift tunnel leading into the ghetto, if the Nazis haven't already blown them up.

I make my way to the park and find a concealed space among a cluster of thick oak trees and hide there, to buy myself time. In the distance, I spot two shadowy figures approaching. I hold my breath as they get closer. I make out twin black-leather jackets. One man is heavyset, the other beanpole thin. They round the park twice. Smugglers for sure, but they could be anybody, paid off by anyone.

The two men spark up cigarettes and stand in place. As I move in for a closer look, relief overtakes me. I recognize one of the men. We crossed paths on at least two occasions. A sewer smuggler, a Pole, who goes by the name Vladek, and the other is not a man but a teenager. They are my only option. And I have just two things to offer in exchange for passage: money and sex.

You also have a gun, I remind myself, as I walk toward them. You can force them to take you back.

Twigs crack beneath my shoes, and Vladek quickly turns my way.

"Who's there?" he whispers loudly. He has a gun too.

I take a deep, anxious breath. This could go either way. Start with the bribe and see what happens. I keep the gun hidden behind my purse.

"Cigarette?" I ask Vladek in Polish. "Cigarette" is standard smugglers' code for passage into the ghetto.

"It's late. How many do you need?" he asks, sizing me up from the corner of his eye while looking past me to see who else might be lurking or hiding.

"Just one." Passage for one.

"When?"

"Now."

He laughs, eyeing me fully. A woman who looks like she is dressed for a night on the town, not a makeshift tunnel connecting the Aryan side to the ghetto, with soldiers everywhere.

He moves in closer, mere inches away, and I can smell his sour, smoky breath. I have two bullets left. I may need them once I'm back inside the ghetto. "There was an explosion," he says. "Gestapo is doubled up at every corner. It will cost you." He doesn't look directly at me, rather over my shoulder, watching for anything amiss, but his voice echoes into the dead of night.

"What do you want?" I ask, knowing exactly what he wants.

"I've seen you before, haven't I?"

"Yes." Our eyes square off. "Name your price."

"Two things."

I sigh deeply.

"One for me and one for him. And six hundred zlotys."

I could kill them both right now, right here, and be done with it. I could blow their lusty brains out, rob their wallets, snag their cigarettes, and wear the clothes of the teenage apprentice. But someone else inside the ghetto may need passage in or out. These men, these lowlifes, are our lifeline. Pay the price, I tell myself. Save the bullets. It will be over quickly.

"I want a guarantee that you will take me all the way to the other side."

"Doesn't work like that anymore." Vladek takes a long drag, expelling a lazy ribbon of smoke, as though we have all day. "Too dangerous. I will take you half-way there. And I will give you my flashlight, which adds to the price. The rest of the risk is on you."

I blow air out of my cheeks. He has me where he wants me, and we both know it.

"Which one of you is taking me?" I ask, then

change my mind. "I want you," I tell Vladek, the experienced one.

"That's what they all say," he laughs lasciviously. His apprentice chuckles. "You're a Jew?"

I roll my eyes, put my hands to my hips. "Do I look like a Jew? My older brother is in there, married to one. I have gone back and forth a few times for my dying mother's sake to make sure he's okay. He wouldn't leave his Jewish wife and children. I'm doing this for her."

Vladek looks at me sympathetically, then his face hardens, knowing that everyone lies. Truth doesn't exist anymore. He stretches out his hand. "Money up front."

I hear the sirens sounding in the distance. "You're right. There are police and soldiers everywhere. Let's not get arrested while we haggle. I'll give you whatever you want underground. All of what I owe you . . ." My eyes bore into his, and he meets my final offer with a nod.

The younger smuggler starts shuffling his feet, turns to his mentor. "I will stand watch."

"Stay away from the street," Vladek tells him. "Keep behind the trees, out of sight. Remember what I've taught you. Don't do anything to give yourself away. If someone stops you, say your mother is very sick." He eyes me knowingly. "And you need to get her medicine. Don't be stupid, okay?"

He already is stupid, I think. You're getting the money, the sex, while he stands watch.

Vladek looks me up and down once again. I get it. I'm not a woman. I'm a commodity. Barter. He starts moving in the opposite direction. "This way."

Chapter Twenty-Two

Vladek and I walk the streets together but not in a straight line. We decide to take the tunnel leading into the ghetto, a safer option than the sewer right now. He gives me his coat to cover up my dress and steers me through two back alleys to get there. The makeshift underground tunnel is forty-six meters long. It stretches from Muranowska 7 in the ghetto to the cellar of Muranowska 6 on the Aryan side—cut off from each other when the ghetto was sealed. I give Vladek twice what he demanded, to keep his mind off me for as long as I can once we enter the dark tunnel with no possibility of escape. When we reach the twenty-five-yard mark, he stops, angles his body toward me.

"A deal is . . ."

"Yes, I know." My heart hammers in my ribs. I have

done this too many times before. I do what I always do. I disassociate from my body completely, to prepare for what comes next.

He pushes me up against the rough surface of the narrow tunnel wall, kisses me hard and sloppy, thrusting a slobbery tongue deep inside my mouth. He feels the top of my dress, squeezes my breasts. His rancid breath becomes heavy, panting, and then he stops, looks into my lifeless eyes, and says, "What is your real story?"

Please, I think, opening my eyes and staring into his murky gaze, just get this nightmare over with. I don't have time for chitchat.

But the smuggler wants to talk. "Your dress." He touches the material. "It's the exact type of dress my wife sews for wealthy, aristocratic women. Who are you really?"

His wife? The guilt is setting in, that's what this is.

"I'm a teacher," I answer with a half truth.

"A teacher . . ." He steps back, drops his hands limply to his sides, as though he is done pawing me. Is he done? "That's admirable. Well, I was once a carpenter. I used to build things. And now . . ."

I try to keep my gaze steady. *I don't care about you or your wife. Just get me to the other side before we both get killed.* And yet, this man feels the need to bare his dark soul. I command my face to soften up. "A carpenter? This must be very difficult for you."

His forehead scrunches, as though pained by his new line of work. "These Jews. Not all bad, you know. I worked for one for years. Generous. Treated everyone equally. Gave me a large bonus every Christmas—triple time. He was that kind of Jew."

Was, I think. We were all that kind of Jew once.

Then it dawns on me. Triple time Christmas bonus. Construction. A man who took pride in treating everyone as if they were the owner of the company. "Maksymilian Landau," I whisper, bracing myself.

His mouth drops open, his eyes light up. "Yes, that's him! You knew him?" His expression quickly changes. "I heard they killed him inside his home right in front of his family."

I fight back the tears. This is the closest I've gotten to my father in nearly three years. "He was my father," I respond, my voice breaking, and I can't stop it.

"Your father?" The repentant smuggler bangs the side of the tunnel with his fist, puts his hand across his heart. "I'm sorry. For all this . . . and for that." That. The kiss, the fondling, and what was about to come after. He hands me back the money I gave him. "Keep it."

I stare at the stack of returned bills in my hands. Bribes, payoffs, so many things that it could be used for.

What would my father do? Then I see the baron's cruel face rise in front of me.

"No, you keep it. You need it too," I insist, feeling the soul of my father run through my veins. *Nothing is for free, Bina, remember that. Never owe anyone anything.* Every jewel coming out of this smuggler's lopsided mouth is worth every damn zloty. "Just get me to the other side safely. That's all I ask."

No more words. No more touching. Just a quiet, careful trudge through the darkness, Vladek leading the way and the click-clack of my tight, painful shoes through the muck the only sound between us.

Chapter Twenty-Three

When I emerge from the tunnel, I find myself in a dark basement beneath a lattice of cobwebs. I inhale the familiar cloying ghetto bunker air as I make my way out of the deserted building and into the street, careful to remain in the shadows. The ghetto labyrinth is embedded in my mind. I know every street, every twist and turn, all the hiding spots. My father used to tell me that I was blessed with a photographic memory, just like him.

As I move past each run-down tenement, I notice that all the lights are out as dictated by curfew. But I can still discern the moving shadows in various windows, illuminated by candlelight for those who can't sleep—the night zombies. So many windows have been smashed during the daily Nazi raids that each façade I encounter is like a glimpse of a face with broken teeth.

In the weeks since I was away on the Aryan side, I changed, and yet here, everything is the same— especially the stench, like rotted meat, permeating the thick air. Sharp, broken cobblestones cut at my bare feet. I dumped those painful shoes back in the tunnel. I mentally hug myself. The soles of my feet are irrelevant. *You made it back. You're home.* Roving surreptitiously like a ghost between buildings, I maneuver as if my calloused dirty feet have wings. I imagine myself Titania in *A Midsummer Night's Dream* as I flit stage right, stage left, upstage, downstage.

I pause briefly at the side of the four-story building that was once my home on Nowolipki Street. Now it is just another broken face with shattered windows. I glance up at the second floor, with its glass blown out, and I see remnants of my kitchen. Keep walking. Don't look back. The air around me becomes increasingly dense with each stride.

I make my way to Mila Street, where Eryk told me that Zelda and her fighters had relocated. The courtyard in front of the building is oddly vacant. My eyes well up as I approach the entryway. Like all doors in the ghetto, this one is covered with dents from Nazi boots and bullet holes. I recall that first day when I demanded to see Zelda, and her young guards tried to stop me from entering their headquarters. Sadness tugs at my heart. The boy with the stutter is dead. And Eryk . . . what do I tell him about Dina?

I turn the doorknob and immediately feel the cold muzzle of a gun pressing against my temple. I let out a sigh of relief when the outstretched arm connects to a teen boy not more than fourteen years old, wearing an oversize jacket and a flat newsboy cap, man-size clothes that clearly don't belong to him. He is standing on his tiptoes to reach me. I can't help it. I smile warmly at him, even though it's difficult to see him in the dark, enjoying the welcome home. "Glad someone is on top of things. Nice gun. Where's Zelda?"

"Who are you?" He keeps the pistol right where it is. I let him do his job.

"I'm Bina Blonski back from the Aryan side." I point to his gun. "The weapon in your hand . . . I sent it to you. I must see Zelda now. Tell her I'm back. What's your name?"

"She is not to be disturbed. Only in the case of emergency." He pauses, deciding. "Sammy."

"Well, Sammy, you're looking at the emergency."

He hesitates, trying to figure out what to do. I shake my head. Children forced to make adult decisions. He slowly removes the gun from my temple but keeps it at my back as he walks me through the doors, where there is a small torchlight on the floor, and I can now see the boy clearly. Small but mighty. I like his style. I spot two more young guards standing at the base of the stairs going up to the first floor—a boy and a girl—look-alike siblings, maybe twins, with their downturned dull eyes, unkempt hair, and rags for clothes, also aiming a pair of guns that I'd sent. I feel the lump forming in my throat. Child fighters. Orphans for sure. If nothing else, my people are now armed.

Sammy and I descend the creaking stairs to the dimly lit basement and my mind races. I pause at the last step, take a deep breath, and view the expansive new space in front of me—a high-end bunker that once served as Manny and his thugs' headquarters. My breath halts. Time stops.

Aleksander. Standing cross-armed in the archway at the far side of the room.

Our eyes lock, and words escape me. "Aleks," I whisper, noting his muscles through his white under-shirt, feeling the instant charge between us. I barely see the others as they begin to emerge one by one out of the woodwork, gathering in the room. There must be two dozen people, maybe more, but I see only one.

"Bina." His lips slowly curve up.

I move past the boy with the oversize coat and dive

into Aleksander's arms, inhaling the strong, intoxicating scent of him, pulling him to me with all my might. But his return embrace is limp, practically unresponsive. I let go and look into his eyes for a clue. But his gaze is averted, focused over my shoulder. I turn slowly, follow the path. I do a double take, then a triple take, grab a nearby chair for support. My legs go weak, nearly buckling, as time folds in on itself. At the other side of the room is a bald, rail-thin man. I rub my eyes. It can't be.

Jakub. Alive.

I hold my chest, unable to catch my breath. My husband who was sent to Treblinka on the death train has miraculously returned—the sole ghetto prisoner in nearly three years to survive the camps and come back here. My mouth struggles to form words, but nothing comes out. Jakub looks like he has been split in half, cadaverous.

He walks slowly, achingly, toward me. "It's me, Bina. It's okay . . . I know how I look. This is a shock, but I'm here." He gently unpeels my fingers clawing the chair next to me and pulls me into a deep embrace. Starved, all bones. Yet, unlike Aleksander, my husband's scrawny arms feel like steel doors encasing me. I fall into him, my body so weak, my mind so tired, my thoughts gone gray.

"Where are your shoes?" he asks.

I manage to look down at my mud-soaked feet and laugh between my tears. Everyone breaks out in laughter. It's not funny, but it's ghetto funny. And then Zelda enters and everything, all sound, stops at attention.

"The Face has returned," she announces, warmth oozing from her liquid eyes as she moves toward me from across the room with wide-open arms.

"Zelda." I pull away from Jakub and run to her. Tears I can no longer restrain fall unrepentantly down my face. She notes my bloody dress with a hard gaze, takes my hand and leads me to the long wooden table in the center of the room and seats me next to her at the helm. She gestures to the others to join us.

"There is much to discuss," she says, never wasting a minute. Never mind that I am dealing with the shock of seeing my husband resurrected from the dead. For her, there are always more important things at hand. She signals one of the younger members to bring me coffee and something to eat. This woman—commander of the resistance—is barely twenty-five years old and somehow manages to control everyone with just a snap of her fingers and a simple nod. She has that effect on everyone. Even Jakub, a nonbeliever, is under her spell. I can tell when someone intrigues him by the way he tilts his head, strokes his chin as he, too, sits down at the table next to me.

"Tell your wife what happened," Zelda commands him.

I turn to Jakub. A million stories are stockpiled behind those worn albeit still sharp eyes as he speaks. "I was in Treblinka. It was hell, Bina. Worse than any of us could possibly imagine. A factory of death, torture, degradation. The ghetto is paradise compared to it. I am here only by chance." He runs his hand over his shaved head, then cups his palm over his mouth, as though trying to muzzle the agonizing words that are poised to fall out. I reach over and take his free hand, a hand that looks as though it belongs to a seventy-year-old man, with its protruding veins and skin so thin and sallow. "When I arrived, there was a man there, a Nazi standing at the entrance to the camp," he continues. "Crazy as it sounds, I knew him. Johann Haas. He was once a journalist, a reporter for *Berliner Tageblatt*. We met at that conference in Amsterdam—remember, Bina?" He smiles to himself, as though attempting to recapture his once fulfilling professional life. "We had drinks together with a group of journalists. Talked, laughed, cajoled. When he saw me in the lineup, I knew immediately there was a ray of hope. A lot happened there . . ." He shakes his head, as though warding away the cruelest of imagery, and I can't help but think of what an odd, egg-shaped head he has without his thick, wavy brown hair. "Well, Haas got me out. He gave me clothes, an ID, money, and an escape route. I had the opportunity to go free, but I came back for . . ." His eyes glaze over.

Me.

He came back for me. Jakub was given a get-out-of-hell pass and he, too, returned here. Home. And then I correct myself. No, it isn't about me. Knowing Jakub, he came back for his precious archives. Those papers are most likely still in the apartment, hidden under the floorboards beneath our bed or stashed in milk cans buried underground. *Stop!* I scold myself internally. Just stop. He deserves better. You know what you did. I glance over at Aleksander. What *we* did.

"Truly a miracle," I tell him, my hot eyes filling with water, not admitting to myself what I'm really feeling. Jakub is alive, which means my relationship with Aleksander is dead. Jakub smiles at me affectionately, then looks at his brother lovingly across the table. It's gut-wrenching. Not the guilt, but the punishment.

"Bina," Zelda says with a light snap-snap in front of my face, breaking me out of my internal spiral. "We heard about the Nazi nightclub bombing and the burning down of Żegota headquarters." She lowers her eyes briefly. "And the girls." But she stops there. Everybody in the room bows their head. The moment seems to freeze. Clearly, everyone knows what happened, how it happened, what I did to make it happen. Murderer, savior, heroine—pick one.

I look around the room. "Where is Eryk?" I ask, breaking the spell, realizing he isn't here and dreading that conversation.

Zelda leans in. "He is meeting with the leaders of the ZZW organization—you remember, the other resistance movement in the ghetto. He's been negotiating with them. The good news is that all the various factions have agreed to cooperate, put our differences aside, and join forces." She glances at Aleksander. "Aleks and Eryk have been coordinating and dividing up the ghetto territories among all the fighters and doling out support jobs to those who can't fight but want to help. No easy task."

I nod my understanding of the grave situation ahead. Hitler's birthday is in less than forty-eight hours. Every man, woman, and child still alive counts and must fight back together. There is no other way.

Zelda's eyes bore into mine. She doesn't hold back this time. "Those girls died with dignity, Bina. You gave them that. I can see it weighs heavily on you."

Taking a quick, shallow breath, I glance around the room, observing each intense face waiting for my response. "Yes, it does. And what came after weighs heavily as well. Our contacts are all gone." I feel my chest caving in. "There was an infiltrator in Żegota, the group that gave us the weapons. The leader— they called him Motyl, whose real name is Stach Sobieski—was taken, tortured, and is believed to be dead. He was once my best friend. His father, Konrad Sobieski, was the leader of the Nazi-Polish alliance and behind his own son's capture. Was . . . because he is now dead too." I pause, look at Aleksander, not Jakub. "I know this because I killed him." I glance around the cold, dank bunker. I point to the few guns that have been laid out on the table. "Whatever we have now is all we are going to get." I turn to Zelda. "I know it's not enough."

She raises her pointy chin. "Not enough to win, but enough to cause plenty of damage and make a stand, which is the only win we've got," she says. "Your work out there changed the landscape for us in here. There were sacrifices, but you did this." Her eyes shine and I feel the standing ovation in each ebony pupil. She is proud of me, like a mother would be. Sadness over-takes me. I glance around the table, at the room stuffed with fighters. Tonight may very well be one of our last all together.

Zelda holds up her hand, indicating we have more

to discuss. It's nearly four a.m. "Today is also the day before Passover." She signals to her teen lackeys to bring her the Shabbos wine, whiskey, and matzohs—unleavened bread that someone must have prepared, stored in a makeshift cabinet in the corner of the room.

"They are coming for us, and you want to drink and discuss the Ten Plagues?" Aleksander scoffs in disbelief.

"Don't be such a downer, Blonski," Zelda says, pouring him the first shot. "Tomorrow, we fight, but tonight we commemorate the Jewish exodus from enslavement in Egypt and toast to our own oppressors' defeat. We are ready for them. So, drink, goddamn it!"

Aleksander concedes, raises his glass to her and to me, then downs the whiskey. Wet droplets linger on his full lips, and I imagine them pressed against my body. I quickly look away, damning myself to hell, too afraid the others will see the blatant desire written all over me, and that Jakub will too. And especially Zelda, with her radar eyes, who knows everything anyway. Guilt hovers over me like a menacing cloud. I quickly lace my fingers through Jakub's, hoping his goodness will somehow swallow my sins.

"So how exactly are we ready for them?" I ask Zelda point-blank.

"For starters, you're certainly dressed for the occasion." She laughs heartily, bringing attention to my bloodstained nightclub attire. Everyone else joins her, laughing in unison—anything to delay the reality of the bloodbath we are about to face.

Slamming down her emptied glass, Zelda stands, swipes her hands across her dusty trousers, signals her fighters to follow her into the adjoining room, where the bombs and grenades are being stored, and where Tosia, our young bomb maker, is busy working around the clock stockpiling Molotov cocktails and other homemade explosives. Zelda feels no need to answer my question. She is a woman born ready.

Chapter Twenty-Four

April 19, 1943

With the first glimmer of dawn, we are as ready as we will ever be. None of the fighters went back to sleep. Who could sleep? Instead, we drank more, laughed harder, shared stories from our pasts— our ghetto past. The past prior to our captivity has long been erased. Zelda, of course, makes the final toast with a rousing "redemption through resistance" speech.

"L'chaim. Here's to life, our lives," she says. But this time, her toast is not with a glass of whiskey. Instead, she raises one of Tosia's dynamite specials high above her head. "Go big, my friends. Go hard," she urges. "We are going to sabotage those bastards as soon as they enter the central gates. We have already laid mines all around the entrance. We will wait until a large platoon is inside, and then we'll set off the explosives. After that, they will surely send in tanks. The goal is to hit those goddamn tanks immediately. Lob those grenades. Blow them up, don't hesitate. Our secret weapon is the element of surprise. We have only one shot at this. Don't stop, don't pause, don't breathe, don't retreat. No matter what."

We all know what that means. Don't stop fighting until you're dead.

Jakub has been assigned to report everything as it unfolds. He will need to move through the ghetto like a mouse and record the details as though he were a war correspondent, which he is. Zelda said it is crucial to get the news of our revolt out to the rest of the Jews in Europe. To tell a different story, that there is another way. No more walking into the ovens like sheep to the slaughter, rather encouraging fighting back like hungry wolves to the end. "Our story is not simply a story, Jakub. It defines our survival as Jews," Zelda tells him. "This is the history we must tell. Now do it."

Jakub is our designated Josephus—Flavius Josephus, a first-century Jewish-Roman historian and military leader, the recorder of heroic Jewish tales. Bald and emaciated, my husband has never been so fired up, so light on his feet. The color has returned to his face. He meets my smile with a smile. I am proud of him, and for the first time in our marriage, he feels it.

It's only been twelve hours. We haven't fought, haven't touched, but we are sharing a renewed appreciation for each other—for surviving. His way and mine. I now respect the pen in his hand, and he knows the guns in our hands are my doing. On the other hand—the invisible one—I am witnessing a new disturbing development evolving before my eyes.

Her name is Tosia.

As Zelda discusses details of our battle plan, I notice Aleksander and Tosia exchanging furtive glances. My heart clinches. The way he is looking at her, and how she twirls her fingers through her reddish curls, the alluring sparkle in her gray-green cat eyes looking right back at him. *Did you two get close when you made bombs together?* I yearn to bang my fists on the wooden table and demand an explanation. What about me, Aleks? I'm alive. I came back for you. Just look at her. All those freckles, you can barely see her pale skin beneath the scarlet clusters. Look at me, damn it. Yes, Tosia is smart, skilled, creative. But I'm smarter, more skilled, more creative. Look at the guns in your hands. I did that, not Tosia. Me.

Zelda's right brow is arched like a bow pulled too far, and her scolding eyes are shooting arrows in my direction. She's warning me to stop the nonsense. I angle my shoulders and cast my gaze downward. I'm being a child. I'm married. Jakub is alive, right here next to me. Aleksander is not mine, never was. My cheeks burn. I excuse myself to the bathroom and dash into the small makeshift commode that barely fits a human.

Examining my reflection in the tiny mirror over the washbasin, I acknowledge what I see isn't pretty. The green-eyed monster has consumed my face. Aleksander's attention is firmly, pointedly, on the bomb maker and not me. He needs to prove that he doesn't desire me. That I'm Jezebel and he is innocent—still the good brother.

I splash water on my face. He is right.

I return to the table as Zelda discusses our advantages over our enemy: the will to fight to the death, that we choose how we die, and that we know all the ghetto's hiding spaces—from fake floorboards to attic passageways, to underground tunnels to bunker hideouts to rooftops. We have geographical advantage, she says. It's our turf. Blah, blah, blah. I hear but don't hear. Aleksander is half smiling at Tosia in the same way he looked at me that night. I could scream.

Zelda stands for the finale, her closing arguments in our makeshift war room. "This is our moment to avenge our loved ones." She smiles broadly, and it is truly her loveliest feature, softening the severity of her resting pinched expression. "Today is payback."

I glance at the youngest members in the room, at their gritty faces, their fledgling fists curled at their sides, ready for action. Zelda turns to the more than one hundred resistance members of all ages packed inside the bunker. "We have enough guns for each of us. Do. Not. Waste. A. Single. Bullet," she commands, acknowledging each face slowly with her piercing, slow-moving panoramic stare, a general sending her ill-equipped unit onto the front lines knowing that every soldier matters. "Make every shot count. If you are hit, shoot one more time. The last word must be yours."

Chapter Twenty-Five

The hours tick in slow motion as we wait restlessly inside the bunker. All the fighters have been divided among the different buildings, spanning all four sections of the ghetto. I am positioned on the third floor of our Mila Street outpost, standing guard at the window as the day bursts forth into a flood of sunlight.

Sammy, still wearing his oversize jacket, was scouting outside, and now runs into the room announcing loudly: "The Nazis are coming!"

Everyone grabs their gun. Zelda heads for the rooftop with her prized possession—"Hitler's buzz saw"—a highly advanced machine gun smuggled inside by Manny, who did not stay and fight. He'd made his own escape into the forest while I was away, taking off after his family was rounded up and murdered. But Manny did not leave the ghetto fighters empty-handed. He bequeathed his massive headquarters and suitcases stuffed with zlotys and a cache of weapons to the resistance. Just before he parted, he gifted Zelda his prized MG 34, a Maschinengewehr 34, a Nazi specialty. It can reach nine hundred rounds per minute. How Manny obtained it—like everything else he did to survive and thrive here—no one will ever know.

Pausing at the door, Zelda stares hard at our small core group: me, Jakub, Aleksander, Tosia, and little Sammy. "No one here is getting on a train today." Her eyes are piercing bullets. "Or ever again." Every muscle in my body draws in tightly. I know this means this is the last I will ever see of her. She is assuming the riskiest position of all: the lone sniper on the rooftop. The most visible and most potent.

I leave the window, run to her, and take this stoic woman into my arms. She is so compact. The gun wrapped around her is practically bigger than she is. I never realized how small Zelda is because in our world she is larger than life. "We will never forget you. All that you've given us." I can't help it. I kiss the top of her head, feel her flinch at the intimacy, but I don't want to let her go. As she pulls away, I see the small bubble forming in the edge of her eye, and then it disappears quickly. Squaring her shoulders, our fearless leader takes one last look at us, nods, and heads into battle.

With a heavy heart, feeling the weight of the gun in my hand, I return to the window. The streets below are still empty and oddly glittery, as though covered with snow, from all the feathers and down bedding once belonging to those whose homes the Nazis smashed up in their daily raids. I will never get used to the sights and sounds of this hellhole, and yet I will fight for it down to my last breath.

I think of my father, sister, and my mother. I touch my barren stomach with the barrel of my gun and tighten my grip. Whatever this is and however it all goes down, it will be worth every damn bullet.

Suddenly, they come. Nazis enter the ghetto goose-stepping in unison and singing! Singing, as though they have already crushed us. Singing, as if they could push us off the map with one eye closed and a mere finger flick. My body ignites. On cue, a series of explosions resounds through the air. Arms, legs, bodies go flying. It's the most glorious sight I have ever seen. None of us utters a sound. What we are witnessing before us on the ground is unfathomable.

Minutes later, the tanks roar in, the backup bullies, and Zelda makes her first power move from the rooftop. She lobs a grenade. Thrown with the precision of an Olympian, it lands smack in the middle of the first armored vehicle. A Nazi tank! *Bang, bang, bang.* And it, too, blows up. The colors—a massive mushroom-like burst of yellow, red, and black—fill the entire window.

"She did it! She fucking did it!" I scream with sheer elation as I watch the monstrous tank destruct, witness more bodies flying out—hearing and seeing with my own eyes Nazis screaming and scrambling, crying out for help. It's magnificent. Feeling drunk on our first successes, I grab one of Tosia's homemade miracles from the floor next to me and toss it through the open window onto the clambering, unsuspecting soldiers trying to regroup beneath us. I watch as Tosia's gem wreaks havoc below.

"Jakub!" I scream at my husband, who is crouched in the corner furiously writing. "Two tanks down. Dozens dead, maybe more! Mark it!"

And the battle begins.

The reverberation of bullets and bombs can be heard on all sides of the ghetto, from every broken, smashed-up window. Everyone who lost someone— which is everyone—carries those souls on our backs as we fight for our lives, fight to take lives, fight for our dignity. I am no longer a woman but a she-wolf starving for blood. Aleksander is shooting wildly from the far window. Aleksander and Jakub, the three of us fighting together. My men, my family.

And then, everything changes.

A bullet flies through my window and right past me. I feel the wind of it whoosh against my face, followed by a young scream behind me. Oh no. I turn.

"Sammy!" I drop my gun onto the closest chair, scoop up the boy, hold him in my arms as the blood oozes from his coat's breast pocket. I press my hands against the bullet wound with all my might, but there is nothing I can do to stop the hemorrhaging. I won't let him go like this, alone, a child. An orphan.

"My coat," he musters. "My father's . . ." His words trail off, his breath rattles. His father's coat. It didn't shield him, but it gave him courage.

"You are so brave," I whisper, as Sammy's eyes begin to roll back. I kiss his wet forehead and wipe my fingers over his thick boyish lashes and gently close his lids. His nose is still running. I cradle his small head, and his newsboy cap falls into my lap. One tiny last breath, and our young soldier is gone.

"Bina, now, goddamn it, we need you!" Aleksander shouts out, his voice cracking. He sees the dead boy. "No time. Get back to the window. Fight!"

I gently lay the child down on the floor, then remove and place his treasured coat over him. Wiping away the

tears rolling down my face with my dirty sleeve, bro-
kenhearted, I return to my window and try to regain
my footing. The ghetto as far as I can see is under siege.

By nightfall, the Nazis, with their state-of-the-
art artillery and enough armament to capture all
of Poland, retreat. Retreat! Surprised by our attack, damaged, and beaten. I will never feel this way
again—this triumph, this victory, this life-defining
standing ovation. I hear the victory howls up and
down the street—wolves to the moon. We did it! My
heart beats recklessly. We took them by surprise and
fought back. Those monsters were afraid of us. Us!

"Zelda!" I scream out our window, hoping she hears
two floors above me. "Zelda!"

No matter what happens in my life—if I make it out
alive—I will never again feel a win as great as this. Justice has been served. Even if it was just one helping.

I picture Zelda above us on the rooftop, dripping
with sweat, her mud-black eyes gleaming like a she-
devil possessed as she wields Hitler's buzz saw. A
young woman led her inexperienced fighters to take
down S.S. Major General Stroop's warriors just in time
for Hitler's birthday. No greater gift.

Today, we won.

I read those exact words ten times. Jakub's last

sentence scrawled on his reporter's page. We all gather around to see it, to witness each curved letter, with our arms draped around one another's shoulders in a close-knit huddle. I glance over at Sammy covered by his father's jacket. In our greatest victory, we say the Mourner's Kaddish—a prayer for the dead—for our Sammy.

We lost, and we won.

Without warning, the door suddenly bursts open and the unimaginable storms in. The one face who will steal this stunning victory right out from under us, with his oily black Luger pointed in my direction, decked out in full Nazi regalia. His mismatched eyes are fixated and furious, but his cold, lying, punishing, traitorous mouth is smiling.

Chapter Twenty-Six

Lukas the driver. The man who helped me give the young girls cyanide, who supplied the dynamite to blow up the Nazi nightclub, who allegedly was Stach's lover, is now surrounded by reinforcements. I look around at the half dozen Nazi soldiers accompanied by two cameramen filming the moment. Surprise. The Żegota mole has revealed himself.

Various gazes ricochet around the room, from our side and theirs, all converging in my direction. Lukas and I regard each other, the moment of reckoning palpable between us. I see his true intentions reflected in his icy two-toned potent glare: He means to kill me. And more than that. He plans to enjoy it.

I keep my face blank using every theatrical skill I possess, refusing to give him the satisfaction, as his soldiers aim their rifles at us, demanding we immediately drop our weapons. I watch the slow release of our precious guns as they hit the floor—*tak, tak, tak*—and are swiftly scooped up by the nearest Nazi and placed in a pile.

Lukas salutes the room with a taut, exaggerated Heil Hitler, a victor's joust, then turns to me with a weak smile. "Irina? Not dressed as the maid or the whore this time? No, dressed as a Jew." He laughs, a sound so cutting that it could slit a throat. "Bina Blonski—that's what he called you. Remember? The baron, the man who ordered his own son's death, only to be murdered by his daughter." He lets that revelation sink in around the room. "Just like in one of your beloved Shakespeare plays."

Lukas's mawkish laughter is echoed by his lackeys and the surrounding cameramen. I don't move a muscle. My head spins, my stomach cleaves. It's out there now. The Nazi's daughter. Everyone in the room is frozen in disbelief, terrified of what comes next. All eyes are on me. Jakub. Aleksander. I have explaining to do.

"You're wondering how I found you?" Lukas stares me down. "I offered one of your own policemen fifty zlotys and a loaf of bread, and he led me right here." His thin-lipped smile is chilling, and I feel myself withdrawing into my body. "And then I shot him dead."

Lukas waves his burnished Luger high in the air, like a black kite. He pauses for a second when he sees Sammy's small, limp feet sticking out from the coat, bleeding out onto the floor around him. He walks past the dead child without flinching. "You know, I've been waiting for this exact moment, Bina/Irina— waiting to see the expression on your face when I found you, and it doesn't even come close to how I imagined it." He places his hand on his heart. "It's so much better."

The smile vanishes and he points to the ceiling with his gun. The rapid fire of a machine gun above us is still going at it. Zelda solo-soldiering on the rooftop at the last Nazi stragglers. If only she could aim down into this room. "We will deal with that situation in a minute. Tie everyone up," he orders his men. "Except for her. She's mine." I feel the small knife Zelda gave me yesterday pressing against the sock in my boot. That's all I've got as backup. A pocketknife—a sling-shot against swords. Not enough to save us.

"Leave them alone," I beg Lukas. "Take me. I'm who you came for."

"You really are such a good actress." He signals to the cinematographer. "Did I mention that I'm a film-maker by trade? Make sure you get a close-up of her face. Just like that: the angst, the fear, the terror of what comes next. You can see her racing heart inside her eyes. Capture that."

He turns his attention to Jakub. "And you must be the husband. I heard you escaped from Treblinka, with help. Johann Haas, was it? Funny, how you survived, and he didn't." He makes a loud clucking sound with his tongue, winks at me, and the rage erupting throughout my body is now apparent on my face.

Spurred on, Lukas slowly, dramatically pulls out papers from his uniform's inner pocket while the cameramen film it all. My heart drops. I recognize the slightly crumpled papers immediately. Jakub's manuscript . . . words I wrote on the back of several of his pages because it was the only paper I could find when I was alone in the apartment for days. The rest of the manuscript is hidden inside the suitcase I had given to Anna. My breath begins to shudder. I must have left those pages on the shelf with the supplies. They must have found them when they ransacked the apartment. How could I have been so careless, so stupid? God, if you exist, please end this now. Kill me before he reads those words aloud.

"No," I plead, trying to divert Lukas's attention. "Stop."

But he ignores me, emboldened by my reaction. "Irina, you are not only a stellar actress but also an exemplary writer of pornography." He glances at

Aleksander. "I couldn't have planned this any better if I had written the damn script myself. All of you in one room. Who knew? So perfect. You, husband!" he shouts at Jakub with an ugly twist to his mouth. "Did you know that your wife slept with your brother?"

Aleksander's face goes chalk white as Jakub's round eyes expand into discs—cartoonishly large on his bald head. *No, no, no. Please stop.* Jakub looks from me to Aleksander, back to me. His chin trembles, his eyes protrude even farther, then his face falls so hard that I can't breathe. *Shoot me now, goddamn it.*

I lunge toward Lukas, but a nearby Nazi is quicker and holds me back.

"The evidence is all right here." Lukas lifts the page in front of Jakub's face, so that Jakub can see his own handwriting on the back—his opus, the manuscript I was supposed to safeguard and deliver to the outside world but failed to do. I stare at the floor. I can't look at Jakub or anyone in the room as Lukas begins to recite the intimate details of the night I spent with Aleksander, using my own words.

I begin to see spots as Lukas exaggerates each lewd detail with intense inflection in his voice. The washing of my body, the touching, the stroking, the sucking, the embracing, the lovemaking, the afterward. Every single exact detail I jotted down so I wouldn't forget anything. Once needed to last me forever. And now once will destroy me and the two men I love.

"Enough!" I beg and scream, dropping to my knees, but nothing comes out, just hollow air. My voice is lost in the recesses of horrors that can no longer be categorized, and instead expand and contract into a kaleidoscope of shady fragments fighting for space in my mind.

"A close-up on the husband right now," Lukas commands the young cameraman nearest him. "Who needs Nazis when Jews betray one another so beautifully." He drops the papers onto the floor in front of Jakub. "Don't feel bad, it even made me blush."

Lukas hovers over me. "Here's what's going to happen. As my comrades take down this silly little revolt, I'm going to give you a choice, just as you gave those stupid little Jewish girls a choice in the synagogue. Oh, and that little Jewess you tried to save . . . Dina, was it?" He shakes his head, purses his lips. "You'll never know what happened to her, will you?"

My heart sinks even further. Eryk. Thank God he's not here. I want to die. Please let me die. I want to throw myself onto the pointed guns surrounding me, but I can't move. My arms are locked behind me. This demon wants me to see it all.

"Like I said, so much effort on your part, the whole

synagogue charade. Truly impressive," Lukas continues. "I'm going to give you a choice now, Bina/Irina."
He spits out my name, signals again to his sidekick
cameraman. "Zoom in. Now, choose . . ." Lukas turns
away from me and aims his gun first at Jakub, then at
Aleksander, then back and forth as if he were holding a
tennis racquet. "Who will live and who will die? Your
husband or your lover?"

"Take me!" I scream.

"Don't worry, I will eventually take it all. But for
now, you must choose," he shouts over the gunfire resuming outside the building. "Choose, damn it!"

"Me," Aleksander cries out, begs. "Shoot me."

"Perfect." And with that, Lukas comes around me,
pushes his way between his guards, grabs my fingers,
forcibly curls them around the trigger of his gun, aims
at Aleksander, then fakes a shot and shoots Jakub
squarely in the chest.

"No!" Aleksander yells with a scream that isn't
human, as Jakub clutches his chest and falls backward
to the floor from the impact. No cry, no blame, just a
hard thud. My head spins, I can't breathe. My brilliant
husband's life is reduced to a dull, heavy sound.

"Jakub!" I cry out, thrashing wildly, trying desperately to pull away from this evil man's grip. He signals for assistance. It takes another two guards to hold

me down, as one cameraman hovers over me, his face blocked by the large camera, zeroing in on my agony.

Lukas eyes me with an approving half smile, then turns and shoots Aleksander in the leg. I scream again and again, until my voice becomes an elongated shrill, like the piercing wail of a shofar on the High Holy Days. "That was for insurance," he tells Aleksander, then points his gun back at me. "I'm coming back for you and for him, for information on the organizers behind all this."

He looks to his men, gestures to the ceiling, where Zelda is still shooting like a wild banshee. "That crazy bitch on the rooftop is quite good," he says. "You should see the film I've taken of her in action from down below. Running in circles tied to a pole like a spinning top shooting at us. It's hilarious. I've never seen anything like it. They will love it in Berlin."

He walks over to Aleksander, who is tied up and slumped against the wall, his face perspiring profusely, using his good leg to put pressure over the bullet wound in the other leg. "You not only fucked your husband's wife, but also the daughter of a Nazi." He gestures to me and leaves his finger suspended in the air. "Yes, Konrad Sobieski is the same man who ordered your house to be razed to the ground, killing your wife and child. I do my homework. That's Bina's real father. So much drama in one family. There's nothing I love more than a great script."

Silent tears roll down Aleksander's face, and it's excruciating. I can't look at him and I can't look away. One by one, like dominoes, Lukas is taking down everyone I love. And there is nothing I can do to stop him.

He signals to the cameraman. "Her face right now. Capture it. It's exquisite."

"By the way . . ." He bends down so that he is at eye level with me. "I'm not only a filmmaker, but I am charged with capturing the highlights of our winning war. My specialty is infiltrating opposition parties like Żegota—filming the takedown, documenting our victories, state by state, country by country, for our national archives."

His cruel face blurs. I try to look past him, but his tormenting voice is still going at it, buzzing with venom. "And you probably are wondering why I allowed the Nazi nightclub bombing. That, too, was part of a bigger plan. Every single member at the club that night was invited personally by Jürgen Stroop, under my advisement. All the invited guests had one thing in common: Traitors. Liars. Dissidents. Those based in Warsaw who did not represent the Aryan ideal." He winks, indicating his men don't know about his sexual preference. "And it was time to do away with those who thought too much of themselves, like that pompous baron—Daddy."

He sneers, and it's as though his mouth is being slowly unzipped. He then motions two of his officers to stay with us and signals the others to join him. "Do not let her out of your sight. Now, let's go take down the Jew bitch going berserk on the rooftop."

Chapter Twenty-Seven

I rub my eyes hard, disoriented, confused by the tangle of gray woolen blankets enveloping me. Where am I? My gaze travels from wall to wall for clues, landing on the few snapshots tacked to a wooden post. Zelda with her sister and brother. Zelda with her parents. Zelda at the center of all her fighters huddled together. I spot my purse in the corner of the room and the nightclub dress I wore hanging on a hook, realizing that I'm in Zelda's room in the bunker. Is she alive? I try to recall the chain of events, how I ended up here.

I force myself to sit up. Everything hurts, especially my head. My clothes are drenched in sweat and covered in blood. Slowly, random images begin to surface. Lukas, the shooting, Jakub, Aleksander, stabbing a

Nazi guard with Zelda's pocketknife, then an explosion. That's where it ends. I press my ear to the wall behind her bed and hear muddled voices on the other side of it. I begin to decipher more facts: Zelda is dead. It took twelve bullets to kill her, someone says. Even then, she refused to die, another voice chimes in, adding that her last word was *Raisa,* her sister's name, as she shot her final bullet, taking a German soldier down with her.

Someone mentions Tosia. How she saved the day. I lie back against the pillow and vaguely remember how Tosia, with her pearlescent skin smothered with freckles, threw a grenade into the hallway as the Nazis made their way down from the rooftop after killing Zelda. Alone, she took out three Nazis while one was wounded and another managed to escape. Did Lukas escape or die?

And Aleksander . . . My heart screams. *Is he alive?*

Nothing else matters. I must know, praying that he is among them. I struggle to get up; my ribs are burning, and my head feels like it is being weighed down by bricks. The voices on the other side of the wall are still recapping what happened. I stop moving when someone describes how Tosia carried Aleksander to the bottom of the bunker, dragging him down the three flights of stairs. Alive! He's alive! And then the same voice recounts how I stabbed a wounded Nazi soldier with my small knife—bludgeoned him to death. Butchered like meat, someone added. I don't recall any of it.

But that doesn't excuse what she did, a familiar voice yells out angrily. Eryk? The others agree. I freeze. They know. Everybody knows. Daughter of a Nazi . . . slept with her husband's brother while he was on a train to Treblinka. Not even buried yet. The voices become a Greek chorus of disgust and blame.

But he slept with me, too, I yearn to shout back in defense. *There were two of us there.* Tears fill my eyes. I am the wicked witch of Warsaw. I killed my husband twice—last night and long before he was sent to Treblinka.

Painfully, I remove my bloodstained shirt—Nazi blood—then grab a shirt from Zelda's small pile of clothes, a loose plain-woven beige blouse. I sniff it. Woodsy, sulfurous, metallic, as though she'd been oiling guns. It smells like her. Tears roll down my cheeks as I put it on. I feel so small, so defeated.

Zelda is dead. Jakub is dead. Sammy is dead. Little Dina—I will never know what happened to her. Get up. Go out there now. Face the firing squad.

I stand in agony, check my purse with the Irina papers and the money still intact. My leg muscles tighten like steel rods. There's going to be a price to pay. Without thinking twice, I grab my purse, take a small satchel of Zelda's, and fill it with a few items from her desk: a flashlight, a compass, two cigarettes, matches, a half-filled flask of water, bandages, the still-bloody pocketknife, and a thick black sweater hanging on a hook. And then I head out.

The talking stops immediately. I focus first on the long wooden table where everyone is sitting, before absorbing the surrounding accusatory faces. The table is covered with grenades, bullets, magazines, weapons, Nazi uniforms, and dozens of wallets filled with deutsche marks and zlotys peeking out of them—a smorgasbord of military booty seized from our enemy. At another time, we would have danced around the table to rejoice, a victory hora. But the loss among us is too great to celebrate. My eyes peel away from the table and toward Aleksander, who is sitting on a chair in the corner of the room, his bandaged leg elevated with a stack of pillows. Then I meet Eryk's angry face next to him.

His hair is matted with sweat and his shirt is covered in blood. His impassioned gaze impales mine, and his voice is slow and succinct as he stands and walks toward me. "Did you lie about my sister? Why did you tell me that Dina was safe, hidden in the forest, and in good hands? What really happened, Bina? Did that Nazi kill her? What if I could have saved her?" he shouts. "I trusted you, goddamn it."

I bite down on my bottom lip. He never could have saved her. Nobody could. But that doesn't matter right now.

"I tried, Eryk, I really tried. I still believe she is alive," I muster, my voice choking. Anna told me that Stach had gotten her out, but then Stach was captured. And Anna never knew for sure what happened to Dina. I just didn't mention that part—the uncertainty. My eyes well up. Eryk is unmoved. They all are.

"I don't believe you. Not one word you say." He glances at Aleksander, whose face is stone cold. "That Nazi said Dina was dead. I believe him."

They believe a Nazi over me.

Aleksander fixates on me. There is hatred in his eyes too. *How the hell could you have written down what we did? You did this. Your words killed Jakub before the Nazis did.* There is a sheen of sweat painted across his forehead, like one of his own textured brushstrokes. "A Treblinka oven would have been a better death for Jakub," he says. His voice is lifeless, numb. "It should have been you," he says. "You, not Jakub."

Those eyes that once sparkled like emeralds are now opaque like pond scum. He is staring at me in the same cold way the Nazis look at us: disassociated and repulsed. The man I love with all my heart wishes me dead, and right now, seeing my reflection in his deadened eyes, I wish that too.

"I'm leaving," I announce. My voice, known for its rich, throaty tone, is timorous, disgraced.

"Just go. Get out of here," Eryk responds icily. I should have told him the truth about Dina, not given him false hope. I broke the circle of trust, and that's all we have ever had here together; the only thing we could count on. "And don't come back," he shouts. No longer a boy but a man. No longer a man but a soldier.

My heart breaks irreparably. Shame slashes mercilessly through me. As I turn to go, banished from those I love, those I fought for, those I came back for, I notice the Browning planted on the far edge of the table squished between two shiny German Lugers. It's mine. I don't deserve it, but I take the gun anyway, stuff it inside my waistband, and no one stops me. As I make my way toward the stairs, I hear Eryk shouting after me, "I'm just glad Zelda didn't live to see this."

Chapter Twenty-Eight

Adrenaline propels me forward amid the flaming, red-lit sky, airborne bullets, grenades, smoke, debris, and madness. I could easily curl up and die, take the fast way out by hurling myself in the middle of the uprising and be done. But something bigger than me is pushing me to stay alive. Self-loathing turns to defiance, becoming the wind beneath me. I run, swerve, move, dodge, and twist, pressing my back against one brick wall to the next, as though performing a ghetto ballet in which I'm the principal dancer.

I run for all that was stolen from me, but mostly for Zelda, whose bullet-ridden body was left dangling upside down by a rope off the side of the bunker on Mila Street for everyone to see. Her rebellious spirit, her stubborn voice pushes me ahead. *Live, Bina, live.*

*You can make this right. The last bullet—last word—
must be yours.*

It takes me a good hour of hiding and dodging, but
I make my way to the convent where I used to teach
drama classes. Beside it is my sewer, the one I used on
multiple occasions to smuggle food and supplies in and
out of the ghetto. The sewer is positioned close to the
park on the Aryan side, nearly adjacent to the tunnel
that Vladek had led me through a few days ago. Exhaling deeply, I take one last look at the ghetto burning
down around me, then slowly, carefully, I lift the lid
and descend into the sewer. Alice spiraling down the
rabbit hole.

Above my head, I hear the violent ripple of gunshots and bombs exploding as I move like a lone gazelle
through the stench, contaminated water, and sludge,
the approximately one-hundred-and-twenty-meter distance from the convent to the Aryan side, not knowing
who or what will greet me at the other end, or if this is
the end.

With what little strength I have left, ignoring the
grinding pain in my ribs, I climb the makeshift ladder
built for our young smugglers and lift the heavy lid.
In the slim space of air, I don't see any moving boots
or shoes nearby. Most likely, all the Nazi soldiers have
been redirected into the ghetto to quash us. Raising

the lid higher, I hoist myself up and out, then carefully refit the lid onto the pavement. I look around quickly. It's now or never. Heart pumping, I sprint toward the nearby park where I hid just a few days ago. I lean against a large, leafy oak tree, make myself as small as I can, and collect my breath. Now what?

I wait.

From my vantage point, I see the fiery bombs arcing like asteroids over the ghetto. I picture our remaining fighters giving everything they've got. My heart is crushed. I should be there, not here. *Aleks, I know you despise me. I know you will never forgive me, but please live. I can't bear a world in which you don't exist.*

Taking a tiny sip of water from Zelda's flask, I carefully search the grounds, hoping Vladek is back out here, scoping his territory for his next customer. I wait for what feels like hours, staring up at the charcoal sky, feeling the cold breeze whip at my face. *Guide me, Zelda. I need you.*

Thirty minutes later, in the distance, a large shadow materializes, moving carefully from one tree to the next. I stay put, watching and waiting. And then the movement stops. The shape becomes shapeless, but the size of it—it's him, isn't it? I can't stay here forever. It will be light soon. I see a lit cigarette like a firefly in the night, and then Vladek appears in his black leather jacket. I make myself seen as well, and he doesn't even look surprised, as if a woman emerging from the trees is normal.

He half smiles. "So, Landau's daughter needs another favor?"

"Yes. I need you to hide me." Before he responds, I step forward and slap a bunch of zlotys into his palm. "Please, Vladek, take this and get me out of here."

"Where?"

"Isn't that your job?"

He points to the ghetto burning. "My job has changed."

I sigh deeply. I have only one place to go. "I have an address. It's not too far."

He replies by stuffing the money inside his jacket—no qualms taking it this time. He points in the direction of the same cluster of trees where I was hiding earlier. I don't think twice. I follow him.

We weave among the trees and the bushes like small children playing hide-and-seek. I remain a good ten paces behind him. He turns, gestures to a truck parked in the distance. I follow him. As I approach the vehicle, I'm surprised that the truck is shiny, freshly painted. The Germans seized everything good, valuable, and new for themselves. And then I get closer and stop cold.

Impossible. Vladek knows exactly what I see and turns away guiltily.

Even in the grainy darkness, I make out the covered-up shadows of the once swirly gold logo concealed beneath the black paint: Landau & Sons. A truck that belonged to my father's fleet. I clasp my hands to my chest. I'm going to be sick. Vladek quickly jumps into the driver's seat. I should shoot him dead right now. I climb into the passenger side. Nothing matters anymore. Everything has been stolen from me. What's one more thing.

Vladek doesn't look at me as he starts the truck. "Crouch down," he orders. "And cover yourself with that." He points to the folded tarp on the seat.

I follow his orders and scrunch into the space where my feet should be and grab the tarp, only to realize that it is not a tarp. It's a pennant. And not just any pennant. Black, oxblood, and white. A swastika in my face. I let out a silent, blood-curdling scream beneath it. A Nazi flag. What was I thinking getting inside this painted-over stolen truck? Either Vladek is turning me in for ransom or he is playing both sides.

I'm an idiot. Why did I trust him blindly? Because he got me back inside the ghetto? Because he didn't rape me that day? Like everything else in this twisted war, you can't count on anything or anyone when survival is at stake. How much money is a runaway Jew worth now? I wonder. And why did I tell him that address? How selfish of me. How wrong. I feel the vibration of the road beneath me. I clutch my purse and satchel, and then remember my gun.

Flinging the pennant off me, I quickly climb into the passenger seat and aim the pistol at Vladek's head. "Who the hell are you really?"

"Put that away now!" he shouts as he drives. "If anyone sees us, sees you . . ."

I thrust the barrel of the gun against his temple. "Why do you have a Nazi flag?"

"Everyone has a fucking Nazi flag. I'm a smuggler. If I'm caught, I need to show that I support them. It's a cover. Now get down and hide, goddamn it."

"Why should I trust you? You stole this truck from my father."

"I didn't steal it," he says. "I took it before the Nazis did. I saved the damn truck. Now get the fuck down!"

Liar. They are all liars. Smugglers always play both sides, loyal only to the highest bidder. But if I shoot him, what do I have left? I can't take this truck and drive across town without getting caught. I tuck the gun back inside my waistband, crouch back down into the space beneath the seat, and cover myself with the Nazi flag. It's Vladek or nothing.

Chapter Twenty-Nine

We arrive at the destination less than fifteen minutes later. Vladek parks and points at the boarded-up two-story house across the street. "That's the address you gave me. See that sign hanging off the doorframe? It's a ballet studio. Are you planning to dance your way out of Warsaw?"

I sit in the passenger seat and pray I'm not endangering Anna by showing up here. She is the only person left besides Vladek who can help me escape, if she is even alive. What if Lukas already got to her too? But I have no one else.

"This is the place," I tell Vladek, unsure of what I'm doing right now.

"Not smart," he says, shaking his head. I know what he sees. A building that is in shambles amid a tree-lined upscale residential street with neighbors who will know immediately if someone is lurking inside the deserted studio. A runaway Jew is worth a lot, probably triple the price since the uprising began.

"I have no other choice," I say.

Vladek smacks his palm against his head, as though wrestling with himself. "There may be another option . . . who lives here?"

Anna. I need to check, to find out if she is still here. "Twenty minutes," I tell him without answering his question. "Can you give me twenty minutes?"

He turns off the vehicle and cuts the lights. "Ten minutes, and then I'm leaving. It's not safe. Neighbors are among the worst collaborators with the Nazis. No one wants trouble on their street."

"Fifteen minutes." I throw down onto the seat a stack of zlotys that I don't even count and jump out of the truck, cross the street, and hurriedly make my way to the right side of the studio toward the back window. I hide in the shadows, trying to recall Anna's instructions that last night in the safe house. The window latch is broken, she told me. You need to jiggle it open to get inside.

Please be here, Anna. I hold my breath as I carefully wriggle the latch. Is my suitcase still here? I wonder. My heart pounds when the window gives way and opens.

I take a quick look around, and once I am certain no one is watching, I step onto a broken brick beneath the window, which Anna must use as well, and hoist myself up and inside.

"Hello," I whisper, steadying myself as I look around the large empty studio space. "Hello?" I repeat, but nothing.

I don't turn on any lights, but luckily the moonlight streaming in through the shutter slats illuminates the studio. There is a long barre perched against a wall-size mirror, an old record player in the far corner, and a parade of colorful costumes hanging neatly on a valet stand on the other side of the room. I picture a young Anna here, sashaying in her pink tutu, twirling on her toes, looking to her beloved Madame Sosia for approval. I imagine that gut-wrenching day when the Nazis stormed in and shot the beloved teacher dead in front of her pupils. I check for any clues of the attack. Nothing. Anna must have scrubbed the floor clean of blood.

"Anna, it's me . . . . Irina," I whisper again. No answer. I walk around, trying to decide what to do first. I have ten minutes, maybe less. I must move quickly.

My suitcase. Is it here, as Anna promised it would be? It is all I have left; the only memories of my family are packed inside. It shouldn't matter, but it does.

I check around until I spot a small hallway next to a staircase leading up to the second floor. There is a large storage closet and a commode. "Anna?" I call up from the base of the stairs, which are cracked and dusty. I take a few steps up, wait for a response. Still nothing.

No one is here. I return to the hallway closet and open it. It is stuffed with blankets, pillows, linen, and shelving lined with tinned food. I remove everything carefully, take nothing, and that's when I see it. My suitcase stashed behind a stack of boxes. A warm feeling overwhelms me. Anna kept it for me. She knew I would come for it.

Gently removing the small valise from the closet, I drag it toward the center of the studio where there is light. I hold my breath as I open it up. Everything is still inside: photographs of my family, Aleksander and Karina, and Jakub's manuscript—minus those pages I had carelessly left behind and that Lukas took when he and his men raided the safe house. And then beneath it all, I feel it, the Behrman family's violin, the Stradivarius. I pick it up. It's heavier than I remember. Something inside of it shakes. I hold it up to the light. Between the strings, inside its hollow body, I see a thin booklet, and eyeglasses? Anna must have put those in there for me. I pinch open the strings as wide as I can without breaking them and shake out the hidden items.

A passport. I open it and read the name: Petra Schneider, with Anna's picture. She is wearing the same thick horn-rimmed glasses. If I put them on, I could easily pass for her. My heart pounds hard. She knew I would survive. She was expecting me. She left me the one thing that could save me—more than food, more than shelter, even more than this valuable violin—a fool-proof non-Jewish identity. Hers.

Petra Schneider.

I strain to read the passport. Petra was born in Hamburg, Germany. She is listed as a student and has a very believable story. And I can tell, just by looking at the few clues, the entire story. Petra's mother has a Polish name. Her father is German. We would play a game in the ghetto to pass time: Give me a name, a fake identity, and I will give you the story. My colorful stories always won. Petra Schneider moved here from Hamburg as a young girl, to spend time with the Polish side of her family and to study ballet. Petra is legitimate, an Aryan Pole. And Petra, Anna is telling me without telling me, is my way out.

This courageous woman has saved my life twice and demanded nothing in return. She could have sold the priceless violin on the black market to feed herself and all her relatives for a year, perhaps even booked her own passage out of this godforsaken war zone. Maybe she is already gone. But Anna went even further. She anticipated my return, believed I would one day make it out of the ghetto and need passage. All the planning she did for a woman she barely knew. My eyes well up. I may never be able to thank her for giving me a second chance at life. I press the passport to my chest. She wants me to live even more than I do.

I quickly shut the suitcase and take it with me, pausing briefly at the costume valet, and make a split-second decision. I open my satchel and remove the pearl hairpin that I wore the evening of the nightclub bombing, which Anna had given me as part of my disguise. It's sharp on the ends, and I thought to use it as a weapon if needed.

Instead, I attach it like a barrette to the strap of the first dress on the costume valet as a sort of Morse code—a sign to Anna if she returns that I was here, made it out alive, and reclaimed the suitcase.

"Thank you," I whisper to the empty studio space encompassing all that Anna once loved, then I quickly leave the same way I arrived, up and out the window like a cat burglar.

I carefully check the empty street before returning to the truck. I look up at the military fireworks still going ballistic across the blackened sky. Warsaw is sleeping, but not the ghetto. It will never sleep again.

My friends are dying while I am saving myself. I break out into a cold sweat as I open the truck door.

"Leave the damn suitcase," Vladek says angrily.

"I am not leaving it," I retort, placing the valise on the seat and crouching in the floor space beneath it. "Can you get me out of Warsaw tonight?"

He glances down at me. "Are you crazy? No one is getting out of Warsaw tonight."

"I can pay . . . a lot."

He points out the car window. "Maybe you are blind or deaf? The ghetto is blowing up, the forest is probably surrounded, the Gestapo is everywhere. They know that any Jews who manage to survive the siege will try to escape. To be honest, that's what I was doing in the park tonight—waiting for runaway Jews. And then you showed up." He gestures to the ballet studio across the street. "Maybe it's best that you stay here. Hide until it is safe to leave."

I contemplate it. I can sleep inside the storage closet—it's big enough. There is food. But the neighbors . . . Vladek is right. They would give me up without blinking. I must get to the forest somehow.

"Vladek, I know you are risking a lot right now. Please, take me to the partisans." Seeing the refusal on his face, I opt for a more conciliatory tone. "Or at least near the border. From there, I will find a way out. Unless you have a better idea?" I make my eyes wide and fearful—a princess in jeopardy—a look men cannot resist.

We both remain quiet for a few moments, contemplating each other. He speaks first. "There is one possibility. But . . ."

I hold my breath. Always a but, always a catch.

"The thing is, well, you see, I'm not just a smuggler." He clears his throat. "I'm a driver."

"Not construction." I state the obvious by the way he is stumbling over his words.

He presses his lips together tightly. "Remember when I told you that my wife was a seamstress? Well, she is now employed as a seamstress for high-level Nazi mistresses. My other job is to drive those same women to wherever I'm told their services are required. I also deliver the dresses. Nazis are always celebrating themselves, throwing lavish parties honoring high-level officials who come to town. And—"

"And you supply the women."

He nods the truth. A smuggler with a conscience. "It keeps my family alive. I do what I must do."

Hence the Nazi pennant. Not just a safety precaution that drapes the truck.

"You're a pimp," I say under my breath.

"This war has turned us all into whores and pimps."

His face boils beneath his scraggly beard. I can see the reddening of his exposed cheeks. "I make sure those women get to and from safely. A protector, not a pimp."

A protector? But then, who am I to judge? The things I've done . . .

"So, let me guess," I say. "Your idea is for me to dress up and then you hand me over to those Nazi bastards on a porcelain platter. From there, I would find my way into their beds and out of hell."

"Not exactly." He sighs. "But yes, disguise you as one of the mistresses and take you out of Warsaw, to the countryside, where those lavish celebrations take place." He clears his throat again uncomfortably. And we both know exactly what that means.

Konstancin. Villas, castles, vacation homes, lush with towering pine trees and picturesque gardens filled with poppies and lilacs as far as the eye can see. "My home," I whisper, feeling sicker than when I discovered Vladek is driving my father's truck. My family home has been taken over by the Nazi elite.

Vladek doesn't respond. He doesn't need to. It's all right there, written in the dead air between us. I will myself not to cry. This is just a truck. My home was just a home. My memories are just memories. All expendables.

"If you have any chance of escaping, that's what I

would recommend. Maybe, stay here for the night until I can arrange a better hiding spot. But . . ."

But. And there it is again. The catch, the complication.

He shakes his head, as though fighting with himself. "I can't do this for free. I'm not a good man. I don't claim to be. This will cost you plenty and require detailed planning and involve more than just me. Right now, the Nazis are engaged in battle. Their fancy parties are on hold until it's over . . . once they win." He points to the ghetto as if it were a mere finger length away. "This revolt buys us at least a day or two to plan. But I can't move forward without compensation. There are too many people to pay off. I'm sorry." He holds my gaze.

Not sorry. The very lucrative business of dead Jews.

"What if the uprising lasts longer than you anticipate?" I ask. "What if it's not just a day or two but weeks?"

Vladek flicks his wrist. "Impossible. The Nazis seized all of Poland in thirty-six days. You think a handful of starving Jews with a few grenades and reject pistols can stand up to the S.S. war machine? I hear Jews are using children to fight." He glances at his watch. *Using children! You have no idea, you bastard.* "Today is Tuesday?" he notes. "By Thursday, the Nazis will be celebrating and demanding their mistresses back in their beds. Two days. I give it two. Tops."

So, my life depends on the quick destruction of the ghetto, I think. Revenge is unbearable, Zelda.

"How much?" I ask. How much is my life worth?

"That's the bigger problem. You can't afford the escape."

I think of Eryk's face, the violin inside my suitcase. It belongs to him and Dina. To save their lives, not mine. I think of Petra Schneider, my new foolproof German-Polish identity. Zelda's face rises before me. *Live, Bina, live.* I make a quick decision.

"I have a violin."

"A violin?" He gives a pealing laugh, then his face waxes serious. "People need food, money, not music. This is war. Ah, you rich Jews have no idea."

You rich Jews have no idea. "The violin is a work of art. It's worth more than a dozen trucks," I counter, thinking of all the corrupt art dealers who took advantage and profited immensely off persecuted Jews forced to sell their paintings and valuables for a pittance of what the art was worth and flee their homes. I think of all of Aleksander's magnificent paintings that his own art dealer stole from him, profiting immensely. "There will be buyers for this violin, I guarantee you."

Vladek shrugs. "Doubtful, but I will check. If you're

right, that would solve that problem. But there is still the other problem, the bigger one." He looks me up and down. "You are beautiful. You look like them, but you are a Jew. Nazi mistresses are all Polish women. Nazis can smell a Jew a mile away. I have never seen anything like it. They sniff out the nervousness, the tics, the hand movements, the scent. They measure the size of pupils. They can catch a Jew with one eye closed. I've seen it a hundred times. Can you play—"

"Whore, seductress, mistress?" My voice rises, and I try to contain the scorching rage, but I'm failing. It takes all my restraint not to use my last few bullets and blow this lout's head off.

"What I'm saying is your life depends on your ability to act—to *not* be a Jew. Can you act under pressure?"

And that's when I laugh, loud and bellicose—an ogre's meaty laugh. A cackle worthy of Macbeth's witches that surely all the nosy neighbors on the street could hear.

Vladek tries to shake me quiet. But I don't care. I laugh until I cry. I sob until I have no more tears left. He eyes me like I am a lunatic. And he's right. There is so much I want to tell this coarse man, this pimp smuggler who means nothing to me, but who is now my sole means of survival.

Everyone I have ever loved is dead, Vladek. All

those rich Jews and poor ones too. All those fighting children, dead, I shout at him silently. Aleksander was right. It should have been me—not Jakub. It should have been me—not Zelda. But here I am still alive, Vladek, and it's all *because* of my acting ability.

What you don't know, what Nazis can't sniff out or tell by a tic or a nervous gesture, is that I am nearly twenty-four years old, and I have portrayed practically every part imaginable: heroine, wife, lover, mistress, daughter, almost-mother, villain, maid, whore, seductress, smuggler, assassin. I am a woman born to become anyone other than who she really is.

BOOK II

HOLLYWOOD

1956

Chapter Thirty

Three vodkas later, my body moves in sync with the fit young bartender from the hotel's seedy cocktail lounge downstairs, Mack or Mick—can't remember his name. Who cares? Doesn't matter. In the decade since I made Hollywood my home, the amount of *doesn't matters* could fill a theater with standing room only.

My hands grasp his firm twentysomething ass, and my breasts press hard against his smooth, hairless chest. He moans, whispers sexy things, and I return the volleys on cue. I know my lines.

The second round wraps up quickly—a collage of mouths on body parts—and the cooldown begins. Only then, when the young man loses all shape and form, becoming nothing more than a function of night, can I finally relax. Closing my eyes with a companion smile, the lover mistakes it for pleasure, the frothy laugh for the satisfaction he thinks he gave me. Feeling generous, I let him have it.

"So good, better than I imagined," he says as he sits up, stretches, showing off his strong abdomen and, thankfully, signaling his imminent getaway. "But break's over. Got to head back downstairs for the late shift. Can't have the boss complaining 'Where's Mick?'"

Mick. I tell myself, *You do need to remember his name. And you do want the boss complaining that he's late.* One more added detail, one more witness.

I watch him strut toward the heap of clothes near the door. He just slept with the woman every man in America desires, and every woman strives to emulate: Lena Browning, Tinseltown's leading lady. Long, supple legs, cat eyes enhanced by thick arched brows that are five shades darker than her highlighted shoulder-length blond hair, with a mysterious half smile that captivates audiences, dominates magazine covers. Make no mistake, not the Girl Next Door. That title goes to Doris. No, we're talking beguiling, knife-in-your-back Queen of the Trysts—*that* actress. At thirty-six (in Hollywood years I'm twenty-nine), I am no longer an actor—not even a person—but a high-paid femme-fatale fantasy.

If only they knew.

The bartender turns to me as he slips on his well-worn loafers. "Dinner next time, perhaps?" he asks with a sly, lazy grin. I force a smile back and let my eyes do the talking: There won't be a next time. I needed you as an alibi. Now go.

The next morning in my trailer, Connie, my personal assistant, places cucumber slices doused in chamomile over my eyes to help correct the morning puffiness. A masseuse is busy working my feet and both women are discussing the homicide that took place last night, the body found floating face down in Lake Placid, about twenty minutes from our movie set.

Connie speaks first. "A bullet right between the eyes . . . father of three. Near his vacation home, apparently." Everyone, especially those in this industry, loves a good murder story.

"I hear the wife is a suspect," chimes in the masseuse. I refrain from rolling my eyes beneath the cucumber slices and bite back a smile. Here it comes. Grist for the gossip mill.

Connie's turn. "A neighbor said she heard the man and his wife arguing earlier that day. I saw her interviewed on the news this morning."

"A nightmare," I respond, sitting up and removing

the sticky slices from my eyes, while mustering the appropriate look of concern and shock.

But inside, I am high-fiving. Thrilled to learn that the wife is now a suspect. This should buy me enough time to wrap up this movie and get out of Dodge before anyone comes sniffing. Because I, alone, know the real story, all the facts.

The dead man, father of three, was an engineer with the U.S. Department of Defense, identified as Ralph Winters. He happened to be taking his kayak out for an evening paddle near his Lake Placid vacation home that day. A man of rigid habit, Winters doesn't happen to do anything. That was the beauty of this kill . . . the predictability made it so damn easy.

Earlier that day, Winters was enjoying a happy hour schnapps or two and a cigar, legs splayed out lazily from his Kelly-green Adirondack chair on the end of his dock, a ritual he adhered to every evening. He finished off the cigar, then took his usual hour-long ride 'round the bend before dinner—his favorite activity and only daily exercise. He loved the quietude as the sun began to set. Just him and his lake. His slice of paradise. While approaching a deserted section of the bend, Winters "happened" upon a redheaded woman in a canoe frantically waving her arms, crying out for help. It looked like she'd lost her paddle. A damsel in distress. (What actress among us hasn't played this demeaning role on repeat?) Whether you are a man or a Nazi or a Nazi-in-hiding like Winters, woman-in-despair works every time. Even the worst among men envisions himself a knight in shining armor on occasion.

Steering his kayak my way, Winters sidled up to help me, his jaw dropping like a dump truck when he saw the barrel of my pistol facing him at point-blank range.

I stared deep into his shocked pale-blue eyes when he realized that the redhead with the gun was the film star Lena Browning. If only I could have photographed that look.

"Why?" he asked.

"Why?" I laughed in his face. "You know damn well why. You're a liar and a murderer. No more hiding. I know who you really are. Saw you with my own eyes riding alongside Jürgen Stroop wherever he went. His bitch. This is for Stach Sobieski and so many others—with love from the Warsaw Ghetto." My all-time favorite line. Cheesy, but I've used it on repeat. I aimed my Browning P35—a replica of the original—and took one perfect shot right between his eyes.

Never. Waste. A. Single. Bullet.

Winters fell sideways, tipping the kayak over with him, and I relished his portly plunge into the icy water. Every pore on my skin rose animatedly, and my heart danced as blood cradled the man's bloated face, his cheeks filling up with water like a puffer fish, a bluish-black halo of plasma encasing his bald head.

The dead man was not Ralph Winters from Darien, Connecticut, a town known for its anti-Semitic history. He was Rolf Wagner, born in Munich, Germany, and rose in the S.S. ranks to become a high-level Nazi engineer, who was sent to Warsaw to serve directly under Jürgen Stroop.

Wagner was single-handedly responsible for master-minding the bomb attack on the Żegota headquarters, setting the entire building on fire, and then a month later, his most memorable explosion: the destruction of the Great Synagogue of Warsaw—signifying the Nazis' ultimate victory over the Jews of Warsaw. It took four weeks for the Nazis to quash my people—not two days, as Vladek predicted. Four full weeks of the ghetto's fighters giving everything they had—slingshots against tanks—to the very end. If only Zelda had lived to see her fighters hanging on until the very last bullet. If only I were there too.

Wagner should have been tried for his war crimes in Nuremberg. The evidence against him was staggering, with many eyewitness reports. But he possessed that little something extra special that protected him and bought him a golden ticket to freedom: superb technological skills and engineering expertise. Instead of hanging by a noose, he was saved by the U.S. government, as part of its Operation Paperclip, a top secret intelligence program in which sixteen hundred high-ranking Nazi scientists, engineers, and technicians were rescued from Nazi Germany, their criminal pasts wiped clean, and given U.S. government employment after the war.

Why waste a brilliant mind, right?

I heard rumors about Paperclip and decided I needed to find out for myself if it was true. I did my research and assembled a list of high-level American leaders who were there at the Nuremberg Military Tribunals—particularly those in the inner sanctum of the American High Commissioner for Occupied Germany—the men in charge of deciding Nazi guilt or doling out clemency. On the heels of the huge success of my film *Moon Over Monaco* in 1953, I made sure I was invited to a prestigious White House cocktail party loaded with military bigwigs to see what I could discover up close.

When I was introduced to a prominent married Pentagon official named Frank Campbell (on my list), who appeared to have a yen for tall, lanky blond movie stars and a penchant for gin and tonics, I knew I'd found my man. The flirty gentleman was perfectly drunk and bragging about his wartime activities to impress me.

We talked about Europe, politics, movies, and I kept making sure that his glass was full.

"Did you have direct dealings with the Nazis?" I asked, playing dumb.

"More than direct." He grinned. "I had a key role serving in Germany right after the war, in Nuremberg."

And that's exactly why I'm here. "There's talk that some high-level Nazis escaped to Argentina and Venezuela. What about on our soil?" I signaled the bartender over for another round.

"Now, that's classified information."

"Now, that's sexy," I said, lightly pressing against his tuxedo jacket, giving him a better view of my cleavage. "Sounds like you are a classified kind of guy. If only I had that list of Nazis hiding here . . ."

"What would Hollywood's most famous star do with a list of Nazis?" He laughed, raising a curious bushy brow.

I winked back. "You mean, what would Hollywood's most famous star do *for* a list of Nazis?" I matched his brow lift, laughed lightly, luring him out of the ballroom into a nearby private alcove.

"I'm serious," he said.

"Well, so am I. The thing is, Frank . . . I'm not just simply curious," I told him, remembering Zelda's words that the best lies are wrapped around a truth.

"Nobody knows this, so I'm trusting you, but I just signed on to star in a top secret role in a new film about a female rocket scientist planning to outsmart her Russian counterparts. The woman will stop at nothing to get to the top, even luring a Nazi rocket genius to help her." I paused, cleared my throat. "I can't reveal more than that, because of my contract. But that's why I'm here in Washington—doing research. And now, lucky me, I seem to have met the right guy." I squeezed his arm, saw his face change colors, and knew it was time to pounce. I leaned in and gave him a deep kiss.

"I can't believe I'm kissing Lena Browning," he panted.

I stopped mid-kiss and whispered huskily, "And I can't believe I'm with such an important military hero. Is there any chance I could see the document? Perhaps there's someone on it who I could talk to off the record for deep background, to really develop my new character." My eyes ignited with hope. "Frank, it would mean so much. I really believe this is my Oscar-winning role. If you do this for me . . ." My voice trailed purposefully, accompanied by a firm press of my hand to his crotch to seal the deal.

A tryst at the Jefferson Hotel was planned for the following night. I exchanged my body for a glimpse of Frank's classified list—a road map of prominent Nazis living free and easy in America, with their real names and locations. I picked one Nazi name from the list, a man who worked for NASA, then Frank quickly slipped the document back inside his briefcase and we got down to business.

I drugged Frank's postcoital gin and tonic with heavy tranquilizers. And once he fell into a deep slumber, I removed the list from his briefcase, took photos, got dressed, and then shook him awake.

"Frank," I told him in his drowsy state. "The evening was lovely, but best for both of our careers and your marriage that this never happens again. Did I mention that the president is a dear friend?" I placed my hand over my heart. "A man who easily trades government secrets for sex is not to be trusted. If I were you, I would watch my back." And then I left, knowing Frank would not only keep his mouth shut, but would be looking over his shoulder for the rest of his life.

Rolf Wagner's death was "payback" number four from my list of names. I will never be able to get to all sixteen hundred criminals, so I targeted only those Nazis I knew of personally back in Warsaw—who'd destroyed my family, my friends, my community, who had made it their mission to crush our existence.

As always, I had a solid alibi in place. Mick, the flirty bartender at my hotel, would be waiting for me right around the time I finished off Wagner. We pre-arranged a rendezvous in my hotel room timed perfectly. And after I was done with Mick, he'd never forget his own satisfying tryst with Lena Browning—something he'll surely brag about to all his buddies, which I wholeheartedly welcome. More witnesses to back me up if anyone tries to connect me to Wagner's demise.

As I watched Rolf Wagner float away like a wet Goodyear blimp under the setting sun, I let out a deep cleansing breath, and for a short, precious time, the part of me that would always be at war was tranquil and at peace.

Chapter Thirty-One

The small window in my trailer is open a crack, and I hear my name repeated by a multitude of frantic lackeys scurrying around the set. Lena needs this . . . Stan said Lena better have that or else . . . Mort will hit the fucking roof if Lena doesn't get . . .

Lena, Lena.

My makeup has been applied, my hair styled and glued into place, and I'm ready to roll. As I step down from my trailer, I see Jack Lyons emerging from his. Wearing khakis and a black Cuban collar shirt, and freshly tanned, my leading man looks particularly yummy. I wave, he winks back. We'll rendezvous at lunch. It's light and easy, no strings attached—just the way I like it. But I am fond of him. Jack is surprisingly warm, funny, kind, and as generous as an actor as he is between the sheets. He never feels threatened if my role or scene is meatier than his. A good apple among so many rotten ones.

This scene, taking place in a small town near Lake Placid, is the climax of the film. Jack and I have been practicing all week in and out of bed. It's our second film together. This one is a love story with strong elements of suspense, my wheelhouse: Can this man love a woman with a dark, secret past? Can she love a man who destroyed her husband? Yes and yes. Guaranteed box-office success. And obviously not a stretch for me.

In this scene, we both know we must break off the relationship or people will get killed. It's the clincher. Tears well up in Jack's eyes as he holds my hand, presses it tenderly to his lips. My return gaze, however, is as dry as the Sahara. The director immediately calls for a twenty-minute break, clearly wanting more emotion from me. I see the disappointment spread across Stan Moss's face as everyone disperses.

"Lena, Lena," he says, wrapping his buttery brown-leather-jacketed arm around my shoulders. "You're the best. Everybody knows it." He points to Jack, who is heading to his trailer. "Your husband's nemesis, a man with his own secrets, has fallen in love with you, and as coldhearted as you are, you can't hide your true feelings for him. I need torment, pain, struggle. Tears,

Lena. Just one, damn it. The shot needs one fucking teardrop streaming from eyelid to cheek to show the audience that you are human."

I glare at Stan and hiss under my breath, "Read my contract."

"I know, I know. Everybody knows. The 'no crying' clause. But I can't have Jack Lyons weeping like a newborn and nothing from you. The audience won't buy it."

I draw out a heavy, exaggerated sigh. "They always do, Stan."

"C'mon." His eyes beg mine.

"Don't worry," I tell him firmly. "You will get your money's worth."

Stan lifts his foggy glasses and mops his forehead with a crumpled napkin from his coat pocket. Someone nearby goes running for aspirin. "It's not the money, it's the artistic value—"

"Spare me, Stan. It's always the money. Focus on my lips." I slowly run a manicured nail over my famous pillowy mouth. "Concentrate on the quiver." I glance over his shoulder and notice that one of the cameramen is still filming me even though we are on break. I point at the intrusive camera. "Who the hell is that?"

He shrugs. "Michael Somebody. From London, I think. Or somewhere else. Who cares? I was told by the studio heads that he's an investor's cousin, great with the camera, and to get him on set. You know how that goes. So I put him on backup to shut everyone up."

"Why is he still filming me right now?"

"Christ, how the fuck do I know?" Stan downs the four aspirins that the script girl just handed him.

"Make him stop."

Stan shouts over his shoulder, "Hey, you, cut it. We'll begin shooting again soon. I'll let you know."

The cameraman nods. The light goes out in his camera, the shutter closes, and I glimpse his face. Plain-featured, sharp-jawed, reddish-brown hair parted neatly down the middle, early thirties. Unlike the other wrinkled, unkempt cameramen and crew, this guy's clothes are perfectly crisp, as though he has a job interview. He stares back at me a little too boldly. His eyes pop a startling shade of silvery gray and then he quickly looks away. I've seen him somewhere before. Not on set, but where? When?

"At least let Elaine put a few drops in your eyes, Lena," Stan pleads, interrupting my thoughts, refusing to let it go. "Glisten them up a bit."

I watch the cameraman exit the set. I will revisit that later. I turn and stare down Stan. "If you ask me again, I'm walking."

Stan's shoulders go limp. He knows better than to

push me; this isn't our first go-around together and is far from our last. He also knows that I have no problem exposing a little skin if the character mandates it, but no crying.

He looks at me with hangdog eyes. My gaze back hardens. Man up, Stan. A clause is a clause. But the truth is, though Stan doesn't know it—will never know it—I need him more than he needs me. He values my opinion, my input on character development, and incorporates all my ideas into his scripts. But most importantly, each off-studio location is Stan's idea, which I'd planted in his head. Men are so easy that way.

Three out of the four dead Nazis got what was coming to them while I was on location on a Stan Moss film. It's amazing to me, but not surprising, that no one—including Stan, who can sniff out anything amiss—has assembled the puzzle pieces. Hollywood's klieg lights tend to blind people.

I eye Jack Lyons's trailer in the distance, decide to shake off some steam. "I'll be back in a few. Don't worry, Stan." I squeeze his arm. "You'll get what you want. I promise."

He throws up his hands. Despite the begging, Stan knows that my quivery mouth will give the climactic scene all the emotion it needs. He trusts my abilities implicitly, and I trust him more than anyone else in

Tinseltown. I have known Stan practically my entire "Lena Browning" life. He is the first director I worked with and my favorite. We've done four blockbuster pictures together, having met three weeks after I arrived in Los Angeles, and thirteen months and three days after my first postwar kill. I always tell Stan a girl never forgets her first . . .

Chapter Thirty-Two

Germany
December 1946

I t was a bitter winter's day when nearly a thousand war refugees boarded the SS *Ernie Pyle*, setting sail from the Port of Bremerhaven in northern Germany to America. Make no mistake, this was not a two-week luxury cruise. The grueling journey would be yet another pit stop in hell, after experiencing many months in dire conditions in various displaced persons camps in Germany on our way to America.

After nearly two years on the run, maneuvering through the forests of Warsaw and ultimately hiding in a decrepit old barn in northern Poland until the war ended, I wound up in Germany with thousands of other wrecked Polish ghosts. We were slivers of humans, with nothing left but the clothes on our backs and a will to survive. The Allies placed me in the Deggendorf DP camp in the Bamberg district of the American-occupied zone for almost six months, with two thousand other Jewish refugees—mostly survivors of the Theresienstadt concentration camp.

Deggendorf, with its "welcoming" barbed-wire fence, was a step up from ghetto life, but not by much—overcrowded, barely any food, contaminated water, and a shortage of medicine and necessities. But there were no Nazis, and that's all that mattered.

Everyone's story on the ship heading to America was some version of the same—death camp horrors, immense loss, and heroic and criminal means of survival. If you breathed the air of a refugee, you would know he or she had already faced their own death long before. Eyes were haunted and unblinking. Everything was seen in too sharp a light. Pain was silent, distrustful, and bottomless. Where we were now headed was shrouded in mystery, but we all knew collectively that nothing could be worse than what was.

As the days passed uneventfully on the ship, I kept to myself, remaining close to the railing, taking comfort in the mind-numbing monotony of the waves slapping against the hull. I wasn't looking for friends. I was looking to forget. But five days into the journey, I saw a face across the ship's deck that sent shock waves down my spine, jolting me awake, forcing me to remember. The face belonged to a Nazi who was masquerading as a Jew.

Rage—the kind that isn't human—filled me like fuel pumping inside an empty tank. This Nazi blended easily into the refugee landscape because he could. In the same way I blended into the Aryan side of Warsaw because I could. He had dark curly hair, eyes the color of spoiled caviar, a scraggly unkempt beard, rags for clothes, and he was painfully thin—the special kind of gaunt appearance exclusive to survivors. It covered you like mold and moss even after you gained back some of the weight. No one would pick the Nazi out of this crowd unless you knew him. When he smiled politely at the woman sitting next to him, his hidden Nazi light burned brightly through his sallow skin like the eternal beam emitted from a lighthouse tower—*I knew.*

I saw the man in action only once, but I would carry his face for a lifetime. That day, after a year or so of living in the ghetto, I was on the Aryan side smuggling medicine. In the distance, I saw a group of Nazi guards gathered around ghetto entrance number 12, located at the northern tip and heavily utilized by our child smugglers, who could fit through the barbed wire and broken bricks in the wall.

The guards were aiming their rifles at three little boys who were no more than seven or eight years old, shouting at the crying children, who had stuffed their clothes with stolen food to bring back to their starving families. They decided to have some fun and began poking their rifles into one boy's stomach, where the shape of a loaf of black bread was apparent beneath the child's thin, tattered white shirt.

I slowly walked toward the children, wishing I could save them, do something—anything—to help them. I mingled with the crowd of Poles gathering behind the soldiers—parents with their own children who were watching the brutal spectacle, like it was a show. A cautionary tale. *See, kids, this is what happens when you steal.*

One of the boys tried to run away, and suddenly one of the Nazis stepped out of the pack, the only brunette among his flaxen comrades. He shot the boy in the back, then turned and shot the other two children execution style. *Tak, tak, tak.* Like dominoes they fell. The stunned crowd grabbed their kids' hands and silently dispersed like ants on a hill. I yearned to pick up the three dead boys and bring them home to the ghetto, but someone pulled me out of harm's way. I was in shock, couldn't feel my feet move, and yet somehow I found myself across the street, hearing the soldiers behind me still jeering and laughing, then chanting in unison—"Heinrich, Heinrich, Heinrich"—as though demanding another round in a beer hall. I turned back, and there he was. Heinrich, the child murderer, smiling proudly, his Nazi comrades slapping his back.

And now the joke's on him. Heinrich was sitting fifty feet away from me camouflaged as a Jew on his way to America. I felt my body elongating, my blood thickening as my calloused hands turned into iron fists.

This time, there would be no walking away. No fraternal pat on the back.

I waited it out another day, carefully scouted Heinrich sitting on the deck, watched him eat the crumbs they doled out to us, followed him from afar, biding my time until the right moment presented itself. And it would. I caught him alone in the late afternoon that sixth day. I purposely sat across from him but didn't look at him. I felt his hot gaze infect me. Slowly, I turned and gave him the look. Chin down, smoldering eyes, lips pursed together. Nazi or Jew—doesn't matter—the look never failed.

Predictably, Heinrich mistook the look for an invitation and walked over to the bench where I was sitting.

He greeted me in Polish. Smart on his part. Most of the refugees on the boat were Polish.

I responded in German and watched him light up like a Christmas tree.

"German?" His eyes widened. "I thought Polish for sure. Where are you from?" He quickly shifted into a gleeful step-skipping German.

You mean where is Petra Schneider from?

"Hamburg. You?"

He paused, gathered his thoughts, his eyes clicking. "Munich. My name is . . . Haim Feinberg."

Haim Feinberg from Munich. A fake identity, which I assume was stolen from a dead Jew. I laughed robustly inside. Zelda would have loved this.

"I'm Petra. Haim," I repeated, throwing him a curveball just to see him squirm. "That was my husband's name."

"Your husband?" His beady eyes calculated the math and grew darker: Was . . . The husband is dead. She's German. Married a Jew. That's why she is here. German women who married Jews were the worst kind of betrayers.

He did a good job of reining in his revealing facial expressions, but I saw it all anyway. The blanching of his skin, the jaw jump, the scrunching of his brows.

"And you?" I asked. This was how Jewish postwar conversation unfolded: single words—a death code—indicated the lives of loved ones lost without asking specifics. "You" translated to: Are you alone? Any survivors left in your family?

He shook his head as though just admitting those mutilating words aloud was too painful. *You bastard.*

"I'm very sorry," I mustered, touching his arm gently. "Do you have family in America?"

"Yes, in New York."

Obvious answer.

I gave him a few moments to observe me up close, taking in my well-worn dark-blue dress and thinking about what's beneath it.

"Well, nice to meet you," I said as I stood up, counting slowly to myself as I walked away. One, two, three.

"Wait."

And there it was, the mouse sniffing the cheese, just before the snap of a trap. I made a small pivot in his direction. "I usually take a walk on the deck late at night to clear my head . . . who can sleep?"

"Who can sleep?" he repeated.

"Care to join me, perhaps?" I lowered my eyes shyly.

"Ja," he said emphatically.

Ja, I thought you would.

It was nearly eleven p.m. when I felt Heinrich's presence creep up behind me. I wore a thick shawl over my coat as I stood against the guardrail watching the surging whitecapped charcoal waves slam mercilessly against the ship. The spangled stars above were bright and shiny, casting a glittery sheen over the water. In somebody else's life, this would have been the perfect setting for a romantic moment. Not mine.

"Petra."

"Haim," I whispered without turning around.

He sidled up next to me, leaving respectful space between us. "Peaceful here."

"Yes. A refuge from the refugees." I laughed softly.

He laughed too. But that's all I gave him, nothing more. The quiet between us was deafening as we gazed out on the expanse of ocean and night. His shoulder grazed mine lightly. I looked around us quickly. The deck had emptied.

My body moved faster than my mind. Zelda's knife, the one I've exercised on numerous key occasions over the past few years, slyly made its way out of my coat pocket and into my firm grip. I hid it beneath the wingspan of the shawl. When Heinrich leaned over the railing after spotting a large fish in the distance, I stabbed him hard in the back, digging the small, thick blade through his coat and into his skin like an ax felling a tree.

Shocked, he cried out for help, but I quickly stabbed him in the throat to shut him up. Not all the way. Not enough to kill him yet. He must know why . . . I heard Zelda's voice bang inside my head.

"Those three little boys at exit number twelve," I hissed into his ashen face. "I was there. You murdered them for trying to feed their families. This is for them, with love from the Warsaw Ghetto, Haim," I spit out as he slumped down, grasping onto the railing for support. Still alive but barely.

He began to beg. Gibberish last-ditch breaths. I spread the shawl wide to shield us from any potential onlookers, then I quickly reached inside his coat pocket, grabbed his identification papers, and ripped off the gold mine taped around his body—thick wads of deutsche marks. I took it all. Heinrich's fresh start in America would now serve as mine.

With all the strength I had left, I pushed the Nazi beneath the cable guardrail and through the open space, relishing the loud splash as he tumbled overboard into the ocean abyss. I stood and witnessed his arms flailing as the unforgiving water greedily devoured him.

My heart racing, I glanced at the fake papers and

pressed them to my chest. Haim Feinberg, whoever you are, that was for you too.

Closing my eyes and clinging to the guardrail, I allowed the crisp night air to wash over me, basking in the exquisite cleansing sensation. I pictured Lady Liberty in the far-off distance welcoming me with her torch held high, promising a new beginning, and I vowed never to leave my past behind.

Chapter Thirty-Three

Hollywood, 1956

Eleven takes later and Stan yells, "Cut!" He focuses on Jack Lyons's watery eyes and my trembling mouth. There is enough emotion to go around. Our final kiss is deeply passionate, the chemistry more than believable. Everybody is happy. Stan apologizes profusely for doubting me and has a vase sent over from Tiffany's to my trailer. I give it to Connie, my assistant. Jack has dinner plans tonight. I will see him later, maybe. It was a long day on set. Right now, I need a tall drink, and most likely, as it goes, more than one.

There's a choice of two bars in this ghost town. I don't want to go downstairs to my hotel bar, where I may run into Mick the bartender. Instead, I finish off a mini bottle of tequila that I stashed in my hotel room, put on a dark wig, glasses, and comfortable slacks, and head over to the closest dive bar a few blocks away.

I walk in and the place is barely breathing. A few rickety pool tables, a jukebox, and a sorry-looking excuse for a bar. I sit on a stool and then spot several of the camera crew hanging out at a table in the far corner of the pub, and wave. They signal me over. Why not.

"How's it going, boys?" I offer my best Lena smile, knowing, as every actress does, that the cameramen are the only ones on set who truly matter. Michael Some-body with the glacial stare is with them. I'm going to find out exactly who he is.

The guys pull up a chair for me and order another round of drinks. They tease me about the brunette wig and glasses for a few minutes. I laugh with them. I know them well, having worked with two of the cameramen on Stan's other films. We share a few more laughs at Stan's expense, but my mind is on Michael, who is busy nursing his drink and not even looking at me. Up close, I notice that he has a long, skinny faded scar down the right side of his face. I wonder how he got that. I order a pitcher for the table and lean toward him.

"You're from London," I say, trying to engage him. "You came with Jack."

"Didn't come with Jack. Not from London." He

speaks as though forced to conserve his words, with just a hint of an odd inflection in his voice that I can't quite place. I'm sensitive to accents. Mine still comes out when I'm tired. I wait for him to say something else. Instead, he gets up abruptly, mumbles a lame excuse, and leaves the bar. What the hell was that?

The next morning, the Lena Browning frenzy begins again with the usual coffee, cold cucumber slices on my eyes, followed by anything else I want. When I arrive on set, the cameraman doesn't even glance up at me or greet me like the other cameramen do. It's as if I'm some throwaway he slept with the night before. Who does he think he is?

I subtly asked around and learn from the makeup artist that his name is Michael Mills and that nobody has ever heard of him before this movie. Something is way off. I admit, he is beginning to make me a little crazy. It's not just the ignoring—it's the way he does it, as though I'm not worthy of his time.

After another grueling day of shooting, a quick dinner, and an even quicker romp with Jack, I find myself walking aimlessly outside. It just rained, and the tree-lined empty streets glisten like a Monet painting. I see my warped reflection in a puddle and step on it. I pass by a bank, a post office, a barbershop, and when

I reach the street-side window of an all-night diner, I stop in my tracks. Inside, the cameraman is drinking coffee alone and writing something. A letter perhaps? This late? He sees me, nods, and looks back down. Dismissive. Damn him. This, whatever it is, ends now. I march into the diner and walk straight to his table.

"Hello, Michael."

He looks up, nods his hello.

"It's late," I say. Not my finest opener.

He glances at his watch. "Or early."

"Can I sit?"

"I don't know, can you?"

I glare at him. No one treats me as though I am an interruption. No one. I sit across from him anyway, order coffee, determined to get to the bottom of this. "So."

"So," he repeats, making me do all the work. I take out a cigarette, wait a few seconds, but he doesn't even bother to light it, even though there are diner matches and an ashtray right next to his elbow.

I reach across him just as rudely, pick up the matches, and light up. "You don't like me, do you?"

He leans forward with those spectral eyes. "You mean *you* don't like you."

That's it. I slam my fists against the white Formica. I could have him fired before he takes another sip of that coffee. "You haven't been in Hollywood long enough to talk to me like that. In fact, no one has even heard of you before this movie. Who the hell do you think you are?"

He snaps his fingers mockingly. "I recognize that line. *Lovers and Leavers*, right?" He leans back against the candy-apple-red cushion, smirking. Up close, there are creases indenting his cheeks, the hereditary kind that must have formed unnaturally early. And beneath the diner's neon lights, that wormlike scar snaking down his face seems to take on a life of its own.

"I'm really impressed that you follow my movies so closely," I counter.

"Don't be." He taps the saltshaker against the table.

I slide out of the booth and stand. I will talk to Stan first thing and get rid of him. "I'm leaving."

"Don't let me keep you from Jack Lyons's bed."

"Don't worry, I was already there." Two points, buddy, and you're so done. And yet, as I turn toward the door, I feel no semblance of victory. Something about him . . .

"How 'bout a tear for the road?" he shouts over the jukebox belting out "Heartbreak Hotel."

I stop, turn, and march right back to the table as he grips the shaker with both hands, as if it's a microphone, imitating Stan Moss begging for a tear on set. "Can anyone get me a tear? The shot needs just one fucking tear. Somebody!" he pleads with a drawn-out whine like a child begging to stay up past his bedtime.

Heat prickles at my eyes. "Someone must have really done a number on you."

"Perhaps."

I lean in, my voice a purr, my signature. "You know nothing about me."

"Wouldn't say that." His lips curl and his features seem to rearrange themselves from bland into something bordering on dangerous.

I want to smack him, slap his stupid, cracked face with that reptilian scar, but I'm too afraid he's seen that move in another one of my films, so I remain perfectly still, my shoes anchored to the sticky linoleum floor, a part of me needing to see this through.

"I know your game," he continues with a finger point, as though he has a right to talk down to me. "Leading man, tabloid shots, bank the money. Every girl in America wants to be just like you. Every guy fantasizes about you. Everyone thinks you're so goddamn alive. But you're dead. See, it's the lighting. It tells me the whole story. Your eyes don't sparkle—they deflect light. Funny, isn't it, how all your admirers praise your beauty, your eyes," he chortles. "Am I the only one who sees what's behind them? Dead, swallowing up light like a winter lake. You don't cry, not because it's in your contract, but because"—he wags that finger again, and I want to slice it off with a butter knife—"you don't have any tears left to shed."

I feel the color drain from my face as if there were a hole in the back of my head. And then I bolt out of the restaurant. I have never run out of anywhere since the day I arrived in America. Since my stratospheric ascent in Hollywood, I have never not had the last word, the last line. I peer back quickly—I can't help it—and see the cameraman still sitting there in the window, a curved silhouette, his head bent to his writing, as though I were nothing more than a disruption, a take five. Go to hell, Michael Mills. I'm not waiting until morning. I am heading straight to Stan Moss's hotel room right now and getting rid of you. I don't care if it's the middle of the night.

Breaking into a sprint, I tear past a run-down movie theater, a nail salon, and a convenience store. One of my own movie posters stares back at me from the sepia-tinted window. Billowy blond hair, pronounced cheekbones like a high priestess, lying dry eyes. Fuck him. I keep running, past my hotel, until I find myself standing under the sign of the cheaper hotel a few blocks down, where the crew is staying. Not Stan. He's at my hotel. My feet are stuck to the parking lot concrete, and I can't move. Michael Mills is clearly someone from my past, I just don't remember where or when, and I can't move forward until I know.

For a good fifteen minutes, I watch the flickering rusty-edged neon OTEL sign, until I see him approaching, hands deep in his pockets, his gaze direct and callous. He walks past me, nods in the direction of his room. Not even a flicker of surprise to see me. Worse, it's as if he expected me to be here. I notice the tiny curling at the corners of his mouth and realize that I am following his script.

Chapter Thirty-Four

The cameraman opens the door to his hotel room, removes his jacket, and flings it onto the bed. He doesn't even turn around when I enter the room behind him and shut the door. I feel sick. Why did I come here?

He tosses his key onto the nightstand, next to an open pack of Camels, and heads into the bathroom. I listen to the infuriatingly slow, even flow of his piss, the flush, the leisurely hand wash. He returns holding an itchy-looking, yellowish two-star-motel robe.

"Put it on," he orders, tossing it onto the bed. "I'll get the camera."

Camera? What is this? I glance down at the cheap robe. I'm not putting that ratty thing on. Startled by his confusing behavior and uncertain of my next move,

I hold my ground. "What do you want from me?" I demand, cross-armed.

He cups his chin, rolls his eyes upward at the cracked beige stucco ceiling with an exaggerated philosophical ponder. "Hmm, what do I want? The one thing that you don't give anyone."

Tears. Is that what this is about?

I glare at him. Everyone knows I don't cry in my films. Articles have been written about it. This is not about the goddamn tears. Something bigger, darker, deeper is going on. I feel it, smell it, know it. My feet dig into the threadbare carpet, and I remain frozen. Goose bumps rise along my body. I know better than to stay here. And yet, the fiercest part of me doesn't want to run away. I need to play this out, to see exactly what I'm up against.

Ignoring my question, the cameraman leans forward, touches my shoulder, and signals me to sit on the bed. His astringent soapy scent eclipses the air around me, and I suck in my breath as I sit. This is not about sex either. Unlike every man who gets me alone in a hotel room, Michael Mills is clearly not interested in Lena Browning bragging rights.

He turns on his portable camera and the glare beams heat over my face. I stare at his one closed eye, his steady hand, the half of his mouth not covered by his equipment. I observe his wiry body, the way it curls behind the camera. My heart pounds. I close my own eyes and wait for it, whatever this is. But nothing happens. He is dead silent.

"What now?" I whisper finally, when I can no longer take the punishing stillness.

"What nothing. Let it out," he says tersely. "I want the tears. The goddamn tears that Stan Moss can't have."

Liar. Enough with this charade. I stand. "This is not about tears. What the hell do you really want?"

He doesn't answer, seemingly more interested in adjusting his camera. The air between us is stifling, but I wait. I'm not leaving this room until I get answers.

One eye remains fastened on me as he takes his time turning off the camera. The *clickety-click* sound of the shutter closing is exaggerated, echoing in the small room like a ticking time bomb. He gently places the camera on the nightstand, walks over to me, standing too close. His coffee breath tickles my face. "You're right. It's not about the tears. It's about truth." His tone calcifies as his reddish-brown brows narrow in, the tips practically touching. "Bina."

And there it is. That name—long dead—resurfacing like a deep-sea diver coming up for air. I freeze and melt simultaneously; my body temperature goes haywire within seconds of hearing it.

I push past him. "Who the fuck are you?" I demand, as I grab my purse and head toward the door. I whip around, feeling feverish.

Smiling a sickly smirk, he remains infuriatingly silent. He reaches for a cigarette, lights it up, and lazily draws in smoke.

"Who am I, Bina? I'm his brother . . ." The cameraman's face begins to lose symmetry, rerouting into a collage of contours and shadows. "Brothers. Seems to be your specialty."

"Whose brother, goddamn it?" I demand, feeling my knees buckle, but I dig my toes into the carpet for balance. My mind begins to whir, itemizing facts like a grocery store register. No one knows Bina Blonski unless, of course, he was there in the ghetto. Was he a guard? He's younger than I am, which would have made him a teenager back then. Michael Mills. A typical American name. And then it hits me. Mills . . . close enough to Müller.

Lukas Müller. His brother. Why didn't I see it immediately? The slitty silver-gray eyes. One of Lukas's mismatched eyes was a similar color. Why didn't I detect the faint accent in his voice? I repeat his brother's name ten more times in my head. Lukas Müller. Driver. Infiltrator. The man who murdered Stach, Jakub, and most likely Zelda.

My enemy's brother is my enemy. And now he's come for me once again.

I take a few small faltering steps backward toward the door, but I hesitate to leave without knowing exactly what he wants. Seemingly unconcerned that I will take off, the cameraman reaches under the bed and draws out a large dark gray duffel bag and places it on top of the bed. He unzips it and slowly removes a photograph from a file folder, then sends it across the top of the low-rise dresser toward me like a hockey puck. Almost hypnotically, I walk toward the photo, glance down at it, and gasp aloud. My heart plunges, and I press both hands to my chest to stop it from bottoming out. But there is no end to the falling now. It's all there in blown-up black and white.

Three men and a woman. That day in the ghetto. Trapped inside Lukas Müller's arms, I am being held against my will. His hands are knotted like bolts around my fingers, forcibly around his gun aimed at Jakub and Aleksander. The photo captures the second worst moment of my life. The worst is what came after that. *It should have been you, Bina.*

I swipe the photo to the floor and its white matte border grazes my foot. I yearn to stomp on it, rip it apart. But that's exactly what the cameraman wants me to do. I will myself not to collapse in front of him. Do not give him the satisfaction. Give him nothing.

"Your accent," I say listlessly instead, trying to buy myself time to pull it together.

"The accent comes out only when I let down my guard, which I don't. Not ever. Just like you," he says, taking another leisurely drag followed by a large smoke ring blown directly at me. He is enjoying this. Making a game of it. How the Nazis love their games—the mocking, the degradation, the demeaning sport of abuse. "I'm going to make this simple," he adds with an amused shake of his head. "Rolf Wagner was found dead in the lake, a bullet to his head . . . twenty minutes from here." He lets this piece of front-page news sit between us, get warm and sour like a bottle of milk left out on the counter.

"Coincidence? I don't think so," he continues. "I came on this movie set solely to observe you closely. From this moment onward, wherever you go, Bina, I go. I'm about to become another clause in your contract. Nonnegotiable. We have much to discuss. The things you have done, the things you will need to do for us, for the movement, which is still very much alive, and the movie you will make . . . But we'll get to all that." He picks up the photo from the floor, holds it to the light, and points to the image. "I took this. I was there that day, in that room, documenting our activities."

I can barely breathe. "It was you behind the camera . . . the close-ups. Another monster in the room."

"It's all perspective."

His brother.

"Is he alive?" I must know.

The warring pools of the cameraman's leaden eyes transform into twin stalactites, penetrating and glacial. Just like his older brother, who stole everything from me and made me into this—a shell, a woman who has made a big life out of playing pretend and can never come back from it. I hug my body, but it doesn't protect me from me. Bina Blonski's tears ran out that day in the ghetto, and this man captured the moment.

Chapter Thirty-Five

It has been two hours, maybe more, stuck in this dingy, mothball-infused hotel room, facing off with Michael Müller as he lays out his terms. I envision Müller not as he is but as he once was: wearing the olive-green uniform adorned with slabs of colorful medals for random acts of genocide, the silver-plated skull-and-crossbones emblem on his visor slung low over his young brow, the gleaming ebony revolver poking out from his hip. I visualize the man before me with a combination of hate and excitement, imagining all the different ways I will crush him. Right now, it's about listening, playing the role he needs me to play: the submissive.

Freed from his cameraman guise, Müller stands over me, bragging a litany of Nazi propaganda. "And

Josef Goebbels . . . pure genius. He understood how to reach the hearts and minds of the people and alter public opinion—not just in Germany but throughout Europe. He was the grandmaster of optics. He had balls and imagination. But between us"—Müller leans in conspiratorially, as though privy to a secret that I am dying to hear—"my allegiance will always belong to the brilliant filmmaker Leni Riefenstahl, a true artist and Hitler's favorite." He presses his hand to his heart, and it takes everything inside me not to heave. *Keep talking, Nazi.*

"Leni embodies the best of us—artist, actress, photographer, and dancer. An exceptional swimmer too. Such powerful strokes. There is nothing that woman couldn't do. Have you seen *Triumph des Willens* or *Olympia?*" He doesn't wait for my answer. "Masterpieces."

He keeps going. "Did you know that Leni was blacklisted by most of the studio heads here in Hollywood, although Walt Disney took a half-day meeting with her when she visited Los Angeles in 1938, when she was promoting *Olympia.* Disney was a friend, and there were other famous friends who embraced our views. Henry Ford. Charles Lindbergh. Coco Chanel, Hugo Boss, Joe Kennedy . . . the list of support is wide and endless. Our Leni was clever. Smarter than all of them. Lived her life like a movie. Simply the greatest filmmaker of our time." He points to himself. "Everything I learned was from her and my brother."

"Is your brother still making movies?" I press again.

Müller's face shutters. His eyes betray nothing. "His work is alive. That's what matters."

As the night rolls mercilessly into morning, Müller's euphoric prattle is exhausting. "Leni's very last film in Warsaw was of Hitler's victory campaign in 1939, and then she left Poland. My brother and I took over from there, continuing the important work she started. That stint in the ghetto—your scene—was all my initiative, my contribution to the Reich's National Archives. I earned my name at that uprising. So you could say I owe that to you." Müller's eyes shine, as though recounting all the medals that had been added to his uniform after the ghetto siege. "I admit, we suffered losses that day, and I filmed those, too, but they didn't make the final cut." He gives me a baleful stare, points to the scar lining his face. "I did receive this little memento on the last day of fighting. My badge of honor." He laughs. "You should have seen the other guy."

I squeeze my eyes briefly, not wanting to think about what happened to him.

"But Leni . . . such an impeccable eye for detail, unlike the inferior director Stan Moss."

I wait it out. I let Müller verbally masturbate to Leni

Riefenstahl. The more I learn about his past, his plans, the more data I can collect about his brother, Lukas, the ringleader. Is he still alive?

Müller begins to pace. "The Allies may have won the battle, but the war is not over for us. Our movement is extremely organized, and we have regrouped. The FBI and its Jewish supporters tried to shut us down once before in the United States, stalking us, exposing the Bund, the National Copperheads, the KKK, the Silver Shirts, First Americans. But we are stronger than ever, Bina." He spits out my name with the full force of his teeth. "We have divided into strategic cells all over the country. My goal is to expand our cinematic presence in America. Instead of importing films from Germany and distributing them here, I want to create original content on American soil. Homegrown propaganda. So much more effective. Americans are such simpletons, so easily convinced." He pauses to light up another cigarette. This time he offers me one. I take it. *Keep talking, you sick fuck. Brag and spill.*

"What does any of this have to do with me?" I ask. Enough. It's time to hear his end game.

"Everything," he responds with a Nazi-style shark circle, then points to the duffel bag. Smiling, he reaches inside the bag of tricks, pulls out a thick, bound script, and dumps it on my lap. I read the cover page: THE

GODDESS OF WARSAW in bold red letters. Today's date, July 25, 1956, is scribbled beneath it. Is this what he was working on inside the diner?

"What is this?"

He takes a beat, still beaming. "Your next movie. You will push aside all other projects and focus only on this." He taps the script. "It is the Leni Riefenstahl story, written by one of our screenwriters, approved by me."

Standing back, Müller gauges my reaction. I force my face to remain blank, but my heart is ticking so fast that I fear he will hear it explode. "It is an ode to the greatest filmmaker of our time. You"—he points his burning cigarette between my eyes—"will play Leni."

I let this nightmare sink in for a few distilled seconds. He's going to use me to build his propaganda base, to hit the ground running with an American starlet to do his dirty work. That's when I begin to laugh. "Me, a Jew, playing Hitler's favorite filmmaker? Now, there's a plot twist."

Müller's nostrils flare. "Yes, you, a Jew, *forced* to play her. It's pure poetry, don't you see? A famous Jew who has fooled everyone into believing that she is the most beautiful, mesmerizing WASP actress in the world portraying a beloved Nazi heroine. Punishment for you, mass publicity for us. We intend to utilize your star power to spread our ideology from coast to coast. Basically, you will be working for me now."

Using his cigarette as a prop, he points it again between my eyes, and I focus on the orange-black tinge. "Picture it." His hands form a makeshift movie-screen frame, and he peers through it. "A major hit from America's favorite actress portraying one of the greatest filmmakers who ever lived. Fucking brilliant. It's going to be my award-winning debut, with many more films to come. And the best part is that we are building our own mega studio lot here in Los Angeles. I intend to become a major power broker in Hollywood, and I have unlimited resources at my disposal to do this."

The burning starts in my toes and wends its way inside my head. My thoughts begin to twist and tangle. Should I hang him, shoot him, strangle him, drown him, or smash him to death with his camera? The options are endless.

"And if I say no?"

He shrugs. "You won't."

I raise my brow, turn my face slightly with a chin dip to my chest, highly aware that this is my notorious you've-messed-with-the-wrong-girl look, photographed in countless magazines and seen in all my pictures. My voice waxes deep and slow. "And how can you be so damn sure?"

He laughs, but it's not a laugh. It's a statement. "The Third Reich playbook. One must always have insurance before you make your move."

Müller's hidden German accent breaks out, dominates the room, and sends shivers down my spine. He glances at his watch. "Tell me, Bina, do you think that this little plan was hatched this morning?" He shakes his head. "Not the way we do things." He reaches back inside the bottomless duffel bag of horrors, and this time produces a file with a large pink triangle on its cover. "Have a look."

I take the file, open it, and slowly scan the images. My heart feels like it's being mutilated. Stan Moss, the man who made me a star, has been secretly photographed in myriad sexual poses with a bevy of naked young men. One compromising position after the next; each shot kinkier than the previous one. If these images get out, Stan's career will be decimated, his marriage shattered. He will be booted out of Hollywood, and perhaps arrested for indecent acts.

Stan's secret lifestyle isn't a surprise to me. But this? He is more than just a director; he is family to me. And yet, we have never openly discussed his closeted sexuality, and I have never revealed anything to him about my wartime past. He knows what everyone else knows: that I grew up in the Bronx and worked as a catalog model for Bergdorf's in New York before coming to Hollywood. He knows nothing about Bina Blonski or Petra Schneider. No one does. A few months after I got off the boat in Ellis Island, I found a discreet forger on the Lower East Side, another survivor, who, for a hefty sum, courtesy of Heinrich the Nazi, provided me with all the paperwork I needed to wipe away any trace of my past.

While I was busy crafting Lena Browning's new life in New York, Stan was a rising, successful screenwriter for Walt Disney Studios in Los Angeles, wanting to break out and make "real" movies his way. Passionate thrillers. Like Hitchcock, but sexier, darker, edgier. MGM tried to hire him. So did the other studio bigwigs, but he decided to go with Flagstone, a fledgling studio with strong investors and an artsy mindset. They offered Stan total artistic control, and he decided Flagstone was where he could grow and build his name. But first, he needed a muse. Every great director has his muse, and Stan was determined to find his.

At that point, I had just moved to Hollywood and was staying at the Hollywood Studio Club, a "chaperoned dormitory." Your basic brothel for young actress wannabes and scouts on the prowl for the Next Big Thing.

The Studio Club was Stan's first stop on his search

for a new face for his debut thriller. He wrote the script himself. He knew exactly what he was looking for. He perused the hotel lounge and patio, searching for a tall, willowy blonde. A strong, smart, calculating leading lady whose career he could nurture and who would carry the film not as an armpiece but as the main attraction. While a bevy of actresses flashed their curves at Stan, I saw the competition that day and decided I couldn't be bothered with such idiocy. I stayed in the corner of the large patio on a lounge chair with my legs crossed and my nose in a book. Stan says he spotted me over the sea of boobs and bouffants and knew instantly that I was the one.

That day we sealed the deal over Cobb salads at the Brown Derby, and I knew I had chanced upon the right man at exactly the right time. A man who made it clear from the beginning that he didn't want to sleep with me but intended to mentor me. A first. Someone who saw in me what I immediately recognized in him: secrets and unbridled ambition. Married with two young kids, Stan, I would later discover on a film set, preferred the company of men, and I tucked his secret safely away. With Stan's guidance and directorial brilliance, we soared together in the business, our studio backing us at every blockbuster turn. We owe our careers to each other. But I never felt that I owed Stan my life—or the memories of those I loved and lost. That's why I never shared my past or felt guilt over using our studio locations as alibis for my side hustle.

But now . . . my stomach twists as I absorb Müller's incriminating photos. Our secrets have finally caught up to both of us.

I look up from the file, meet Müller's piercing gaze. He tilts his head, smiles at the sordid photos. He most likely hired the young men himself to entrap Stan. "Like I said, insurance. You see, I need everyone on board. *The Goddess of Warsaw* is going to be a Stan Moss film starring his muse, Lena Browning. My hunch is that you don't want your highly disturbing past to rise to the surface either. All those Jewish girls you murdered in the synagogue basement. And then killing your own husband while saving your lover, his very own brother? Cinematic, I assure you, but it certainly will not expand your audience."

He clucks his tongue with amplified disgust, reminding me of his brother. "I've got all the footage, the proof. The way I see it, you are going to convince Stan Moss to make this film, to push aside all his other projects for mine. *Goddess* has big-picture potential. You will star in it, and I will handpick the rest of the cast and crew and guide the production. I will be behind the scenes acting as both director and producer. Everything must pass through me. Everything." He pauses,

scratches his head. "I understand you and Stan are con-
tracted through Flagstone studio. Tricky, but it will be
his problem to figure out. The beauty of this film is that
it's already fully funded. I have investors clamoring to
be part of this venture. Money is no option. Our movement is extremely lucrative. As always, we can count
on our banker friends in Switzerland. Magicians with
money and art." He pauses again for another cigarette.

"And if I don't agree to this?" I interrupt him. "If
I blow your cover, expose your blackmail, your Nazi
propaganda, and go public with my friends in high
places . . . the White House, the Pentagon?"

He glances at his fingernails, bored. "You won't."

"So sure?" I move toward this twisted, evil man. I
point my finger between his eyes this time. "This could
also be your greatest mistake."

"I don't make mistakes." He grins creepily. "Nazis
don't make mistakes. It's those around us who are weak
and falter."

"No mistakes, huh?" I meet his smirk with one of
my own. "Need I remind you of the 'perfect Aryan
child' campaign—the quintessential Gerber Baby of
the Reich that your friends in Berlin used in their propaganda? Need we revisit that colossal slipup? We all
laughed ourselves silly in the ghetto when we heard that
the Nazi baby's photograph was splashed everywhere:

postcards, posters, newspaper ads, magazine covers." I smile even broader, as Müller's face goes red. And I'm loving it, savoring the moment. "Yes, yes!" I exclaim with a loud, exaggerated hand whack to my chest. "As it turns out, the Reich's 'Über Baby' was a Jew!" I shrug. "Oops."

This rattles him, and Müller begins to stomp around the room. "I see how this is going to go. Unfortunately, you're forcing my hand here a little earlier than I intended. I don't like problems. I like things to move on time, run smoothly, and be executed exactly the way I want them done." He stands in front of the bag of horrors once again. "Here's a little something extra that should give you all the incentive you need to make this movie. I was saving this for later but . . ."

I hold my breath, anticipating this psychopath's next play. Like a magician who knows his audience, Müller rolls up his sleeves, pulls out another picture, and voila, flings it at me. It falls to the ground.

"Insurance."

I pick it up. Another white-bordered image. A boy and a girl, twin redheads around ten years old.

"Do they look familiar?" he asks.

"Cute kids, but they mean nothing to me." I fling the photo back at him.

"Look again, Bina." He holds the image up to my

face. "Those children belong to a couple named Ariel and Tamar Barak. See, I think those cute kids mean everything to you. They are Zionists." He spits out the word like it is spoiled fish. "They live in Israel. Their parents used to live in your old neighborhood. Their former names are Aleksander Blonski and Tosia Selmowitz. Familiar?"

Smile, grin, beam, sneer, leer—whatever movement Müller is doing with his mouth right now I no longer see. I feel a thousand deaths at once. That's when I fall backward onto the bed, a total collapse.

I can no longer hide nor fake confidence. My acting slips away and the shell I've called home cracks into a million unfixable pieces. He's alive. Aleksander married Tosia. They have children. They have made love countless times in the last decade. Not just once—a memory recycled over and over to feel something, anything. They live freely as Jews in the Holy Land with Hebraized names. They created those beautiful children together, a life beyond the ghetto wall, while I am stuck here behind another iron wall—visible to the whole world, and yet, no one knows the real me. Except for this megalomaniac. I am being blackmailed by my executioner's brother, while Aleksander and Tosia are farming, laughing, galivanting together in the Land of Milk and Honey.

I stare into my blackmailer's eyes at the bottom-less hate, and instead of breaking me, his dark energy begins to embolden me. The jealousy that was chok-ing me just seconds earlier stops cold, the maelstrom of emotion twisting within me starts to disentangle, and my deflated heart expands and elates.

Aleksander is alive.

After everything that they did to destroy us, they couldn't kill him either.

"Water or cyanide?" Müller inquires with a wink, relishing every second of what he thinks is his upper hand. "As you can see, we know a lot, Bina, Irina, Lena. Always have, and that's our edge. Here's the final plan. You will make my goddamn movie. You will tell no one about our agreement. Or else Ariel and Tamar's happy little life and legacy will be shattered, and Stan will be evicted from Hollywood. Your choice. We intend to finish the job we started in Warsaw unless you fully cooperate."

Our eyes lock, as mine once did with his brother. I take the despicable script, turn, and exit the hotel room. Müller wins. This round.

Chapter Thirty-Six

S tan Moss can usually be found in one of three places: his sprawling executive suite at Flagstone Studio in Culver City; his private "starter" office on Brighton Way just above a coffee shop, where he sorts his mail and "thinks"; or at his permanently reserved corner booth at Chasen's. I chose the Brighton Way location to meet him. No secretary, no parade of assistants, no interruptions. Old school. Just us.

The stairs creak beneath my high heels as I climb up the three flights to Stan's office, carrying my large Hermès bag. This place is on its last legs, but I like it here. I like that Stan keeps this office exactly as is, for nostalgic purposes. No renovation, no hoopla, just discreet and private. It's built for a Someone who wants to hide out and be a Nobody for a few hours.

The door is left open for me. Not surprised. Stan knows that I am always on time, and he probably heard the staircase orchestra as I clacked my way up. I enter and see him sitting at his desk, head bent, surrounded by mounds of papers. Scripts, most likely.

He looks up and smiles when he sees me, holds up a finger to indicate that he is in deep thought, jotting down a few last-minute notes. I inhale the intoxicating cinnamon aroma emanating from the lone candle flickering on the coffee table in the corner of the office. It smells like a bakery. This place is so homey, chock-full of Stan's personal mementos and knickknacks. The opposite of his sprawling show-off digs with the magnificent view at Flagstone Studio headquarters. When I'm here, I meet the real Stan Moss. Exhaling deeply, I wish I could turn around and save us both the pain.

Stan puts down the pen, seemingly satisfied with whatever he was writing, gets up, observes my sheer mulberry chiffon wrap and matching form-fitting dress with an approving nod. He gestures me over to the couch. I swallow hard, envisioning the compromising photographs in Müller's pink triangle folder tucked inside my bag. Did he bring those men here? I feel sick for what I'm about to do.

"You look nice, Lena," he says. "You should wear that color more often. It's bold."

"My stylist calls it my 'statement dress.'" I slipped it on today, purposely needing the extra confidence.

"What kind of statement are you planning to make?" he jokes nervously. I hear the slight tremor in his voice. He could tell by the tone of my voice on the phone earlier that whatever this meeting is about, it's serious.

You have no idea.

"My guess is that this conversation calls for drinks," he says, walking over to the bar on the other side of the room. Stan pours us both a vodka on the rocks with two lime wedges in mine. He knows my drink, of course. He hands me the glass and we both clink quietly. He sinks into the armchair across from me and waits for it.

"Any word on the dailies?" I ask, buying time before I drop the bomb.

He smiles broadly. "I was just going to tell you. I heard that MGM and Warner are squirming. Word on the street is that we are going to smash them at the box office come Christmas. And Billy called and said Howard—that anal-retentive prick—is very happy, which means . . ."

"Everybody at the studio is happy," we say simultaneously and laugh. Howard Mehlman, our crotchety pain-in-the-ass studio head, is never happy, perpetually driving Stan and everybody else nuts with his endless demands and critiques.

When Stan laughs like that, he reveals beautiful teeth. I love his laugh; it always fills the room but doesn't occur often enough. He is never relaxed; only when he is here. I sip my drink and study him. Ten years older than me, Stan is bookishly handsome at forty-six, his thick, freshly cut, wavy black hair is laced with gray. The elegant way he carries himself reminds me of Jakub—too sophisticated and creative for a city bursting with narcissistic assholes. Stan's eyes are an entrancing powder blue behind large aviator glasses. I picture him in another life as an English professor, the dreamy kind that students would fall in love with. Slim, slightly shorter than me, he is stylish no matter the occasion. Today he has on a tan cashmere V-necked sweater, loose pleated trousers with cuffs, and buttery brown loafers, no socks. A Sunday outfit on a Tuesday.

"Now that we are done shooting, are you heading to your usual South of France getaway?" he asks, slowly sipping his drink, totally unaware that this conversation will force him to drink most of the bottle later.

I smile wanly and shake my head. No St.-Tropez. No getting away anywhere, anytime soon. Jack Lyons flew back to London a few nights ago, so that's over. Since Michael Müller appeared in my life, I am trapped, too afraid to leave Hollywood. I've been busy taking precautionary measures. I met with my banker to hide a large sum of my money in a Swiss bank account, in case I need to run. I have been plotting and strategizing next moves and potential outcomes, and in between I have been reading and reliving the nightmare called *The Goddess of Warsaw*. I need to know what I'm up against. I glance hard at Stan. What *we* are up against.

"I'm in town for a while, longer than planned," I respond vaguely, gathering up my nerve. "How 'bout you?"

A heavy, drawn-out sigh. "I'm taking Joanna and the kids to Vermont for a few weeks, spend some quality family time together. I owe her that, apparently." He shrugs helplessly, and I get it. For a workaholic, two weeks is prison time. For a homosexual married man this means the extra burden of playing it straight. If things were normal, we would have shared a good laugh about secretly making our next movie on a nearby ski slope so he could sneak out. But not today. There are no ski slopes or sandy beaches in the cards.

I guzzle my vodka as Stan quietly observes me. He and I have been living shoulder-to-shoulder lies that are about to be exposed like a silent film turned talkie. Life as we both know it is officially over.

"Something has come up." I place the finished drink

on a kitschy coaster of a Malibu sunrise surfer scene, lean forward, elbows to knees. "We've been friends a long time. I wouldn't be here without you."

"Are you breaking up with me?" Stan gives me an out-with-it gesture. His eyes go cold and hard. "Stop beating around the bush."

I blow the air out of my cheeks. "We are being blackmailed."

"Blackmailed?" His face turns instantly flush. A man who lives a clandestine life lives in fear of this exact moment. It's a matter of when, not if. "Go on," he says in a measured tone.

"I was not born Lena Browning."

His shoulders go slack, visibly relieved, mistakenly thinking that my nom de plume is the issue at hand. He closes his eyes briefly then dismisses me with a flick of the wrist. "You think Rita Hayworth was born Rita Hayworth? No one gives a shit."

This is going to be bad. "What I meant is that I was not born here in America. I've lied about my past—lied about everything—for good reason. I was born in Warsaw and my entire family, including my husband, were murdered by the Nazis. I spent most of the war years trapped in the Warsaw Ghetto. A lot of bad things happened there. I'm Jewish."

Stan's mouth drops open. This, he wasn't expecting.

Just wait until I tell him the rest of it. He is Jewish, too, nonpracticing, and surely no stranger to the horrors of the Holocaust. We've never discussed it before for good reason. "I had no idea. Jewish? I mean, look at you—"

A Jew who looks like an Aryan. "I needed to put everything behind me to survive, to go on. I spent a full year getting rid of my accent before I came to Hollywood and built a new life story for myself. You know how it is here."

He nods. Everybody knows. Rampant anti-Semitism in Hollywood—even among Jews. The dirty little secret is that you shouldn't be too Jewish in Hollywood. You can be a Jew, but a Christmas tree Jew. Secular. An assimilator. Ironically, so many of the big machers here—particularly the founding producers, the pioneers of Hollywood—are Jewish. Having been snubbed from practically every other industry in America, they gravitated to show biz. Hollywood itself was formed less out of the love of film and more out of pure survival, a collective of ostracized Jewish men clinging to driftwood, creating what would become the American dream—that is, if you don't flaunt your Jewishness. And I don't need to tell this to Stan, but too Jewish and too homosexual is the most lethal combo of all. Total banishment.

I remove a cigarette from an open pack of Lucky

Strikes on the coffee table in front of me, the first smoke of what most likely will be many more this afternoon. Stan has packs stashed in every corner of the office, like a child with strategically placed pacifiers. "I came to this country with nothing but my looks, talent, and a will to live," I explain. "I was an aspiring actress there, too, before the Nazis invaded Poland. Even during the war, I acted." I pause, breathe. The secrets glued inside me begin to pry open and I cling to them with all my might. "Unspeakable things happened there. Worse than anything you've heard or could possibly imagine. I did what I had to do to survive."

Stan is silent and pensive as I slowly begin to reveal myself. A man privy to every emotion on my face in the close-up frames of a camera, who understands the way my body moves like no one else, now realizes that he knows nothing true about me other than that I take two limes in my vodka and that I tend to sleep with my costars. I lean forward. "Nazis have invaded this country with rock-solid cover stories. Many were high up in the Nazi Party, particularly scientists, engineers, and doctors. War criminals whose despicable histories have been whitewashed by our government. How did America go from fighting Nazis to lauding Nazis?"

Stan's eyes pop open, as though meeting me for

the first time. "I'll tell you." I answer my own question. "This elite brand of Nazi offered up superior expertise—lots of practice with gas, ballistic missiles, and rocketry. The Americans recruited these elite Nazi scientists to help us beat the Russians and to escalate our space program and other technology. We sold our souls. I heard about a clandestine U.S. program called Operation Paperclip from someone high up in the Pentagon." I take a hard breath. "But it's not just scientists, Stan. Nazis are here among us, in our business, hell-bent on perpetuating their ideology. Nazi filmmakers . . . on our very own set."

Stan removes his glasses, rubs his eyes, a gesture he makes repeatedly, especially when he is tired or frustrated. "Who, goddamn it?"

"For starters, that backup cameraman. Michael Mills. Real name Müller."

Stan waves his glasses at me. "I knew there was something fishy about that guy. The way he dressed like an accountant, and how he stared at me like a fucking zombie. You saw it too, right?"

I stand, begin to pace. "Müller and his cronies have targeted us—you and me—specifically."

Stan waves it off. "Targeted? Please. He's a nobody, a nothing, Lena. One call and I'll have that mamzer blackballed from every studio."

I feel my stomach lurch. "He's got us by the balls. Me . . . and you," I emphasize again, as I return to the couch, reach inside my bag, and pull out the folder with the pink triangle on its cover. I gently place it on the glass coffee table in front of him. "I'm so sorry."

You could hear a pin drop as Stan stares at the triangle, slowly traces its charcoal outline with his forefinger. His face changes colors as he opens the file. I can't watch this. I just can't. I turn, move across the room, away from this unfolding humiliation, my back facing Stan, giving him space. I walk to the bar, pour myself another vodka, straight up this time, no limes—who can think of fucking limes?—as he reviews the contents of that repulsive folder.

The room is silent, except for the flipping sound of each photograph. I hear Stan's breath turn heavy and then staccato. He knows that I have already seen the pictures, and I can feel his hot shame radiate from across the room. It's heartbreaking. I take my drink and walk behind his desk, scoping out the myriad promotional posters and stills from all his films mounted on the wall—many taken from movies we did together. I peer at his memorabilia shelf, crowded with tennis trophies, film awards, and family photos: his wedding picture under a floral chuppah, another on a beach with his lovely wife and their two young children—a handsome strapping blond boy who looks just like her and a lovely dark-haired girl, all Stan. A perfect mix of both parents. I hear the folder snap shut behind me.

"What was your name?" he calls out, his voice looming at my back.

I turn slowly toward him. "My name?"

I see Stan as I have never seen him before. Frozen featured, deadly calm, the color drained from his face. His secret life fills the room like a carbon monoxide leak. All his fears have come to fruition inside one incriminating folder.

"Bina Blonski," I whisper.

He nods painfully. "What does Mills have over you?"

"Like I said, his real name is Müller. He is the younger brother of a brutal Nazi I once knew, the man who killed my husband." I blink at Stan. "More than he has on you," I add without divulging the details.

Stan's shoulders crumple before my eyes, the shock of the revelatory photos sinking in. I place my drink on his desk, walk to the armchair to stand over him, then pull him toward me, pressing his head to my stomach like a mother consoling a child. I stroke his thick, perfectly cropped hair and feel his clean-shaven cheeks slicked with tears. We remain like this for a few minutes, maybe more, until he finally disengages.

Looking up at me with bloodshot eyes, he says, "This is why you don't cry."

"Yes," I say. "I have no tears left."

"How long have you known?" His gaze is downcast. Tiny droplets are trapped in his lashes. He can't look me in the eye.

I cup his chin and lift it upward. "Since the beginning," I say. "It was during filming *Moon Over Monaco*. You didn't see me. That young actor, the French one, Bernard—"

He briefly squeezes his eyes shut, as if that image were being projected on the wall behind us. "You never brought it up, outed me, gossiped, told anyone. Never betrayed me." He stands, faces me. "Why?"

Over his shoulder, against the wall, I see another passionate embrace, the distant, obscured faces of Stach and Mateusz fervently kissing inside the theater storage room, a forbidden love that they paid for with their lives. "Because it doesn't matter to me." I take his hand. "You took a chance on me when I was holding on to life by a thread. I care about you, Stan, not who you sleep with. But this will ruin you. Joanna, the kids, your career, everything you've built . . ."

He nods. We both know the rules. "What does Müller want from us?"

"This." I release his hand and reach into my bag once again, then hand him the despicable script. "He wants a movie."

"A fucking movie?" he shouts.

I shake my head. "Not just any fucking movie. A Nazi propaganda film about the German filmmaker Leni Riefenstahl. He wants me to portray her, you to direct, and he will have total creative control on set. Apparently, lots of Jew haters are fighting to be aboard this project. Müller plans to use us to spread Nazi ideology here. That's what he wants in exchange for keeping our secrets. Our souls."

"Do you trust him to keep up his end of the deal?"

"Not even a little."

I feel faint and fall helplessly into Stan's armchair. He stands in front of me, fists balled at his sides. "This is impossible, you know that, right? There's no way in hell that Flagstone is going to make a Nazi tribute film. That's studio suicide." He begins to pace in front of me, then stops midstride. "What happens if we tell this prick no go?"

"He will put all his threats into motion, destroy us, and enjoy every minute of it." I think of my exquisitely decorated mansion in Beverly Hills and Stan's sprawling estate in Bel-Air. "You have a lot more to lose. Joanna, the kids."

"What if we destroy him first?" Stan asks, just as someone like him might. A rewrite of a bad script.

I'm one step ahead of you. "That's the plan—my plan. I will stop him for good."

"For good? How?" Stan raises a brow. I see the doubt clouding his eyes. "You're just an actress," he says. "You portray assassins in your films. Don't get confused here, Lena. That's not real, in case you haven't heard." His eyes challenge mine, and I don't look away. Instead, I stand and move in closer so that mere inches separate us. I want Stan to really see my face, to understand that the roles I play are not acting.

As the midday sun lances through the window, casting stripy shadows across me, Stan is entranced. Can he see the half woman, half predator? The real femme fatale living inside my eyes? I spread my arms wide. *This is me, Stan, Lena Browning playing Lena Browning.* He takes a step back, and by his wide, unblinking gaze, I can see that I terrify him.

"Lena," Stan whispers, his eyes smarting. "Who the fuck are you?"

Chapter Thirty-Seven

Michael Müller is constantly barking orders on set. "Own it, damn you!" he shouts at me. "You are not believable! Leni Riefenstahl was not just a director, an actress, a photographer. She possessed the inner strength of ten men. Look at that mountain ahead." He points at the fake mountain scenery behind us. "She alone turned mountains into a movie genre. Command. Show it in your eyes and do it now!"

He then jumps in front of Stan, practically pushes him out of the way. "Move!"

My mouth drops open. If anyone else ever did that to Stan, there would be hell to pay. I glare at Müller and don't bother to hide my contempt. He does this Bina Blonski taunting routine at least twice an hour during filming to belittle me in front of the cast and crew—his people. The public mocking at my expense is received with a burst of giggles. Nazis have always worked in packs.

I let Müller believe that he's got me where he wants me. Reduced. I allow him to think that everything is going exactly as planned on "his" movie set. And to the onlooker, it appears that way: Stan Moss is directing but taking orders from him, Lena Browning is the leading lady who Müller bosses around mercilessly, the film crew is in his domain, and the studio honchos are surprisingly on board, having been hoodwinked by Stan (who pitched them a slightly different script that he wrote himself and managed to push through). Stan also brilliantly outsmarted the studio execs by insisting that for "authenticity purposes" he would film off-site in Germantown, Pennsylvania, which all but ensured that the studio's spies would stay off the set. No one leaves Los Angeles for Pennsylvania. This location initiative also pleased Müller, given that Germantown, six miles outside of Philadelphia, is one of the most historic German neighborhoods in the United States.

Bolstered by his newfound power trip, Müller drives around in a customized golf cart wearing black Ray-Bans and a ridiculous belted leather trench coat reminiscent of Third Reich fashion. His trendy Nazi chic is not meant for us, I explained to Stan, it's for them, his followers. The coat is symbolic. The Nazis believed it represented virility, strength, power, and prestige. They issued that same leather trench to all S.S. officers who ranked Hauptsturmführer—captain or higher. Müller even dropped his meticulously cultivated American accent and spoke only in German on set, except to Stan and me. A führer in the making, right before our eyes.

I also insisted that Stan play the part of subservient Jew. *It gives Müller a hard-on,* I told him. *Don't look him in the eye. That's key, Stan. Stare at your shoes when he speaks to you. That's what he wants, the dominance, the control. It won't be long, I promise.* I feign total confidence. The piece I haven't yet revealed to Stan is that I still don't have a solid plan. I need to find my hook, the chink in Müller's armor, before I make my move. Always have insurance—straight out of the Nazis' own playbook.

And then, miraculously, two weeks to the day after we started shooting *Goddess* in Germantown, my opportunity arrived.

I was in the bathroom, saddled in the farthest stall from the door at a local hamburger joint. I had gone for a long walk after an intense day of shooting and needed to clear my head from portraying the Nazi filmmaker who saw "beauty in destruction." I popped into the local restaurant to pick up takeout to bring back to my hotel, and made a brief stop in the ladies' room while I was waiting for my order, when I heard voices that I vaguely recognized enter the bathroom. I immediately curled up my legs onto the seat and listened.

"That girl never shuts up," one woman said.

"You must have something in Wardrobe to muzzle her."

Both women broke out in laughter, and I realized who they were. One was Agnes, Müller's head of Wardrobe, a middle-aged plant straight from Berlin. The other, Monika, Müller's personal assistant, a svelte twenty-five-year-old with a long blond braid roping down her back like Rapunzel. Her parents apparently came to Los Angeles from Germany before the war. She dressed like a sexy schoolgirl in her daily uniform—a short plaid skirt, starched white blouse, sturdy black heels, and a clipboard permanently tucked under her arm.

They used the two stalls adjacent to mine. I held my breath and exhaled only during the flush. "Forget about her. I have something more pressing to discuss," Monika told Agnes as they washed their hands. "I have been waiting to get you alone. Remember that estate I told you about in Pacific Palisades? Well, I was there last weekend with Michael for the first time during the break. Agnes, you would melt over the sheer size of it," she gushed. "Twenty bedrooms, horse stables, and even on-site coaches teaching marksmanship and hand-to-hand combat. It was everything I dreamt it would be—a magnificent, self-sustaining compound."

"I heard whispers about it and wondered if it really existed," Agnes said in a low voice.

"Yes, it's a top secret location, for obvious reasons. Only VIPs are invited there. Michael calls it 'Hitler's West Coast White House'—Das Haus for short. Apparently, it's where they hold high-level meetings. Just recently I heard, and I shouldn't mention names but . . ."

"It's in the vault," Agnes begged. "Tell me."

"Well, the architect of the V-2 rockets back in Germany paid a visit recently." Monika's voice became quieter. "You know who he is. The man is spearheading NASA's rocket engineering program. It's also where . . . Can you keep a secret? Michael is building a major movie studio. I'm telling you, Agnes, Das Haus is where the real power lies. And that's not all that lies there." She giggled.

Das Haus. I made a mental note to check it out when I get back to LA, and clearly, Monika was more than

Müller's assistant. Monika was now the one to watch closely.

"Here, Mika, use this," Agnes said sweetly, calling Monika by the nickname that I've heard Müller use on occasion. She turned off the faucet. "Try this red shade instead of that one. It will look good on you. It's by L'Oréal. I notice you've been using Max Factor. It's garbage. Dump it." Agnes didn't need to explain her contempt. The meaning was clear to all parties in the bathroom. The founder of Max Factor was a Jew. "L'Oréal's founder, Eugène Schueller, was a friend during the war. And we never forget our friends, and we certainly don't support our enemies."

I heard something hard drop to the floor and bounce.

"Good to know. I won't use that brand again," Monika said, then cleared her throat. "Michael and I are planning a special event for Christmas at Das Haus. An exclusive party, and I need your help. It's going to be elegant—a throwback to the old days. Gowns and uniforms, with, get this, a special reenactment ceremony on Christmas morning. So Michael suggested that I talk to you about borrowing—"

"Uniforms from *Goddess*!" Agnes exclaimed, clapping her hands together. "Absolutely brilliant. Tell him yes! We have an entire battalion in Props that he can use."

"Yes, uniforms. And of course, you must come," Monika added. "Michael was very specific. We need four general uniforms and at least twenty privates—representing Hitler's birthday—four twenty. You know how crazy Michael is about numbers and symbols. The reenactment ceremony is for prestigious members of the organization. Though we do need more women in attendance." She lowered her voice. "I was thinking of asking Connie to join us. I have been recruiting her."

There was a long pause. "Really? Connie, her assistant?"

My Connie? My heart dropped.

"Yes," Monika responded as if she heard me. "She's been glomming on to me, and it's clear she has a crush on Paul Schweiger."

"Who doesn't?" Agnes chuckled. "If only I were ten years younger."

"He's dreamy, I agree. And Connie is smitten. She told me just that, confidentially. I feel sorry for her, the way that woman orders her around."

That woman. Me.

"How much does Connie really know about us?"

"Not enough. But she's learning and very curious. And Paul is on board. He knows what he needs to do to make Connie feel special."

Connie. My trusted assistant for the past five years.

Thirty years old. Reserved, kind, smart, trustworthy, resourceful Connie was testing the Nazi waters. Always watch the quiet ones, my mother used to say.

"She could be very useful," Monika said, and then I heard the snap of her purse shutting. I felt the lump growing in my throat. Connie was no match for these calculating women.

"I like how you think," Agnes responded, and they both exited the bathroom.

I waited an extra fifteen minutes in the stall after they left, just to be sure. I stretched my legs, exited the stall, and spotted the discarded Max Factor gold-tubed lipstick on the floor. I quickly left the restaurant through the back entrance, forgoing my takeout order in case Agnes and Monika were still inside the main dining area.

I zipped up my coat and hid my face with my scarf and walked vigorously back to my hotel, knowing that knowledge comes with a hefty price tag. I had found the chink in the Nazi armor—and her name is Connie.

Chapter Thirty-Eight

Three weeks later, the *Goddess* cast and crew are back in Los Angeles for a five-day Thanksgiving break, and then back on location. I hear Connie at my front door, letting herself into my home to discuss next week's schedule and packing options. She heads straight to the kitchen, brews us tea, and enters the library with blueberry muffins and the newspaper.

"Morning, Con," I say, smiling, betraying nothing. She is being groomed, and I am going to allow it to happen and play along. For now.

"Hi, Lena. I take it you've been up for a while." She sets down the tea, muffins, and paper on the coffee table in front of me.

"Yes. Couldn't sleep." I gesture her over. "Join me for tea."

"Okay," she says uneasily. "Just wanted to get all the details settled. I wasn't planning on staying long."

"Of course not," I say, pouring her a cup of tea. "Tell me, what's your plan for the holiday?"

"Plan? What plan do you mean?" She stiffens, and her eyes bulge, reminding me of Bambi's mother just before she gets shot.

"Oh, you know, are you seeing family? Or doing what I'm doing—taking time at home to decompress before we go back on location."

"Home. Nothing . . . special." Connie is jumpy, guilty. I make her nervous. Good.

"Why don't you take a few days off from coming here as well. A real break to catch up on your own life. I can manage my affairs. Come back on Sunday. We can prep and pack together late morning." And until then, I will be following your every move.

"Thank you. That works." She appears visibly relieved. Her eyes shift with calculated excitement. I know what she's thinking: Paul, Müller's leading man. A young Nazi American portraying his hero, Jürgen Stroop.

"It's none of my business," I begin slowly, "but is there someone new in your life these days?" Connie had a long-term boyfriend the first year she worked for me, but they broke up six months later. And since then, a few random dates, but no one special.

"No," she says too quickly. Good thing you're not an actress, I think. You mean yes. Paul, who has been flirting shamelessly with you, using you. I have been watching closely on set every day since that bathroom encounter. I see the way you smile, flip your hair at him whenever you walk past him. I also see that your hair is now a few shades blonder than usual. And I can't help but notice that you've been wearing short skirts these past few days like Mika, and brighter lipstick. Probably L'Oréal.

But I say nothing. Instead, I faux-smile at Connie, thinking those master manipulators know exactly what they are doing. They picked the right girl to brainwash. It took them less than a few weeks to turn her. Throw a handsome, doting man at a lonely woman, and she will believe what she so badly wants to believe: that a man like him could desire a girl like her. And then, they will use her to betray a girl like me.

Connie is smitten and malleable. It works for them. And for now, it works for me too.

The next morning, I rent a black Chevrolet, wear a disguise, and stake out Connie's apartment. I follow her blue-and-white Buick around town all day as she does random, monotonous errands: supermarket, gas, library. In the evening, she heads downtown to a biergarten called the Brown House, named for the Nazi headquarters in Munich. I spend three hours sitting in the parking lot directly across the street with binoculars monitoring the comings and goings, the who's who of Hollywood's Nazis, several of whom I recognize from the *Goddess* cast and crew. When Connie finally emerges from the Brown House around 10:00 p.m. with her arm looped through Paul's, she appears, admittedly, happier than I have ever seen her look. A different Connie. A Connie with a skip to her step. I snap pictures for later referencing, so I can study them up close at home.

This meet-up happens again for the next two nights, from 7:00 to 10:00. Connie is clearly in the thick of it, emerging from the biergarten both nights with Paul. On Thanksgiving Day, Paul picks her up at her apartment. I tail them straight to the biergarten and wait. At 10:40 p.m., the duo emerges from the premises. Connie is no longer glowing from the Paul Effect, she's neon. I follow them to an apartment complex in West Hollywood—must be where Paul lives. I wait a few hours outside the complex, when I realize that Connie is spending the night. So I leave.

On Friday, I track her again. This time a foursome appears at the biergarten's entrance, and I know my luck is about to change. I sit bolt upright in my car as

Connie and Paul, Müller and Mika leave the premises together, laughing and visibly tipsy as they squeeze into Müller's two-seater Thunderbird. I glance at the glove compartment, grateful that my gun is there, if needed. I wait two minutes and then follow Müller.

From the biergarten, he drives to Sunset Boulevard and then west to Pacific Palisades. He turns right on Monaco Drive, takes the roundabout to Capri Drive, another right on Casale Road, and then, when I see him slowing down and there are no other cars in the vicinity except for mine, I pull over, park, and wait. Using my binoculars, I see the glimmer of the Thunderbird's taillights. I tail them once again but very slowly, with my headlights turned off, following their path on Sullivan Fire Road along the eastern edge of Topanga State Park. I kill the engine, because there are no other vehicles on the road, and I wait.

Up ahead, Müller stops his car in front of a tall wrought-iron fence surrounded by fifteen-foot-high hedges and with four armed guards at the entrance. He leans out the car window at the base of a long driveway leading up to a sprawling estate and speaks to one of the guards. A minute later, the gate parts like the Red Sea and the Thunderbird disappears inside. My breath speeds up, my chest constricts. I know exactly where I am: Das Haus.

I wait another hour, maybe more, contemplating my very limited options. It's a private road. I take my chance and drive past slowly and see lights and shadows merging in the lit upper windows of the estate's second and third floors. There is no way I can get inside. But at least now I have an address for the base of their operations and an understanding of how it works. The kids all meet up at the biergarten for drinks and networking, but the adult table is right here inside this Bavarian über-schloss transplant. Once again, bad actors plotting against the innocent. Once again, these villains have invaded my ghetto.

This time, I think as I drive away, they are not going to get away with it.

When Connie returns to my house on Sunday morning to help me pack, I immediately notice the change. She is polite but nothing extra. She doesn't ask about my holiday, inquire about my health, or partake in any of our usual banter. She takes notes and does her office tasks perfunctorily, continually checking her watch as if she has somewhere else to be. I see her expression grow bitter when we go upstairs into my bedroom to pack. When she thinks I'm not looking, I observe her in my vanity mirror, eyeing me in the same way they do—with hate-fueled filmy eyes, projecting one lone spiteful word in my direction: Jew.

My anger rises. I can feel it mask my face. *Don't fuck with me, Connie.*

"I'm famished," I lie, having eaten just before she arrived. "How about you make us one of your fabulous omelets—the kind with fresh garlic, yellow peppers, and Gruyère cheese. Sally is off today. So it will be just you in the kitchen. I can finish the packing from here and we can have a bite together before you go. Sound good?"

Her mouth tightens with resentment as I quickly lead her out of the bedroom, after spotting her purse leaning up against my chaise. The omelet prep buys me snooping time.

Once I hear her downstairs banging around, I lock my bedroom door and lunge for the purse. There's nothing much inside of it except for a wallet with forty dollars, a comb, some hard candy mints at the bottom, a lipstick—surprisingly, Elizabeth Arden. I laugh to myself. Clearly, Connie didn't get the memo that cosmetics mogul Elizabeth Arden, like Max Factor, is also a Jew. I pull out some crumpled receipts and an extensive grocery list. I let out a whiff of disappointment. Nothing important or telling. And then I realize something. I reexamine the grocery list closely and catch my shocked expression in the vanity mirror. It contains a wide array of German delicacies, enough to feed an army. Certainly not a list for a single working woman.

Brot & Brötchen
Käsespätzle
Leberklösse
Schnitzel
Currywurst
Kartoffelpuffer
Rouladen
Sauerbraten
Riesling
Schnapps
Jägermeister
Pralines, Eclairs, Strudel
Edelweiss

A party list. I fall backward onto my bed. And not just any party, but the Nazi Christmas bash taking place at Das Haus.

Connie, I realize as I hear her trudging up the stairs, is no longer my assistant. She has officially crossed over. She's theirs.

Chapter Thirty-Nine

"S tan, you look terrible," I tell him as he joins me in my trailer during a break on set. His hair is longer than his usual neat trim, his skin looks sallow, and his eyes are baggy behind his glasses.

"I can't take another day of this shit," he says, plopping onto my small couch. "I don't sleep. I can't eat. I'm lying to everyone. The studio heads, my wife, and that dictator . . ."

I roll my eyes. "Müller is insane. Hold on a little longer. Trust me, okay? This is all going to go away very soon." I sit down next to him costumed as Leni Riefenstahl in beige wide-leg trousers and a practical white button-down short-sleeved linen blouse. "But I do need something from you." I lower my voice to a whisper. One never knows who is listening outside the trailer. "How can I get my hands on some real props?"

Stan lifts his glasses, rubs his eyes. "Real props? What kind of real props?"

I sit back, drape my arm over the back of the couch. "The kind that do real damage."

His eyes sharpen. "Jesus, Lena. What do you want? A cannon? How about a tank while you're at it?" He slaps his forehead, leaves his hand there. "I know you think you alone can defeat the battalion of Nazis on set, but you can't. Honestly, that Monika/Mika character terrifies the crap out of me. She's got a prison warden vibe. Every time she looks at me, I want to run and hide."

I spit out a burst of laughter at the tragic absurdity of our situation. Stan laughs, too, then his face turns serious. "It's time, Lena. Let me in on your plan. Maybe I can help. How do you intend to get rid of these monsters, shut down this goddamn production, and send those assholes back to Germany?" He gets up, pours us both a vodka on the rocks, two limes each. I accept the drink eagerly.

"See, that's the thing," I say, weighing my words. They are not going back.

His glass touches his lips, but he stops midsip. "What's the thing?"

Don't trust anyone until they've earned it. Zelda's first rule. I trust Stan, but he has never experienced the horrors of war, never had to fight for his life. Film rights, yes, but not his life. Until now.

He folds his arms and crosses his legs, waits for an answer.

I hesitate. "I saw the Nazis' LA headquarters. I spent all of Thanksgiving tailing our cast and crew from a biergarten to this mega compound, which is bigger than any studio backlot I have ever seen. The amount of land, Stan . . . Armed guards at the entrance. My plan is to destroy it, and I need real 'props' to do it."

"Do you actually know how to use explosives?" I can see that despite his misgivings, Stan is visibly impressed.

I think of the Nazi nightclub that I had a hand in blowing up, Kapitan, Dabrowski, the baron, and the others, here, on American soil. "I have some skills," I say simply.

"Basically, you became a household name as a femme fatale, and you actually are one?" His eyes amplify like a little boy seeing his first horror film.

"Yes, Stan, basically. How do you think I survived the war? By flashing a smile, showing some cleavage? No one survived unless there were extraordinary measures involved."

"How did you get out?" he asks.

"I don't talk about it."

"Only because I never knew to ask you about it. But now I want to know."

I finish the vodka. "I had some help. I escaped the Warsaw Ghetto through a sewer." Stan's face scrunches up. "Yes, me in a sewer. Many times. From there, I paid off a smuggler, pretended to be a high-class Polish call girl to entertain Nazis in the house where I grew up—a home that was a mansion twice the size of yours that my father built and that the Nazis seized. We were the token neighborhood Jews. Twenty-five rooms, three sprawling gardens. I knew every nook and cranny. Once I got into the house, I was able to escape through the basement into the surrounding forest. From there, I joined the Polish resistance. I thought I was safe. Except the price for my safety—no surprise—was sleeping with men. That's how girls who looked like me survived. I was tired, Stan, so goddamn tired." I emit a pained breath. "I killed both men—members of the resistance—who pinned me down in the woods, and then I lied when their comrades came to our rescue, claiming that we were attacked by traitors, and that I was raped, left for dead." I shrug. "Yes, Stan, even then I gave a stellar performance. To their credit, those men cared and brought me from the forest to a sympathetic Polish couple, farmers, who helped me because I have this face. A beautiful Polish girl who was raped was worth protecting, not a Jewish one. I stayed hidden in their barn until the end of the war. They gave me food, clothes, and shelter." I pause, look away. "But there, too, I paid a heavy price. I had to sleep with the farmer to stay alive, and there was no way out. I couldn't kill him because it would alert their neighbors that I was there, and I had nowhere else to go. Nearly two years hiding in that barn and enduring that fat fuck. The wife was lovely and caring. Men are animals, Stan. But some men are monsters."

"And then what happened?" he asked, squeezing my hand, knowing the story is far from over.

I purse my lips tightly. "The same night that we learned that the Nazis surrendered, let's just say the farmer didn't make it home to his wife. I was ready for him. I slit his throat." *With Zelda's pocketknife.* I show Stan my faint scars, the ones along my inner arm that I always cover with makeup, and then I lift my shirt to reveal the long pink scar at my hip—all self-inflicted. I lied to the farmer's wife and told her that her husband died a hero, trying to protect me from looters who were everywhere, and we were both stabbed. She saw blood all over me and believed me, of course. In her deep grief, she nursed my wounds and let me stay there with her in her home until I healed. We hugged and cried when we said our goodbyes. One of my finer performances. Through twists and turns, I ended up in a displaced persons camp in Germany and then found my way to America."

"Jesus, Lena." Stan's mouth is agape.

I then shared the conversation I'd overheard between Agnes and Mika in the bathroom, the Christmas reenactment, Das Haus, and my big plan: the Day of Reckoning.

"Connie is with them," I say finally.

His jaw goes slack. "Connie Simmons? Your Connie?"

"She is their Connie now. And she is sleeping with Paul, Müller's actor playing Stroop."

Stan's face reddens. I'm sure he wishes that he was sleeping with Paul the actor. I move in closer. *Is he?*

"Stan? You and Paul?"

He covers his mouth, shakes his head. "No, I'm not. But I won't lie. I've thought about it. I mean, look at him. Like a Viking warrior. He's not sleeping with her."

"How do you know?"

"Because I know. I've spent my life with actors. I guarantee Paul's not shtupping Connie, but perhaps making her believe that he will. Poor girl. He's clearly in love with Mika—anyone can see that." Stan's hard gaze conveys that he is done with Connie and on to bigger issues facing us. "Let's get back to the real problem at hand and possible solutions. First, your plan is not going to work. There are too many holes. This bombing . . . how the hell do you intend to do a full-scale operation at this so-called Das Haus: strap explosives to your chest and parachute in?"

My eyes expand. Not a bad idea.

"The details don't matter. I need dynamite. Lots of it," I say. "I remember you telling me once that you consulted with veterans for that war movie you did." I snap my fingers, searching for the name. "*The War File*. Remember, you told me that you stockpiled enough ammo at the studio to blow up—"

Stan holds up his hands. "*The War File* was a shit movie. I was brought in to save the studio from total disaster when the director was drinking so much that he developed alcohol poisoning. It tanked at the box office. So this is your grand plan? Christ, Lena. It's not going to work for a lot of reasons."

"Name one."

"Mostly, because you are not in control. You are on their turf."

My eyes bore into his. I see where Stan is going with this. "What I think you're saying is that I need home-front advantage."

"No, Lena. That's *exactly* what I'm saying."

Chapter Forty

Dressed in costume as Leni Riefenstahl, I have never felt more like Bina Blonski than I do right now, watching my home—the ghetto scenery—razed to the ground. Müller would not rest until every detail was exact, as it once was. The studio set even smells like death. It is so realistic that it is unbearable.

This is the final scene, the one Müller can't wait to film. The Nazi victory over the Warsaw Ghetto uprising. We left our Pennsylvania location and are now back at the Flagstone Studio lot to film it, and for good reason. We needed fake weaponry and enough explosives to create the realistic finale that Müller demanded. The studio has all the goods stored in its armory. Stan did a superb job convincing Müller to film the final scene here, on our home turf. The key was letting Müller think it was his own brilliant idea.

The Great Synagogue of Warsaw constructed behind me is a precise replica of the real one, and it begins to gut me. Müller, that bastard, got every physical detail right for his grand finale, except for one thing: the twin five-foot-high brass candelabras perched at the entrance that had been saved by the rabbi and smuggled out of Warsaw before the Nazis destroyed the synagogue. Müller was determined that history be his version of history. He didn't want to showcase any Jewish victory, even the smallest of triumphs. He intended to stage the fall of one thousand years of vibrant Jewry in Poland in one giant explosion. Hence, those symbolic candelabras would be blown up with the rest of the synagogue in Müller's film.

Leathered up, Müller prances around the set like a sleek black panther. "Bina," he instructs. "Stand still, with your back facing that." That. He points to the synagogue. "I want this shot to be a powerful yet artsy silhouette. Leni wasn't physically there at this final moment. Doesn't matter. Her vision was with us until the end, and that's what counts. We only get one take, so do it right!" He plants himself in front of me. "The ghetto is burning. Picture Leni Riefenstahl standing in the forefront, and then"—Müller scurries past me to peer into the camera frame, pushes aside the cinematographer, then looks up at me—"think Statue of Liberty. Hold your hands out wide. Show the magnificent triumph in your face, a goddess bearing witness to the Führer's greatest victory. Do it now!" he commands.

I do exactly what Müller tells me, but I am envisioning my own interpretation of what's about to happen on set—not his.

"Yes, yes, exactly that." He clasps his hands together, glances up from the camera. His eyes are wild. "We are almost ready. This last scene will be filled with a legion of Nazi heroes, standing behind S.S. Gruppenführer Jürgen Stroop. Truly miraculous."

Müller's expression changes instantly with violent force. "Mika!" he shouts. "Are all the Jews off set—except for Bina Blonski? No Jews are allowed for the victory scene. It must be authentic. Where is goddamn Stan Moss?"

"Off set," Mika confirms, eyeing her clipboard and checkmarking it.

"Where's that Jewish spy from Flagstone?"

"Back in his office. A fake emergency that I called in." Checkmark.

"And Connie?"

I hold my breath. Mika's cornflower-blue eyes

bore into his. "She is prepared, Michael. We all are. Everything was ready to go last night exactly as you asked. It will be a lovely surprise for the cast and crew." She smiles seductively.

A lovely surprise indeed, I think. I try to decelerate my pounding heart, but the beats only seem to grow louder and faster.

Müller calls for a thirty-minute break before the final scene so that he can collect himself. He wants to check once again that every detail is accurate. I planned for this too. So did Mika. I saw the thirty-minute break noted on her clipboard schedule when I broke into Wardrobe last night.

I head to my trailer, and Connie is there inside.

"You're here?" she says with surprise. She didn't know about the break.

"It is my trailer."

My heart aches as we face off. She has betrayed me, but still. It's Connie. Five years by my side. A woman I once called friend. No matter what she's done, I've got to give her a way out—one last gesture. Anything to save her from herself.

"Connie," I say softly, desperately searching her face for remnants of the old Connie.

"Yes." Icy, contemptuous eyes return the volley.

"Don't go back on that set. Take the rest of the afternoon off."

"The afternoon off? Why would I do that? I have responsibilities here," she snaps. Her newly platinum-blond hair is styled in a side braid like Mika's today, only much shorter. She is wearing a short skirt and a bright floral blouse with a double strand of pearls, just like Mika. "I want to be here for the finale."

No, you don't.

"You seem to have made friends on set. I understand," I say, hoping for a breakthrough, for any connection. "But perhaps they are not the best influence on you."

"What do you mean?" she asks, hands placed firmly on hips.

"I mean Paul."

Her face turns a thousand colors.

"You used to tell me things, Con. We used to share details about our lives. We were friends, confidantes. What's going on? You can tell me." *Don't do this. You are better than this. Better than them.* I move in closer, and she backs away as if I'm contaminated and then stops moving.

New Connie is here.

She points a manicured finger at me for the first time ever. "Don't tell me who is a good influence or not. It's really none of your business." Her hazel eyes blacken. "None of your goddamn business!" She corrects herself, practically shouting. I am taken aback. I have never heard her raise her voice or swear before. She is always calm, a problem solver; nothing rattles her. A rarity. In this high-stress business, everything rattles everyone.

"My private life remains private, and all mine," she continues. "This movie is the best thing that has ever happened to me. I'm leaving you after this shoot. I'm going to assist Michael and Mika and be part of their new studio. Consider this goodbye." She takes the pitcher of iced tea off the small corner table and dumps it out in front of me, smiling at the puddle flooding my shoes and the floating lemon wedges. She swipes her hands and walks toward the door.

"Five years, Connie," I call after her. She stops in her tracks, turns.

"And now I'm free." She exits my trailer and stomps down the two steps and out of my life.

Twenty minutes later, Connie walks onto our set like a Pan Am stewardess holding a tray filled with dozens of shots of schnapps. Müller stands by Paul. Mika is on his other side. And Agnes from Wardrobe is adjusting something on Paul's uniform. They all smile at Connie, who is blushing from all the attention. I'm sick to my stomach. But now, it's out of my hands. Connie made her bed.

"Lock it up. Quiet on the set!" Mika barks.

"Paul," Müller says to his leading man, loud enough for everyone to hear, "this is the defining moment of Jürgen Stroop's Warsaw campaign." He pulls out a tattered olive-green notebook. "What I'm about to read to you is straight from Stroop's own diary, recounting the exact moment after they blew up *that* on May sixteenth, 1943. Simply legendary." He points to the synagogue structure behind him. "Now listen."

"Quiet on the set!" Mika cries out. The most irritating human on the planet. I will not be sorry to see her go for good.

Müller takes a deep inhale, adding to the dramatics. The set is silent. "What a marvelous sight it was," he recites in German. "A fantastic piece of theater. My staff and I stood at a distance. I held the electrical device that would detonate all the charges simultaneously. I glanced over at my brave officers and men, tired and dirty, silhouetted against the glow of burning buildings. After prolonging the suspense for a moment, I shouted, 'Heil Hitler' and pressed the button. With a thunderous, deafening bang and a rainbow burst of colors, the fiery explosion soared toward the clouds, an unforgettable tribute to our triumph over the Jews. The Warsaw Ghetto was no more. The will of Adolf Hitler and Heinrich Himmler had been done."

Müller snaps shut the book, hands it to Mika, then walks over to Paul, uncomfortably close, practically body to body. "This, Paul, will be the most important 'Heil Hitler' of your career. It will set everything I have planned for us in motion." He then nods at Connie, who proceeds to walk toward him with the schnapps, slowly, carefully, like a bride to her groom.

"Thank you." Müller winks at her. "Bring the drinks in there and wait for us." He gestures to the synagogue, then turns to the cast and crew. Only his people are still on set. Anyone connected to Stan or Flagstone has been dismissed. "We are all going inside that to toast to our first feature film here on American soil. Toast to a magnificent day in our history: to Leni Riefenstahl, the Führer, Goebbels, Stroop, and for me personally, I will raise a glass to my brother, Lukas Müller." He looks at me and smiles the family's sickly signature grin. "Now get the fuck off my set, Bina Blonski. Your job here is done. I want to be Jew-free for this milestone in cinematic history."

As I turn to go, Müller's parting words whip at my back. "By the way, Lukas is alive and very, very well."

I walk out and must restrain myself from skipping.

Lukas Müller is alive. Thank you for the confirmation. Because in about thirty minutes, Michael Müller, you won't be.

"Music!" I hear Mika shout out. Suddenly, Wagner's *Siegfried Idyll* plays from surround-sound speakers, hailing straight from Auschwitz.

I quickly make my way off set, and one by one, Müller's people file past me as if I don't exist, their hypnotic gazes focused on only one person: Michael Müller, the Hollywood Hitler.

I pick up my pace and pray Stan is ready, knowing with every inch of me that he is. I can just hear him now: *Let's give those bastards the ending that they deserve.*

When I get to the parking lot, I stand next to my car, lean against it, observing the impressive dome of the Great Synagogue protruding from the set. I picture Müller and his followers ensconced inside, downing their celebratory schnapps, toasting themselves. Their last drink is filled with the poison that I shot directly into each of the bottles' corks last night, bottles that Connie had stored in Agnes's Wardrobe trailer, per Mika's instructions. I picture Müller at center stage, giving a rousing tribute to the longevity of the Third Reich and the new day dawning for Reich cinema. They will struggle together, cast and crew, gasping for breath, clutching their throats, screaming for help that won't come. Finally, they will tumble to the ground, a pileup of costumed Nazis and their megalomaniac director. My heart rises with the image, then drops with a hard plunk. And Connie.

And then, the insurance.

On cue, I hear the massive explosion and look up to see the dome blowing off the synagogue. It pops off into the air, just as Jürgen Stroop had described it. This time, it is *my* doing. Instantly, the sky becomes a black hole, bursting with flames, debris, and smoldering chaos. This time, the unheeded screams are not ours. They are theirs. Nazis leveled to the ground inside *that*—one of the most important synagogues in history.

Dropping to my knees, I peer up at the inky sky smothered in smoke, filled with a spectacle of stars that somehow manage to burst through the shadowy haze. I smile back at Zelda and the others standing and clapping. Yes, I poisoned them and blew them up—leaving nothing to chance. The Nazi victory film is destroyed along with its fanatical creators. *It's over.* And the young Bina Blonski, who lives and fights within me, rises to take her final bow before the only audience that has ever mattered.

BOOK III

HOLLYWOOD

2005

Chapter Forty-One

Sienna Hayes is not acting. For a girl who never finished high school, never met a Jew until she landed in Hollywood, she has done the work. She tells me constantly how much she enjoys the research, delving deep into the Third Reich, Jewish history, and my life. For the past six weeks we have spent full days together discussing my past, chain-smoking (despite warnings from my squad of doctors) and drinking my usual vodka with two limes (to hell with them) and her dirty martini with three blue cheese olives. Sienna asked me early on in our meetings if I should be smoking with the cancer. I asked her if *she* should be smoking with my cancer. We laughed, happily closed the subject, and jointly lit up.

That's the thing I relish most about our tête-à-têtes:

the laughter. I can't remember relishing anyone's company in years as much as I do this young, curious, and surprisingly intuitive starlet, whom I, admittedly, misjudged.

I also like the new pattern in my life that she provides. The early wake-ups, the getting dressed for our daily interviews. The way she rolls into my circular driveway each morning in her two-seater silver Jaguar, sporting oversize Jackie O sunglasses with her long blond hair tied back in a ponytail, the loose tendrils framing her perfect face like a sunflower. Sienna reminds me of a modern young Grace Kelly in her sleek array of smart, colorful pantsuits, carrying a briefcase with a recorder, a notepad, and folders stuffed with historical documents.

But today, it's not about the cigarettes or martinis or stories from the past. Sienna clearly has something pressing on her mind. I can tell by the way she crosses and uncrosses her legs repeatedly and rapidly tip-taps her yellow pad with her chewed pen cap (an annoying habit I've tried to ignore).

"It's been six weeks and four days, Lena," she begins firmly, and I can also tell by her newscaster approach that she rehearsed this. The tapping picks up momentum. "It's time to really fill in the blanks."

"Ahh, the blanks." I smile demurely. I know there

are holes in my stories—more like craters. I purposely put them there. I lean back, drape my arms lazily over the back of my hunter-green velvet couch, which is more comfortable than it looks. I will do and say what I want about my life, not what she wants. But I admire the girl's tenacity. I take an extra slow sip of my vodka to cut the tension closing in.

"There's only one problem with that," I add with a slight growl, a sound that the media hounds dubbed "wolfish"—especially in my later years when my smoker's rasp had taken its toll. I will never forgive them for that insult. "If I tell you . . ."

Sienna throws up her hands dramatically. "I know, I know, Lena. You will have to kill me."

We share a laugh, but I note by the sharp break in her voice and crossed arms that she's serious.

"I quite like your outfit today," I say, buying time, nodding approvingly at her stylish burgundy pantsuit with a thick black belt over the long jacket, and the choker with a silver-dollar-size onyx pendant. Masculine, yet feline and feminine. My style, and hers. A woman should dress up for the truth, I think. Lies are casual, jeans and barefoot. But a good, belted suit with shoulder pads and stilettos demands truth.

"You are trying to divert me. Not going to work this time." She leans forward, using her chewed pen as an accusatory pointer leading the way. Her almond-shaped eyes narrow. "I'm serious, Lena. I need clarification. How did you and Stan Moss really get away with the on-set explosion? Help me understand the cover-up behind what has been called the worst on-set 'accident' in cinema history." She air-quotes the word "accident" then waits a few elongated moments before dangling a cigarette in front of me. Her version of a bribe. Oh, what the hell. I take it.

I light the cigarette, tuck my perfectly molded still-blond waves behind my ears, revealing large sapphire studs, a gift from the studio after *Moon Over Monaco* killed it at the box office—and still my favorite pair of earrings. I examine my nails and spot a chip, take my time, and see Sienna growing itchy. She does the leg-crossing thing again. Twice.

"I learned early on that you must make a plan that works, not one that you hope works," I explain. "No stone was left unturned. Stan and I were prepared, Sienna. We could write the script in our sleep. We grew up at Flagstone and knew every inch of the studio's back lot and all its storage units—even where the extra toilet paper was kept. It was more of a home to us than our actual homes. Müller didn't stand a chance once we exacted revenge on our own turf. Stan was right about that." I smile to myself, still impressed by how we pulled it all off without a hitch. "One take," I tell her, lifting my signature left brow. "All we had was one shot to get rid of Müller and his followers, and it had to be flawless. 'A war film that goes awry'—that was our logline and lifeline. There was no room for a single mistake."

I stand because truth requires two feet on the ground. I see Sienna admiring my outfit too. It's no different from yesterday's garb or the day before, just a variation of what has always worked for me. A creamy silk neutral dress shirt with shoulder pads, open at the neck, tucked into high-waisted, wide-leg black pants, with a long gold chain dangling against my sternum, never mind that my aged neck looks like it has tree rings. Never mind that I have worn this same uniform since the fifties. *Vogue* christened it the "Lena Browning Look"—so why reinvent the mousetrap?

"As I told you, I learned to make bombs in the ghetto. I was taught how to create something out of nothing, using rudimentary materials. But at the studio that day, I was able to make something out of something. Everything I needed for 'stagecraft' was already in storage, tucked inside the studio's armory. We weren't the only war movie being filmed on set at that time. Stan took what we had in stock, and I made it work for us. I wired the synagogue scenery with real explosives the night before the last scene, replacing the fakes Müller was planning on using. I couldn't have done this without Stan, who had keys."

Keys to everything. Stan's unfettered access to the studio's inventory was the only way we could have accomplished our mission discreetly and implemented it so seamlessly.

"We also knew that Müller was his own worst enemy. He bragged about his abilities on set constantly, and witnesses later testified that he would go on and on about planning an 'authentic' explosion. Those exact words. Only Stan and I knew that the explosives were indeed real, and that Müller's arrogance could later be used against him. Stan didn't know about the poisoned schnapps, by the way. That was my added touch—insurance. I kept that part away from Stan in case it was discovered. I was willing to take the fall. Ultimately, he and I would be exonerated of any suspicion of foul play and Los Angeles would be rid of two dozen Nazis. Win-win."

Sienna's Cupid-bow lips part wide open. Yes, it was all meticulously premeditated, and now she knows. But I can tell by her raised brow that she is still not satisfied. The pen tapping bit starts up again. "How could you possibly get the timing exactly right?" she presses. "So much could have gone wrong."

That's when I break out into a fit of laughter. "Timing, Sienna? That was the one sure thing I could depend on. Nazis have one distinctive quality above all others," I tell her. "Write this down: Nazis are always on time. Always on schedule. Predictable. The trains to Treblinka and Auschwitz were never late. Nazis were always just following orders, always completing their tasks in a timely manner—no matter if it was murder or rape or robbery or arson. And God knows, those bastards wrote everything down. Every death, every bullet, every stolen painting, every asset, every bank account, every home they looted and destroyed was tallied. Why? you ask." I feel my eyes distended like a cartoon character's, and I know it's not an attractive look. "Bragging rights. Evidence! They were determined to showcase the superiority of the Aryan race, how step by step they annihilated us. And Müller was no different. He was raised on Nazi breast milk and insisted on a minute-by-minute schedule. He ordered Mika to record and save everything—proof of his brilliance as a filmmaker—for his own Third Reich studio archives. Mika, Stan and I both knew, was the key to our success; our on-set stopwatch. My job was to get my hands on her daily schedules, which, of course, I did. And the rest is history."

I resume my place on the couch again, kick up

my mules onto the coffee table, and close my eyes briefly, recalling the details of how a few days before the film's final shoot, I snuck into Agnes's Wardrobe trailer where Mika had kept her daily schedules and studio notes neatly organized on a desk in the corner. She was so anal-retentive. "I knew that everything I needed would be there, recorded on Mika's checklist," I explain, laughing again, not in a way that's funny. "I still remember the key item circled in red: 'five p.m. to five twenty-five p.m. Connie/Schnapps for Cast/ No Jews!!!' Three exclamation marks. 'Synagogue explosion five thirty to five fifty p.m.'" I shake my head. "Ironically, the 'No Jews on set' policy saved us, not them."

"Weren't you scared?" Sienna whispers.

"Scared? Hah! Fear is the heart of the whole damn story, young lady. I learned long ago that the secret to fighting back is to become empowered. If you run on fear, you lose, period. I did what I did, Sienna, to never feel scared again."

Leaning forward, I jab my manicured nail into her yellow notepad on the coffee table. "I had to bring down Müller before fear won. It was him or me. That's survival. It always comes down to a choice, never a compromise. The choice is ugly. A normal means to an end won't work. It is those things that one would never do that one must do to survive. I'm not a psychopath. I am an avenger. There's a difference."

"You are in your eighties, Lena. Do you know how to do normal?" she asks boldly. Normal. That's where I draw the line.

It is now a face-off. Sienna does not avert her gaze, and nor do I. Turquoise eyes battle it out as though an ocean tide crashed into the sea. She wants to know if I'm the real monster here. If there is an expiration date on avenging.

"I'm turning eighty-six. Normal?" My voice rises mercilessly. "Normal ceased the day I was dragged out of my home by my hair, the day I lost . . ." I stop. It's enough. She knows it all.

Sienna exhales hard, making room for more questions, more hole filling. My entire body is fired up. Normal? You want to go there? C'mon, Sienna, ask me real questions. I know you want to. What will be my last act? How much more venom could one person possibly have inside herself? When does someone like me call it a day?

Sienna picks up the yellow pad, shuffles her notes nervously. "Let's get back to the scandal surrounding the explosion. Twenty-one people dead on set," she says as the recorder's wheels spin.

Splat. I shake my head, disappointed. I gave her an

opening to what comes next, to what really matters right now, and she didn't take it. Back to logistics.

"And one of the dead was Connie."

"Yes." I acknowledge my assistant's unfortunate death. But that's all I say. Connie's death still weighs on me. I tried to stop her from sympathizing with the Nazis, but she rejected my help repeatedly. There was nothing else I could do.

Sienna knows by my stony expression that this subject is now ironclad shut. She glances again at her notes, decides to veer in a different direction. I can see even from my end of the couch with my failing eyesight that the word "Vultures" is underlined twice. "Vultures" is code for the Hollywood press. "But the media didn't believe you. They wouldn't let the *Goddess* scandal go for months. There were hundreds, if not thousands, of news stories wrapped around it," she points out.

"Yes, gossip was fierce, as expected. Think about it: You had the top studio, top director, and me, involved in a terrible 'on-set accident'—and none of us were considered suspects. All those conspiracy theories . . ." I roll my eyes, my voice hardening. "So, Stan and I decided to do what anyone facing a Hollywood firing squad would have done."

Sienna leans back with a cock of her head. "You made another movie, of course, at the peak of the rumormongering. Hollywood scandal guarantees box-office success. The money always wins."

"Always."

"*The Accidental Affair* with Jack Lyons came on the heels of the *Goddess* disaster," she announces, as though I don't know my own movie lineage.

"And that wasn't an accident either," I tell her. "Jack was such a lovely, kind man back then—still is— but don't let that fool you. He is as shrewd as a Swiss banker."

I close my eyes yet again, savoring the image of our beautiful affair rekindled for the duration of that movie too, and the several times after that when we rendez-voused in London and when Jack was back on location in Los Angeles. I care about him, always will. Natu-rally, our on-and-off media-hyped love affair faded with new movies, new costars, new love interests. "Jack understood that with all the press surrounding *Goddess*, everyone would clamor to see my next film. In fact, it was Jack who sent me *The Accidental Affair* script and begged me to do it, and of course he pleaded with Stan to direct. We knew it was our next move and ran with it."

"And then Stan went on to win an Oscar that year for best director and Jack won best actor," Sienna states, like she's the top student in class giving a book report.

Then her face drops, chin to chest. "But there's more, isn't there, Lena?" She searches my face; her eyes squint deeply like spikes of sea glass. "I know there's more."

"There's always more," I echo. My mouth feels dry. Stan is now dead and so are all the others involved. Why not give it to her? I take a deep breath and release the air slowly like a pricked balloon. "A few weeks after the 'accident,' Stan and I arranged a private meeting with the FBI. We told them all about Müller and how he blackmailed us. How Nazis in Los Angeles were trying to resurrect the Third Reich into a 'Fourth Reich.' I even gave them the address of Das Haus—and left the rest up to them. We later learned that the FBI ransacked the compound and discovered massive amounts of weaponry and illegal explosives—all serving to bolster our case, underscoring our 'innocence.' We told them that we had warned Müller not to use real explosives on set, but he insisted that the last scene must be 'authentic' and demanded that only Nazis be allowed on set to experience 'the true destructive beauty.' Of course, everything we shared with the FBI checked out. As I said, Müller did not make a secret of his bitterness toward Jews on set. There were so many witnesses to back up all our claims, even the cleaning crew testified. When the FBI finished with us, their report put all the blame for the explosion on Michael Müller. Stan and I were completely absolved of any wrongdoing." I smile at the memory. "Poetic justice."

I see the shocked look pass over Sienna's face. "Yes," I tell her. "We played two truths and a lie with the FBI. But since you're finally asking some good questions, there's more. The heads of Flagstone begged us not to go public with the story that we told the FBI. Nazis being given the green light on their studio back lot was the kiss of death for them, not to mention their own insurance claims. In exchange for our silence, Stan and I demanded a three-movie deal, top salary, the best crews, a large percentage of movie sales, distribution approval. And I—"

"Became the highest paid actress of your time."

I clasp my hands together like cymbals. "And now you know why."

"But—" Sienna stops herself.

"You can say it." I feel the tightness inside my chest. "I lost for best actress the same year that Stan and Jack won. To Susan Hayward. I lost four more times after that. The highest paid actress, nominated for numerous Oscars and awards, has never won the gold."

Sienna nods quietly. "You should have won."

I run my hand through my hair. "The only guarantee in Hollywood is that there are no guarantees." I stand once again and take a seventh-inning stretch. I am tired, it's getting late. Today's discussion depleted me. Sienna stands, too, knowing it's a wrap for the day. But I am proud of her. She's no pushover.

"Look in my eyes, Sienna," I tell her as she gathers her things. "It's time to ask the final question. I mean, really look. Tell me . . . do I look like I'm done here?"

Her breath catches in her throat. I can see the lump rise in her bare, beautiful, lineless neck. We both know I'm not talking about being exhausted, needing a catnap before dinner.

She presses her sensual lips together, then lightly licks them. "The last act," she whispers. "Whatever it is that you're planning is going to happen on my watch, isn't it? In real time." She points her cigarette at me. "You want that Oscar."

"Clever girl," I say with a penetrating gaze. But, sadly for you, not that clever.

"Oscar is the only man in Hollywood I never slept with. So yes, I intend to make his bed my last one."

Once again, two truths and a lie—my specialty.

Chapter Forty-Two

I am not a morning person, but Sienna is. All sparkly and bright, ready to go. I can tell by the animated look on her face when she enters my house that she has news. After eight weeks straight together, we know each other's looks, pauses, twitches, gestures, and various smiles. Each tiny movement has its own special meaning.

"You have something to tell me." I note her long, confident stride into the library as though she'd rather run than walk. I have staff, of course: a butler, cleaning lady, and a chef. But they have all been instructed to leave me alone during the Sienna sessions.

Today she wears celery-green bell bottoms with a black-and-white polka-dot blouse tied at the waist and a thick gold rope chain necklace with a large diamond-studded dangling *S*. A little on the tacky side, I think, but I keep that to myself.

"There's something you must see." She points to the couch. "Sit, Lena. I think you should sit."

"Well, that just makes me want to stand." I hate surprises.

"Fine, stand." She places an article, a double-page spread, on the coffee table. It's in Polish, and from the *Gazeta Wyborcza*. I look at her. "You don't read Polish," I say, putting on my reading glasses.

"True, but I read translations. There's a historian who I've been in touch with at the U.S. Holocaust Museum. I told her if there is anything new about the Warsaw Ghetto or the resistance to let me know about it. Well, she sent me this article the other day translated, and . . ."

But I don't hear her right now. Staring back at me from the page is a black-and-white image of an elderly, elegant, full-figured woman sitting on a piano bench, wearing a long, black velvet gown with an expensive-looking pearl choker. Her dark hair laced with gray is pulled back into a tight chignon at the nape of her neck. My heart palpitates. It's not the woman who steals my attention at first. It is what's perched behind her in a glass case. A violin. Not just any violin, but the

Behrmans' Stradivarius. How is that possible? And the woman in the photograph . . . pianist Diana Mazur.

I read the photo caption twice, but the words don't register at first, even though I know exactly what I'm reading, who the pianist is. I bring the newspaper close to my face—my lips practically touch it. Can it be? Well preserved in her early seventies, possessing soft, dark eyes, high cheekbones, and a patrician nose. She looks like an older version of her mother. I grab Sienna's arm to prevent myself from falling.

"Yes," she whispers, holding on to me tightly. "It's her. Dina Behrman. She goes by Diana Mazur. The Warsaw National Philharmonic Orchestra is honoring her parents' life's work sixty years after the war. A commemorative original symphony was created. Mazur, a celebrated pianist, will accompany the orchestra for a one-night-only performance in two weeks. Apparently, Diana rarely plays publicly, just records her music. But this . . . she agreed to perform."

Little Dina lived. As Sienna rambles on, giving her assessment, I close my eyes, feeling the tears push up against the back of my lids. Tears I cannot shed but are there anyway, chafing the folds. Little Dina who feared her own shadow, the only child in the synagogue basement who didn't take the poison, somehow, miraculously, survived. And so did the violin. I press my shaky palm to my pounding chest as I read the article slowly. I peer up repeatedly at my ornately wallpapered ceiling. *Eryk . . . Dina is alive,* I tell him. *I kept my promise.*

Dizzy and disoriented, I must have fainted. I feel a wet cloth pressing across my forehead, sprinkling stray droplets onto my skin, waking me, bringing me back to the present. Opening my eyes, I see the most beautiful face looming over mine like a full moon. Ethereal beauty that reminds me of what once belonged to me but is now all hers. I cling to Sienna's hand like a life preserver.

"Lena, are you okay? Do you hear me?" Her voice fills with worry. "What do you need? What can I do?"

"You gave me what I needed. What I've always needed," I whisper. "Dina is alive. The violin is . . ." But there is no end to the sentence.

"I will go there with you, to the performance."

"No, no, I can't go back there." I sit up, my voice sounding much younger and higher pitched than its years. "Impossible. I simply can't."

Sienna kneels on the floor next to me. "Dina is alive because of you. This moment must be in the film. I must capture this." She looks at me, this radiant doppelgänger of my youth, this unstoppable pain-in-the-ass young actress-*cum*-director who is making her life's work *my* life.

"Never. Not even for this." My mouth trumps my heart, as my hand pulls away from hers.

But Sienna doesn't take no for an answer. She reclaims my fingers with a tenderness that feels something akin to daughterly love, though I have never raised a child. This must be what it's like. Look at us, I think, a childless woman and a woman who is motherless. Somehow, we found each other, two puzzle pieces meant to fit. The answer is still no.

But Sienna, trailer-park tough, is not having it. "Well, that's too bad, because I already bought us tickets." Her eyes are glued to mine. "We are traveling together in my plane, accompanied by my security team. I will be with you every step of the way."

I open my mouth to protest, but she is ready for that too. She hands me a cigarette already pulled out of the pack to shut me up, and reluctantly I take it. As I inhale the comforting smoke, we both know that any fight I put up now is futile. Working with her is like looking in a goddamn mirror.

Chapter Forty-Three

Warsaw
Two Weeks Later

When Sienna and I enter the magnificent National Philharmonic Hall located on Jasna Street, there is no one clamoring for my autograph or hers, no one notices us at all. We are both heavily disguised, thanks to her skilled makeup artist, who accompanied us on the journey. No one pays any attention to an elderly woman with a short gray old-lady wig (never would I ever), whose black silk-covered arm is looped through her granddaughter's, also unrecognizable in a short dark-haired wig, oversize eyeglasses, and a frumpy dark frock.

"See, I told you," Sienna whispers triumphantly, as we settle into our third-row center seats.

The packed room silences immediately as the lights dim, and I realize I am barely breathing as the musicians file into their designated spots, awaiting the appearance of the reclusive Diana Mazur, whose work I never heard of before because I shunned anything Polish the moment I landed on Ellis Island. But once I learned Dina is still alive, all I have listened to from morning until bedtime are recordings by the gifted Polish treasure, Diana Mazur. Buried beneath every single haunting note, I see them: Eryk; her parents playing in the ghetto square; the girls in the synagogue. I have cried so many invisible tears with each glorious strike of her piano keys, feeling and remembering it all.

A hush engulfs the auditorium as Dina walks across the stage. I press both hands to my chest, as the lovely enchantress makes her ethereal, sweeping entrance. She is tall like her brother, her dark glossy hair is elegantly laced with zebra stripes of gray hanging loosely to her shoulders in soft, easy waves. She emits a regal presence in her midnight-blue silk gown, wearing the same pearl choker she wore in the picture accompanying the newspaper article. She also carries a silver beaded clutch purse with her. Who carries a purse onstage?

And then, the inconceivable occurs. Dina, standing in front of the baby grand piano, opens the purse, reaches inside, and unfolds something that looks like a rag. The audience gasps when she displays the frayed cloth for all to see. It's a faded white armband affixed with a washed-out blue Star of David. Our Nazi-imposed badge of shame: Jew. Garbage. Vermin. Disease. Beware. Dina holds out the band for several uncomfortable moments and then slips it onto the right upper sleeve of her dress, as we were once forced to do. The Nazis made sure we stood out like a warning, a walking, talking contagion for all to see, despise, and avoid.

Dina begins to speak. Her voice is rich and melodious, unrecognizable from the timid little girl I once knew, and surprisingly commanding.

"Good evening. You know me as Diana Mazur, but tonight, I am who I once was and will always be—Dina Behrman, a Jewish survivor of Nazi tyranny. My parents were forced to cut ties with this beloved orchestra when the Nazis invaded Poland in 1939. This orchestra hall was once my parents' sanctuary, their passion, their whole life. But in November 1940, we were seized from our family home just blocks from here. My parents, my older brother, Eryk, and me, imprisoned in the Warsaw Ghetto with more than four hundred thousand other Jews. We were stuffed inside a room as big as a closet. My parents, as you know, were brilliant musicians and an inspiration to so many. Despite our hellish existence, they would not stop the music no matter what, even though their music—all this—was stolen from them." Dina's voice amplifies and chills course down my spine. "No one—not even those criminals—could steal their passion, their God-given talent. My parents played in the ghetto's central square every Sabbath to bring light to the darkness, to remind everyone of what we all once cherished together: the music."

The rich Polish language that I shunned for decades fills my soul. Each word, each nuance coming from Dina's mouth is like fresh air pumping through me. No one moves, no one blinks. I glance over at Sienna, whose eyes are fixated on Dina.

"My parents were murdered in cold blood in the Treblinka concentration camp," she continues. "My brother, Eryk, only seventeen, was forced to take care of me and protect me until"—she squeezes her eyes shut, cuts off her own story—"we were separated. He died fighting Nazis. Died a hero. He will always be my personal hero. After escaping the ghetto, he refused to give up the struggle and insisted on helping others rather than claim his own hard-fought freedom. He searched for me day and night. And then one day"—she inhales deeply—"we learned of each other's existence."

I squeeze Sienna's arm so hard that she muffles a cry. Eryk knew Dina was alive, my heart shrieks with joy. *He knew.*

"Sadly, my brother died just before our reunion, after bombing a platoon of Nazis at a railway station. He was shot dead by a traitor among his group. This"—she points to the armband—"was his. After the war, a brave Polish soldier who was in the forest fighting alongside Eryk saved this, found me, and gave it to me. A Polish hero who has since passed, but his son, Milos, is here tonight." She pauses, smiles at the audience—her mother's radiant smile that lights up her entire somber face. Everyone turns as Milos stands with his palm to his heart. There's not a dry eye in the house—except, of course, mine.

"My name is Dina Behrman," she repeats loudly, her voice vibrating throughout the auditorium. "My brother's last words were: 'Find my sister.' This first composition is for you, Eryk, for my parents, for the Polish heroes who stood up to evil. Some who are in this very room."

Her eyes land on me. Am I imagining it? She turns to the musicians behind her and nods. They respond with music. Little Dina, scared of her own shadow, sits at the piano in total control.

I close my eyes, swept away by the evocative rapture

of the melodies. When she hits the final note of her performance, the crowd stands and roars. She touches her necklace, and I know what that means: This is for you, Mama. She looks down at the piano, rises, and turns to the audience.

I clap and clap and clap until my hands ache.

Dina silences the audience, gestures for everyone to resume their seats, and reaches inside her purse once again. I know exactly what she is getting. I don't even need to look. I feel it, smell it. The note. From the synagogue basement. Her promise, her responsibility to the girls who died there. It happens right here, right now.

Dina clears her throat. No one moves.

"How was I saved?" she asks. "How could I go through what I endured and stand here tonight and play piano?" Her voice reverberates amid the excellent acoustics. "I am here only because of those who risked their lives to save me. It began with one courageous woman and ninety-three young girls—religious Jewish girls—who had been seized from their school in the ghetto by Nazi soldiers and taken to the basement of our city's most beautiful synagogue. We were hosed down, deloused . . . and prepared." She points over her shoulder, and it's as if the Great Synagogue of Warsaw is materializing in the auditorium before us. "I was one of them. Barely ten years old. We had two nights to-gether before we were to be turned into sex slaves, Nazi whores. One brave woman snuck inside the synagogue, disguised as a maid, and offered the girls a way out of hell—with poison and a choice: die with dignity or die after being used and abused. That was the only choice. Not *if* we were going to die, but *how* we were going to die. We chose dignity. And me"—her eyes glisten like water pearls—"I was appointed the designated survi-vor, to one day tell the story if I survived the war. I was the youngest and the smallest so I could hide. Believe me, I wanted to die with the others. I was afraid of the dark, afraid of spiders, afraid of everything. I hid for hours alone in a storage closet."

The silence in the auditorium is deafening. "I was saved by a man I will never know and given the gift of life." She sighs deeply. Her heavy harnessed breath is heard loud and clear. "But you see, I couldn't tell the story. The truth became buried with everything else in my life. I only survived because of this." Her hand ten-derly grazes the sleek black lacquer of the piano behind her. "But I carried this note with me every single day." She waves the tattered piece of paper. "And today, as I honor the memory of my parents, I am reminded that it is time to honor the note too. A sixteen-year-old courageous girl named Lilah, representing all the girls, scribbled this before her death and stuffed it inside my shoe. 'Don't let our deaths be in vain, Dina,' she told me. 'You must tell the world what happened to us.' Here are Lilah's last words:

"'I do not know when or if this letter will reach someone sometime. But if it reaches anyone, we shall not be alive by then. Please recite Kaddish for ninety-three clean, innocent Jewish girls who decided to take their lives in their own hands and not be mutilated and dishonored by the dirty S.S. officers.'"

Dina looks up. "Those girls all died by poisoning. I saw each brave girl's last breath with my own eyes. I was there, the sole witness. And now I'm here, on this stage. I survived for them. Playing piano is survival for me."

Sienna's cameraman captures the entire performance from the side of the hall, where the other international journalists and crews are standing. Much later, I would learn that the cameraman was given alternate instructions by Sienna. He was told to zero in on Dina's face and then mine, back to hers, back to me, showcasing a tennis match of unfiltered emotion. This exchange would later become one of the most poignant moments of her film.

When the performance ends and the musicians take their leave, there is a light tap on Sienna's shoulder accompanied by muted instructions. She leans over and whispers to me, "Diana Mazur will meet you in her dressing room. It has been prearranged. She is waiting for you, Lena."

I cling to Sienna's arm as we make our way to the dressing room, terrified my shaking legs will give out on me. The security guard knocks and Dina answers. He steps aside and we face each other. Time, past and present, slams together. We both don't move.

"Dinale," I whisper. Little Dina.

"Bina."

She knows. She saw me in the audience. Sienna had sent word earlier that we were there. She ushers me inside the dressing room, and we fall into each other's embrace—two old women, two young girls merging—forgetting time's passage and those milling around us. Our clinging bodies express everything we need to say, and we are unable to peel away from each other.

I look into her teary eyes when we finally break apart, and she leads me to the small couch in the corner of the room. She instructs her assistant, Sienna, and the cameramen to leave the room. They were permitted to film the moment we reunited, but now the rest is ours alone, she told them.

"Did you know about me . . . Lena Browning?" I ask her once the others have left the dressing room.

"Yes." She averts her lovely gaze. And I get it. The tarnished memories, the note she never shared with the world, and the guilt of surviving prevented her from reaching out. "I knew," she admits, but that is all she says. I don't push it. It doesn't matter. We are here now. Survival is about secrets, about extraordinary measures taken to stay alive. The equation is absolute: If you survived, it meant others did not. The trauma of a second chance at life, a second act, is at once miraculous and unendurable.

"The violin," I say softly. My heartbeat quickens. How do I tell her that I traded in her parents' prized possession for my life, when it was meant for her? For once, I choose truth. "I saved it, Dina, hid it for as long as I could. And then I was forced to trade it to get across the border. I had nothing else. I'm so sorry."

She leans forward, places a gentle finger to my lips to stop the words from running. "What matters is that I got it back. I searched for it for ten years after the war and then learned through a colleague—a prominent violinist—where it landed. It was sold during the war to a crooked art dealer, and ultimately it ended up in the hands of someone who didn't know its history.

An old friend of my father's, who was high up in the government, helped me get it back." She bites down on her bottom lip, and I know without her telling me that it must have cost her everything.

"Eryk knew you were alive," I say, and change the subject.

She presses her hand to her heart. "Yes, he knew."

Over the next thirty minutes, puzzle pieces from our past meld together. I tell her all about Stach and Żegota, that he was the one who rescued her from the synagogue basement. That I'd heard she made it to the forest, but never knew for sure—one of my deepest pains. A long excrutiating silence passes between us. Blame, perhaps? I see the agony growing inside Dina's wounded eyes. The toll of the past has become too heavy. It is time for me to go.

I say the thing that normal people would say, *If you ever come to Los Angeles* . . . but we both know, given our age, our history, that this is it, our lone moment of reconciliation. I rise slowly, wanting to leave, yet yearning to stay. "The girls, Dina. You made them proud."

As the tears stream down her lovely face, I take her genius hands in mine for a final embrace, and then we hold on for just a little longer.

Chapter Forty-Four

I rina . . . Irina."
I whip my head around at the sound of that name, just as I approach the waiting limousine outside the symphony hall. *That name. That voice.* Like a magnet to steel, I feel her presence, and then I turn and see her. I rub my eyes, thinking I am hallucinating.

"Stop," I command Sienna before she gets into the car. "Stop right now."

Sienna follows my gaze. "Who is she?"

"Anna . . . the dancer."

Sienna holds back her security team as I stare at the elderly woman in the distance, standing near a group of symphony stragglers congregating close to the entrance of the auditorium. I leave Sienna and begin to walk toward her almost hypnotically. Piercing azure eyes, white fluffy hair to her shoulders, a silky blue clingy dress with a matching scarf that she is not wearing but I envision on her anyway. Anna the ballerina, the woman who saved my life, who, with Stach, helped save Dina's life.

She is here for Dina too. A witness to the living miracle with her own eyes.

Anna is flanked by two stylish young women, one who looks exactly like her—the Anna of sixty years ago. I can barely breathe. They must be her granddaughters.

From the corner of my eye, I see Sienna approaching and signaling her cameraman to film this encounter. "Stand down," I turn and hiss sharply, my voice scolding and louder than I intended. "This is not to be filmed or this project is terminated immediately."

For once, Sienna listens. She takes a few steps back as I walk over to Anna.

"Anna," I whisper. "It's you."

Her granddaughters look at her, then at me, and I understand. Her name isn't Anna, the way mine isn't Irina or Lena. The way Diana Mazur isn't Diana. The way Sienna isn't Sienna.

"Petra," she says, her eyes illuminating. Of course. Petra Schneider. The name that ultimately saved my life. She turns to the young women at her sides. "Girls, please give me a moment. This is a dear old friend."

"With emphasis on old," I tell them in rusty Polish, and they both laugh.

Anna pulls me aside. "Irina, I knew it was you beneath that wig. I was sitting a few rows behind you." She is momentarily speechless. "I would know you anywhere. I saw you walk toward the dressing room after the performance. I waited until you came out."

"And you . . . So many years. I can't believe it." My voice is trembling, too, crackling fragments of sentences.

"So much to say." She glances over at her granddaughters. "They don't know anything about my past. Nothing. But not here, okay? Can you meet tomorrow morning?"

"Yes, where?" I ask excitedly, as though I'm still twenty-four and could run through a sewer or wear a coat laden with dynamite into a Nazi nightclub.

"Where else?" Her smile lights up her face and I feel the familiarity of its reassuring warmth, like a muscle memory, protecting me once again.

Chapter Forty-Five

The next morning, Sienna insists that her personal driver and security guard—a former Secret Service agent—take me to see Anna, and she would wait with him in the car. No cameras, no filming, she promised. But she refuses to let me out of her sight. *You are still Lena Browning. No one knows Bina Blonski, but everyone in the world knows you.*

My heart and head pound in sync as we pull up in front of the ballet studio, now renovated with white brick and bright aqua shutters. My heart skips a beat when I see the same pale-pink sign hanging front and center over the doorway: BALET SOSIA. All these years and Anna kept up the studio, honoring the memory of her beloved mentor.

Sienna looks worried as she accompanies me up

the studio steps, but that's all I let her do. I stand at the doorway and wait until she gets back in the car. I turn the doorknob first, and it opens easily. I forgo the knock. Anna is expecting me.

Entering the studio, I remove the Hermès scarf covering my real hair. I had tossed that godforsaken wig into the garbage bin as soon as I returned to the hotel last night. The truth is, I want Anna to see me as Lena Browning. Yes, I am vain, but it's much more than that. I want her to know that the risks she took to keep me alive were worth it.

"Anna," I call out softly. "Petra," I correct myself.

"I'm here," she says warmly, walking toward me, hand outstretched. She is still so lovely. Age has certainly taken its toll on both of us, but there are still strong remnants of the young women we once were. We are both wearing black slacks and neutral-toned blouses. We laugh at our similarity, and revel in the lightness of the unfamiliar sound. It's a first for us. There was no laughter back then.

"Tell me everything," she says, leading me to a quaint bistro table in the corner of the studio preset with coffee, tea, and pastries. "I wasn't sure if you had had breakfast. Please." She gestures to the chair. "And don't leave anything out."

For the next hour or so, I spill it all, not necessarily

in order, but as each image appears inside my head. The uprising, the escape, Vladek, returning here to the studio, looking for her. She says she found the pearl hairpin that I attached to the costume and knew I had been here and taken the suitcase.

My eyes well up at the mention of the suitcase. I thank Anna for the identification card that saved my life and tell her that I held on to the suitcase filled with precious items, including Jakub's manuscript, for as long I could, but was forced to leave it behind when I joined the resistance in the forest. I managed to save only two photos from the past: my wedding day with my whole family surrounding me, and the one with Aleksander and me by the sea.

Anna is silent, then softly says that she still has the hairpin. But that was the last she knew I was alive until several years later, when she saw me splashed across magazine covers, in newspapers, and of course—she smiles while touching my arm—in every one of my films. She has seen them all.

"I wanted to reach out to you one hundred times but . . ." she says apologetically, the sentence trailing off to nowhere. Just like Dina, I think. The "but" is loaded. War makes you want to forget what was and focus only on what is, what will be.

I tell Anna how I escaped Warsaw by masquerading

as a Nazi escort to get over the border, using her impeccable documents, first making my way to the forest near where I grew up, and then finding refuge on a small farm, where I hid until the war was over. I then tell her about the farmer, enduring his nightly rapes—until I stopped him for good. She holds my hands in hers, eyes closed, not surprised. She would have done the same thing, her hands say.

"Lukas," she says finally.

Just his name. It is enough. We sip our tea quietly.

I tell her how he hunted me down in the ghetto, killed my husband and others. I recount everything I can remember. Even . . . about Aleksander. I talk about my feelings for him in a tiny whisper, and she leans forward, her face near mine, never asking me to speak louder. The deepest pain is always the quietest.

Finally, I fill her in on the details about Lukas's brother, Michael Müller, whose sole purpose was to control and destroy me in Hollywood, and how I put an end to his blackmail—the only person outside of Sienna and Stan to learn the truth. And that's when she stops me. She holds up her hand like a traffic patroller.

"Lukas Müller shot me," she reveals in the same hushed tone I used when discussing Aleksander, "right after he dropped you off that night in the alley. I haven't spoken about this to anyone since it happened."

I keep my eyes focused on her tortured expression. "He thought I was dead," she continues. "I should have died with the two bullets in my chest. He shoved me out of the car and threw his bloodstained coat over me." She sighs heavily. "I still have that bloody coat as a reminder, up in the attic." She points to the ceiling of the studio, indicating that remnants of the war are hidden up there.

"I lay bleeding to death on the side of a road when a young man found me, carried me back to his family's apartment nearby," she continues. "He was a medical student—can you imagine my luck? His name is Antoni. He saved my life, and I married him. We have two children and five beautiful grandchildren. I made him swear to never discuss it. Because I wanted to live, experience joy, and forget the damn war. That's why I hung up the phone every time I thought to reach out to you. Each time I saw your face on-screen, I saw the war." Her eyes well up. "I couldn't . . . I'm so sorry."

The morning passes quickly as we shed our skin for each other. Finally, I peer out the studio window and see my loyal blond lieutenant in her dark-haired wig and sunglasses still waiting patiently for me in the car, not budging. It is time.

"I must go now," I tell Anna. "This has been . . ."

Her face drops, her mouth tightens into a thin, resolute line, and I can tell she has more to say. "Lukas Müller is still alive. He lives in Buenos Aires. He is—"

"Armand Arias." I finish her sentence and her mouth drops open. "A director. A celebrated enigma. No one sees him, just his movies."

"Yes . . . so, you saw it then too?" Her voice trails in disbelief.

I nod. "That's how I knew for sure it was him, that he is still alive. I have been searching for him for decades with no luck, no leads. And then, that movie. *The Impostor*. The minute I saw the last scene, I knew."

Her gaze is unblinking. "Yes. Two women, a corrupt member of the Argentinian aristocracy, and an 'impostor' in a getaway car after a bombing occurs in a nightclub. Every word of that conversation was ours—the exact same dialogue."

I nod again, having watched the movie at least a dozen times, as Anna continues to describe the last scene. "The aristocrat is shot dead by the woman in the back seat. The driver lets that woman out of the car, gets rid of the aristocrat's body, then shoots the other woman still in the car, throws his bloody coat over her dead body, then pushes her out the door and drives off. The End." Anna pops off the chair. I can see the trauma in her eyes. "I could barely breathe, Irina. I'm sorry, I mean, Lena. My husband took me to the hospital the night I saw the film. They called it an anxiety attack."

I had previewed the movie before it even hit the theaters, after all the critics hailed *The Impostor* a shoo-in to win at Cannes and every other international award. My agent had sent me an early copy of the film. Right after viewing *The Impostor* I began devising a plan for Lukas Müller, and then Sienna and her biopic came into my life, and I knew the perfect plan had found me.

Anna interrupts my thoughts. "Do you think Lukas wanted you to know that he lived his life to the fullest and got away with everything?" Her cobalt eyes search mine like burning torches.

"I've wondered the very same thing," I say carefully.

"Do you think he knows you killed his brother?"

"Yes," I say unequivocally. "I've often speculated why he never came after me again all these years, and then I realized that a narcissist cares more about himself, preserving his own life more. I think this film is—"

"His way of showing you that he won." Anna finishes my sentence, parroting my thoughts.

"Exactly."

She folds her arms and assesses me, eyeing me just as she did back then in the tiny safe house after bringing me supplies and giving instructions. "I found some older photos of him," she says. "His face has been surgically altered, those crazy-colored eyes are darkened with contacts, but . . . ."

"You never forget the face." I have those same photos.

"Never." Anna is smart. Not just smart. She is an animal like me, all instinct. She leans forward. "I can see it in your eyes . . . Is there something more I need to know about Lukas Müller?"

I feel light-headed. A woman who I have not seen in sixty years sees through me as though I'm translucent. A woman who saved my life. A woman who was shot and left for dead while risking her own life against the forces of evil. She merits the truth, deserves to know my final plan. I clear my throat, slowly sip some water first. "I have spent my life as an actress. It is the only way I could breathe. Like you, I kept my past hidden from everyone. But on the side, I did what I had to do—serving justice while the world looked the other way. It is the only thing that has given my life meaning . . . purpose. Do you understand what I'm saying?" I search her timeless oval face, her still-sparkling eyes, fierce mouth, flared nostrils, and I know she does. "The war is long over, Anna—I hope you don't mind if I call you that. But not for me. Never for me. Not while Lukas Müller is still breathing."

Anna's voice is practically imperceptible. "Müller finds me too often in my nightmares. He is living as a celebrated filmmaker and his criminal past has been buried. This movie, I hear, is up for many awards."

"Yes, it is," I say coldly, my eyes never veering from hers. She begins to see exactly what I'm not telling her.

"And I also heard that he has been nominated for a major prize at the Venice Film Festival, and by all accounts, that undeserving bastard is slated to win. They say the Venice event will be his first public appearance in years." Her eyes are scorching. She opens and closes her fists. "Müller has lived too well, too long."

"I promise you . . . he will not win that award."

She nods with tacit approval.

I rise from the bistro table and so does she.

"Wait," she says, holding me back by my arm.

She moves across the room with the agility and grace of a much younger woman, and I can picture her here once again, the girl dancing her heart out with Madame Sosia clapping in time. Anna stands in front of the small desk in the corner of the studio, unlocks a drawer, and returns to me. "Take this—our good luck charm. Do what you must do."

I stare at the jeweled hairpin reclining in my palm, sandwiched between my hand and hers. I hold her gaze, squeeze the pin, and allow its slim sharpness to prick at my skin. My last act is for both of us.

Chapter Forty-Six

Venice

Three Months Later

S ienna and I decide that her biopic, aptly titled
Femme Fatale, would be announced at the Venice
International Film Festival, taking place the first
week of September, where she would be a presenter.
I, of course, planted the seed right after our trip to
Warsaw. She loved the idea and suggested that I come
as her plus-one. It has been at least fifteen years since
I have done the Venice circuit. I was a presenter back
then, and sat on the jury in 1967, when Catherine
Deneuve won for *Belle de Jour*. My presence will
certainly make a splash. Once the paparazzi see us
riding the gondola together and our secret project is

unveiled, the media frenzy will be sensational. We are both ready for it.

Me, especially.

Sienna and I coordinated our outfits for the week, a showcase for the "young Lena Browning" to be inextricably tied to the old one. How I wish we could trade places and I could be that youthful again, stand in her heels, not mine.

Before traveling to Venice, I made sure that all important details were implemented. My financials are all in order. My house is ready. The few key personal items from the past—particularly photos of those I loved—are here with me, protected in one of my half dozen suitcases. All the things that matter to me have been organized for what surely will take place after Venice. I have lived my life my way, and in the end, I am a very rich woman. Sienna doesn't know it yet, but I appointed her my executor. I trust her, and I don't trust anybody.

Descending the plane into the private section of the Venice Marco Polo Airport, Sienna and I twin in our large Jackie O sunglasses, wide-leg trousers, cream-colored blouses (mine unbuttoned two down, hers four), with matching thick gold rope chains. My hair is freshly dyed, and hers is natural and beachy looking with fresh highlights. We are quite the Hollywood duo, and within minutes of our arrival at the festival, waving from the gondola, the word is out, and the media goes wild.

We hold an "impromptu" press conference, and I smile proudly at my young doppelgänger as she talks to the press and explains our work in progress. I feel the familiar heat of the cameras flashing on all sides, and admittedly, I relish the attention. It's been a long time coming. The story is too good, so Tinseltown juicy. They just don't know it yet. But they will.

I'm sorry/not sorry for what is about to happen, I tell Sienna with my eyes. But the experience you are about to cultivate would have earned rave reviews from my dear old friend Stella Adler. Her theory was that actors needed to build up a wealth of resources beyond their own knowledge and experiences, so they could more accurately and convincingly portray a wide array of characters.

Watch and learn, Sienna . . . watch and learn.

We enter the Palazzo del Cinema after the exhausting three-day media whirlwind. I should be drained from all the interviews, but I feel quite the opposite. Younger, lighter, leaner. I am no longer the Hollywood has-been tucked away in the Hills with her penciled-in brows and parade of double-lime vodka martinis. No, tonight I am relevant once again. I don't walk into the grand theater, I float, feeling serene and beautiful in my shimmering custom-made high-necked ivory Oscar de la Renta gown. Sienna is at my side in a form-fitting beaded match. We are both dripping in Harry Winston. The princess to my queen.

"How do you feel about seeing Jack Lyons again?" she whispers in my ear amid the flashbulbs, glitter, and glitz, the myriad mics shoved in our faces. And yes, I do enjoy the burst of side comments, all some form of "Lena looks better than ever." Damn straight. Still here, people. Fat Lady ain't singing yet.

"Thrilled," I tell her. "Jack is presenting the Golden Lion for best film. Kind of perfect, right? Lyons meets lion." I laugh giddily. A little too forced. Perhaps I overdid it.

Sienna pauses with a hard side-eye. She has lived, breathed, studied my movements, the timbre of my voice and its myriad meanings. The way I tug my hair back just so when I have something to hide—every nuance is embedded in her head for when she plays the younger me in her directorial debut. She is more aware of Lena Browning's mannerisms than I am.

The look she gives me now is more of a pierce than a pause. I turn away quickly, wave to a French director who was once a close friend of Stan's. "Bonjour, Luc!" I call out with an exaggerated wave.

"It's happening here, isn't it?" Sienna mutters under her breath.

"What are you talking about?" But feigning stupid is not one of my qualities. I can't even act it.

"Lena, just stop."

"Follow my lead," I say, noting the lights flickering on and off, our signal to find our seats. The ceremony is about to begin.

If only Stan were here. "You couldn't write this shit, Lena, if you tried," he would have said. "No one would believe it. But it's all here, primed for the taking, isn't it? The buildup, the climax, the clincher. Can't wait to see what you're going to do with this." My heart thumps with bittersweet excitement. *I can't believe it's been four years, Stan. I hope you're watching from your front-row seat up there. God knows, I miss you.*

Once we take our seats on the far-left side of the front row, I admit to Sienna that Jack Lyons and I are planning a little something special tonight, and I wanted to surprise her. She raises a brow, but I ignore it. It's more of a surprise to Jack, I think, but I leave that part out.

Just before the ceremony begins, I greet old friends who pay their respects to me. How happy they are to see me back in Venice, blah blah blah. A collection of shiny new actors passes by me as though I am scenery and instead they chat up Sienna. But I keep one eye planted on the doors, peering over the expensively perfumed shoulders and aftershave-doused tuxes. I throw my head back with feigned laughter and disburse warm pleasantries one after the other like an usher handing out stage bills as I wait for the "guest of honor" to arrive.

And then I see him.

It's as if eternity is contained in this singular moment. Still slim in his designer tux, but bald and dried up—he is a man who has lived too well, but time got to him anyway, like the rest of us. He makes his grand entrance as the very last guest to enter the packed auditorium, surrounded by a posse of sycophants and security as though he were the president of Italy. A worshipful silence fills the room, followed by surround-sound loud whispers: the elusive emperor of cinema has arrived. Oz revealing his face: Armand Arias, aka Lukas Müller.

Müller at ninety-two smiles tightly while taking in the adulation, the obvious angling for his attention. A beautiful, much younger Argentinian woman is planted at his side, and a handsome young man at the other. His latest wife and, most likely, his lover. His film's stars and producers welcome him with wide-open arms, a multitude of air-kisses. No one touches him. They know better. Everyone in the room understands that this is Arias's night, his last roar. His golden lion. *The Impostor* is the opus of his much-discussed covert albeit prolific career. Critics salute the film as "Arias's most authentic work"—so real, so emotionally packed, "as if he were there."

Ahh, but he was. The film is not only autobiographical, but also a thinly veiled ode to the Third Reich. And I am the only one in the room who knows the truth.

He sees me. He knows I'm here—everyone does. His fake brown eyes—those liars—latch on to mine. I smile amiably in return, pretending that I'm just like the others, in the presence of greatness. Duped. Everyone knows Lena Browning, but no one more than you, Lukas Müller. *Enjoy this moment,* I tell him silently, *believing that you still have the upper hand.* That you are still the superior race.

Adrenaline surges through my veins like youth serum. I have waited my entire adult life for this moment. I squeeze Sienna's hand next to me. She squeezes back, misinterpreting my excitement.

The orchestra begins. And the master of ceremonies, a beloved Italian comedian, begins the show by telling a few bad jokes that earn uproarious laughter. The guests are ready, knowing that a camera can randomly land on you at any given moment. Rule number one and two: Never pick your nose or dig something out of your teeth during an awards ceremony. Never argue with your plus-one or show your disappointment that you lost. It will be captured.

The next few hours move too slowly, until it is finally time for the most prestigious award of the night: the Golden Lion for Best Film. Jack Lyons walks onstage accompanied by a young Italian siren at least forty years his junior—the ideal (typical) matchup.

It has been several years since we have seen each other. Jack has aged. His overly tanned skin is leathery and bloated, and he's had obvious plastic surgery. But when he smiles, there it is, that everlasting eye twinkle. And when he speaks with that gorgeous rich British voice of his, immediately years are chipped away, and he is everybody's celebrity crush once again. Jack, forgive me . . . but it must be done like this.

I count to sixty in my head, then slowly rise from my seat.

Sienna holds me back by my arm and whispers, barely moving her lips, "Lena, what are you doing?"

I smile for the cameras that I know are on me, and murmur back through my teeth, "It's part of the presentation. Must go."

Surprised by my unplanned interruption, but always the gentleman, Jack extends his hands when everyone sees me walking toward the stage un-prompted, perhaps believing that I am having a senile moment. He silences the audience and says, "If the magnificent Lena Browning has something to say to me and it's not about my lovemaking skills [laugh, laugh], well, then I'm here for it."

Always a class act. His copresenter's thick, dark eye-brows narrow with a this-is-not-what-we-rehearsed-Jack horrified look. But she's a newbie and no one pays attention to her, and he is Jack Lyons, a two-time Oscar-winning legend. And I'm . . . well, we all know who I am.

"Ladies and gentlemen," Jack announces. "May I present the incomparable Lena Browning—God's gift to cinema." An ovation, of course. Even Lukas Müller is forced to stand and clap. I couldn't love this more. The way his fraudulent eyes blaze with fury and his face splotches red, wondering what I'm up to. I ignore him purposely. Look at everyone in the room but him. I smile, wave, wink, then hold my arms out wide. *Yes, Lena Browning is in the house.* And then I lower my chin, raise my legendary filled-in left brow, and turn to Jack, who is not quite sure what's happening but is game anyway. He hands me his microphone, and I blow him a return kiss.

I'm sorry, Jack. I'm ruining your moment to take mine.

Sienna's hand is cupping her mouth. She also knows that the cameras will zero in on her, too, so she shifts slightly, offering up her best angle. *That's my girl.* From this vantage point, I see so many familiar faces that have touched my career over the years. I take my time and walk in front of the podium, center stage, smack in front of Lukas Müller. "When I was a little girl, all I ever wanted to be was an actress," I tell the adoring audience. "But"—I glance at Müller with a playful smile, press my jeweled hand to my chest—"I am an impostor." A play on words, of course. Laughter erupts in the theater. I wait it out, soak it up. "You see, I am not Lena Browning. My real name is Bina Blonski, survivor of the Warsaw Ghetto. And that man"—I point to Müller while projecting my strongest Lady Macbeth voice—"is not Armand Arias. He is Lukas Müller, a high-ranking Nazi who murdered my husband, my friends, and countless others. He is the impostor."

The audience goes wild, believing that I am reenacting a scene right out of Müller's movie—the usual "hoax" skit that happens at every awards ceremony, no matter what country you are in.

Müller's face is explosive. He can't hide it now. He can't leave. He is stuck, fists clenched, boxed in with nowhere to go. His trophy wife seems to be trying to calm him down, asking what's wrong, and he swats her hand away. I pray the cameras caught that.

I walk closer to the edge of the stage, perfectly in line with Müller. "I have been searching for Lukas Müller for nearly sixty years, but once I viewed *The Impostor*, I knew I'd found him." I wave the mic like it's a magic wand. "The highly acclaimed last scene—the one that the critics deem 'so authentic'—was taken from my very own life. I was there in that car. Lukas Müller was that driver. I was the girl who shot the criminal in the passenger seat. But the real criminal was the driver, the impostor all along." I aim my mic at Müller.

"Armand Arias, you got away with your war crimes and have been admired for years, fooling us all. But not tonight, my friends. Not tonight."

Müller is whispering something to the man to his left, who begins to stand.

"She is still fucking great," I hear someone quip as I peer directly into Müller's camouflaged eyes. And before anyone can stop me or Müller's bodyguard can shut me down, I reach under the long slit at the side of my dress and pull out my treasured Browning—my namesake—nestled inside a slim holster wrapped around my leg, and I shoot the enemy point-blank in the chest. Bull's-eye. Exactly where I intended. The shot heard 'round the world.

One bullet. *That's for you, Zelda.*

The audience roars, clapping voraciously, believing the blood is ketchup, that this exquisitely performed scene is all preplanned. That the world's most celebrated femme fatale is paying homage to the world's most reclusive director. I know the charade will last merely seconds until reality sets in. I touch Anna's hairpin in my hair with my free hand as a gesture to her, knowing she is watching this spectacle from her home.

"That's with love from the Warsaw Ghetto," I shout into the mic as Lukas Müller takes his final breaths, and the echoes of my voice are the last words he will ever hear.

"Lena, no!"

Sienna charges onto the stage, a blond pit bull unleashed, pushing past the security guards who are now rushing my way, understanding that this was not an act. She grabs me, shields me, removes the gun from my relenting hand. Flash, flash, flash. The optics—so damn good—are not lost on either of us.

In the fleeting moment that Sienna turns away from the audience and locks eyes with me, I perceive the ever-so-small curl in the corners of her lush ruby-red mouth—one of a dozen Sienna smiles I have come to know. This barely visible triumphant grin tells the story of a trailer-park kid who rose from the ashes of abuse, drugs, and neglect, and did what she needed to do to survive. A woman who, like me, understands to her core why this had to be done exactly this way. That tiny implacable smile is applauding. *Brava, Lena. Brava.*

A stillness sheaths the theater into a collective bubble of disbelief before all hell breaks loose. The great Armand Arias has been assassinated point-blank by the legendary Lena Browning. A femme fatale's final strike. The paparazzi lap it up, pigs in shit, greedily capturing a cinematic golden shocker in real time from every possible angle.

Minutes later, as the approaching sirens wail from outside the theater, all I can think as the police enter and come for me: *I won.* The last bullet, the last line, was mine.

Epilogue

Venice
Eighteen Months Later

I never won an Oscar. But Sienna did. *Femme Fatale: The Lena Browning Story* won for Best Director, Best Leading Actress in a Drama, and Best Film. I watched her win the triple-gilded victory from the prison's TV room, surrounded by my new friends, guards, and even the warden.

The televised murder of Armand Arias/Lukas Müller has taken on urban legend status, especially here at Casa di Reclusione Femminile, the jailhouse for women in Venice, located behind the high walls of what, ironically, used to be a convent. My new home far away from home.

I am the only convict here who everyone witnessed commit her crime in real time; a justice killing before millions of viewers. Basically, I am a goddess on the prison hierarchy, and silver lining, my Italian has improved immeasurably.

Mealtime discussions here are lively and philosophical. *Is it a crime to murder the murderer? A crime to slay your rapist? A crime to avenge your abuser?* We discuss these moral issues at length in the dining hall, in therapy, and late at night on our cots with our own consciences.

I have no regrets. Murdering Müller was not an option—it was a mandate. I accomplished everything I set out to do in one fell swoop: exposure, vengeance, payback, and most of all, I sent a powerful message to those Nazis still living free and easy among us: You can hide, but you will be hunted. Even an old lady with barely there brows can take out a Nazi on national television.

Would I do it again? my new friends ask over lunch. In a heartbeat.

Sienna, however, is not convinced. She visits me regularly and is working with an A-list team of defense lawyers both here and in Los Angeles on an appeal to get me extradited back home, to receive the appropriate medical care, and ultimately be set free.

Not possible, I tell her. In addition to Müller's murder, our film exposes the truth behind Hollywood's greatest on-set "accident." I admit my guilt on camera. But Sienna is determined to keep up the good fight. I repeatedly tell her that she is wasting her precious time on me, when she can be out enjoying her life, her youth, her talent, her beauty, her superstardom. I also tell her that she may have won three Oscars, but I won her. She likes hearing that, and I like watching her face when I say it. The soft blush fanning her flawless skin—a motherless girl likes to hear those things.

"Bina," the prison guard calls out, interrupting lunch. Yes, I've gone back to Bina, insisting that everyone here call me by my real name. "You have a visitor."

I enter the Visiting Room and I stop abruptly in my tracks. My breath puddles in my chest. I want to turn around and run back to my cell and hide, but my worn-in shoes are glued to the linoleum floor. I can't feel myself. The guard walking too closely behind me bumps into me, but I don't feel that either.

Aleksander.

My heart tears straight down the middle at the sight of him after so many years. I never asked him to come. But he's here anyway, sitting in the far corner of the large, cold room, hands cupped, facing the stained cinder block wall with the other visitors.

Our eyes lock and I am untethered. Heat cloaks my body. In a matter of seconds, time stops, starts, and disappears. Aleksander's hair is now silver, still thick, too long for a man almost ninety. His neck, visible in his royal-blue crewneck sweater, is sun-kissed. I try desperately to find my equilibrium as he takes me in. My hands are cuffed, and I wish, for the first time in the nearly eighteen months that I've been locked up, that I was wearing makeup, that I was still beautiful, that my lips were glossed a pearly pink, and my body was still taut and lithe. That I'm not this, but still that.

"Aleksander," I say as I slowly walk toward him. Not as a word, or a whisper, or a poem, but a breath.

He smiles. And there it is. The stars, the moon, the sun, up close.

"Bina."

He stands as I slowly sit across from him. The guard takes his leave, plants himself in the corner where he can watch me. Aleksander sits and places his hands over my cuffs, and I see the guard's stern gaze—knowing, without him shouting at me, the prison's no-touching policy. Our eyes barter silently. *He can touch you for one minute, but I want an autograph for my mother.*

Done, my eyes transmit back. The language of prison life is all about silent gestures, favors, quid pro quo exchanges.

Aleksander speaks first. *God, he is still breathtaking.* His weathered, handsome face is lived in, crinkled in all the right places. "I wanted to come sooner," he explains in heavily accented English, neutral territory. Polish is the past for both of us. "I saw what you did. I didn't see it that night, but I heard about it, and then watched it." He looks away briefly, and then his eyes return. I lose myself in the bottomless jade, the color of the sea at its most tumultuous. "I watched it repeatedly, dozens of times." His voice trails softly. "You landed the bullet in the same spot where he shot Jakub." He knows. An eye for an eye. "I can sleep now, Bina."

"Yes," I say, never having slept better in my life than I have in the months I've been incarcerated.

"I should have come sooner," he whispers, as I melt inside him, dancing across the scratched-up table while not moving an inch.

"You're here now," I say, trembling. "Tell me, I must know, Aleks, how did you— When did you—"

He sighs hard, folds his arms. "I escaped with Eryk and Tosia through the sewers. No one was left. Everyone was dead, Bina. Smugglers helped us get to the forest—not by choice, of course, but with guns pressed to their heads. We fought with the Polish resistance for a while, and then Eryk was murdered, and Tosia was wounded badly in the leg." His hardened gaze is faraway, back there. "She had a limp for the rest of her life. We decided it was time to stop fighting and find a way to escape the war alive." His jaw remains clenched. "Through a series of events, I returned to Warsaw and held the owner of my art gallery hostage at gunpoint. Do you remember Daneusz? Well, that bastard made a fortune during the war off my paintings. I threatened to murder his whole family if he didn't help us find a way out of Poland. He knew I was serious, because"—Aleksander looks away, over my shoulder—"I held a gun to his daughter's head. I'm not proud of that, but Daneusz understood that I was not backing down. He used his contacts and got us out of Warsaw to Switzerland hidden inside large art crates. In Geneva, Tosia and I met with members of the Israeli Haganah. We decided to join them and settle in Israel." His eyes soften. "Aside from enduring more wars, more battles, I've had a good life there. I married Tosia . . ." He searches my face for the hurt he knows this admission will cause. But I already know all this, already felt the debilitating pain. I reel in every muscle I own to hide it.

"Tosia was a bomb maker until the end. Only on a

much larger scale. She was one of the founders of Israel's aerospace industry and helped design advanced missile defense systems. Her work and legacy are immeasurable." I see love and pride written all over Aleksander's face, and the jealousy swelters savagely inside me. *And I'm just a movie star.* But I stamp it out, determined to prevent the green-eyed monster from consuming my face in front of him.

"She passed away three years ago. We have been blessed with two children, a son who is a highly respected physicist and a daughter who is a wonderful pediatrician, four grandchildren. We live in Ein Hod, an artist's colony in northern Israel. It is gorgeous and peaceful. I am a farmer and an artist." He smiles. Teeth still white; a smile that trumps any leading man's I have ever encountered. Aleksander has lived a good life. Family. Love. Births. Weddings. Without me. My chest pounds. "Tell me more about your children," I say to buy myself time, buy myself breath.

His face colors slightly. "Yakov and Zizi. Redheads like their mother."

Named for Jakub and Zelda.

"Oh, Aleks." It's as if someone is pulling apart every organ I own, tugging at my heart, kicking my stomach, clasping my throat, stomping on my lungs.

His voice chokes now too. "I traveled here to thank

you for what you did and . . . I wanted to come many times before. I knew you were alive. I saw your films." A flush begins to spread from his neck to his cheeks. Mine too.

"You're here now."

His eyes change color, the golden flecks begin to dominate the jade pupils. He clears his throat, shifts in his chair. "I also brought you something. Something I've kept with me all these years . . . something I could not leave behind."

He places a neatly folded piece of paper on the table. It is so delicate that it looks like rice paper. He smooths it open and pushes it toward me.

I stare at it and then look up at him, as I once did across a bunker, seeing and feeling nothing else around me but his presence. My cuffed hands prevent me from clutching the fragile paper with both hands. Instead, I run my fingertip slowly along its worn edges before I allow myself to fully imbibe the image. Every inch of my body is on fire as Aleksander gauges my reaction. A body too old to feel this young and lusty once again.

It's a sketch. I can see that he has gone over it re-cently, preserved it. The image is of a young woman bathing. Her eyes are closed as she takes a small pre-cious bar of lavender soap and lightly dabs it to her droplet-glazed skin, knowing that the bar must last for three people, knowing that she traded her body for this little piece of luxury and a handful of potatoes to keep her family fed. The woman's waterfall of golden hair is pinned up like a cameo, exposing her long, lithe neck. The arch in her back emphasizes the fullness of her breasts tipped with erect rose-tinted wet nipples, her tummy is flat, nearly concave from malnutrition. But it doesn't matter. She is beauty personified, a woman deeply in love.

My breath dissolves. My heart stops. Aleksander spied on me as I bathed just as I secretly watched him through that broken hinge on the kitchen door. Jakub wanted to fix that door, but I insisted that he leave it as is, and Aleksander had surprisingly backed me up and now I know why.

A tsunami rises behind my eyes, presses relentlessly against the old folds of practically lucid lids, demanding once and for all to be set free. And then suddenly, without warning, the trapdoor opens, and the tears imprisoned for decades leak out through my lashes, spill down my cheeks and onto my lips. I taste the unfamiliar salty wetness, and it's heavenly.

Aleksander's voice is a deep whisper now. "Tosia was a wonderful wife, brilliant, loving, and brave. A perfect mother to our children and grandchildren. I was blessed twice, Bina." He closes his eyes, and I see what he sees: curvy, dimpled, fun-loving Karina and their baby girl. "But I saw you, too, that very first time at the school social. I knew you pretended not to see me, that you were playing hard to get." He breaks out into a nostalgic grin at our shared memory. "I also knew that Karina would be a better, wiser choice. With her, my life would be happy. You were too wild, too restless, so full of drama and dreams. Stubborn, selfish, creative, exciting. I saw it in your eyes. You wanted it all and more. You were too much like me." His voice totters. "It was a split-second decision. And then while I was deciding, I saw how my brother looked at you, how Jakub's studious face lit up. And I thought, she will bring life to him. Two artists are too volatile. We would have destroyed each other. But"—he looks away, then turns back shyly—"I felt everything you felt. You weren't alone, Bina. I loved you, too, from that first moment. And that night we shared together . . ." His voice halts. "And then, Jakub came back from the dead. Who escapes Treblinka? My scholarly brother whose head was always buried in his books managed to outsmart the enemy and escape. He was alive, and I slept with his wife. There was no bigger sin of betrayal. I knew that whatever I allowed myself to feel about you had to die. And then Lukas Müller murdered everything with one bullet. You, me, and Jakub."

Our fingertips touch now, both gentle and electric, filled with everything we lost and found. Aleksander's revenge was living a life built with love, creating a family, a legacy, proving that those monsters couldn't destroy all that was good. My path was the opposite. I built a meteoric career—rising so high that I could use my vantage point to topple those who destroyed everyone I loved. Our loss, the river of pain running through us, is the same. He chose love. I chose hate. Look at him, look at me.

Which way is better, his or mine?

The answer, I now know, lies in the gray. Somewhere between Zelda and Jakub. My husband wanted the world to witness our history, exactly as it unfolded. Zelda wanted the world to know that we stood up, fought against our fate, determined to change the outcome no matter the consequences. Revenge wins battles, but love wins wars. What did I win in the end?

Peace of mind, perhaps. And yet . . . Aleksander is here at last, and just the two of us remain. Can he see through the part of my fortified heart that is defenseless, putty—that belongs solely to him?

I glance over at the guard pointing toward the large overhead clock. I know, I know. Five-minute warning. This is it, closing time, all I've got left. My fingertips loll against Aleksander's elegant veiny hands for what most likely will be the very last time. "I love you," I say, feeling the mighty resonance of my own voice, as though a packed theater were listening in. "I have always loved . . . only you."

Aleksander's eyes don't veer away this time. Reaching across the table, he wipes away the tears free-falling down my face, and holds his hand there, tender skin matted against the wetness. Forbidden love tore us apart. And yet, it was a true love all the same. It was ours. *Once.*

Author's Note

When I began writing *The Goddess of Warsaw* over two years ago, I had no idea how eerily similar the world I was writing about eighty years ago would be to present-day world events, both in detail and in scope. As a daughter of a Holocaust survivor and an author of World War II historical thrillers with a sharp lens on both "then and now," I am struck by how relevant this story is, especially amid surging antisemitism worldwide.

This novel tackles what may be considered the most important Jewish uprising in World War II history through the eyes of a fierce young woman who survives the war using her brains, beauty, and acting abilities, rising to become one of the most famous actresses of our time but never forgetting the lessons of her past. I knew, even before I put pen to paper, that my fiery protagonist Lena Browning (née Bina Blonski) would have the last word, last act. Once you "meet" Bina, you know that she wouldn't settle for less.

Through Bina's journey, I was determined to explore various questions relating to Holocaust history: What is the fine line between the pursuit of justice and the hunt for revenge? Is there an expiration date for avenging those you loved and lost? What is the price tag for survival?

As I dove deeply into World War II research, I was inspired by real-life events: the fascinating internal workings of the Warsaw Ghetto, the Ringelblum Archive—a collection of documents of daily life in the ghetto led by a group whose code name was *Oyneg Shabbos*, S.S. commander Jürgen Stroop's heinous edicts, which included turning Jewish women into Nazi sex slaves, the suicide of ninety-three Jewish girls who chose death over submission to the Nazis, the destruction of the Great Synagogue of Warsaw, Operation Paperclip, Hitler's favorite filmmaker Leni Riefenstahl, the Nazis presence in Hollywood post–World War II, and most importantly, the heroic Warsaw Uprising itself—Jews versus Nazis—the quintessential David versus Goliath battle.

I put everything I possess as a writer into this book,

and it is perhaps, my most personal, meaningful work. There are so many people to thank in the creation of *Goddess*, who supported me throughout the writing process and helped bring this story to light.

My family is always my first stop. David Barr, my love, I am so grateful for your unconditional support, our beautiful bond, and raising our amazing, loving, independent daughters together. Our girls—Noa, Maya, Maya (Barski) and Izzi (our furry fave)—being your mom and "Bonus Mom" will always be my greatest accomplishment, the very best chapter of all.

The creation of a book takes a village. Mountains of gratitude and appreciation for my HarperCollins/ Harper Perennial "dream team" led by my brilliant editor Sara Nelson. This is our third book together, Sara, and I'm so grateful for all that you do—always encouraging my voice and standing strong behind my stories, guiding and shaping my work into its finest form. Many thanks to Edie Astley, Amy Baker, Doug Jones, Lisa Erickson, Bel Banto, Heather Drucker, Suzette "I owe you a croissant big-time" Lam, and Jane Cavolina. Ahhh, this magnificent cover. . . . Art director Robin Bilardello—you truly captured Bina's essence. I am honored to be part of this extraordinary literary family.

Stéphanie Abou with Massie & McQuilkin Literary

Agents—my agent, gladiator, and lovely friend. Thank you for your all-around badassness—strength, depth, and care—always believing in my work and making my book dreams come true, both here and abroad. *Merci beaucoup!*

Kathleen Carter, you are a rockstar—so grateful for having you on my team, kicking butt, and promoting *Goddess* with your grace, warmth, and elegant touch.

Big thanks to my web designer Steven Franzken, Amanda Kim, my talented intern, and Sophie Tangel, the goddess of Tribe Marketing.

I couldn't have kicked off this novel without the all-star Beta Book Club—my earliest readers who gave *Goddess* an intimate read when it was still a seedling: Bonnie Schoenberg, Lisa Eisen, Beth Richard, and Josh Gray. I incorporated every one of your suggestions into the manuscript. I am so appreciative of your feedback, provocative questions, and honesty. It made me a better writer, the book a better story.

I am blessed with a BIG beautiful extended family, who keeps me afloat with their love, support, and cheerleading. Special shout-out to Jon, Terri, Bethy, Matt, Jimmy, Revi, Jason, Laura, Bons, and Stevie. Much appreciation for the strong support of my parents and my wonderful in-laws, Susie and Richie, (who advertise my books all over town), and to the most fascinating squad of nieces and nephews (so damn proud of you guys—I know you know).

My lifelong friends keep me sane, grounded, lifted, and loved year after year. Thank you, beautiful (inside and out) women, for always having my back: Lisa Eisen, Lisa Newman, Julie Kreamer, Rebecca Fishman, Randi Gideon, Leslie Kaufman, Amy Klein, Bonnie Rochman, Dina Kaplan, Cathie Levitt, Julie Samson, Sharon Feldman, Staci Chase, Lauren Geleerd, Carla Kim, Melissa Van Pelt, and Laurel Hansen.

Writing can be a lonely gig at times, but *not* when these fab Book Mamas are in the house. Among friends who were part of this book's process: Francie Arenson Dickman, Rochelle "YM" Weinstein, Sam Woodruff, Jackie Friedland, Amy Blumenfeld, Lauren Margolin, Alison Hammer, Renee Rosen, Andrea Peskind Katz, Abby Stern, Zibby Owens, Lynda Loigman, Jamie Brenner, Leslie Zemeckis, Jaclyn Goldis, Jamie Rosenblit, Sam Bailey, Erika Robuck, Alyson Richman, Patricia Sands, Corie Adjmi, Erica Katz, Allison Pataki, Amy Poeppel, Elyssa Friedland, Brenda Janowitz, Kerry Lonsdale, Kristy Harvey, Kristin Harmel, Jennifer Anglade Dahlberg, Julie Maloney, Susie Schnall, Leslie Hooton, Sara Goodman Confino, Jenny Share, and Ali Wenzke.

A note of profound gratitude to these gifted authors and friends who paused their own very busy book demands to give *Goddess* a golden launch. I am truly humbled by your words: Jenny "The Goddess of Manhattan" Mollen, Natalie Jenner, Liv Constantine, Danielle Trussoni, Nguyễn Phan Quế Mai, Jean Kwok, and May Cobb.

Hugs to my girl Malina Saval—a dazzling editor, reporter, activist, and my former (and fave) intern. Her award-winning article, "Too Jewish for Hollywood: As Antisemitism Soars, Hollywood Should Address Its Enduring Hypocrisy in Hyperbolic Caricatures of Jews," was extremely insightful, historical, spot-on, and a big help to *Goddess*.

Judy Batalion's masterpiece *The Light of Days*, in a league of its own, provided great background and intimate details of the Warsaw Ghetto, especially its powerful female leaders and fighters.

Dan Kurzman's *The Bravest Battle: The 28 Days of the Warsaw Ghetto Uprising* was an excellent source of background and I highly recommend it.

Estelle Laughlin, a survivor of the Warsaw Ghetto and author of the deeply moving *Transcending Darkness*, I will always cherish the gift of our special afternoon together and interview. It has been an honor and privilege getting to know you and learning about the extraordinary circumstances of survival.

So much appreciation to my loyal, caring readers, the uber-creative book influencers, bookstagrammers, podcasters, online book sites, libraries, and all the literary event planners who have chosen my books for special events. Much gratitude to bookstores nationwide and abroad for carrying my work—and especially to my homies: The Book Stall, The Lake Forest Book Store, and the Book Bin.

The Illinois Holocaust Museum and Education Center provided key research background materials for *Goddess* and has been hugely supportive. Many thanks to Lori Fagenholz. The Jewish Book Council and community, particularly the incomparable Suzanne Swift—I am so grateful for your support and celebration of my books across the country. And to all the authors and friends involved in the Artists Against Antisemitism campaign—it has been a privilege working together and being part of this important movement.

That Little French Guy, *merci*, Ben, to you and Le Staff *extraordinaire* for providing my morning fuel—an endless supply of savory croissants and cappuccinos—to get me through the daily book grind.

And finally, the cherished memory of my Grandma Rachel is always with me. Her legacy as a Holocaust survivor showed me the beauty and joy of Judaism, motherhood, family, and tradition. She will forever be the voice in my head, the hand that guides mine.

About the Author

L isa Barr is the *New York Times* bestselling author of *Woman on Fire*, *The Unbreakables*, and the award-winning *Fugitive Colors*. She has served as an editor for *The Jerusalem Post*, managing editor of *Today's Chicago Woman* and *Moment* magazine, and as an editor and reporter for the *Chicago Sun-Times*. She has been featured on *Good Morning America* and the *Today* show for her work as an author, journalist, and blogger. She lives in the Chicago area with her husband and three daughters.

HARPER
LARGE PRINT

We hope you enjoyed reading
our new, comfortable print size and found it
an experience you would like to repeat.

Well – you're in luck!

Harper Large Print offers the finest in
fiction and nonfiction books in this same larger
print size and paperback format. Light and easy to read,
Harper Large Print paperbacks are for the book lovers
who want to see what they are reading without strain.

For a full listing of titles and
new releases to come, please visit our website:
www.hc.com

HARPER LARGE PRINT

SEEING IS BELIEVING!